Sophia Khan has an MFA from Sarah Lawrence College. She lives in Islamabad.

Yasmeen

Yasmeen

SOPHIA KHAN

HarperCollins *Publishers* India

First published in India in 2015 by
HarperCollins *Publishers* India

Copyright © Sophia Khan 2015

P-ISBN: 978-93-5177-276-7
E-ISBN: 978-93-5177-277-4

2 4 6 8 10 9 7 5 3 1

Sophia Khan asserts the moral right
to be identified as the author of this work.

This is a work of fiction and all characters and incidents described in this book
are the product of the author's imagination. Any resemblance to actual persons,
living or dead, is entirely coincidental.

HarperCollins *Publishers*
A-75, Sector 57, Noida, Uttar Pradesh 201301, India
1 London Bridge Street, London, SE1 9GF, United Kingdom
Hazelton Lanes, 55 Avenue Road, Suite 2900, Toronto, Ontario M5R 3L2
and 1995 Markham Road, Scarborough, Ontario M1B 5M8, Canada
25 Ryde Road, Pymble, Sydney, NSW 2073, Australia
195 Broadway, New York, NY 10007, USA

Typeset in 11/14 Adobe Caslon Pro by
Jojy Philip, New Delhi 110 015

Printed and bound at
Thomson Press (India) Ltd.

To my family

My heart, my fellow traveller
It has been decreed again
That you and I be exiled,
go calling out in every street,
turn to every town.
To search for a clue
of a messenger from our Beloved.

— Faiz Ahmed Faiz

PART I

1

I wonder now if you receive these, and if you do, whether you still care. Do you see my face in windowpanes? Do I cross your mind on snowy days? I wonder if you think of me, if late at night you jolt awake as I do, grasping desperately at empty air.

I know my mother is dead the day I find the box. It is with a feeling of numbness that this certitude assaults me. Hunched in the darkness of the crawlspace, I feel nothing beyond the box's metal edges digging into my thighs. They say when lightning strikes it can take a while for a person to process what's happened. Victims have been known to wander yards from the site of the strike before falling unconscious or howling in pain. I imagine they experience something akin to flash blindness, only the world stays white and empty until their minds can assign meaning to the shadows again. With the box safely in my lap, I wonder if I've spent years inhabiting an echo.

It's on a Sunday in January that I find it. Heavy snow has stilled our already slow town of Crawford. The lack of anything better to do has found me crouched in the crawlspace over my father's study almost nightly. I have memorized the gradient of his receding hairline, the irregular click-clack of his untutored typing, the particular slump of his shoulders when he's stuck on a sentence of the book he's been writing my whole life. Tonight, it seems, he has arrived at something of an impasse. I peer through the peephole and I see him idly forking around rice on the plate

3

of biryani I laboured over all afternoon. He shovels down a mouthful and swallows quickly without tasting. The biryani may as well have been made last week. It may as well be ninety-second supermarket rice.

I straighten up and fumble for the cigarettes, placing the nearly empty bottle of Chanel in my lap so I don't lose it in the dark. The box begins to put my legs to sleep, but I ignore this, figuring that if I stay just as I am and pretend today is just like any other, I'll eventually figure out what to do, how to feel.

When I first started coming up here, nothing was more than an arm's length away. The insulation has now begun to recede along distinctly me-shaped lines. This is how I found the box: a corner of it suddenly protruding from a shoulder-shaped hollow. It is strange to imagine I was ever scared of being up here by myself in the dark, but I was. When I first noticed the ill-fitting plank above the toilet, I was too frightened to do more than look around. I was eleven and my mother had been gone just over a year. It was with her in mind that I'd quickly shut the trapdoor and leapt from the toilet's top that first day. She didn't like me to be invisible, to lurk in dark places she couldn't see. More than anything, it frightened her to be alone. Back then, of course, I didn't know she was dead.

Afternoons downstairs were long and empty after school. I kept seeing my mother's reflection in mirrors, her imprint on the living-room chairs even though she wasn't there. In the crawlspace, there was just me. One day I bore two holes in the floor: one over the hallway; the other over my room. I would watch the empty house from above for hours, hoping to catch a glimpse of whatever made it seem my mother was still there. I never did. Instead, I learnt to live my life without really having to be there. I would imagine other-Irenie going about her life below, watch other-Irenie do her homework and make drawings for her mother. Though I never went so far as to imagine other-Mamma, I knew other-Irenie was sure she was in the kitchen, or the bathroom, or halfway up the stairs.

I settle back against the heating vent and pluck absently at the rift in the insulation. My left foot, which is asleep, brushes against the small tape player I keep stashed up here. I stay still, worried that an involuntary twitch might send it flying. Down below, my father shifts in his seat but does not get up. I wish he would at least fart or something, but my father is not much of a farter. A sigher and a stretcher, yes, but nothing more interesting than that.

'Poking into other people's business will get you nowhere,' my mother always used to warn when she found me hiding behind doors. But I am not doing that now, not really. I am not up here simply hoping for a fart. It's true that I drilled the hole over my father's study with an intent to spy. What was it that made him rush straight up each day after work? What did he have in there that was so compelling he'd be halfway up the stairs before I could respond to his perfunctory hello-how-was-school? Perhaps I thought he'd pore over secret files pertaining to my mother, make whispered phone calls, slip out the window and slide down the drainpipe. Perhaps I just hoped to see him relishing the dinners I had learnt to make for him once my mother was no longer here. But he did none of these things. He just sat at his desk and typed, or stared blankly at the screen, or slid his chair over to the window to sit and read. Then, as now, he'd let his dinner grow stone cold before devouring it in large and mindless bites. It isn't spying if there is nothing to spy on.

My foot has woken to stinging pins and needles and my back is growing stiff. The box is leaving deep grooves in both my thighs, but I'm not ready to address that yet. I estimate that I've been up here for almost an hour. Usually, I pop up, do my thing and climb back down, but with my winter project finished and Celeste in Florida, there's not much else to do. I wipe off my glasses and take another look through the peephole. It seems my father is similarly listless. I light the cigarette. It's time to shake him up.

The first time was an accident. I was rifling through my mother's bureau, looking for a safety pin, when I spied the top of the bottle poking out of the tissue box. My mother was always absently sticking things in strange places, where no one, herself included, would ever think to look: shoes in the crisper, keys in my backpack, perfume in a tissue box. After she vanished, I'd spent weeks looking for the perfume. When I was sad, she'd let me take a whiff—sometimes she'd even dab a bit behind my ears.

In my eagerness to get it open, I somehow tipped perfume all down my front. Suddenly my mother was all around me, holding me in her arms, stroking my hair, putting me to bed with a story and a goodnight kiss. Then I opened my eyes. The room was empty.

Hours later, I awoke in the crawlspace, the perfume still in my hand. Even now, I cannot remember having climbed up here. When I heard my father come in, I edged closer to the peephole. I remember wondering if he'd call my name, look for me when there was no response. The house was dark and he must have assumed I was next door at Celeste's. He came up to his study with a jar of peanuts and quickly lost himself in a book. When he was a quarter of the way through the peanuts, I felt the beginnings of a sneeze. I whipped my shirt up over my mouth to stifle it, inadvertently dragging the perfume-saturated cloth over the peephole. My father slowly put down his book and extricated himself from his chair.

'Yasmeen?' he'd whispered softly, sniffing at air.

It was the first time I heard him say her name since she'd gone. I wanted to hear him say it again and again. I wanted to be sure that he wouldn't forget her, even if he'd forgotten me. I was suddenly furious at him for letting my mother go away, for never talking about her, for acting as though she'd never existed. I wanted him to miss her as I did, to visibly grieve over her absence.

And so it all began.

In the beginning, it was just the perfume. As I got older, I grew more creative. I played the Nusrat qawwalis she listened to, smoked Turkish Golds, and whisperingly recited poems from the earmarked anthologies she kept stacked along the front room's walls, sticking mostly to Faiz and Dickinson because they were most heavily underlined. By the time I was thirteen, I'd learned volumes by heart, and even now find myself silently reciting them as I climb stairs.

My father has never said anything to me about these spectral happenings. I am convinced he wants to keep this wisp for himself. So I continue to leave traces for him, all the while thinking that it's really me who has her. It was always me who did.

I blow a mouthful of smoke through the hole and drop the cigarette into the syrupy dregs of the chocolate milk I brought up earlier. This is a mistake. My father hears the hiss and straightens in his chair. I jerk back into the darkness.

'Irenie?' he murmurs. I don't answer. Years or moments later, when it feels safe to move, I peer down at my father. He pecks away at his keyboard, oblivious. The box weighs painfully on my ankle. For the first time, I look at it closely. It is made of metal, maybe tin, and is about the size of two shoeboxes put together. In the dark, it appears to be heavily decorated with some sort of fluorescence. One latch is broken, the other secured with an ornate lock. It's just as I remember it.

I knew what it was from the moment I first felt its contours in the dark: my mother's secret. The one she never told me. It entered into my memory so long ago that it seems always to have been there. I remember it on my mother's lap in the bedroom when the art room at school had caught fire and Mrs Ronson drove me home. I remember it on the pantry floor with my mother hunched over its contents on those rare afternoons I defied her and refused to sleep. I remember it that one time on the kitchen table when I had a sleepover at Celeste's but came home scared. Each time, my mother would smile and close the box, ignoring my questions and merging back into life as though the faraway look so recently on her face had never been.

'What's hidden in there?' I'd ask, but she'd tousle my hair and put the box someplace unreachable. Whenever she was busy, I'd search the house hoping to find it. My mother was an expert at hiding things and she knew where I'd look. After she disappeared, I looked for it obsessively. When I couldn't find it, I was sure she'd taken it with her, perhaps to someplace happier.

I see the tiny speck of light coming through from the study go out as I lower myself from the ceiling. I'm holding the glass between my teeth and the box in my left hand. Catching sight of myself in the mirror, I feel positively James Bondian and all at once the realization hits: I have found my mother's greatest secret. Will whatever's in the box tell me why she left or where she went? I want to know her every particle, every thought she ever had. In the urgency of this longing, I lose my footing and clutch at the shower curtain for balance. The glass falls from between my teeth and shatters in the tub, but I do not drop the box.

'Irenie?' comes my father's voice. He knocks gently at the door.

I hurriedly shove the panel back into place and look for somewhere to stow the box. Under the sink, perhaps. My father *never* opens the cupboard under the sink, not even if the toothpaste has run out. He cuts the tube in half with his nail scissors and uses whatever he can get. Before my mother left, the toothpaste was either fat and new or a neat caterpillar with a curled up tail.

'What?' I ask rather loudly. I cut my finger on a shard of glass as I hurry to clean it up. Washing blood and ash and chocolate dregs down the drain, it occurs to me to wet my hair. 'I'm washing up.'

I do not hear him move. Hasn't anyone told him that women need their time? I strip off my filthy dress and quickly don a towel.

'Well, when you're through I'd like to brush my teeth,' he says, still there.

I throw open the door and he stumbles slightly. To my extreme irritation, I see he has been leaning his forehead against it. 'Done,' I tell him.

He looks at me oddly, but says nothing. As I brush by him in the doorway, he shrinks away more than usual and stares at the floor. When I get back to my room, I see my hand has left streaks of blood all up and down the towel.

That night, I keep waking up thinking of the box. I want to go get it, but what if my father finds me in the hall? It has been five years since I've seen my mother, a third of my life, and I can't quite remember how her face looked not frozen in a photograph. My father had her two years longer. He is the one who let her go, maybe made her go, when I was in Florida with Celeste and unable to protect her. I will not let him take this from me.

I dream my mother is in the kitchen, slicing banana over my cereal even though she knows I hate it. I dream that she's ironing my father's shirts, letting me spray starch. I dream I'm wandering through the house in the dark looking for her, but I'm not scared because I know she'll be there. I finally give up trying to sleep at around five and go downstairs to make myself a cup of tea. It's only then that it finally occurs to me *just* what finding the box means: if my mother were alive, the box would be with her.

My father chooses this morning to go late to work. He lingers at breakfast, even though I'm too distracted to manage anything more than a buttered toast. On Mondays, he usually gets an omelette. He reads the *Journal of Late Antiquity* and struggles through that single piece of toast.

'Won't you be late for school, Irenie?' he asks. My father and I rarely eat together and I sense he'd prefer to be alone.

'Won't you?'

'Add/Drop week,' he mutters. 'Office hours in the afternoon.'

I sit playing with the honey pot until I'm sure I will be late even if I sprint the entire way.

2

To think there was once a time when I imagined I could never be without you. To think I imagined I would simply disappear. It's been years now and somehow I'm still here.

The first day of school passes in a blur. All through my classes, I worry the box will vanish into thin air like a dream of a thing that never was. When the final bell rings, I rush home to check on it, not waiting even for Celeste.

Bringing it out in the light, I see it's elaborately decorated, if rather battered. My mother must have painted it before I was born, maybe even before she met my father. Painting, she used to say, is something that requires passion. During my lifetime, it seems she never felt any. I never saw her lift a brush, not even during the lessons she gave.

I rattle the lid and tug at the latch, but it holds fast. I notice then that it is an antique Ottoman lock, whose filigree perfectly matches the pendant that has hung from my bedroom mirror since my mother left it for me five years ago. She never took it off until she took off forever. When I sat in her lap I would play with it, mesmerized by the interlocking spirals. Even then, it seemed to me it must hold secrets though I'd never guessed it was a key.

The box, once unlocked, opens smoothly despite having been shut for so long. I hold my breath as I open it, almost expecting a climactic soundtrack to play in my mind. But the room stays silent. Inside it lies a parcel wrapped in what appears to be an embroidered sheet. It is full of letters. 'Dear Ahmed,' I read across the one stuck to the lid, the only one that's out of place. It's my mother's handwriting, though bigger than I remember it and casually untidy in a way her penmanship never was. It's on the old-fashioned airmail paper that occasionally used to arrive from Islamabad. She was always delighted when it came and would open it slowly, worried she'd rip out a word of the letter that had been its own envelope.

'Be still Irenie,' she would scold as I climbed all over her, trying to peep at words I couldn't yet read.

I flip over the letter and look at the address. Ahmed Kakkezai. London, England. It was sent in 1992, so how did it get back into this box? 'Love, Yasi,' she's scrawled along the bottom. I don't remember my mother ever mentioning an Ahmed or having any particular affection for London. When we passed through on our way to Islamabad, she was always eager to go on. If my father suggested a stopover in Ireland to visit his mother, she'd say, 'I just want to get there.' We'd only been once and I don't think any of us had enjoyed it. Like my father, Granny seemed at a loss for what to do with us. As far as I remember, my mother's only visits to London were spent pacing around Heathrow during layovers. She was never a good traveller, despite having been back to Islamabad almost every summer. And she never wanted to travel anywhere else, despite all the travel pamphlets she collected describing this place and that.

'Everyone I love is either here or there,' she would say. 'Why would I want to go anywhere else?'

But she'd loved Ahmed in England and we'd never gone there.

The top letter of the pile is almost twenty-three years old. The one beneath it is a week older: from Ahmed to Yasi. His is typewritten and the ink has begun to fade. There are two stacks of letters in the box, each thick as a phone book, and I wonder how far they go back, whether they're all Ahmed and Yasi or if she had other correspondents. So many letters, my mind screams.

So many secrets. I must not panic, I tell myself. I must proceed systematically. It's better to ease into it. Before I begin, I will establish a context. If the letters are just between the two of them, I must be prepared for the fact that my mother exchanged ten pounds of letters with a man I don't know. I must begin at the beginning and end at the end. I will peruse the stacks before I read them, looking just at the date and the addressee. I'll establish a count and order them chronologically.

Before I'm even a quarter of the way through, it's apparent my mother was one step ahead of me. The letters are arranged from oldest to newest, first hers and then his. There isn't a single letter from anyone else.

My mother must have ironed the letters before she put them in order. The creases look pencilled in on pages so perfectly flat they seem never to have held a fold. There are hundreds of pages in the box. How long did it take her to leave them all so perfectly? Did she lie in bed at night waiting for morning when she knew she would be free for this arduous task? I would like to believe she left them so well ordered for me to find some day, but the dearest of delusions are often the most fragile. This box and its secrets were hers alone: when it came to its contents, I suspect she didn't think of me at all.

The sheets accordion across my floor by the time I finish counting. There are two thousand four hundred and fifty-six pages in front of me. The earliest ones are brief notes they sent to one another during their college years. It must have been there that they met. The later ones are much longer, going on for pages. But I want to start from the beginning. At the bottom of the box is a newer-looking manila envelope stuffed with something and taped shut. Why would my mother attempt to seal away something in her box of secrets? The sense of dread that's been creeping up on me all afternoon intensifies. For a second, I'm unsure if I really want to know about all the skeletons my mother hid so carefully in her closet.

It's too late to back out though, and I find myself lifting up the envelope as though in a dream. My fingers mechanically pull back the scotch tape, leeching yellow from the paper and leaving fuzz along the strip. Now she'll know I've been into this, I think as I flick away the tape. She's never coming back, I remind myself. She has left you this time for good.

The envelope contains an awkward bundle wrapped in an old handkerchief of my father's. I unwrap it to find a stack of cash. There's a little over seven hundred dollars there, plus a cheque from a Mrs Randolph for another two hundred and forty: the forgotten dividends of her painting classes. She started them around the time I first began school and continued until about a year before she left. Her students were elderly local women and the unemployed wives of other professors. Occasionally, a college student enlivened the generally subdued group with wild stories of failed love affairs and late nights. While these lessons were in session, I was prohibited from entering the front room—or the 'studio' as it was called during those times. I lurked in the kitchen, eavesdropping as I stuffed myself with varying iterations of the Tollhouse cookie. The crackle of the fireplace and the syrupy afternoon sunlight that streamed through the wall of windows seemed to put the women at ease. They often paused, paintbrushes suspended mid-air, to confide indubitably important but unendingly mysterious things like that since they'd turned forty white cotton panties were all they could be bothered with.

After the last of her students left in their clouds of perfume and patchouli, my mother would lead me to the rapidly cooling front room to assess their work.

'What do you think of Meredith's use of yellow here?' she'd ask, cocking her head and resting a hand on her hip, as she stepped back from a painting. 'It strikes me as slightly garish, but I can't decide if that's her point.'

I'd consider the canvas in question with what I hoped was a thoughtful look and reply, 'Yes, I think so. To me, it looks like she meant it.' I loved it when my mother asked my opinions on things. Her students painted a lot of abstracts, which seemed to me far inferior to the intricate little girls with poufy dresses and elaborately bowed hair I painted in art class at school. I knew my mother hated my little girls, but a streak of unusual stubbornness made me persist with them anyway.

'They look like little wedding cakes,' my mother would say. 'Children don't look like that in real life. Where are the scabs on their knees and the dirt in their hair?'

At times like this, I came close to hating my mother. How could she not see that the children I was drawing were perfect, just like I wanted to be for her? Maybe if my hair was always neat and my skirts stood out in starched penumbras, my mother wouldn't cry at the breakfast table and drink whiskey in coffee cups. Although I never told her, I couldn't stand the crazy, chaotic messes of colour her students produced. They seemed dangerous to me, too difficult to understand. I forgave them though, for the crisp parcels of cash their creators brought in and for the chance they gave me to be an adult with my mother.

'Let's go for ice cream,' my mother would sometimes say on the coldest of winter days. 'We need to remember that summer exists.' She seemed to me to use her earnings primarily to finance unplanned adventures. Once, she picked me up from school in the middle of the day and took me to the city for a multiple-fork lunch. Sitting across from her, over the sparkling white tablecloth, I felt like the luckiest girl in the world. Every man and woman in the restaurant sensed my mother's presence and couldn't help but watch her from the corners of their eyes. The busboy was at our side to refill her glass every time she took a sip, and the hot rolls in our basket were continually refurbished. My mother was the centre of my world, and it pleased me to see how she could so easily become the centre of everybody else's, while still being all mine.

I put the money back in the envelope and pencil the grand total across the top. My father will be home soon and I want to clear all this before he gets back. I don't think he's been in my room since my mother left, but I don't want her secrets lying around when he's in the house. Maybe he'll sniff them out and I'll be forced to share.

I put the letters back in the box, careful not to mess up the order, and push it under my bed. Celeste will never understand why I haven't read them yet, but it's my mother's life in this box, and though I'm determined to invade it, I won't launch my offensive in a way that would displease her. Right now, it's time to start dinner. My mother was never late with dinner, not even when she'd spent all afternoon weeping quietly over the latest addition to the box.

3

My love for you is a firefly on a starless night. It is a mother's first look at her new-born; it is the aurora borealis pouring in through an ancient's trepanned skull, a rainbow in wintertime. It is the Mariana Trench, the Lacandon Jungle, the snow-covered peak of K2, the Pacific Ocean, the Atlantic Ocean, all the oceans that come together so really are just one. It is simultaneous supernovae, your face in each pulsation. It is the universe and in my universe there is only you.

James got home just as his dinner was beginning to congeal. He nodded at a pair of architecture students photographing the trellis out front, but did not invite them in for a cup of tea as Yasmeen might have done. Inside was hardly warmer. The kitchen was comfortable enough so long as the stove was on, but a draught from the laundry room that he'd long meant to fix rendered it icy moments after the cooking was through. Irenie had left him a breast. She knew he would have rather had a thigh. He had told her on multiple occasions, but she'd say, 'People your age should not be eating thighs.' James couldn't help but wonder if she cared.

There was no sign of his daughter now. There was no sign that the meal had not been cooked elsewhere and spirited in by ghosts. The thought of this struck James's fancy for half a second but he was not a fanciful man and his mind quickly moved on. It had been a tiring day. Every day was tiring during the first week of the semester. There were students to meet, schedules to be made, special exceptions to be considered. James disliked complications that necessitated violations of his routine. That afternoon, two students had come in to complain about being wait-listed for his intro class. The first was a pretty girl who gave off the distinct reek of profound stupidity; the second was a young man with brambles on his collar. All considered, they seemed neither more promising nor less than the students already in his class. He would not have given them a second thought had Doris not told him on his way out that their admission was entirely up to him this year. He just taught the classes; he did not wish to decide who got to take them. But if the two stragglers were not admitted, he might get a reputation for being too unbending. People might feel the need to speak to him about it. It was James's way to choose the course which would require the least interaction.

He considered the chicken breast again. It lay in a pool of reddish sauce from which a thin rim of orange grease was beginning to emerge. It had tinted a small section of his rice already and now threatened to infringe upon the eggplant's space. He wondered how long it had been sitting there, how long ago it had been made. Irenie's school had just begun; perhaps she hadn't had the time to cook dinner. Perhaps the chicken breast had been recovered from a tin-foiled dish at the back of the fridge, set out for his consumption just as it was on the verge of going bad. But the kitchen smelled of frying onions and spices that had never ceased to strike him as foreign. The chicken had been cooked that night. He had been allotted a breast either for health reasons or out of contempt, and his tardiness was the sole cause of it looking old. James sighed and began the lengthy process of disentangling himself from his winter clothes. He was surprised to see the snow on the shoulders of his coat; he hadn't noticed it was snowing. He shed his layers onto the hatrack and took his plate upstairs.

Passing Irenie's room, he noted all her lights were on. So she was home. He briefly considered knocking to tell her he was back but she would have heard him on the stairs. If she'd wanted to say hello, she would have come out by now.

He continued to his study and gently shut the door. He retrieved his dressing gown from the peg and set his dinner on the desk. In the warm light of his desk lamp, it looked somewhat less grotesque. It wasn't that Irenie wasn't a good cook but that the plates she left for him when he was late always seemed to glare at him in accusation. She cooked the same complicated curries her mother once had; only hers were seldom passed around the kitchen table in serving dishes, never salted with family conversation. They were left instead in single servings to grow cold and quiet on the counter. James would have been happier with sandwiches, though it was something he knew better than to profess.

James, as always, forgot to bring his cutlery. Some days he would brave the trip back to the kitchen for it, but tonight he was too tired. The kitchen was his least favourite part of the house. When Yasmeen was still with them, it was always full of clamour and laughter and tempting smells. Even when she wasn't cooking, she could often be found reading by the stove. He had once caught her with her stocking feet propped inside the oven. 'I was cold,' she'd smiled and shrugged. That was when he'd fixed the fireplace. When she couldn't sleep, she'd go downstairs with the excuse of tea. Waking up alone had never alarmed James then. He always knew where he would find her. Now her absence was in everything: the silence of the kitchen, the empty gloves beside the kitchen sink, the cup beneath the bathroom mirror that still held her last toothbrush. Once, James had suggested to Irenie that they leave the little yellow house.

'How will Mamma find us when she comes back?' his daughter wanted to know. She glared at him as though it was he who'd chased away Yasmeen.

'How indeed,' was all he could say.

He nudged his dinner listlessly with a fingertip. It was now completely cold. Oh, stop being such a baby, Yasmeen seemed to be saying bemusedly from the photo on his desk. Her eyes said different things each night. Though eighteen years his junior, Yasmeen had always delighted in calling him a child.

Fine, he thought, fine, I won't be. He triumphantly brandished the teaspoon that he'd just recovered from a mug beneath his desk. Even cold, his dinner was delicious. It always was.

He remembered the first time Yasmeen had made him dinner. It was a chicken dish very much like this one but it wasn't delicious. He had pulled her into the coat closet for a kiss and it was left simmering overlong. They attempted to skim the unburnt sauce off the top and had then resigned themselves to rice. It was one of the best meals he could remember. Oh, stop feeling sorry for yourself, Yasmeen's eyes seemed to be saying now. He tried but failed and found he was no longer hungry. Pushing his plate away, James picked up the photo frame that held his wife. It was one of the few photographs he had of her. Irenie wanted it desperately, he knew, but he couldn't bear to let it go. He couldn't even bring himself to place it in the living room. Irenie had Yasmeen every time she looked into a mirror: her small and straight nose, her delicate chin, her smooth and slightly burnished skin. James wanted to keep this one thing for himself.

The photograph was taken not long after they first met. A drunken art student had intercepted them and had begged Yasmeen to pose. It was early in their courtship and he counted every hour he got to spend in her company, so he resented the intrusion. But Yasmeen, as always, had been obliging. The student dragged them all over campus. In the end, all he took was that one photo: Yasmeen beside a snow-covered pine tree brushing away a bough with the familiarity one generally reserves for one's own hair. A print turned up in her mailbox a few weeks later with neither a signature nor any note of thanks. Yasmeen didn't like it. She had asked him to remind her never to wear that cap again. But James found the photo charming. She told him he could keep it as long as he promised no one else would ever see. To his knowledge,

only Irenie ever had. It was hard to believe that seventeen years
had passed. To James, falling in love with Yasmeen never seemed
like something that had happened long ago.

The first thing he had noticed was the sound of her step, a
sharp tic-tic across the slippery, polished marble. He would be
trying to concentrate, grading a paper or preparing a lesson plan,
when the click-click of her sharp heels would drive mercilessly
into his mind, distracting him from whatever he was doing. Finally,
halfway through the semester, he leapt from his desk at the sound
of those shoes, intent on admonishing her about the need for
silence in academic buildings, and caught his first glimpse of her.

He was not prepared to be impressed. Women in high heels
had grown passé for him over a decade ago. A woman he dated for
a few months, Agnes, was so self-conscious about her stature that
she insisted on wearing high heels even when she knew their plans
for the day would entail a great deal of walking. She'd insist they
go out on the town, walk rather than take grimy cabs (and god
forbid he even mention the subway), but then she would whine
ceaselessly about her shoes biting. She invariably invited herself
back to his apartment after these outings for a nightcap and
her shoes would be off before they were through the door. He'd
attended to her various injuries without complaint, and afterwards,
much later, she'd rest her head on his chest and draw her long
manicured nails across his ribcage, sighing that no one had ever
looked after her as well as he. When, finally, he suggested more
practical footwear, she regarded him with the long-suffering air of
some patron saint of ailing extremities left out of every catechism
he'd ever read, and sighed, 'It's not my fault you're so tall. If I wore
shoes any lower, my nose would be level with your navel.'

They broke up a week later. He didn't understand her needs,
she said. He had been wary of high heels ever since. (He once
thought, absently recollecting the relationship some years after his
marriage, that Yasmeen would have been twelve then, or maybe
thirteen, probably longing for her first pair of heels as she scuffed

her way through a dusty schoolyard in her shiny black Mary Janes. He had tried to ask her about her first heels once, but she was short with him, reluctant as ever to discuss her past. The next evening, she'd met him at the door in stilettos and little else, but really all he'd wanted was her memory.) So when he burst from the chaos of his office into the tomb-like foyer he had been flustered, faintly annoyed, and not at all prepared to meet Yasmeen.

'Pardon me, Miss,' he'd said sharply, in a voice somewhat too loud for the space, 'would you mind...'

She turned around, startled by the decibel of his voice in the otherwise silent room, and his irritation left him all at once. She didn't look as though she belonged in her sombre suit, in his mundane life, in this mouldering university building at nine a.m. on a Wednesday morning. Even in the dimly flickering fluorescence, she seemed to glow. Somehow, her outline was more vibrant than everything else in the room. She was clearer, sharper and more real than anything he'd ever seen. It was as though he'd been living in two dimensions and all at once something had inflated, grown round.

'Yes?' she said, looking at him askance.

'Nothing,' he'd managed to stammer, 'nothing at all.'

Over the next few weeks, he'd made a number of what he'd thought were discreet inquiries into her identity. Charles Faber, a swarthy and rather garrulous Latin professor who had, to his irritation, recently moved into the office next to his, was more than happy to oblige. In the cramped coffee room down the hall where Faber spent most of his non-teaching hours smoking French cigarettes, flirting with secretaries and gossiping, James had learned that the woman's name was Yasmeen. Though she had attended a small liberal arts college in New England, she had grown up somewhere in Asia, perhaps India or Pakistan, but she did not speak of it. She was working somewhat half-heartedly towards a master's degree in literature. The tutorial she taught was related to Professor Chafen's notoriously tedious academic writing course.

Her students adored her, and often came to her outside class to discuss the various trivialities which college freshmen are wont to suffer. She was frequently seen sitting patiently at the campus coffee bar with a toasted onion bagel and a teary co-ed. There were rumours that she was wildly promiscuous on weekends, that she drank heavily and perhaps even used drugs and was occasionally to be found in the society section of the local paper draped over the arm of some languid young heir, disinterestedly surveying the intrusive photographer. On Monday mornings, though, she was perfect, never a hair out of place, and there was no one who could claim to have personally seen any of her supposed lovers or substance-fuelled frolics.

James learned all this with little prodding. Yasmeen, it seemed, was one of Faber's favourite topics. He would expound at length on the particularities of her face in a certain sort of light that only ever filtered through the smoke-stained windows on those rare days which are rainy and bright at once. James could sometimes hear him scuttling to his office door when the tell-tale click-click gave Yasmeen away, hoping to catch a glimpse of her through the frosted glass. Though James himself might have liked to peer at her clandestinely in this manner, his general disdain for Faber prevented him from doing so, and he took to going down the hall for coffee every morning when Yasmeen's tutorial was scheduled to end, hoping she might come in and fetch a cup for herself. He would offer her the sugar bowl, perhaps mention the weather in passing, and tell her silently how much he loved her. But her tutorials often ran late, her students clamouring for more of her, far beyond their allotted time, and there was only so long he could spend in the dark coffee room without wanting to strangle Faber.

One day, quite without warning, Faber interrupted himself in the middle of a melodramatic monologue detailing the relations between a certain sociology professor notorious for predilections closely approaching pederasty, the teenage son of a member of the religion department, and a highly controversial artist-in-residence whose paintings of mutilated children engaging in unspeakable sexual acts had been featured briefly in the Guggenheim before they were promptly removed to serve as evidence in an obscenity case being waged against him, and asked, 'Have you ever even spoken to her?'

James, who had been paying only cursory attention to him as he mentally reviewed the texts he'd selected for the Fundamentals of Homeric Poetics course he was slated to teach the next semester, was so alarmed that he dropped his mug. Relieved to have a reason to not look Faber in the eye, he bent to gather up the iridescent blue remains glittering in the dull murk of rapidly cooling coffee.

'What?' he asked nervously. 'Whom do you mean? Which her is this?'

Faber gave him a look but remained eerily quiet, tapping his foot impatiently and not offering to help with the mess. James gathered up the last of the pieces, quite without idea of what to say, and went over to the sink for a dishtowel to wipe up the spilt coffee. The two men stayed silent in this strange tableau for a few minutes: James kneeling by Faber's left foot, scrubbing at nothing in particular on the tile, Faber leaning against the fridge, mug clamped tightly in a surprisingly dainty fist and resting on his large belly. Finally he gave in, cleared his throat conspicuously and muttered, 'To Yasmeen, of course.'

'No, not really,' James admitted, standing up in relief and adjusting his spectacles. Yasmeen was beautiful. Everyone in the building must have noticed her by now, spoken to her, or wanted to. Faber himself often accosted her in the hall to offer up inanities about the university, the weather, the particularly becoming colour of her dress that morning, though James couldn't imagine where Yasmeen would find a colour that was unbecoming. Even after they had been married for five years, he would insist that she looked lovely in a particularly abhorrent puce blouse that he had bought her one Christmas because he knew she liked the designer. He considered feigning surprise at Faber's line of inquiry, brushing it off as he would any of his lewd speculations or sly insinuations, but it was too late for that now. He'd already shattered his mug, spent far too long crouched on the floor, mute as a phrenology dummy.

'Well, perhaps you should,' Faber responded, with the practiced pseudo-sagacity that so impressed the dim-witted posse of undergraduates who regularly followed him around campus, spouting obscure Latin epigrams and epigraphs no one but they and Faber cared to know. 'The year's almost over and she won't be teaching that tutorial next semester.' James was impressed and faintly unnerved that Faber had registered his existence, let alone his secret longings, during the months of his seemingly oblivious ranting. Sitting down at the small and slightly crooked table that held the sugar bowl, Faber rather smugly informed him that he was easier to read than a gossip magazine. Having never been tempted to peruse such a periodical, James was unsure of just how transparent he had been. It wasn't that he asked *that many* questions about Yasmeen, Faber said, but that he'd never asked about anyone else. Perhaps no one else had noticed, but Faber was astute. He had a nose for this kind of thing. Yes, indeed. He was truly intuitive. James was obviously smitten with the girl and he should do something before it was too late.

Faber lectured at length. James couldn't stand his confidential tone, the warm brush of his breath as he murmured fatherly advice, an old man to a younger one, as he described with surprising emotion how he'd met his wife, the irreplaceable Irma, who had tragically succumbed to gout after a long battle with various illnesses, both imagined and real. Since then he'd been on his own, with only his work to sustain him. His grown children called only on high holidays and his grandchildren lost interest the moment the shiny presents he came bearing each Christmas had been unwrapped, exchanged, abandoned for more delectable delights. Excusing himself hurriedly to get to his afternoon seminar on time, James resolved that the man was less obnoxious than he had thought.

James took to getting his coffee earlier in the morning after his talk with Faber, not wanting to have to endure his winks and giggles. Fortunately, he never arrived till after ten, so James felt safe spreading out his newspaper on the sticky little table and leisurely sipping his second cup of coffee while scanning the books section one damp day in November. It was one of those hushed winter days when it feels too early to be awake even in the middle of the afternoon, and he wasn't quite ready to go to his office and begin work. He was reading a special feature on an author whose historical fiction he occasionally enjoyed on long plane rides when Yasmeen swept into the room, spraying raindrops and stray leaves. She was wearing galoshes today and he hadn't heard her coming.

'God,' she exclaimed. 'It's absolutely miserable out there. I had to get the bus a full hour earlier so I'd have time to dry off before my tutorial.' She paused for a moment to take off her raincoat and put it down on the chair across from him, really looking at him for the first time. 'I'm so sorry,' she said. 'I'm Yasmeen. I have a tutorial in the room next to yours.' She went over to the dish drainer and began to inspect the motley collection of stained and chipped mugs: Happy 85th Birthday Great Aunt Gertrude; George Washington High School Sailing Team, 1974; cartoon kittens in a beribboned basket.

'I know,' he replied softly. 'Careful about the red one. Charles Faber put it in there. When it's filled, the bottom snaps open.' She smiled and selected a plain green one. Gold rim. 'I'm James,' he said after a pause he hoped was not too long.

'I know.' She smiled charmingly. 'The mystery member of Orchard Hall. I hear the rest of them scurrying about, nattering about this, that or the other without stop, but you're always in your office with the door shut. I was beginning to wonder if you weren't a genuine recluse.'

She had poured her coffee now and was rummaging around in the fridge for milk. Would she sit down with him once she found it? He prayed she would. He prayed she wouldn't. She didn't. Instead,

she put her coffee down on the table and leaned her elbows on the
back of the chair, peering at him like an inquisitive child.

'So you teach classics?'

'Yes. Greek. To a disinterested audience mostly.'

Had she really been curious about him or was she just being nice
to the poor ageing academic stammering through this everyday
interaction? He wanted to look at her, as if to drink her all in, but
he was sure that a hundred men had stared at her just like that and
he didn't want to be one of them. What is it like to be a beautiful
woman? Your face like a badge you can never remove, a red flag
attracting attention at every turn whether you want it or not. Even
now, wet and dishevelled with damp wisps curling darkly from the
dignified knot at the back of her head, she was perfect.

'Would you like my handkerchief?' he offered gallantly,
perhaps a little desperately, as he pulled it from his breast pocket.
'It probably won't be much help, but you can dry your face at least.'

She smiled. 'Thank you.'

Were handkerchiefs antiquated concepts, he wondered. She
might think him a geriatric. At least this one was quite nice:
monogrammed cream cambric with his initials embroidered in
simple navy script across the top. His mother ordered them from
a special clothier near Cork and each Christmas they would arrive
in neat packets of five with no note or greeting. Other than the
occasional illegible letter detailing the latest developments in her
garden or his scholarship, it had long been their only manner of
correspondence. With her second husband, she seemed happier
than he remembered her being since his twin, Irene, died when
she was just nine. America didn't quite agree with Grace Eccles,
especially after her husband died. She stuck it out for five years
after that. A few months after James left for Yale, she announced
she was selling the house and moving back to Ireland. It wasn't
really a surprise. He was all she had here, and they had never
been close. Less than a year later, a letter arrived informing him
that she had got engaged to William McKenna, a retired jockey,

whom she met at the butcher's when he attempted to lay claim to what she had determined was to be *her* kidney, so could he come that July for a small ceremony, just family? William was amicable at the wedding, and James liked him, although they had met only a handful of times in the twenty-five years since. Both he and his mother detested travel and had little to say to each other beyond what could be conveyed in their brief biannual epistles. He was glad she was happy though, and blessed her now for her annual gift.

Yasmeen had finished wiping her face with the handkerchief and made to hand it back to him, but it seemed somehow unchivalrous to reclaim a lent hankie. 'Keep it,' he told her. 'Maybe you'll need to dry your face again on the way back to the bus stop.'

'How sweet,' she said, and meticulously folded it into a tiny square before tucking it neatly into her jacket pocket. 'My mother was forever pressing them upon me when I was a child, but I'd lose them or rip them or stain them faster than she could keep up with. When I left home it just seemed too much of a bother to procure them on my own.'

He suspected she was lying, just a little fib to assure him of his worth in some small way. Yasmeen did not seem like the type of woman who would grow up to abandon habits ingrained early. Even now, her nails were short and her hair was neat. Surely she thought him grey and dull, tiny unreadable print on a smudged newspaper from some other time, some other place, that had nothing to do with her.

'Going home for the break?' he asked rather abruptly, uncertain of how this interview could gracefully end.

'No, unfortunately not. It's much too far,' she replied, spooning three teaspoons of sugar into the temporarily forgotten coffee and stirring choppily.

He had thought she would be graceful in everything.

'India?' he asked.

'No,' she said, 'we aren't all the same breed of brown.'

'I'm sorry,' he stuttered, but she was already gone, the slim shadow of her back disappearing in the corridor. She hadn't bothered to take her coffee with her, so he brought it back to his office and drank it, gagging on the sweetness of each sip.

Chastened by their earlier interaction, he did his homework before approaching her a second time. A respectable two hours after the last class ended, he made his way over to the registrars' through the icy December air. Most students had long since left, turning in finals early to extend their Christmas holidays, and the paths were largely unploughed. The short walk left his trouser cuffs drenched. A bell tinkled jarringly overhead as he let himself into the smoky, wood-panelled room, and he found his heart racing. He felt as though he was about to commit a terrible crime: abusing his position for personal gain, cheating the system, incipient molestation. In all his years as a tenured professor, he'd never once done anything even faintly questionable, never once caved into a whiny student's demand for an undeserved grade or skimmed over that last exam graded late the night before it was due back.

He cleared his throat, drawing the secretary's attention from her chain-smoking, romance-reading idyll. The bell seemed not to have alerted her to his presence.

'Oh, Professor Eccles,' she said, looking up, 'still here, are you? No grand plans for the holidays? Well, I suppose we can't *all* be rushing off early when there's work still to be done. How can I help you?'

He considered his options. It wasn't too late. He could still say he needed some form, the class listing for next semester, even an envelope. 'I need the address of a student,' he said. 'A Yasmeen Khalil.'

'Ah, Yasmeen,' said the woman, Beatrice perhaps, exhaling a vast cloud of smoke. 'Lovely girl. Always asks me how I am and wishes me a nice day. Is she in one of your classes, Professor?'

'Well, yes,' he lied. 'My Wednesday tutorial. She asked that I send back her last paper over the break. I'm not yet done grading it.'

If she checked, Beatrice would know Yasmeen was not in his Wednesday tutorial, nor in any tutorial he had ever taught, but she seemed disinclined to do any such thing. She tapped her novel impatiently on the desk.

'Would this be her permanent address or her address here?'

'Her address here.' And then daringly: 'Sending it all the way to Pakistan would be a bit of a bother.'

'Yes, I suppose so,' Beatrice responded. 'By the time those third-world postal systems get it there, she'll probably be back here ready for a new semester. Let me just go get that for you.'

He spent much of the winter holiday trying to write a suitable apology and then debating over whether or not he should send it. In the end, he sent her a few typewritten lines asking if he could take her out, perhaps for some coffee, to make up for it. Years later, when he learned of the Ahmed letters, the question of whether or not she had kept that letter began to gnaw at him. Slightly drunk after a long Christmas party, he'd asked her.

'What letter?' she asked, tired and disinterested.

'The first one I sent you.'

'Of course not, Mr Casaubon. I thought you were quite mad. I'd planned to avoid you from there on out.'

4

Even then I loved you, as I filled your life with stories you did not want to know. Even then I longed for you, a stranger beside me in my bed. Even then I dreamt of you: all night, just you and me. And even now I miss you, the days and years and memories that separate us no more material than steam.

When I was a child, my mother would leave me in line at the deli counter and come back to find blue-haired strangers in shower caps telling me how their husbands of forty years just left them for secretaries, strippers, neighbours' underage sons. She would step into the kitchen to brew tea and return just in time to censor Mrs Harper's tales of the sex acts her husband had been demanding since he bought the red corvette. In shadowed corners of the library, she'd discover me intent on strange men's stories of how their little girls had turned out.

'There are things you shouldn't know,' she scolded when I protested being led away. 'You shouldn't seek out secrets.'

But I didn't seek out secrets. I just stood where my mother put me and the secrets came by themselves. Old ladies dug out butterscotches, thick with lint, from the bottoms of their bags and the sad-eyed men who stumble through the world half-awake would stop to pat me on the head.

'It's like she's born to listen,' these strangers would sometimes tell my mother.

'Born to listen,' she would later scoff. 'What little girl is born to listen to things like that?'

My mother was jealous, I often thought, of letting strangers share my ear. I *was* born to listen, but just to her. I heard the things she never said and fixated on what she did. Strangers were just idle practice for the stories I really hoped to hear. I listened like a card shark plays gin rummy with his kids: something fun enough to pass the time, but nothing like the real event. I spent hours under bushes and behind doors, straining to listen just in case there were things my mother wasn't telling.

'Some day you'll learn something you'd rather you didn't know,' she cautioned, finding me beneath the sofa or crouched small on the basement stairs. To me, it wasn't a matter of what I did or didn't want to know. Some things hurt my feelings and others made me sad, but isn't it better to know everything you can? My first memory of my father is from a sojourn on the stairs. The fourteen caryatids buckling beneath the banister were my earliest best friends. Whispering to them, I could keep my mother within my sight. If she chopped her fingers with the chicken, I could be right there. When slicing onions made her cry, I had a handkerchief and it wasn't spying because she knew I was there. My father should have known as well, but he never saw me very well or perhaps he just forgot.

'She's gone to bed?' he asked as he came home that day and pulled my mother to his chest. She. Not Irenie, just she. Four words so eager, filled with relief that I wasn't there.

'Irenie's on the stairs,' my mother replied a little frostily, but without pulling away. It was my father who stepped back that day, the glow gone out of his eyes. For a moment he'd been warm and young, but then he was just himself. The way he'd said 'she' made me cry, but wasn't it better I found out that my father wanted Mamma for himself and I was just something in the way?

I thought there was nothing I'd prefer not to see, until years after my mother was gone. Though she had resigned herself to my prying, I have no doubt the crawlspace would have been verboten. For the first few months, I felt guilty being there, but the draw was just too great. I relished the invisibility and the chance to observe my father without letting him see me.

I was twelve, almost thirteen, when I saw something I truly believed would have been better not to see. It was the day before a geography test and I couldn't get to sleep. I wasn't used to failing and I was sure I'd fail this test. Fear kept me up long after my light was off, long after I'd heard the last creakings of my father. I thought perhaps the confines of the crawlspace might compress the worries haloed wide around my head into something small enough so I could sleep.

Light still glowed through the hole over my father's study. What, I wondered, is he still doing up at three-thirty in the morning?

At first, I thought he was just sitting at his desk looking at something. His back was to me and I saw the collar of his dressing gown was frayed. I wondered if he'd noticed the baldness encroaching from the centre of his head. There seemed nothing special about the photo on his desk but he closely stared at it. It was an old Polaroid, warped and fuzzy, the kind people took when they were photographing something they wanted no one but themselves to see. I couldn't quite make it out, but I thought it was a woman floating unclothed in the sea. I focused so intently that everything around the desk went black, but I couldn't see the face. Even without it, I knew it was my mother. I knew from the posture and from the thin brown arm. Perhaps I knew even before I looked, but just didn't want to see.

My father made a strangled sound and brought out his handkerchief. The photograph had seemed to flicker as the desk lamp shook, but now everything was still. I stayed frozen in the dark, not even wanting to breathe. It was centuries or seconds before he rose. He put my mother in a drawer, but forgot to switch out the light. When he turned around, his eyes were red and there were tears in his eighteen-hour stubble. His nose ran with the snot that comes when nothing else is left and he just let it run.

As I learn more and more from these letters, I wonder if there was a side to my mother I'd have been better off not knowing. Once the college notes conclude, they are so angry, these first letters. She seems to hate Ahmed and he her, yet the letters number in the dozens. Ahmed's best friend, a man by the name of Mustapha, is somehow in the middle of it all, or so it seems. They blame and berate, taunt and torture. They imply all manner of betrayals committed in vengeance and outline the grotesque details of a great many more. He has left her, or she him; I cannot tell who did the leaving or why—and why, despite hating each other, they continue to write.

5

I have never yet awoken to a day where I did not regret all the ways in which I've hurt you, when I did not regret all the ways in which you tried to hurt me back, but harmed mostly yourself. Yet hatched somehow from all that hurt is a purer, stronger love.

It has been raining all day and my father has called to say he is stuck in the office. I am perfectly happy to have the house to myself, and have already twice ignored Celeste's suggestion that we spend the afternoon at her house with hot chocolate and old movies. The instant I realized my father was out, I called Mrs Winterbourne at the library and told her I wouldn't be in today. She responded with her usual indifference. My position there is strictly voluntary.

I wrap myself in the old sheet and begin to read. I'm relieved to find these letters are far more pleasant than the ones at the start. Their anger seems to have quietened enough for them to exchange highly personal chronicles of their respective lives. I come across a number of passages about me, and I'm happy to find only pleasing descriptions. She tells Ahmed what my first words are, that I love to drink grape juice and suck on my toes. There's even an incoherent scrawl at the corner that she claims is my baby-hello to him. Although I am expecting it, almost dreading it, she never once bemoans that having a baby has latched her to an unhappy life. In fact, she doesn't even seem unhappy. In one of her letters, from when I was about two, she scolds Ahmed for not spending more time with his children. I am strangely proud of my mother, extolling family values to the man she loved, for a family that was not hers.

The letters I read this morning are all in that vein: detailed descriptions of children and of homes. It seems Ahmed did take my mother's advice, and became much happier for it. There are no more professions of undying love or desperate pleas but it seems to me these things no longer need to be stated. The letters are full of reminiscences, of descriptions of snowy afternoons in libraries and card games that were played late into the night, of long weekends at my mother's friend's beach cottage and bracing walks in the Massachusetts hills. I can't imagine my mother so carefree. It makes me want to cry to think that she had that and lost it.

For about a year the letters are replete with remember-whens, but I guess they made my mother and Ahmed as sad as they're making me and they soon switch back to the everyday. Before they do, I get a sense of their youth, spent forever rushing from one thing to the next yet somehow clinging tightly to each other. As far as I can tell, they do not meet again following whatever drove them so violently apart in 1983, though a letter of Ahmed's dated 13 June 1985 makes a brief reference to the possibility of a meeting in Islamabad later in the summer—a possibility my mother does not address.

I've given up reading and am sobbing into the musty sheet with a hopelessness I know is not my own, when I hear the door slam downstairs. I jump up, wipe my face on the sheet, and let it settle over the disordered mound of letters in a single motion. How could I have let myself be caught unawares like this? What if my father had popped in to say he was home? What if he asked why I was crying? What if he'd seen what I was reading?

I am still crouched in this bush fighter stance with my eyes red from crying and the masses of hair I haven't yet bothered to braid, standing all up on end when Celeste sweeps through the door.

'Wow,' she says, 'You look *just* like the Unabomber in his mug shot.'

'I was going for Ginsberg,' I tell her, smoothing down my hair.

She laughs and puts her dripping mackintosh on the floor. I glare at the plastic-checked mess spreading its wetness close to the blanketed letters until she sighs, pulls the plastic bag from my dustbin, and shoves it in. Peril is temporarily averted.

'The letters again?' she says. 'You know, I don't think your mother would want you to be sniffling your way through the best days of your life as you pore over hers.'

'It's raining, Celeste. It's a miserable day. There's not much else to do.'

'We could be watching a movie. We could be plotting a coup. We could be doing the homework you claimed to be doing.' She settles herself gracefully on my bed and draws the blanket around her shoulders, queen-like even damp. There's no getting rid of Celeste when she's decided to stay. The first day I met her I thought I could, but it was impossible then as it is now. Six years ago, when I learned a little girl my age had moved in next door, I was not excited.

'Why don't we go over and say hello?' my mother had urged. 'It would be nice for you to have a friend so close by.' My mother never tired of talking about the importance of childhood friendships. She missed her best friend Shireen though they'd lived across the world from each other for years and years.

But I didn't want friends, and certainly not ones who'd always be there. I had my mother, and that was enough. The play dates she arranged with mothers she met at the supermarket or outside my school were painful enough. I'd be shepherded into strange houses where dutiful little girls would play Barbie while I'd watch the clock. I should be home right now, I'd think, Mamma might need me at any time. Sometimes, the little girls were less than patient with me and I would recount how Amy had smacked me in the face with her colouring book or May Beth had slyly suggested that everyone at school thought I was weird. My mother would sigh and look defeated when I returned with these reports, but she seldom made me go back. When it was warm enough, I'd sometimes spend summer afternoons cycling around adjacent blocks with kids from the neighbourhood or floating serenely in somebody's pool, which seemed to satisfy her so long as I continued to present myself for schoolmates' birthday parties during the year. Though my own birthday parties were always sparsely attended, my mother seemed to think that turning up on weekends at whoever's door with a beautifully wrapped present and the birthday wishes she'd force me to recite in the car was a binding social obligation I couldn't ignore. So, until Celeste St Clare moved in next door, we'd managed to negotiate an unstated stalemate that allowed me to stay by her side but for occasional birthday party assurances to allay her fears that I would grow up to be socially inept.

For months, I struggled daily to come up with reasons why we should not stop by next door. Whispers were travelling down the halls at school loudly enough that even I had heard: her brother, who was only six, had been sent home twice already for using language that made his teacher blush; her mother, who had just opened a flower shop downtown, was often seen roaming the streets in her nightgown, a crown of nasturtiums and nothing else; Celeste herself had appeared on Halloween in hot pants paired with pompom roller skates and at the Christmas carnival she had used the excuse of some moulding mistletoe to kiss Jason Franz (a suspected homosexual since his second-grade enthusiasm for his elder sister's dress in the year-end play). They had handed out horehound sweets for Halloween and the siblings often arrived at lunch with tins of condensed soup or pungent wedges of Délice de Bourgogne. Given my own shaky social status, I didn't want to do anything to disturb the mantle of invisibility I'd been cultivating.

My mother and I were in the midst of one of our tea parties when the day finally came. She had rinsed out the good china, tiny teacups from my Irish grandmother who died shortly after our only visit, and set me to massacring lemons for lemonade. As I wrung the skins dry, she'd prepared cucumber sandwiches and made old-biscuits-made-new again with Nutella and jam. We'd set up a blanket with my play vase of plastic flowers between us and were bantering about the weather, our ailments, and the misbehaving children we'd spied on from our porch. I was telling her how I'd seen an unkempt first-grader ease an impressively large glob of snot from his nose and store it surreptitiously in his lunchbox that day at school, when I noticed my mother had stopped laughing and was beckoning welcomingly in the direction of the hedge. I cut my story short and turned quickly to see who was coming. There, making her way carefully through the thorns, was Celeste.

I no longer remember how that first tea party with Celeste went, but I do recall barely managing to stifle my sulkiness. To my great dismay, Celeste fit right in to our game, and she and my mother seemed to be getting along splendidly. Our new neighbour had dressed for the occasion in a torn lace tablecloth, of which, I must confess, I was terribly envious. As the afternoon drew to a close, panic curled me deeper and deeper into myself. What if this girl decided to come every day? What if she never left us alone? By the time her mother and brother appeared in front of the house, apparently eschewing Celeste's tactics of topiary espionage, my hackles had risen high. Blake busied himself bashing the cherub in the fountain with a stick and my mother drew Selene St Clare into the house for some real tea. I thought I might explode.

'I hear you mother is crazy,' I announced the instant we found ourselves alone.

'Yes,' she replied. I had hoped she would hit me, or at very least begin to cry but she just sat there looking at me, licking the jam off a biscuit expectantly, as if waiting for me to say something else.

'So why don't you live with your father instead?'

Celeste seemed pleased by the question. 'He's dead,' she said. 'And as for Blake's, who knows?' At the mention of his name, Blake threw a rock at us and missed. Since Celeste could remember, they'd travelled around with a varying array of her mother's boyfriends, punctuated occasionally with extended sojourns at her grandmother's. The Grandmother had moved to Florida last spring. She bought her daughter a flower shop in the suburbs and flew south to enjoy the last few years of a life she was sure her daughter's antics indubitably had shortened.

'That wasn't nice,' I said.

Celeste shrugged. 'Have you ever lived in a yurt in Yellowstone?'

I decided then and there that I'd allow her occasional visits. However, she appeared at my house every day for the rest of the school year. By the time summer vacation began, I had long since given up trying to get rid of her and occasionally had to explain to my mother that Celeste was *my* friend and if she needed us we'd be up in my room telling secrets and creating our wonders with glitter and glue.

Celeste, perched on my pillow now, says, 'Seriously though, you're a mess.'

She rifles through my wardrobe for a solution and selects an old dress of my mother's: my closet used to host her overflow. The dress is dotted Swiss and spring-like, but she forces me into it anyway. It's less Victorian, she says, than the kilt and cardigan look I've kept up since my mother left. I just buy what she used to buy for me, larger sizes every year. I'm surprised to find her sundress is a little tighter and shorter than it was on her, and Celeste, of course, approves.

'I'm worried about you, Irenie,' she says when I am satisfactorily attired. 'It doesn't seem healthy for you to stay cooped up in your room doing this all the time. I mean, when did you find this box? Two, maybe three weeks ago? I don't think there's been a single day since then that you haven't gone rushing home from school and shut yourself in with them.' She pauses briefly for breath. 'And there's this business of how you organize them. It's bizarre. You act like she's going to come back and find out if every corner doesn't line up. I understand you miss your mother, but this isn't going to bring her back.' She stops abruptly after she says this, afraid, perhaps, that she's gone too far.

'I'm not trying to bring her back,' I insist, smoothing down the dress. 'I just want to know what she was like. When she left, I was too young to see her as anything more than my mother, but now I have a chance to know her as a person.'

Celeste doesn't quite know what to say. She's seen her own mother as a person for far too long. We spend the rest of the afternoon making chocolate chip cookies for a school bake sale in which she has developed a sudden interest. This interest may be predicated upon one Dionysius Blue: senior, sports star, high-school god involved in everything from baseball to bake sales. Dionysius is a devout hobbyist, famous for having debuted his efforts at flame juggling at last year's fall fair. This month, his hobby is impressing Celeste. Will she make memories with him, I wonder. Will they write longing letters to each other years after they part? As I slide the cookies onto the cooling rack, I struggle to understand what it is that draws people to each other in this way. Soon, Celeste will pack up our efforts and go home. I'll read the letters until I know.

6

It's funny, isn't it, how they say absence makes the heart grow fonder? With each passing year, mine grows only more forlorn. I look for your smile in the faces of strangers. I scan newspapers, now foreign to me, hoping I might find your name there. I look for you everywhere and yet find you nowhere.

James always looked forward to Fridays—not for the weekendly reasons of most of his colleagues, but because Friday was the day his in-laws called. At first, James looked forward to hearing from them because they and Yasmeen shared the same blood. As time passed, however, he began to appreciate his conversations with them. His mother-in-law in particular could be extraordinarily charismatic. Sometimes James would find himself prattling on to Tehmima, whom he'd long ago christened 'TM', like an excitable child. Irenie was similarly affected by her grandmother's charm. She would say more to her in their half-hour conversations than she'd say to James in several months. It was only through eavesdropping on them that he ever learned anything about his daughter's life.

And so it was that they came to be facing each other across the kitchen table one unseasonably warm February morning. It was half past eight, nearly an hour after TM usually called. Irenie had the day off but James was due at work. He'd have to leave by nine to make it in time. The phone rang and he leapt for it.

'Hello?' he said. Silence. 'Is someone there?' The caller took a deep breath and then hung up. They had been getting these calls for a while now. James suspected it was an admirer of Irenie's, but when he asked her if she knew who it might be she'd glowered and said, in an unpleasantly insinuating voice, 'I haven't got any admirers. It must be one of *yours.*'

'I hope everything's all right,' he said, looking nervously at his watch. 'It isn't like her to be late.'

Irenie looked up from the strawberry jam into which she'd been dipping a teaspoon then pulling it out. Had James been a different sort of father, he would have told her that the sound it produced was giving him a headache, but because he was who he was he just regarded the spoon pointedly.

'She probably went somewhere and lost track of the time,' Irenie said, sticking the spoon deeper into the jar and giving the jam a stir. James hoped she wasn't crushing the strawberries; they were his favourite part. 'People go out, like for tea or whatever, you know?'

Her superiority annoyed James. So she had spent every one of her first nine summers there while he had visited just twice. How did that make her an authority on the social mores of the whole country? 'It's not a particularly safe place,' he told her.

'It's safe enough. Mamma was always fine there, wasn't she?'

At this, they both fell silent. True, Yasmeen had been fine there. And to succumb to what? James glanced at his daughter surreptitiously, wondering how much she knew, but the girl's face was blank. You should tell her, said the right side of his brain. It's much too late, said the left.

Tring tring, said the phone.

Irenie leapt for it, then remembered who it was that had to get to school.

'Hello, TM,' James said. 'Yes, I can hear you quite well.'

Irenie, as it turned out, had been right. His mother-in-law had got stuck in traffic on the way back from Lahore. There was a new road, she told him, a motorway so broad fighter jets could use it to take off, but she was a traditionalist and preferred the old route, the one she knew.

'Always wise,' he said. 'Stick with what you know.' At this, James could feel Irenie rolling her eyes. TM spoke at length of her grandchildren and of the happenings about the house. Then Yasmeen's sister, Mehreen, took the phone and spoke briefly of a gory root canal she'd performed that morning. Like James, Mehreen was naturally reticent, yet each week she made an effort to talk to him. He wondered if she knew how like Yasmeen's her voice was, if she knew how great a kindness she was performing granting him these five minutes of her time. She probably did not, he thought. Mehreen was nothing like her sister, and it would no doubt have surprised her to learn that he found them alike in any way.

'Well, dear,' said TM, when her daughter had handed back the phone, 'don't you think it's about time you and Irenie came to stay?'

She asked this at least eight times a year but James was never prepared. Grading, he thought. A manuscript due. A summer position. Any excuse would do. 'I have an, ahem, a fellowship,' he said. Irenie was staring straight at him, waiting for her turn with the phone. Now he'd have to find a fellowship. Or come up with a non-humiliating reason why he lost one. As much as he enjoyed talking to Yasmeen's family over the phone, he wasn't ready to visit her home without her.

'She'll have to learn the truth eventually,' his mother-in-law warned him.

'No doubt, no doubt,' stammered James.

'Tell me, darling, is Irenie happy?'

James regarded his daughter, who was frowning slightly as she massacred the jam. She had seemed more preoccupied than was usual these past few weeks, as though another life were transpiring behind her vacant gaze. He wondered briefly what had brought this about, what change, if any, had recently occurred in her young life. 'I guess,' he said.

'Maybe sending her here for a few months would be a nice change of scene?' suggested TM. 'With teenagers it should be clearer than a guess.'

'We'll see,' James told her, somewhat miffed. He handed the phone to Irenie. Half an hour later, she was still leaning against the kitchen wall, now chatting with her cousin Naaz.

7

I ripped up every photograph I found of me and you and burnt the half that was just you. I sought out your visage in bars and clubs and subway cars and slept with every echo that I met. I left them naked, still asleep, in unfamiliar, empty beds. When a hundred mornings brought no peace, I did the last thing I could think to do: burnt the halves that were just me, ripped apart from you. Animus and invisibility cannot wrench you from my heart. My love for you persists even stripped of tenderness, roots beneath the earth.

It takes me over a month to read all the letters. There are two reasons for this. I could have read them much faster but, for once, I understood why Mrs Winterbourne always tells me to take my time: when you turn the last page, the book is through. I grew afraid of this when I reached 1992. Ahmed was diagnosed with lymphoma and the prognosis was poor. I stalled over a week on those short, sad missives, terrified I'd lose a man I'd never even met. I realized it was this I'd been hoping for all along: to meet him, my mother's Ahmed, to see what he was like and in seeing that, how she'd once been. But I will never meet him. I'm fairly sure he's dead. He made a miraculous recovery in '92, but by '96 he was sick again. The last letter he sent her was a farewell.

I finish reading the letters sometime in March, on a day as cold and dead as the one on which I began. The snow still seems a permanent feature of Crawford's topography but winter has taken its leave, like a caretaker after beach season no longer bothering

to whitewash the picket fence. On sunny days, the filthy piles
of snow seem strange, lumpen Rip Van Winkles along the road,
unkempt now that their sojourns have extended so long beyond
they were meant. But sunny days are cold still. When you go
outside, the fog is still in your breath. Perhaps the only signs that
spring will be upon us soon are in the high-school halls. It starts
in early March when, despite carefully regulated climate control,
the air goes soft and warm. The raucous clamour of the hallways
takes on a certain fluidity, as though the noise is filtered through a
pool of silent water. Girls' cheeks flush through winter pallor and
their suitors strut and preen. So many eyes are glassy, so many lips
slip into dreamy smiles. The fluorescent lights seem gentler; the
simple smell of wet wellingtons is made complex by the addition
of dying flowers, a cloying scent emitted by unwanted Valentine
bouquets left in lockers to decay and also, more mysteriously, in
the sighs of the girls most starry eyed. Groundhogs may have
forecasted spring for Pennsylvanians two hundred years ago, but
in Crawford, adolescent girls are the best predictors. This year,
even Celeste shares their collective blush.

That her date with Dionysius Blue was a success is the second
reason the letters took me thirty-seven days to read; had he not
been there to distract Celeste from me, it would have taken twice
as long. The first night, he introduced her to his latest passion:
Flamenco. Afterwards, they snuck into Selene's greenhouse and
she introduced him to hers. Ever since, he has been by her side
constantly. She doesn't seem to mind and, oddly enough, neither
do I. He taught me to whistle and tie a square knot. On the day I
finish the letters, however, I want to talk to Celeste without him
there.

'Come over after dinner,' she tells me when I call. Blake has
been coughing a lot lately and she's taking him to see the doctor
this afternoon.

Sunday is slower still when it's spent waiting. I go over a
world history paper and spend several hours experimenting with

Nani's nargisi kofte recipe. Mamma always complained that it was impossible to get American ground lamb to stick in thin layers around the hardboiled eggs. With a few tablespoons of breadcrumbs and an egg yolk, I find it sticks quite well. I try not to be depressed that I will never be able to tell her this.

Light plays through the gauze and the world looks soft. White curtains in every room. My mother would exclaim to Nani a decade ago about how there were no great gusts of dust to turn them all brown. They're yellowing now, but I like them better this way. Before, they were the airy, ersatz bright of sanatorium whites—false promises, failing health. Now they're a fleeing bride's train as she leaves her man at the altar. When sunlight filters through, it feels warm even in winter. Absolutes have always made me uncomfortable: light with no colour, skies with no end. I don't like to think how much I'll never know. The old curtains have history; they're filled with our dust. We create our surroundings and in turn they create us. My mother would tell the worst fairy tales when I was a child: stories of lovers separated by circumstance resolvable only by death. They all ended up poisoned or drowned or swallowed by the earth itself. The stories I told myself about my mother late at night were even worse—not because they ended badly, but because they seemed so possible, yet I knew they wouldn't come true.

I knew I'd never see my mother again the day I turned ten. I knew because she didn't call. Celeste and I spent all day at the beach, making sand cakes along the shore. The Grandmother drank Sidecars on the porch, certain enough of our swimming skills to ignore us for her book. We took turns burying each other in the sand, sculpting mermaid tails and mountainous breasts a more attentive adult would have found obscene. Even though we could have swum out as far as we liked, even as far as Jamaica, we stayed by the shore. Without anyone else's nerves to test, there was little point in testing our own. I had a new swimsuit—an early birthday present from my mother—baby pink with a ruffled skirt.

Until we found a real jellyfish dead and drying on some rocks, I'd liked to imagine I looked like one of them. Celeste, bold as her neon bikini, flung it back into the sea with her bare hands.

On my birthday, there were cupcakes crowned with pastel frosting for our lunch. Celeste and I ate nothing else. We devoured half a dozen each and then lay flat on the beach. A woman with a Labrador wandered into the private cove and asked if I was Hawaiian, I'd grown so brown. Jealous, Celeste almost drowned herself in coconut tanning oil, which made the sand stick even more. We rolled around in the sand with the dog until the Grandmother sent her gardener to evict the trespasser and then spent the rest of the afternoon playing Bathing Beauties, a game Celeste had invented in which the Beauty had to bound across the beach in slow motion and rescue the Bather without getting her hair wet.

We spent an hour in the tub that night, having been instructed by the Grandmother to scrub off every last grain of sand. We put on white sundresses that almost matched and light cardigans in shades of baby blue. I wanted to wear lace socks with Mary Janes, but Celeste said that was babyish so we wore our sandals instead. We even painted our toenails mauve. If the Grandmother's surgically secured face could have shown surprise, it might have when she saw us then. The whole time we were there, we'd run around with tangled hair in bathing suits and tattered shorts.

That night, she took us to a fancy restaurant where the menu was in French. When we were done eating, a tuxedoed waiter brought out a birthday cake with a sparkler instead of a candle. At the time, I'd thought it unimaginably exotic to celebrate one's birthday in a restaurant. Even the Grandmother smiled a bit when I ignited the brandy in her glass thinking it would stop the sparkler from sparking. She gave me a beautifully wrapped box with ten kinds of taffy, one for each year, and a delicate gold bracelet with ten pearls spaced out evenly along the chain. Though I knew she was only doing it all because Celeste had refused to come unless

I came and I had refused to come because I'd miss my birthday,
I had a lot of fun. But not so much fun that I didn't notice my
mother hadn't called.

'She's giving you your independence,' Celeste tried to persuade
me when we'd checked the answering machine at least ten times.
'You're in the double digits now.'

But I knew Mamma would never do a thing like that. I tried to
pretend I was having fun the last few days of our trip, but I wasn't.
I'd begun to remember a time three years ago when my mother
wasn't there. I remembered Jo Anne the Sports Fan and how I'd
known at once, without knowing how, what had made my mother
leave when I saw my father and my babysitter entwined upon
the couch. My mother came back that time though; he hadn't
managed to get rid of her for good. But this time, I was sure,
he had. I knew my mother wasn't strong like most adults, even
small things made her sad. This time when he got rid of her, she
wouldn't have it in her to come back.

'Where is she?' I demanded as soon as I returned. His face
confirmed what I'd already known. Adults were good at keeping
secrets but when it came to keeping guilt a secret, they were no
better than us kids. I'd seen guilt on my father's face many times
before and I recognized it then.

The first time my father tried to get rid of my mother, he said
she wasn't well, that she was in the hospital. But the hospital I
went to with Mary Anne looked more like a hotel. And what
kind of hospital didn't allow children? Melinda Yao's father had
died of cancer the year before and she'd missed school to go to
the hospital all the time. I was sure my father had my mother
locked up in a dungeon somewhere and the hotel was just a trick.
Now, of course, I know that Fairhaven Centre is one of the best
addiction centres in the country, but back then I thought it was
a resort where rich people went to relax. If my mother really was
in there somewhere, I'd thought, it was in a basement, scrubbing
sheets.

The second time my father got rid of my mother, he didn't even have an excuse.

'She's gone,' he said. He didn't say anything about when she was coming back. A few weeks later, he gave me the pendant that had always hung around her neck, the pendant which would one day unlock the secret box.

Sighing, I look at the clock. Only five-thirty. It's not so much the last letter that I want to discuss with Celeste as it is all the rest. The last one is only a few lines long. Ahmed writes that he doesn't expect to live much longer, that he'll love my mother even after he's dead. It is an unsatisfying conclusion to the nineteen years of my mother's life I've lived in these last few weeks. It tells me nothing about what happened at the very end. Where did my mother go? How was it that she died? I don't know. All I know is this: Ahmed loved Yasmeen and Yasmeen loved Ahmed. They intended to get married but something went awry. Ahmed married a woman name Mehrunissa and Yasmeen married James Eccles. They missed one another until they died.

When the phone rings me back into real life I find I've been scoring the side of the kitchen table with a knife.

'Irenie?' my father asks when I pick up, as though anyone *else* would answer our phone.

'Yes?'

'I've just figured out a way to rewrite chapter fifty-eight so it brings together the whole book. I think I'll be in my office pretty late.'

'Congratulations.'

'What?' My father can't tell sarcasm from my attempts to be polite.

'On having figured out how to bring it all together.'

'Oh. Thank you. I just wanted you to know I won't be home in time for dinner.'

'Okay.'

'Goodbye then.'

It's a wonder my father managed to get married in the first place, let alone conduct at least one extramarital affair. The letters exonerate him a little, but I still blame him for my mother's death. She stopped writing to Ahmed when they met and she didn't write to him for years. She didn't write till I was almost one, and even then only to say how sorry she was about his parents' death. If my father had made her happier, perhaps she wouldn't have responded to the long letter Ahmed sent in return. Perhaps she wouldn't have responded to his next letter, about how unhappy he was with his life, or the next, about how much he wished to see her again. If my father had made her happier, she wouldn't have needed Ahmed again, she wouldn't have welcomed his melancholy invasion. But even though she did, letters are not the same as love affairs. I'll feel so much better when I hear it from Celeste.

I've put off discussing them with her until now and it's strange to have a secret. Celeste has always known everything that's happened to me. It was she who gently announced it was time for training bras and then took me shopping for them as soon as we could get a ride. It was she who led me down the women's hygiene aisle of the drugstore and explained the facts of life. Celeste knew about when I was so worried about wearing a bathing suit in front of boys that I nearly failed gym in seventh grade. She knew when I tripped over Timmy Bigg's backpack and flashed the entire class. She's teaching me to be a woman, she says, and I her to be a lady. I'm not sure either of us is doing very well.

At half past seven, I find her and Blake sitting at their dining table with a plate of saltines, a bottle of ketchup, and an old jar of grape jelly. The table is beautifully laid, a lace runner down the middle and what I imagine is Dionysius's latest floral tribute as a centrepiece. They're using the Grandmother's wedding china and drinking root beer out of her crystal champagne flutes. Selene is nowhere in sight. They accept my offer of the orphaned koftas, the projectile possibilities of which Blake fortuitously does not realize until they are almost gone. I do my best not to be offended when

Celeste stirs ketchup into the curry and struggle to find a starting point for my story. After a few false starts and fumbles, I finally find where to begin: on New Year's Eve, 1979, Ahmed Kakkezai kissed Yasmeen Khalil on the seventeenth-storey balcony of a friend in upper Manhattan.

And then the story takes off of its own accord. Celeste, usually a bad listener, manages to keep quiet except for a few irrepressible exclamations of surprise. Blake gets bored halfway through and abandons us for QVC.

'Your mother was amazing!' she says as soon as I am through. 'I mean, I always thought she was wonderful, but this is astounding.'

Needless to say, it is not quite the reaction I was expecting. For weeks, I've been worrying about how I'll defend my mother to Celeste. 'It is?'

'It's like the stuff of fairy tales or something. And even then, she made sure you didn't know.'

'I fail to see how that's a good thing.'

'Irenie, do you know how many of Selene's boyfriends I've seen come and go? Do you know how many times I've watched her lose it over some idiot?'

'But Mamma did, well, lose it.' I cringe.

'When Ahmed was dying. The rest of the time, she kept everything to herself. She never dragged you out of school to chase him halfway across the world or left you with your grandmother because she was too distraught to bother with a child.'

'At least your mother always came back.'

'So what? Your mother was, like, the ideal of motherhood. I don't know if I ever told you this, but when we were little I used to pretend she was my mother too. She gave up everything for you.'

'It's not as though she had much of a choice.'

'Of course she did. She could have run off with Ahmed anytime she liked. But she didn't.'

'In the end she did.'

'You don't know what happened in the end.'

'I suppose.'

'So what are you going to do now?' She's so excited she's bouncing in her chair.

'What do you mean?'

'Don't you want to find out what happened?'

'Of course. But how? I've scoured the letters for clues.'

'What about the best friend? Ahmed's? What was his name again?'

I hesitate. Something about Mustapha has left me uneasy: in the early letters he is everywhere and then, after months of silence, neither my mother nor Ahmed ever mentions him again.

'Well?' demands Celeste.

'Khalid,' I mutter. 'Mustapha Khalid.'

'And you said he might be in Boston, right?' She runs to fetch the phone. 'How many Mustapha Khalids can there be in Boston?' she asks, dialling information.

None, it turns out. Or at least none that are listed.

'What about your mother's roommate?' Celeste suggests, undeterred. 'Claire? If she shared a room with your mother all through college, she must know something. Do you know her last name?'

I can't recall, though I do remember my mother being away for her college roommate's wedding the day I broke my arm. I was only five then and the concept of a roommate was mysterious to me. 'If we know that Claire from the class of 1982 got married in 1991, perhaps the office of alumni affairs can provide us with an address,' I tell Celeste. She looks at me with admiration—usually I am not the one to come up with the bright ideas—and procures from the kitchen junk drawer a piece of the watermarked writing paper her grandmother sends her, in pointed suggestion, every birthday.

Selene returns as we're debating over whether to use business or personal address. Celeste thinks we should sound friendly and I argue that my mother was always somewhat formal. We hurry to hide the papers as Selene drops her hobnailed boots by the stove, though she doesn't seem to notice us at all. 'Something smells yummy,' she says absently. There are flower petals in her hair and I see no sign of her having worn a coat.

'Blake had a doctor's appointment today,' Celeste informs her coldly. 'He was very upset that you weren't there.'

'Oh, sweetie, the hyacinths.' She gestures vaguely and strokes her daughter's shiny yellow hair. 'Hi, Irenie.'

Celeste twists away. 'The hyacinths? They had to x-ray his lungs.'

Selene suddenly turns sad. 'So purple they were,' she mutters. 'Purple clouds and purple skies. Purple Haze!'

'Like the song?'

'Yes, Irenie. Like in the song!' She looks at me as though I've just rescued her cat from a flaming tree.

'Your son has mycoplasma pneumonia,' Celeste tells her tonelessly.

'Oh dear,' Selene sighs. 'Oh dear. Did they give him a lollipop?'

'They gave him a prescription.'

'And a lollipop?'

'Yes.' Celeste gives up. 'A purple one.' It occurs to me that her notions of impeccable maternal behaviour are perhaps somewhat skewed.

'How nice. Purple is always better.'

'Do you remember what went on at my house the time Celeste and I went to Florida?' Somehow the question just slips out. Celeste glares at me. Selene often responds poorly to inquiries into the past.

To my surprise, though, she answers, 'Oh yes! Yes, of course I remember. He didn't like the coffee but the flowers were very nice.'

Celeste rolls her eyes. 'I'm going over to Irenie's. You really should go and talk to Blake.'

'Yes,' Selene says vaguely, picking at a grain of rice. 'Have fun, sweethearts.' She smiles, but not at us. Her gaze is directed at the world over our shoulders, the world in which she seems to live. I often wonder if Celeste would be less upset by this if not for the days when Selene wakes up and solidifies from the shadow she is to the person she must once have been. She wants us to bake cookies then, or to go out shopping for new clothes. She scours the kitchen counters and makes terrific French toast. When she hears a joke, she laughs. When you speak to her, she turns her head. She is sprightly and bright. She takes keen interest in everything her children say and do, looking at them as though wanting to sear their faces into her mind. It took me years to realize that this is exactly what she's doing. She can't really see them through her usual mental fog; the snapshots are all she has.

8

Darling, all afternoon a line of verse has been running through my head: 'Little do men perceive what solitude is, and how far it extendeth/For a crowd is not company, and faces are but a gallery of pictures/and talk but a tinkling cymbal, where there is no love.' Bacon says it better than I ever could, though he seems not to think as I do that without it we may as well be dead.

April arrives unexpectedly, still cold and damp, cruel only in the most literal sense. My mother always hated April here. Accustomed to flying kites in February in welcome of the spring, she'd pander to the weather gods all through March with winter coats and woolly scarves. On April first, she'd say beseechingly: now it *has* to get warm. Without very much hope, she'd pack away her overcoats and shiver through school functions and afternoon walks dressed in just sweaters and thick socks. By the time warm weather actually arrived, she'd inevitably be struck by a winter chill.

I tug my hat further down over my ears as I fight the gusts eight long, cold blocks to the library. The wind blows so hard it knocks my stride askew anytime my mind strays from the task of walking straight. Contemplating tonight's dinner, I am propelled into a pole. If I float off inside my head entirely, I might well find myself spread-eagled on the road. The thought is almost tempting for a second: let the winds take me where they will,

but the enfilade leads nowhere new and nothing good has ever
come of flinging blindly from the course. When did I grow out
of adventures? When did the inside of a golden globe become no
more than the cramped underside of a never-dying bush? There
used to be magic in the shrubbery outside the library, in the trees
behind my house. Acorns were ingredients for fairy spells and
neat saucers for imagined cups of tea. Stones, if round and white,
were messages from a secret world. Dead branches, dancing now
across the street, were relinquished sceptres of defeated queens.
The whole world today is grey and dead, the tempest just a whirl
of unforgiving souls. Wind whips wetness from my face and I lose
track of whether it's my eyes or nose that is bleeding in the cold. I
could've, maybe should've, stayed home today, but something has
occurred to me and I require use of the library.

In the overheated library foyer, my head of snow-queen icicles
soon melts into an uninspired mass of tangled hair. I watch the
winter redness of my face slowly surrender to the warmth in
the glass-paned double doors. Ordinarily, I am afraid of being
apprehended: one of those narcissists who cannot pass anything
reflective without taking a good, long look, but the library seems
empty; Mrs Winterbourne hasn't even switched the main lights
on. No one in their right mind would brave this cold just for
something new to read. It is a day for well-thumbed favourites
and for infomercials on TV.

Mrs Winterbourne makes her way into my reflection so quietly
I'm startled to see that it's her face in the glass and not my own.

'Are you going to stand there looking at yourself all day?' she
asks with a feigned impatience.

I go in, mildly embarrassed. Mrs Winterbourne is well inured
to the strange things people do. She has overheard encyclopaedias
of secrets silently shelving in the stacks. The library is as it was over
a hundred years ago: dark wooden shelves ascend almost up to the
roof, ladders roll well-oiled on ancient runners. The faded carpets
betray former plushness and the windows still have drapes. It is a

splendid place to whisper things you want no one else to know. But not a word uttered in this library escapes Mrs Winterbourne's attentive ear. She catalogues the town's infidelities and unplanned pregnancies with disconnect and to her, people are little more than the trite secrets they unwittingly reveal. She disapproves of everything not black and white on a page, but I think she likes me quite despite herself.

'Is there much to shelve today?' I ask, hoping there's not. Usually, I don't mind it. As we work, Mrs Winterbourne tells me stories. Today though, I'm here for something else.

'There are two carts by the magazines,' she tells me, 'and the Ws need dusting. That idiot they sent me from your school only wiped the fronts.'

I quickly put the books away while Mrs Winterbourne putters about in the records room. All births and deaths and marriages of Crawford are noted in those files. She takes her role as their custodian very seriously. When she's almost through, I rush up to her to ask where an antique atlas belongs.

'Come,' she says, frowning. Her disapproval is well worth it: she neglects to lock the door. By the time we move onto the Ws, Mrs Winterbourne has forgiven me. She tells me how *Othello* ends. She is appalled that I haven't read it yet. An elderly woman with a newspaper tucked under her hat straggles in halfway through. She wants a book on raising baby mice. Her grandson has adopted an orphaned litter and nothing they've tried yet will make them eat. Mrs Winterbourne shows her to the reference section and I slip into the records room. Births are in the corner by the window. 1986 is a lower drawer. Though I double check, I see no sign of the name 'Eccles'. I check 'Khalil' and nothing. Holding my breath, I flip through to where Kakkezai would be, but there's no sign of that either. According to the town of Crawford, Irenie Eccles was never born.

By the time Mrs Winterbourne is done with the old woman, I'm back at the Ws, innocently wiping an Edith Wharton. 'Just disgusting,' she mutters. 'They're lenient with children to the point of absurdity and then they come back five years later requesting books on the causes of violence in youths as though they have no idea why their children are out of control.'

I snicker through the dust of many Ws. Mrs Winterbourne detests children of all sizes and sorts. They smear chocolate on picture books and chase through the stacks after story hour. When I first came in without my mother, she made me read by the corner of her desk. No matter how much I begged and pleaded, she wouldn't let me take a single book out without an adult present to guarantee its prompt return. A year passed and she grew used to me there. Another passed and she began to offer the occasional recommendation. She let me stay past closing hour if I was at a good bit and showed me how books should be shelved so I could exchange one for another without getting in her way. When I turned twelve, she finally decided to let me check out books for myself, but by then I was so in the habit of spending afternoons at the library that I came just to help out. If she was glad to see I still came, there was never any sign. She just handed me a rag one afternoon with only the most taciturn instruction. At first, all I did was dust, but now she lets me do anything she doesn't feel like doing herself. Anything except file in the records room. Can I ask her? Will she know? I hand her a high-shelf W and wipe away the dust left in its wake.

'I think we can close up early today, Irenie. Don't you?' she asks, passing me a final well-dusted book. 'No one's going to come in on a day like this.'

'I suppose not,' I concede, though I'm none too eager to go home early and I can't imagine why she would be. We do not discuss things like that, however, so I bundle up to leave. We do not talk about our feelings or our plans or what we've had that day to eat.

'Mrs Winterbourne?' I ask quietly when we're on our way outside. 'Are all birth certificates stored here?'

She regards me piercingly and I feel she knows every hope and thought I've ever had. 'You have your father's eyes, Irenie,' she tells me, and marches into the gale.

9

Do you remember when you told me that if you love someone you must sometimes let them go? You hurled that pithy adage out like pennies for a wish. I held my tongue all those years ago; I didn't say a word. I let that age-old idiocy stand uncorrected and now I am alone.

James hadn't liked it, he hadn't liked it one bit. Why would Yasmeen happily send Irenie off to Florida with some girl they hardly knew when she'd barely let their daughter out of her sight for almost ten years?

'She's so excited about the trip,' Yasmeen had pleaded when he'd questioned her decision. 'For once she's found a friend she actually likes.'

Did his daughter like this girl? She sat in silence at the dinner table as Celeste regaled them with tales of things that happened to her that day at school. She followed wordlessly when Celeste led the way upstairs. Was it just play-acting for Yasmeen who so wanted her to have a friend?

'But don't you think she'll be frightened, so far away from home?' James asked. From you, he'd meant. He wondered if he cared. Irenie's feelings had long ceased to be anything more than background noise. The nights she woke up screaming, she wanted only his wife. When her small accomplishments deserved acclaim, she never turned to him.

'Tell Papa what Mrs Green said about your essay,' Yasmeen would urge.

Irenie would sigh as though she were the mother, impatient with a proud child that wanted to tell the whole world what it had done. 'She said it was three grade levels above anyone else's,' his daughter would report in dutiful monotone. Certainly no one could fault her on her manners, this strange and silent child of his.

'That's fantastic,' James would falter, unaware until Yasmeen rebuked him later that a more sincere response would have been to ask to read the essay. But what could he learn from a third-grader's essay, an essay the author would prefer he never see? It was true, for all Yasmeen's protests, that his daughter regarded him with not a hint of interest. She didn't want to see his office or be taught by him to tie her shoes. If something made her sad, she'd prefer her father never knew. Sometimes James wondered if Yasmeen made up the minor delights and upsets she reported their daughter encountered every day. Irenie was stoic, stone-like, whenever he was around. And although he found her silence somewhat discomfiting, he'd no doubt have been at far more of a loss with a lively child, a child who smothered him with hugs anytime he came in through the door, a child who wanted praise for spelling tests or kisses on skinned knees.

If Irenie became homesick in Florida, James would never know. She would never call up, crying, and beg him to bring her back. He had trouble even imaging his daughter sobbing. Years later, it occurred to him that what had worried him was not Irenie's leaving but Yasmeen's allowing her to go.

Yasmeen sighed and rolled her eyes then. 'I think we should encourage independence. It's you who's always saying I need to loosen the apron strings a bit.'

It was the one disagreement they had. James thought Irenie and Yasmeen were unnaturally attached. What little girl would rather spend afternoons stirring curries with her mother than going outside to play? What woman would rather drink imaginary tea at a table full of stuffed toys than lunch with friends old enough for real caffeine? During one of their uglier arguments, James had accused Yasmeen of basing her entire happiness upon their little girl. It was a comment born of jealousy but that didn't mean it was untrue. It was unfair for a child to bear a weight like that.

'You shouldn't stake so much on her, she's just a little girl,' James had reminded Yasmeen time and time again. Irenie was just a little girl, hard though it was for him to see. When she fell asleep in the car and he had to carry her to bed, he was always taken aback by how little she weighed.

'You should talk, staking so much in little girls,' Yasmeen once snapped when he reminded her that Irenie was just a child. It was the night after they found her hunched over the kitchen table, after Irenie emerged from the basement and Yasmeen began to scream. James had just tucked their daughter into bed. Brushing a lock of hair out of his daughter's mouth, the spider-shadow of his hand had cast her whole head in darkness. Placing his palm ever so gently over her face, James saw that his fingers wrapped nearly all the way around her skull.

'Let's just get you into bed,' he'd told his wife that night, thinking she really was delirious. If anything, he ought to stake much more. It wasn't until many years later that James realized Yasmeen hadn't been talking about their daughter.

10

Why are some paths left untravelled if they are the ones down which we are meant to go? Why are some roads inevitably not taken though they might be smoother, better lit? Why can one not just retrace one's steps to take a different fork? Why am I yet without you when you are all that imbues my life with worth?

The new gym glows October gold although it's almost spring. In daylight the building is cold glass and steel, at night a sterile laboratory display of subjects running at their wheels, but at dusk it is a fairy castle, lit up inside and out. It looks too pristine to believe that ordinary beings sweat and shout behind the brilliant orange doors. Elfin types with pointy ears and flowers in their hair should be celebrating in the courts, while ribbon dancers with wings of gossamer scatter confetti made of sunbeams and edible diamond dust. A group of sporting girls stream out, loud in matching sweat suits with palm tree ponytails erupting from their heads. The sun dips as I pass and I see there's only more of the same inside.

My father has an evening class this year from six to nine. He likes to have his dinner during the fifteen-minute break he's forever forgetting to announce. Sometimes he's waiting when I come at seven; sometimes I catch him by the microwave at home. Celeste doesn't see why I bother delivering these dinners when my father doesn't take an interest in what he eats. Just give him a container of leftovers in the morning, she tells me.

I like to bring him dinner though. If I can do everything my mother did, perhaps we can pretend she's still here. She would be there every Tuesday with a hot, fresh plate of food. Even now that I know she won't be back, I don't want to let her down. Walking across campus as night falls, I feel as though I'm on a vital mission. The boys with basketballs don't see me and the perfumed girls push by as though I am not there. Their world is small, these few square miles, and I am not a part. If they know that there's anything beyond them, they don't seem very much to care. World news is a two-keg party in Bleaker Hall; trauma is a ten-page paper some heartbroken girl hasn't yet begun. If tater tots are served at dinner, word spreads fast and students mass towards the dining hall. They come on bicycles, in sweat suit pants, with binders spewing notes. They collect as though in a rally in this strange, small world where childhood can return. Fried potatoes are once again exciting and Frisbee makes a comeback. It's fine to cry outside the library when you've done poorly on a test. Coming here is like stepping into a snow globe where I'm sure not to be seen. Slipping through the chimerical campus landscape is even better than playing with the fancy dollhouses my mother never bought me when I was a child.

The only people who do see me here are Doris and Charles Faber. Professor Faber is my father's nemesis and only friend and he always stops to show me his latest squirting flower or trick deck. Doris is the department secretary, who has plied me with small presents since I can remember. Doris and Professor Faber believe I am a kind and unselfish young girl. I imagine them at faculty parties telling everyone how sweet Professor Eccles's daughter is, how well she cares for him. I would hate for these shadow people I haven't seen in years to suspect I'm a problem child. I would hate for them to say 'that poor James' in quiet corners. There will be no poor James-ing as long as I'm around. He doesn't deserve sympathy and I'll see that he gets none. Tonight, all he'll be getting is chicken biryani with a side of chhole and a small dish of cucumber raita.

Orchard Hall is dark and quiet. Nothing that has been dead a thousand years demands the urgency of midnight oil. Of the classics faculty, only my father habitually works late. I let myself in through the back with the key he so often reminds me I'm not supposed to have. I doubt his colleagues would be angry, though, if they knew. The most valuable thing here is probably the box of tea bags in the lounge. Even the paintings on the walls are rejects from the art department.

Orchard Hall is less a hall than a half-hearted Gothic construction converted into offices. My father's is in what once was the attic, or the penthouse, as my mother called it. She claimed he got the office as a privilege because the fourth floor is the only floor high enough to offer any views. As far as I'm concerned, all it offers is a creaking climb and an excuse for the rest of the department to pretend my father isn't there.

The pile of junk on my father's desk has grown noticeably since I was here last. Papers are everywhere and at least half a dozen disposable coffee cups lie undisposed of on the floor. Though he has a wall of bookcases and a row of filing cabinets famous for their order, my father's office is always a mess.

I put the plate on his chair, thinking there's nowhere else that he'll see it. I'm proud of myself for hoping only a little that he'll sit in it by mistake. Then, out of nowhere, I feel terribly guilty that wishing my father harm only offhandedly is something I'm proud of. For all the dinners I bring and the shirt collars I starch, I am not really good to my father. Those sorts of things weren't what my mother meant when she urged me to give him a chance. I pick up some coffee cups and throw them away. There's a rag by the computer, so I wipe clean the screen. My father's finicky shelving system seems to order books by some combination of author, translator, publisher and publication date, but I haven't spent the past five years under Mrs Winterbourne for nothing. I figure I'll tidy his office, unasked and unplanned. That is a nice thing for a daughter to do, isn't it?

The books fly into place quickly once I've figured out how my father arranges them. It would make a lot of sense if they were all actually kept on their shelves. At first, I keep expecting him to burst in. I doubt he'd be angry; he just wouldn't know what to do. We would have some stumbling conversation and he'd get in the way trying to help. I'd rather work in solitude, disappearing into the night when I'm through.

A surprise awaits me in the filing cabinets: my mother's handwriting along the tops of most files. I don't know why this strikes me so. She ordered everything at home, so why not here also? I suppose I just always thought that since my father's life was so separate from mine, it was separate from hers too. Perhaps she walked over with lunch for my father every day of the week. Perhaps she stood behind this very chair and pressed his cramped shoulders when he said he was tense. It would have been a great game for my meticulous mother, to make sense of this mess. I imagine her chewing her lip as she filed, waiting for my father to come back from teaching a class. Did he pluck flowers for her in spring? Snitch her ancient sweets from the brightly foiled collection Doris displays in cut glass bowls? Did she jump up to kiss him like she did to me?

'Yasmeen and Ahmed'. A file, almost buried at the back. It's not her writing. Could this be my birth certificate? Does the truth of my origins lie within? I want to open it but it's not something handed to me and it's not lying somewhere I might be expected to look. I'll take it out only if I get everything else put in place, I reason. If I'm to absent myself before nine, it's not likely I'll even finish.

But this unoffered tip for services unsolicited proves great motivation. If I could do schoolwork so fast, I might already be a snow-globed student somewhere myself. By quarter to nine, the office is so neat a dropped pin could be spotted from five feet away. I've even dusted the bookshelves and wiped down the desk with a damp paper towel. If I weren't meant to find the file, I could never have finished so soon, I tell myself. If I weren't meant to find it, I'd have let my father eat food from last night. I would have been glad to leave his plate where he might sit on it and left without second thoughts. Maybe this is what I get for being nice: a file instead of a thank you. But there isn't anything nice about taking something in return, especially something not offered and not meant for you.

Who am I kidding? I'm not nice. I haven't even done anything nice. All I've done is try to subdue the guilt my mother can still sometimes arouse in me even though she isn't here.

The file is slim, almost empty. It does not contain my birth certificate or anything else pertaining to me. In it are three yellowing newspaper clippings from almost five years ago. April eighth, April thirteenth and April twenty-seventh. Unidentified Vehicle Plummets from Dover Cliff reads the first. Families of Mystery Vehicle's Passengers Located, reads the second. And finally, Search for Dover Drowners Abandoned at Request of Families. It's almost nine. Scanning quickly, I see 'inclement weather', 'reckless speeding', 'swerving to avoid oncoming traffic', 'two adults, one male and one female', 'Mrs Yasmeen Eccles of Crawford, New York, and Mr Ahmed Kakkezai of London'.

I'm running across campus, through groups of students heading towards important places, places perhaps important only to them. Unseeing, I hurtle along the quaint cobblestone paths, past the grand statuary of auspicious intellects. I upset an armload of red plastic cups, essential accessories for any Wednesday night affair. And Thursday night, Friday night, even Monday night if you go to college here. But I don't stop to pick them up.

'Watch it, asshole,' someone yells as I leave them behind for the quiet streets of Crawford, empty for the night.

I race down Mayburn Street and take a left on Smith, running as though I'm in a dream. I don't feel it when my lungs begin to ache or acknowledge the protestations of my limbs. The road beneath my feet is elastic tonight; I spring off it, ever faster forward. The only sound is my sneakers on the ground, the only sights blurred into vague nothings by speed and by the night. It should be raining, I think. My hair should hang in wet tendrils when I fall to my knees at an intersection and scream *no* or *how* or *why* at the cold, indifferent sky. But tonight is dry.

Out of nowhere, there is a car before me, its hood hot beneath my hands. And then the horn: a banshee wail so long and loud I think my eardrums might explode.

'Crazy kid,' I hear, as I turn down my street.

The door is unlocked, as I'd left it, the phone still on the kitchen wall. It seems that things should have fallen into disrepair as I ran, the moment of realization crystallizing cinematically in a series of tastefully shot speed-frames: plants withering in seconds, paper peeling in fast forward from the walls, the hands of an old grandfather clock whirring into a blur as clouds and suns and moons race across a sky framed in boughs, sometimes bare, sometimes in vibrant bloom.

The ringing of the phone startles me, but when I answer there's no one there. I hear a breath, maybe the clicking of long distance. Or maybe I'm just imagining things when there is nothing there. 'Why are you doing this to us?' I shout and slam it down.

11

Hope, I've found, is a funny fellow. He loves to play a joke. He burns brilliantly through tempests and in sunshine fades to a gentle glow. He leads you here and there and everywhere, then abandons you in darkness, all alone. He seems to desert you when you need him most, an apostate of the soul. But cruellest of his many tricks is that he never truly goes.

The secrets of people you know are like dust on a mantle: they quietly build without you ever noticing they exist, but once you know they're there, they are infinitely distracting.

My father's secrets have never been of much interest to me. I know that he sometimes puts used handkerchiefs in his pockets even if they're caked with snot and that he's had three short affairs since my mother left. I know he hides a handle of off-brand scotch in his closet so he can refill the Glen Livet bottle downstairs and pretend he only rarely drinks. I know he eats stewed prunes for his constipation, not because he likes the taste. And I know where he hides the Christmas presents Doris selects for me each year. What I didn't know was that my father's been keeping secrets I might actually find compelling. Not secrets of his own, but of my mother's.

'You cleaned my office, Irenie?' he asks four days after the fact. I'm halfway through the bathroom door and wearing just a towel, so it isn't the best time to bring it up.

'It was quite a mess,' I tell him with my mother's sweet severity. I don't think he looks suspicious, but his face never really gives anything away. Whether or not he is my real father, I know my blankest gaze is his.

He's caught off guard by my tone, or perhaps by the realization that his office was indeed a mess. 'Yes,' he affirms slowly. 'Yes, I suppose it was rather untidy. Thank you. Maybe I should unleash you on my papers here.'

If my father had a sense of humour, I might take this to be a joke, but since I've yet to see any sign of such a thing, it's an insincere invitation, and one I'm happy to accept.

When my mother vanishes, I become obsessed with light. The April when she is suddenly gone is particularly rainy, and sunlight never quite permeates the shadowed corners of our house. When I get home from school, I rush from one room to the next, switching on every light. Even so, the house feels too dark. Dimness can leak from unexpected corners and take over a room before you know it. It is a miracle I don't burn down the house. Waiting for another stab at my father's study, I'm proud not to have turned on a single light before it is dark. He needs some sort of grotesque dental procedure and will be spending Saturday at the hospital, sleeping off the drugs. I offer to go along after he frets about it all week, but thankfully he declines. I wonder if he'll come back with dentures, shiny straight and white. I wonder if I'll know. Or if, years from now, I will discover the smile he so rarely smiles floating in a juice glass by the bathroom sink.

I've been making discreet advances into his study for a while now, but have never been so confident of his absence that I can properly pry. My birth certificate is nowhere in sight. It seems every aspect of my mother's life has been catalogued except that which is most important. There must be *something* I am missing. Celeste offers to help me search and turns up with Dionysius in tow. He is building a ship in a bottle and has got stuck on the sails. It seems he cannot sew. In exchange for his assistance, I volunteer to embroider them for him. My cross stitch is impeccable.

We chat amiably as we search and I find myself hoping Celeste's relationship with Dionysius will not be shortlived. He'll be going to Brown come September, but perhaps they can make it last. He retrieves and replaces things from high shelves without making a mess and Celeste has an eye for objects that might be of interest. Two walls of my father's study are bookcases. They extend from cabinets, about three feet high, to the ceiling. Books and papers are shoved into shelves haphazardly, even more untidily than in his office. I had planned to shake each one out just in case there's anything hidden, but I soon realize that would take a year. Dionysius and I do our best with the books while Celeste takes on the row of filing cabinets. We find student papers from the seventies, twenty-year-old wedding invitations, manuals on mah-jong for beginners, but nothing pertaining to my mother. Celeste unearths her Crawford diploma, but that she studied there is hardly news.

'Is this anything?' asks Dionysius, handing me a yearbook. Amherst '81. My mother would have been a junior. There are two photos of her in it: a candid one of her at an art show in impassioned debate with a young man who's no more than a blur in the foreground. Ahmed, I think! Her eyes are alight with love. But the only name beneath the photograph is hers. In the second one, she poses with her arm around a severe-looking auburn-haired girl. Pumpkin carving contest winners: Yasmeen Khalil and Claire Benson.

As Dionysius reaches up to return the yearbook to its place, a piece of white cardstock flutters to the ground. It's a wedding invitation: Claire Benson's. Now her name is Seck.

I tuck the yellowed invitation into the pocket of my moth-eaten argyle cardigan and tell them we'd better finish searching the office. In the cabinets, I find bronzed baby booties so caked with dust they must have been my father's. There's an album full of photos of his parents when they were young: my grandfather tall and proud in an army uniform; my grandmother laughing as the camera catches her pausing to sniff a rose; both of them smiling in wedding clothes and then solemn on a boat; a formal portrait with two light-haired babies, the one in trousers crying, the one in a dress smiling. Irene. There are photos of them side by side in a hammock, crawling through grass, on bicycles, Ferris wheels, horses' backs. There are first-days-of-school photographs with her in pigtails and him in pants, birthday cakes and summer camps. Sometimes it's hard to tell which one is which. The last photos in the album are twin school shots, professionally taken and perfectly posed. My father is serious in a bowtie-waistcoat affair. Irene smiles so wide her face seems ready to split apart at the seams. You can see she's recently lost a tooth. I know she drowned the winter she and my father were nine, so this would have been, I guess, third grade. I struggle to remember my third-grade photo. I smile tight-lipped over half-grown front teeth and look like I'm in pain: much less like my exuberant namesake than her grim and sombre twin.

'I think I've found something,' Celeste exclaims, rifling through a sheaf of papers. 'Letters from your mother.'

There are only a few dozen of them, arranged, like the Ahmed letters, by date. My parents were seldom apart. They're all postmarked Islamabad. One of the earliest ones, from the summer of 1987, mentions an invitation from Ahmed, which she says she will not even respond to given 'what happened last time'. Since my father's responses are absent, I cannot see what he said. Other than that, her letters are uninteresting, if surprisingly tender. I learn nothing from them except that my mother missed my father quite a lot during their summers apart. Scanning them, Dionysius pulls Celeste closer and kisses her gently on the head. Instead of pushing him away as she would normally do, she gently squeezes his hand. The nature of love is something I may never understand.

12

When I was younger I yearned for a time machine with which to visit the past. I would swoop in on you, I thought, perhaps even watch you undress. I would count every caress, pay homage to every last kiss. I would record for posterity each syllable that slipped from your lips. The mind, I rued then, is little more than a sieve. Now that I'm older I see that this isn't true. Despite your long absence, each step that I've taken has been in some way related to you.

James had never been good with birthdays. The first birthday he spent with Yasmeen had been her twenty-fifth. He didn't know it was her birthday then and she hadn't said a word. She'd laughed off his failed cookery, sucked down her four-dollar plate of Yeung Ching's Special Noodle good-humouredly. They'd watched the skaters on the pond, walked around the Square until it was too cold. Afterwards, she invited him up to her apartment where she fed him cardamom tea and slept with him almost dutifully. He was mildly embarrassed to have enjoyed it as much as he did, but she'd seemed as pleased he had. It wasn't until the next morning, as she served him scrambled egg with onion and instant coffee she ran out to purchase just for him, that she'd told him: 'Yesterday was my birthday. I just turned twenty-five.'

How young that seemed to him now, only ten years older than their daughter was today. The thought that Irenie would soon be going out on dates with men, perhaps giving them their heart's desire as instinctively as her mother once did, made James unexpectedly uncomfortable. He suddenly wished he'd got her the sweater Doris had suggested instead of the ridiculously expensive book on gardening he was sure she wouldn't like. The feeling was familiar by now though, the feeling that he'd gone wrong with a gift. Although Yasmeen didn't tell him it was her birthday all those years ago, James felt he should somehow have known. That very afternoon, he'd rushed out to buy her the first gift he ever gave her: a fancy stainless steel percolator that made foam. It wasn't until almost eight years later that he came upon his wife drinking coffee in the kitchen one afternoon and found himself unaccountably surprised. It struck him then that for all the time he'd known her, Yasmeen had never drunk anything but tea.

But the percolator still worked, it was down in the kitchen now. And the gardening book was a classic; Irenie could refer to it years and years from now.

'Almost ready, Irenie?' he asked her, tapping on the door.

'Told you … can't find it anywhere,' he heard her whisper. He heard giggles, a scrambling for shoes, and then she threw the door open, red-faced and laughing with Celeste. As he fumbled in his briefcase for the gift, he elbowed someone in the nose.

'Can Celeste come?' his daughter asked, knowing he'd say yes. Another birthday without her mother, how could he deny her this?

He took the girls to Il Bello Canario, where he took Irenie every year. As always, his daughter laughed delightedly at the aging maître d's story of how the owner named the restaurant for his pet canary because his wife looked like the back end of a bus and his children were no better. James laughed too, no longer bothering to think the owner was unkind if the story was true.

The girls decided they'd share the veal piccata. To start, they'd have insalata mista and vongole oreganata. He didn't know Irenie liked molluscs; he suspected they'd been ordered to impress

Celeste. James ordered lobster ravioli for himself and a glass of the house white.

'Can we have some wine?' Celeste asked, somewhat flirtatiously, he thought.

'Why not?'

Irenie's eyes widened. If she had ever asked him for a glass of wine before, it wouldn't have occurred to him to refuse. As it was, he was glad of something that loosened her up a bit, be it the glass of wine or the presence of Celeste.

James had thought this annual ritual would be more awkward than ever with Irenie's friend there but, to his surprise, she made it better. He had thought the girls would spend the whole meal whispering, giggling over insights he couldn't hear, but Irenie was, as always, unerringly polite. The meal began with a stilted exchange about their lives. Dutifully, his daughter answered the questions he asked about her school. Dutifully, she asked about his classes in return. But this year, Celeste was there to interject with anecdotes about the boy who ignited a fart underneath the school's most sensitive fire alarm. She was there to tell him about a certain Mrs Jansen who thought Irenie's ceramic sculptures showed real promise. She told him about the pep rally where the Crawford's mascot, a crab, inexplicable but for the alliteration, had slipped on a pool of spilt soda and lost its head just as George Washington scored the final basket of its seventy-two-point lead. In turn, she seemed to take real interest in his courses, asked him to explain the logistics of the Trojan horse. She even inquired after his book. Celeste's loquacity seemed to spur on Irenie, who was more animated than he had seen her for several years. Much to his surprise, James found that he was having fun.

'What's the plan for the cake?' Celeste whispered when Irenie got up to use the women's room.

The Eccleses didn't do cakes—or hadn't since Yasmeen. Never much for baking, his wife had delegated birthdays to a French bakery in the next town. After she left, there had been no one to call a week in advance, to describe it in specific detail. Irenie never mentioned his neglect of this. Dinners out had seemed enough to dissuade her from the spiteful vendettas launched the year that he forgot. But now Celeste thought there should be cake. Of course there should be a cake, James realized. On his birthday there was always a special sweet—not a cake these days, but a batch of his mother's bread pudding, and Irenie always stuck candles in that, now that his birthday was in her charge. She even made his mother's Sunday roast for him, stringy beef with all the trimmings, his birthday being the one day Western food was cooked for dinner, just as it had been when Yasmeen had run their home. And he hadn't even arranged for her to have a cake.

'Don't worry,' said Celeste, sensing his distress. She slipped away for a few minutes, and returned with a quick wink. When their dinner plates were cleared away, the maître d' hobbled over with a generous wedge of tiramisu. He led the waiters and a handful of friendly patrons in a chorus of 'happy birthday'. Irenie smiled, embarrassed, and blew out the candles in one go. In the brief light of those candles, she looked like a photograph from long ago.

'Happy birthday,' he said, handing her the gift. All around them, strangers clapped, no doubt thinking, 'What a darling family.' What a lovely chap that man is to have taken his young daughter out. What a lovely girl that daughter is, beaming at him over her not-cake. She was lovely, James noticed for the first time. She wore her mother's periwinkle silk dress, her hair was pinned up neatly and her glasses were nowhere in sight. James so seldom saw his daughter smile that he hadn't realized its effect: when she smiled, Irenie could have been Yasmeen. Her features were ever-so-slightly off, like a mimeograph of the original that's inevitably inexact, but the light her smile brought to her face was the same light that had once made her mother glow. James had to look away. It was Celeste Irenie was beaming at anyway, and she didn't seem to notice.

'Do you like it?' he asked her later, putting coffee on to brew. Yasmeen's percolator, he thought. Celeste was flipping through the book.

'This is great, Mr E,' she told him. 'It's something she can always use.'

'It's great,' his daughter echoed, seeming less enthused.

'My mother had that book.' James cleared his throat. 'Besides the Bible, it was the only book she ever read. I had to have it special ordered.'

'That was nice of you,' his daughter looked at him appraisingly. Was she wondering if it was true? James had always found her facial expressions unsettling: utterly unreadable, yet so much an echo of his wife's. Had he been able to read Yasmeen's expressions? He thought so, but wasn't sure.

'If you don't like it, we can have it exchanged,' he offered awkwardly.

'I like it,' she said. He couldn't tell whether she meant it or if she'd just said so to be polite. 'Celeste and I should go to bed.'

James was left to Yasmeen's coffee all alone.

As birthdays went, he reflected, it could have been far worse. There had been the year he'd got her the view-finder goggles, forgetting that without her glasses she couldn't see a thing, the year he'd got her a party dress at least four sizes too big, the year it had slipped his mind altogether, of course, which he doubted she'd ever forgive. Though he'd got slightly better at selecting presents for Yasmeen as the years passed, children's gifts always found him quite at sea. When James was a child, he received a statement of credit at Cornelius Crinkle's Book Emporium for every occasion on which it was customary to give gifts: birthdays, communions, commencements, Christmases. He vaguely remembered a time of toy soldiers and stuffed bears, of late-night exchanges: baseballs for jump ropes, nonpareils for chewy mints. But after Irene had died, time spent in the toy store made his mother too sad. Every Christmas was the first, third, fifth without Irene, every birthday worse. October sixth became their own Dia De Los Muertos. Decades later, James thought Irene would have been amused by sugar skulls, bright marigolds, risible reminiscences of the things she had done before she was dead, but back in the stifled fifties, their birthday became a time of silent grief. Irene's death broke their parents in a way more final and more devastating than any of the other hardships they had previously withstood. It was as though their being together gave them the freedom to fall apart, where alone they had unfailingly endured.

His parents' marriage had been a pleasant one before they lost Irene. James remembered his father mimicking his mother's Irish brogue and how his mother would laugh and laugh. He remembered outings and picnics and trips to the beach. Theirs was a childhood carefully constructed to make up for all their parents hadn't had. Back then, it hardly even mattered that Irene was the good twin, the one who was better at everything they did. That only became an issue after he let her drown and he saw the question in their eyes: why wasn't he the one to die?

When that question came into her eyes, Grace gave up singing while she cleaned. Christopher no longer bothered trying to hear whether she did. He made something of a success of himself with the hubcap factory, but it was a success that ultimately delivered his untimely end: he was struck in the head with blown gasket just before James and Irene would have turned thirteen. After Christopher's death, the house was even more silent than it had been. There was no longer even anyone to snap at James, to tell him to be more of a man, to criticize him in ways that really meant why aren't you Irene?

So birthdays were a bitter time, a time when he was guiltier than ever for falling short of the child he knew his parents wanted him to be. Even now, now that the birthdays of consequence were no longer his own, now that a decade had passed since Grace's death, almost five decades since Christopher's, James couldn't let go of the notion that he'd been somehow disappointing.

He poured himself the last half-cup of coffee though already he'd had three. What difference would a half-cup make when three already guaranteed he wouldn't sleep? James liked his coffee very strong and with just a hint of cream, but he found himself spooning in two heaped spoons of sugar, as though the half-cup were for Yasmeen. Lately he'd found himself making his coffee like this, though it invariably caused him to gag. Coffee just like Yasmeen's the day he met her; James could at least have this. He thought of his daughter with Yasmeen's eyelashes, Yasmeen's meals, Yasmeen's almost-but-not-quite face. Did she know Yasmeen liked her coffee extra sweet? Yes, she probably did. She probably even liked coffee the same way, if she'd grown to like coffee yet at all. James sighed and rose to pour the coffee down the sink. What an empty gesture, drinking breakfast beverages too sweet.

'Hey, Mr E, can I have that if you're going to throw it away?' Celeste. In a nightdress Irenie had outgrown years ago. On the much taller Celeste, it was generous even to call it a nightshirt.

He handed her the mug. She had been wonderful tonight, not at all unruly and rude as he would have presumed. Celeste was just a child really; perhaps he shouldn't regard her with such suspicion. Why, look how she stretched, just like a child, not caring that the skimpy nightgown rode so high he could see where the crotch of her underwear began. Perhaps she wouldn't lead his daughter astray after all.

'Nice and sweet. It's just how I like it.' Celeste smiled.

Then again, perhaps she would.

James excused himself and went to bed.

13

Your absence has opened a void in me, a chasm deep beyond all account. It has rendered life meaningless. It has blocked the sun out. I ache for you daily; each centimetre of my skin yearns for your touch. I cannot live without you. I miss you so much.

Women had always liked James. It had started when he was in Montessori: 'So blonde and pink and docile,' others' mothers would gush, stooping to pet his curls when they came to collect his classmates for the day. 'Just like a baby angel, a cherub without the wings.'

'Mine!' Irene would shriek when she caught them with their fingers in his hair. And later: 'How *can* you let them poke at you like you're just a stupid teddy bear?'

But Irene poked at him too. James didn't mind a bit. She chose his clothes when they played dress-up and drew bright stripes across his face with their mother's discarded lipsticks when they played outside in the lawn. She tossed him into the swimming pool in summertime and smeared popsicle all around his mouth when she dyed her own lips red. Her favourite game was Nasty Auntie, where she'd stuff him into their old perambulator, cooing absurd endearments and pinching his cheeks as she pushed him up and down the drive. In the end, James got to leap out and 'poop' on her skirt. The poop was Hershey's kisses, which she'd always let him share.

All Irene's best girlfriends were best friends with James too. In their games, he'd be the baby bear, the last little fairy who got lost in the woods, the princeling who had to be rescued from the evil stepmother's plots. It was always James who was saved, never one of the little girls. At the time it made sense: Irene was four and a half millimetres taller and they were always the shortest two in their class. Even after Irene died and James began to grow—to grow and grow until he was the tallest of all the boys in school—girls still wanted to take care of him. They wanted to pull his tie straight in the playground and smooth the mad mess that was his hair. Despite Irene's no longer being there, they never ceased to see him as the playmate most in need of help. Or perhaps it was *because* Irene was no longer there that they wanted to baby him long after they'd outgrown their baby games: without her to protect him, who would make sure poor sweet James wasn't left in the enchanted dungeon to be chewed to death by mice?

For the most part, boys his age left him alone. They had all been lectured long and hard about treating the Eccleses with kindness after the tragedy they'd endured.

'Queer, pansy,' someone would sometimes shout, but James didn't care. He was taller than them all.

'Libertine, lady-killer,' they teased a few years later when puberty took root. 'How do you do it?' an awed classmate would sometimes whisper in the locker-room after physical education. James could not have said. His large group of girl friends had all wanted to become girlfriends around the seventh grade. They gave him their cookies in the cafeteria and fought over who got to sit next to him on the bus. Sometimes pigtails were pulled, ribbons ripped from hair, but no one ever said a harsh word about it to James. To him, Lucy, Miranda, Mildred and Jeanine at three were no different from Lucy, Miranda, Mildred and Jeanine at thirteen. Late in his high-school career, he'd sometimes find himself being pulled under the bleachers for hurried kisses by some of the bolder girls, but it didn't change a thing. He treated each girl just the same.

At Yale, things persisted as they'd always been. James had secretly hoped that he'd finally escape the constant female attention at a university where there were only men, but there had been more young women than ever once he'd left high school. They would come for football games, dances, towards the end for wild parties and protests from Vassar, Smith, Mount Holyoke, Wellesley and sometimes even Sarah Lawrence. James would dance with them, sip cider on icy bleachers, spend nights out on the town. But when he looked into each of their faces, he saw only how Irene might have looked had she lived to be his age too. It wasn't until his encounter with his landlady, a woman much older than himself, that he was finally able to look into a woman's face and not see his sister's peering out.

By the night of Irenie's fifteenth birthday, it would not have been unfair to say that James Eccles was a man of many regrets. Perhaps unsurprisingly, most of these regrets were related directly to the women in his life. He regretted letting Violet Sinclair kiss him after their high-school graduation when he knew Emma Wilson would see. He regretted riding Emma home from school on his handlebars often enough that she shot herself at twenty-three, insisting in her suicide letter that she'd never loved another man. He regretted Caroline Fischer and all the nice-enough girls in college whom he'd never let into his bed. He regretted leaving his landlady in Pittsburgh without saying goodbye, telling his first girlfriend after that it was over in a note, dating the scores and scores of other women who'd been little more than wastes of time. He regretted his faithlessness to Yasmeen, his having been unfaithful to her memory, his disconnect from her daughter—the girl he often had to remind himself was his daughter as well. For almost the entirety of his life, however, James's greatest regret had been that he'd let his sister die. It was almost half a century before another regret swept into first place: not having called the police the second time Yasmeen had disappeared.

Selene, Celeste's mother—both regrets James would never have—had stopped by a few days after the girls had left for Florida to discuss the possibilities their daughterless existence might present with James's wife.

'Well, where is she?' she had wanted to know when James had said she wasn't home. James had said he didn't know. It was true in that he had no proof, but he was fairly certain of the aptness of his guess.

'You'd better call the police,' Selene had urged, thinking him a proud husband embarrassed by a runaway wife. 'Something terrible could be happening to her each minute that she's gone.'

But James hadn't thought so. He'd thought she'd say goodbye to Ahmed, be back before Irenie ever knew that she'd been gone. So he hadn't called the police. He hadn't reported her missing or suggested that authorities be on the lookout across the Atlantic. He hadn't even left messages for her to call, to say he loved her, to beg her to hurry home, though he could have made a handful of wise guesses as to where they should be left. He'd just waited for her to come back. He could have caught up with her at customs, the hospital, the rental agency, but instead he'd sat in his study, staring at the calendar until the day there was the call. James would never forgive himself for that.

Several days before their daughters were expected back, Selene St Clare had appeared on James's doorstep a second time.

'Any word from Yasmeen?' she asked.

James hadn't been able to answer. He'd simply left the door ajar and let her follow him into the kitchen. Earlier that morning, he'd received word that the car which had gone over the cliff had, indeed, been the rental registered to Yasmeen. It would be two weeks more before they abandoned the search for the bodies, but, even with no sign of them, James knew his wife wouldn't ever be back.

'Coffee?' Selene asked, seemingly familiar with the kitchen's layout.

James nodded.

She made the coffee in silence—a rare thing from what James could tell. When she used the crumpled dish towel by the sink to clean up a spill, he had to bite his tongue so as not to yell. Yasmeen had let it drop there when she kissed him goodbye on the morning that she left. The egg cup that she'd left in the sink still sat there untouched as well.

'Still no sign of her?' Selene asked, putting a mug near where he sat. Her coffee was at once scorched and weak. Without having been asked, she poured herself a cup and sat down directly in his line of sight. She was not something he especially wanted to see. It wasn't that she wasn't pretty—she was, though not as pretty as her daughter soon would be—James just wasn't in the mood for a woman's face right then. Selene St Clare was young, he knew, probably no more than twenty-six, but the morning light made her look old. Old and haggard, as though she'd weathered a lot, which, he supposed, she most likely had.

'She's gone,' he told her hollowly. 'I got the call just today.'

It was then that James remembered what his wife had told him about their new neighbour: she was fragile, unpredictable. One never knew what might send her into a fit of nervous collapse. He wasn't sure quite what he'd do if this strange woman suddenly decided to lose her mind. But Selene didn't lose her mind. Instead, she looked at James as though he'd just lost *his*.

There was no choice then but to tell her about the call. He told her about the car, the cliff, and where his wife had been, though he did not say with whom. He figured their neighbour didn't need to know the intimate details of their lives. To his surprise, Selene didn't seem curious as to the details of the crash. She didn't ask, for instance, what Yasmeen had been doing in England or why he was so certain she wouldn't be back.

'There should be a memorial,' was all she said.

They held it late that Saturday, in the indeterminate pink minutes between daylight and night. It was Selene who'd held it, really; all James had done was to attend. She had asked him for Yasmeen's address book, wanting to invite her closest friends, but James had refused her this. Instead of guests, there had been hyacinths, what seemed like thousands of them, scattered over the backyard. In the years to come, James would marvel at Selene's collectedness on this occasion, how a woman who would fairly frequently leave for work in her stocking feet could have been so put together. It was, he realized, the sort of small miracle his wife had quite often inspired.

A priest in Selene's acquaintance had said a few brief words and Faber, the sole invitee for reasons quite beyond James's account, had eulogized at length. For once, the man's verbosity had not been irksome. James had almost envied him the baroqueness of his grief. When it was his turn to speak, James couldn't say anything at all. He simply stood there amongst the flowers, thinking how Yasmeen would have loved the magic their neighbour had done to the lawn. When it was over, they ordered pizza and picnicked under the stars. It was too cold for this by far, but no one was ready to leave behind all the hard work Selene had done. They did not, as one might have expected, share memories of Yasmeen. They simply chewed their food in silence, all lost in their own thoughts. They might have sat there all night had it not been for Mrs Winterbourne, that taciturn librarian in whose employ James's daughter would soon find herself. Something, perhaps the candlelight or the ghost of a sigh, had led her to the gloomy assemblage in the backyard. She hadn't gasped when she'd seen them or even seemed surprised.

'It arrived,' she'd said, holding up a book, the title of which James would never know. Somehow, he didn't *want* to know. In that moment, it seemed very important to him that he not see what his wife had wanted to read just before she died, what

literary precedent she may or may not have been following when
she did. Seemingly sensing this, Mrs Winterbourne tucked the
book away inside her large handbag. She declined Faber's offer
of a slice of pizza—she'd never been one for that type of stuff,
she said, and for a second stared straight at James. Eons seemed
to pass in that gaze and when he looked away he felt she had
understood everything, she *knew* everything. Faber, during this
extremely brief interval, had discovered that there was, in fact, no
pizza left to offer. He and Selene began to clear up trash as Mrs
Winterbourne took her leave. Briefly, they were all so involved in
the mechanics of clearing up the yard that James almost didn't
notice Mrs Winterbourne turning back to say something all but
inaudible to everyone.

'She'll be deeply missed,' Faber later told James he'd thought
she'd said.

14

My love for you is cherry wine. It's camembert, not brie. It's Sunday morning sparklers and Claire's dandelion tea. My love for you is starlit swimming pools, drives with Iftiqar and Shireen. It's afternoons of nothing, the two of us together in the heat. It's monsoon rains and mango trees and campus greens in May. It's Murree and Trail Three. I loved you first when I was just fifteen; I'll love you when I'm ninety-three.

Dr Faber dies on the first day that feels like spring. He steps off a kerb outside the hospital after hearing his heart's still working well and is flattened by a bus. My father does not see fit to tell me so until the morning of the funeral.

'Where are you going?' I ask him as I eat my toast and he flails around the kitchen. He's dunked his tie into the coffee pot, brown stains spread fast over his chest. He scrubs at them with a moistened potholder, muttering, 'Is it vinegar or salt?'

'Vinegar,' I tell him, though he'll have to change his clothes. Something reddish from the potholder is streaked over his shirt.

'Thank you.' He looks up, surprised.

'What is it?' he snaps into the mouthpiece when the phone rings a second time, clearly convinced it's our mystery caller once again. He proceeds to apologize profusely to poor Doris and assures her he'll be there. *Where?*

'I'm a little flustered this morning.' I note the socks he's wearing aren't a pair.

I don't bother to comment.

'I never liked the man much, but it always comes as a shock. Especially when it's so sudden like this.'

I have no idea what he's talking about so I just nod and turn a page.

'What's that you're reading, Irenie?' he asks, looking as though he wishes he could dismiss the whole scene with the turn of a page as well.

I tilt the book so he can see the cover. *Beowulf.* 'For school.'

'Are you enjoying it?'

I look at him askance. My father never asks me what I'm reading, much less what I think. He probably thinks I'm half illiterate, given all I know of Greek.

'Not especially,' I tell him.

To my surprise, he laughs. 'I never liked that one much myself. Faber did though. How he went on about the injustice translations did! Well-established translations too! Not that he ever bothered to do one himself, of course.'

I eye my father warily. Why is he telling me about Faber's opinion of *Beowulf* at seven o'clock on a Saturday morning? Though the classics professor is, as far as I know, my father's only friend, he's always pretended not to like him. And why is he wearing a suit? I'm not yet quite awake enough to put it all together.

'I like Dr Faber,' I say neutrally. And I do. He always tells me I look just like my mother even though I don't really think it's true. Whenever he stops by, often and unannounced, he asks me how I'm doing, whether or not I like school, what my favourite subjects are. When I was younger, he even used to invite me to his house in summer to go swimming in the pool. His grandchildren are about my age and when they visited he had trouble thinking of things for them to do.

'Did you?' asks my father absently as he gives up on his shirt. 'Oh that's right, you did. He always had a soft spot for you— thought you looked like Yasmeen, I guess.'

It irritates me that he says Dr Faber only likes me because I remind him of my mother even though he's probably not wrong.

'You do know he died?' My father begins unknotting his tie.

'What? When? How would I have known?'

'Oh, I thought I'd mentioned it.' I glare at him. 'Perhaps not. The funeral's in an hour if you'd like to come along.'

How typical of him to forget to tell me, I fume, how typical of him to just casually say 'he died, I guess I forgot, funeral's in an hour' as though the whole thing couldn't possibly mean anything to me.

I consider staying home to search the house yet again, but decide there's nothing more to be found within these walls so I attend as an emissary for my mother. Dr Faber always did seem rather blown away by her. I used to think it was kind of sweet, watching this cute old man fawn over her. I put on a black crêpe dress that once belonged to her and a strand of fake pearls Celeste somehow coaxed from the clutches of a supermarket claw crane machine. Then I worry I look like a child attempting to appear sophisticated so I hunt down my old argyle cardigan, finding it eventually wedged between two stacks of school sweaters. It takes me less time to get dressed than it does my father to find a new shirt, but in the car he blames me for making us late. He doesn't even have to say anything; I just see it in his sourpuss expression.

As we're driving there, I begin to wonder if perhaps I should have stayed at home. It might put me too much in mind of my mother. It would be beyond humiliating to begin weeping uncontrollably at the funeral of a man I barely knew. But my mother never had a funeral, I reason, there is no common ground. As it happens, I am not the one to embarrass the Eccles family on this day anyway.

The word 'funeral' leads me to expect an airless church reeking of old incense and grief-stricken matrons clawing at their breasts, boring bits read from the Bible about blood of lambs or some such and insincere relations struggling to think up kind things to say.

And afterwards, a luncheon meat buffet with mayonnaise-heavy salads on the side. Perhaps even ambrosia.

Dr Faber's funeral is nothing like this. In fact, I'm not even quite certain whether one should really call it a funeral at all. First of all, apparently to the surprise and disgust of many, he's had himself mummified—not mummified neatly in the manner genteel funeral homes call embalming, mind you, but mummified like King Tut. What we're led to believe is the body of Dr Charles Faber has been wrapped in umpteen linen layers and painted brilliant gold. A passable portrait is where one can only assume the face is and two disembodied hands clutch a gilded book, some sort of odd-looking astronomical device, and a professor's cap. Instead of having had himself placed in a coffin, or at the very least a sarcophagus, like any other decent dead person, Dr Faber apparently stipulated that he wanted to be stood atop a marigold-draped pyre at the centre of the gathering. My father and I find several score of aging academics milling bewilderedly around this monstrosity when we pull up. The funeral, or whatever one might call it, is being held in Crawford's old South Field. Everyone is ankle deep in dandelions and sinking slowly into the mud. Several attendees look bemused, many more look quite annoyed. I recognize Professor Williams from the physics department, puffing earnestly at his pipe, and old Millicent Steinerwald, who still believes she teaches fine arts, sipping surreptitiously from a silver flask. People disassemble and regroup, refilling pink plastic martini glasses with warm white wine at the bar.

'What is going on here?' I hear several people ask.

'What is it we're supposed to do?'

At half past nine, an hour late, a young woman dressed tip to toe in black velvet climbs on to the pyre. Good lord, not sati, I think briefly, but all she wants is to give a speech. Dear Charles, she tells us, requested his loved ones celebrate the life he lived rather than go into mourning when he died. It appears he was envisioning something of a bacchanalia. Hundreds of students seep steadily

from the woods, many dressed in the most outlandish garb. There
are togas and tailcoats, fairy wings and I think I even spy a nun.
Two champagne fountains are set up beside the pyre and kegs
appear as though of their own accord. The small bar to the far
side of the field somehow becomes at least four times as long. It's
tended by opera singers, or at least music majors with ambition,
who compete against the electric chamber quartet. The older
crowd, already tipsy from the hour spent waiting uncertain in the
field, begins to loosen up. A dance floor gives way to one side of
the pyre and several couples waltz. A group of kids, whom I soon
learn are the grandsons, headbang rather anachronistically. My
father, who has been muttering 'oh dear god' almost continually
since we arrived, downs his fifth drink like a shot and abandons
me to discuss the comic genius of Menander with a Spanish-
speaking night janitor. I watch the spectacle unfold.

Several students whom I've never met sidle up, claiming they
remember me from a class I never took. They offer me a hit of acid
and look offended when I refuse. I help myself to pink champagne
instead and blearily discuss my life plans with anyone who asks.
I tell a German professor I'm considering Julliard for the cello, a
cafeteria card swiper I've always hoped to drive a tank and some
random kid dressed up as Santa Claus that I'd like to be an elf. By
noon everyone is smashed.

During the grand finale, which is, of course, setting Dr Faber
ablaze, it becomes apparent that he had fireworks and false body
parts wrapped up between the layers of his 'shroud'. The Crawford
County Police Department appears to investigate the noise. Just
when the chief steps up to shut us down, what ought to be the head
blows off and he's hit in the face with a piece of burning plastic
ear. Fortunately, the carnage is contained to a ten-foot radius so
body parts don't rain down upon us all. A hundred different legal
codes have been violated on this day. The crowds begin to flee. I
see Emeritus Professor of English Literature Maxwell Boatwright
empty a freezer bag of marijuana behind a tree and Felicia

Crawford Professor of the Musical Arts Joan McClintock hitch
her kilt up halfway to her crotch as she sprints madly to her car.
Irenie Eccles, faculty brat, spreads out her sweater beneath a holly
bush and curls into a ball. After some time, she becomes aware
of something digging into her thigh and extricates from beneath
her a crumpled wedding invitation. *Claire Seck*, she remembers, I
must find her as soon as I go home. Tenured Professor of Greek
Language and Literature James Eccles is nowhere to be seen. He
finally calls his daughter from the parking lot of Stop & Shop
where he went to sleep. When he gets home, still muttering some
nonsense about hyacinths and spring being the secret season of
death, I fix him a Bloody Mary and smile as I hand him an icepack
for his head.

15

*When I tell a joke I still wait for your laugh. When I order fries
I still expect you'll eat half. When evenings turn icy I still reach
for your hand. Though I know I must continue without you,
there are parts of me that just won't understand.*

James didn't remember the funeral or the days that led up to it.
He remembered matching red mittens looped around both
of their necks with a string. He remembered her ice skates had
pink pompoms and his were plain white. Their mother did all she
could to remind Irene she was a girl, but with their matching hats
pulled down over their brows and the pink pompoms discarded
by the side of the pond, they'd looked just alike. Watching Irene,
James sometimes thought she was his own reflection, swooping
low over the ice. The only way he was sure she was not was that
Irene ice skated beautifully and he often fell. That day had been
different though; he'd been as graceful as she.

'Look, Irene, look,' he'd called after two loops of the pond all
on his own. But she had been looking even before he had called.
She knew something was different because he wasn't holding her
hand. Until that day, James had refused to go skating unless Irene
held his sleeve tight. He felt safer knowing she would not let him
fall and he would not pull her down.

'Hurry up, slowpoke,' she'd yelled, trying not to show she was
proud. Irene's cheeks were chapped and she could almost taste the
hot chocolate their mother would make when they came home.

James knew because he too could almost taste it. He also knew Irene would stay there and watch him until he was ready to go.

'Five more minutes,' he trilled, flying past so fast.

She'd been tapping her left skate impatiently, heel-toe heel-toe, at the very edge. When she saw her brother's face so aglow beneath the winter red, she shook her head and skated off on an icy tangent of her own. Keep moving: it was the only way to stay warm outside once the New England winter set in. That fall, they'd loved adventure stories about people who'd survived against all odds: the Iditarod racer who'd been attacked by wolves and walked two hundred miles with a broken leg and arm, the Arctic explorer who'd danced naked on an iceberg until his party had come to rescue him with something dry to wear. Irene was not the type to succumb to a particularly inviting bank of snow.

Five minutes passed, and then ten more. The children gave up on time. Night further dimmed the snow-dark sky and flurries began to frost their hand-knit caps. James's had a dropped stitch somewhere below the crown, but Irene's was uniform all the way around; it was more important for a girl to be perfectly turned out. In the failing light, passing fast, there was no telling which was which. They looped apart, sped towards the dark, and then turned to race back at each other. In a game they'd never played and hadn't planned, they brushed left skates as they overlapped for seconds in the middle. James lost track of whether he was the skater on the right or left, the one who fell or the one who didn't. Irene was him reflected in the ice and he, in turn, was her. They were a motion blur photograph, an adventure comic alien who could be in two places at once. Uncertain of which was her and which was him, James was happier than he'd ever been. It was later said the skate tracks came so close that only a miracle could have prevented them from crashing.

Irene was disinclined to crashing, she never even fell. She learned to roller skate without even a skinned knee and rode her bicycle no-hands. James crashed alone that day, just as he always did. If hurtling towards his sister at high speed was like a pleasant dream, tearing away towards the deepening dark was just the opposite. As the shadows lengthened in the woods, James began to hold his breath every moment he faced away from his sister. He couldn't turn around quick enough to race back to the centre. Though Irene could manage all manner of abrupt turns and even one-legged pivots, a gentle arc was the best James could do when he wanted to change direction. Mistaking a withered, leafless bush for a forest demon poised to leap, he attempted one of his sister's brisk about-faces, which sent him flying head over feet.

James lay face down in the snow, waiting for Irene to come help him up.

'Mr Too-big-for-his-boots,' she would tease, 'you think you can do fancy tricks just 'cause you've learned to skate in a straight line?'

He could feel his elbows bleeding beneath all the layers of wool and cotton their mother had dressed them in before she let them out to play. When he swallowed, he tasted blood. A few feet away, the tooth he'd been too afraid to pull was half-buried in the snow. Irene tied her loose teeth to the bathroom door and forced James to slam with all his might when she got tired of prodding at them with her tongue. She'd been teasing James about this tooth for days, begging him to let her yank it out so their grins would gape alike.

'My grown-up tooth is coming in,' she'd cautioned. 'In a few days our smiles will never be the same.'

James smiled to himself through the snow. Now his smile was Irene's too.

His face had gone numb and the snow on his hat was beginning to melt cold trickles down his neck. Where *was* Irene? Was she punishing him for giving up, for being one of the travellers that went to sleep in the snow? James lay still a few minutes more—it would serve her right to think I'm dead, he thought, I really did get hurt, but his fear of things lurking in the forest soon sent him scrambling to his feet.

Irene was nowhere on the pond. She wasn't struggling with her laces near where they'd left their boots or crouching by the blood spatter on the ice, looking for his tooth.

'Irene?' he called uncertainly; could she be playing some kind of joke? 'Ireeeene,' he called again when no one spoke. 'Irene!' he bellowed, skating towards the side where she'd been headed, no longer caring if night time monsters heard his call. She couldn't have fallen down too, could she have? She couldn't be lying in the snow with bloody elbows waiting for him to come give her a hand? 'Irene,' James wailed into the silence, faltering now and fumbling as he skated over the ice.

When they found him, they thought he was dead too. Blood had seeped through the patches on his elbows and frozen wide red spots around him. His face, though caked with blood and snot, was strangely beautiful in the final moments before night. Tears had frozen, diamond-like, all down his cheeks and his eyes were black with grief. He lay on his stomach, halfway into the hole, incognisant of the icy water lapping at his fingers as he clung to two scarves, his and hers knotted together, floating in the black water.

16

I wish for a time-travelling Pegasus to ride in the night, in the dark, our roadmap retrospect. It is easy to see just where you should be when you're years from the fork that led you so off course in ways it still pains to recollect. 'Take me back,' I could scream, oh how I could scheme, but it would be non-circumspect, it would not change a thing.

'I made roast chicken! And dressing! And *broccoli*!' Irenie announced the instant James set foot through the door. 'I *steamed* it!' At this, she wrinkled her nose a bit. Like her mother, Irenie did not approve of steaming. Or boiling. Or serving vegetables of any sort that were neither sauced nor spiced. Also like her mother, she knew James had been unable to shake off his childhood taste for soft, tasteless side dishes.

'Is it my birthday?' he asked, smiling at his daughter. It was warm in the kitchen and her cheeks were very pink. She was wearing Yasmeen's clothes again, this time a brightly coloured flowered dress.

Irenie grinned at him, shrugged. 'I just thought I'd try something different for once. Are you hungry? It's all ready now.'

James wasn't hungry—he hadn't been, inexplicably, since Faber's funeral—but that night he went back for thirds. Irenie barely touched her food. She chattered endlessly about Celeste and school and the upcoming holiday in a most un-Irenie-like manner. James could barely fit in a word edgewise, which was quite all right with him. This new persona of his daughter's was baffling to him. For weeks now, she'd been remarkably un-dour. She would smile at him in the mornings and make idle conversation as she waited for her tea water to boil. He'd heard her singing in the bath on more than one occasion and there had been a decidedly happy look on her face the few afternoons when he'd seen her straight after school. Last week, she'd even made trifle without his having asked for it. And Irenie *hated* trifle.

'So what do you think?' Irenie asked, finally pausing for breath. James realized he hadn't been listening to her. He'd been enjoying her cooking, her company, the sound of her voice, but he hadn't really paid attention to anything she'd said for a good ten minutes.

'Think of what?'

A familiar look of annoyance flitted across his daughter's face. 'What do you think of me going to Florida for Easter break?'

'No,' he said, before he'd had any time to think. Irenie's ebullience evaporated in an instant. She looked almost as though she might cry.

'Oh,' she murmured.

Why on earth shouldn't she go, he thought then. His refusal had been instinctive: last time she'd left, Yasmeen had left too. But Yasmeen was gone now. It wasn't as though Irenie's coming or going could in any way affect that. The poor girl had seemed so excited by the prospect and he'd crushed her happiness without a thought.

'Actually, go ahead,' he said. 'Go have fun. Why don't you write yourself a cheque?'

'Thank you.' She smiled, but her heart wasn't in it.

James left the table feeling yet again that he'd failed his daughter. Somehow, his reconsidered assent wasn't the same as spontaneous approval of her plans. Later that night, as he tried to find a comfortable position in bed, he was plagued by the familiar certainty that he wasn't what he ought to be.

'Catch, Jamie, catch,' his father would urge throwing a ball at his head, and Irene would jump up and catch when he was too slow.

'Go, Jamie, go,' she would urge as she taught him to ride his blue bicycle months after she'd already mastered her pink one.

Irene had walked first and talked first. She'd been born four ounces heavier and with a full head of hair. But, in everything, she waited for him to catch up. If he couldn't connect with a softball, she wouldn't hit either. If he was afraid of the dark, she insisted her nightlight stayed too. He followed her everywhere and did whatever she said. Her handkerchiefs all bore his blood on the corners where he'd taken over the needlepoint their mother insisted she learn and her baby dolls were prematurely bald from the brushings she insisted he administer. They taught themselves to roller skate hand in hand, each with one foot in a skate. They camped outside on summer nights, under a sheet in the yard. When his daughter grew old enough, surely James could do these things with her. He'd learned how to already, from the girl for whom she was named.

So he gratefully relinquished Irenie's babyhood to his wife. He would spend time with his daughter when she grew into a person.

James missed all her firsts: her first step, her first word. Months before he ever heard her utter a phrase, Yasmeen had called him at work, breathless and pleased. 'She said sock.' Everyday words were added to the repertoire: Mamma, binkie, bear, no, but he never heard a thing. When he was home, Irenie stared silent and big-eyed from her place on the floor.

'Say papa, say daddy,' her mother would urge, but she would just blink. Shortly before Irenie's third birthday, James began to wonder if she really did speak. Wasn't three old enough for her to talk without being asked? Could his wife just be imagining words to make up for their daughter's unnatural silence?

Had Yasmeen not contracted meningitis and been forced to spend a week in their bedroom, a cool towel on her head, James doubted his daughter would have let him hear her utter a word.

A creature of habit though, she had toddled firmly up to him at precisely quarter past five and demanded 'juice'. And as an afterthought: 'please'.

With this proof of her person, James took a new interest in Irenie. He tried to engage her in conversation and to teach her the hazily remembered games of his childhood.

But it was already too late.

Irenie hid behind her mother when James entered a room. Anytime he caught her nattering away about something, she fell silent as soon as she saw that he'd overheard. When he tried to pick her up and swing her through the air as he'd seen a colleague do to the delight of his young son, she stiffened like fast drying glue.

'Irenie doesn't like me,' he confided morosely to Yasmeen one evening after his attempt to play dolls with his daughter had reduced her to tears.

'Of course she likes you,' Yasmeen replied dismissively. 'All little girls love their daddies. Irenie's just shy; she's shy just like you.'

Shy just like me, James had mused, perhaps she's as wary of me as I once was of her. He thought then that they might be allies; the two of them together shy of the world. He'd be the James to her Irenie as his sister had been the Irene to his James. But Irenie was shyer of James than she was of anyone else. She was eternally wary, as though always waiting for him to do something wrong. He knew she couldn't possibly remember him dropping her out of her crib or scalding her skin in the bath, but it sometimes seemed that she did. She watched him like a seasoned mall guard with his eye on a shoplifter. Irenie wasn't just shy of him; he realized eventually, she was suspicious. She watched him with Yasmeen as though he might whisk her away and never let her come back.

'It's hard for Irenie,' Yasmeen explained. 'She has me to herself all day long and then you come home and we're suddenly talking about things she can't even begin to understand.'

It's hard for me too, James sometimes wanted to say. It seems I'm always unpaired, from Irene and now you. 'James and Irene: for always and forever,' they had once scratched into a new sidewalk when the concrete was fresh. That one extra 'i' turned everything on its head.

17

Life and I sat down to chat and this is what I asked: why must your currents take me away from my love, why can my love and I not last? I tell him, give me nothing but you. He gives me nothing, not you. I fear that in this way we'll argue until my life has passed.

The bus has mirror-tinted windows and no lights on the inside. I can't tell which traffic's real and which is a reflection. More than once, I sit up straight thinking we're about to drive over a small, unseen car. I feel like I've fallen into a future world, a post-apocalyptic mess. Everything is empty black except the artificial lights. Robots rule the earth tonight. Their trajectories are efficient and they never stop to chat. They speed along to unknown ends through a night that's cold and black.

It's Good Friday, 3 a.m., and I'm somewhere outside of Philadelphia. It's the deadest hour of the night, the most ill-fated date of the year. I'm barrelling farther west than I've ever been, on a bus crammed full of sleeping strangers. Some ten hours hence I'll disembark into the arms of a woman I haven't met. It wasn't hard to get here, but now it's hard to see why I tried.

How do you greet a woman you've never met, a woman who knows you only from old school photos and a single phone call just over one week ago? A woman who knew the version of your mother you've been trying so hard to find, a woman who knew the other half of her, a half you had not even imagined until some months ago?

I see her before she sees me. She carries a parrot-headed umbrella and what looks to be a cloak made of brownish tweed. Her hair is still vermilion, but it's much shorter now than it was in her senior portrait, cut almost like a man's. Her face has grown more mannish too, settled into the lines and angles of middle age. But I recognize her still. Claire Benson, now Seck, is the first mystery I've unravelled.

When I called and asked to see her, Claire didn't sound surprised. She didn't ask me if I'd come alone or if my father would come along. She told me to come down for Easter, that if I had questions she wouldn't mind. She'd pick me up at the Greyhound station and I could stay for as long as I like. And here I am in Middle America, or in Florida, according to everybody but Celeste, and I almost want to turn around.

'Irenie?' she asks uncertainly, dispelling my doubts. She's seen me now. I am here. I've made my mother's letter-self real.

'Claire Seck?' I ask.

She nods, takes my hand and shakes it firmly. 'Pleasant trip?'

'It was all right. Long. Maybe I should have flown.'

Claire smiles at this. Smiling, she's gentler and somehow handsome, like someone who might sometimes have fun. 'You're your mother's daughter, aren't you? Yasmeen never flew if she could avoid it. She was always taking all sorts of outlandishly long bus trips.'

I took the bus because flying seemed too complete a rending of Mamma and Yasmeen Khalil. Watching the route unravel overland left me Hansel-Gretel breadcrumbs, Ariadne's thread by which to wind my way back home. But this is too stupid to tell someone like Claire Seck. Dr Claire Seck. 'I wanted to see the landscape,' I say instead. 'I've never been west of New York before.'

'Never been west of New York? Good heavens!' She sounds more tickled than surprised.

Claire's car looks like she chose it to match her person. It is long and solid and painted beige. It is a rich person car, but an old rich person car, with a backseat large enough to accommodate walkers, wheelchairs or, very easily, my small suitcase.

'The trunk's full of my husband's samples,' she explains, swinging it behind the driver's seat. I wonder if he's a doctor too. 'He's in Odessa for the night.'

'Oh?' I say politely.

'The children are away too. Gone to see their grandparents. So I guess it's just you and me.'

We spend the rest of the short drive in silence. Like the car, Claire's house matches her person: a tasteful off-white split level with a large, manicured lawn in front. The only thing unusual about it is a gold embossed sign by the door reading 'Le Podiatrist'. So that's what the doctor is for, I think, but why the French?

'A little joke of my husband's,' Claire explains when she sees where my gaze has drifted. 'He's a lepidopterist. He thinks that sign is hilarious. Thank god I never see patients at home.'

'A professional lepidopterist?' I didn't know there were such things this century.

'Indeed.'

Claire leads me down a flight of stairs, through an immaculate family room, past a study, to what she tells me is the guest room.

'The bath's attached. Why don't you freshen up a bit and we can have some lunch? Or are you tired? Would you rather take a nap?'

'I'm fine,' I tell her. I don't think I could sleep. Young Yasmeen is right here, right in this woman's mind. And Ahmed is here too, first time more than just in letters.

I intend to take a quick shower, but Claire Seck has put out a wider range of toiletries than the Grandmother. Of course I have to experiment with everything. There are scrubs and masks and shampoos. Cuticle creams, under-eye ointments and lotions just for elbows. The towels are plush and monogrammed; the hair dryer looks like something from science fiction.

I deliberate over what to wear as though I'm about to face a jury. I've packed my mother's clothes, my own, and even an old shalwar kameez just for dramatic flair. In the end, I decide Claire's not the type for drama and pull on a version of the skirt and sweater outfit I wore on my way here.

Back upstairs, the house seems empty. I wonder if Claire's gone out. Perhaps I took too long. Absently, I look over the photos in the front hall. The first to catch my eye are of a beautiful ebony-skinned man with features so perfect I mistake the photographs for prints. But then there's the same beautiful man standing next to Claire, then the both of them with four coffee-coloured kids.

'I see you've met the family,' Claire says, startling me.

'They're beautiful.'

'I suppose they are. Beauty has always been a passion of Etienne's. Come, you must be hungry.'

'How did you meet?' I ask, following her into the gleaming kitchen. Over a lunch of salad composed of types of greenery whose names I cannot even guess, she tells me.

Etienne Seck and Claire Benson first met in medical school. They shared the same cadaver, a young man whom Etienne christened Dante Vigilante and whom Claire spent months slicing open as she tried to ignore the grandiose tales he imagined about the corpse's life. Ultimately, she chose to specialize in podiatry so she wouldn't have to cut open people with histories and he dropped out to study butterflies.

They met again during her residency. He had pulled a tendon in his foot and she was on the night shift. They reminisced over Dante Vigilante and Etienne asked Claire to join him for breakfast when her shift was done. A few months later, she accepted an offer to take over an uncle's practice in Columbus. Etienne moved there too. He was tired of the East Coast, or so he claimed. While Claire passed her days fixing feet, he scoured the Midwest for butterflies. She was sure one day he would forget to come back, just drift off on a wind, but he never did. All flighty creatures need their fixed points and Claire Benson was Etienne's.

'And that is how it went,' Claire concludes, waving aside my offer to help her clear the plates. 'None of the gallantry of your parents' first meeting, but we're happy nonetheless.'

'My parents'?'

'James gave Yasi his handkerchief and told her to keep it. Isn't that sweet?'

Having seen first-hand the state of his handkerchiefs after some weeks in his pocket, I decline comment. 'What about Ahmed? How did they meet? Do you know?'

'You know about Ahmed, do you? I'd wondered if that's what this was about.'

'I didn't. I'd never even heard his name until a few months ago. I found their letters.'

Claire raises an eyebrow. 'I can't imagine those would have been entirely pleasant reading material.' I cock my head, wondering how she knows this. 'They adored one another, but even back in college they had their fights. And they were merciless when they did.'

'Yes,' I agree uncomfortably, not yet wanting to pursue this particular topic. Discussing it with Celeste was bad enough. 'But how did they meet?'

To my surprise, Claire laughs. 'It's a funny story, really. You do know your grandparents wanted Yasi to attend university in London so her sister could watch out for her, don't you?' I shake my head. 'Well, they did. But for some reason, she was intent on the States. She wanted to go to the University of Chicago. When she got into Amherst instead, she became intent on that. Her parents finally agreed because some relative of her brother's through marriage had a son who would be going. They figured he could keep an eye on her.

'Yasi, of course, was outraged. She didn't want some cretin, as she put it, shadowing her every move. Several times during our first semester, he stopped by our room, wanting to buy her a coffee, but she had me make excuses. He asked me all kinds of questions about her: what she was like, what she liked and I confess I told him because he seemed so sweet. I told her she ought to meet him, but she could be stubborn, your mother.

'That winter, she spent the holidays with my family in Englewood Cliffs. I'd always felt a bit cheated being an only child and that winter it was as though I had a sister. My mothers simply adored her. They even let us go into New York City to celebrate the New Year. One of my moms, Catherine, worked in the theatre district, but even then I was never allowed to go into the city by myself at night. That was all Yasi's doing.'

Claire tells me about the shopping and the dresses and the haircuts. About how my mother insisted they paint their toenails even though nobody but the two of them would see. She had never been to a New Year's party before, not one with attendees her own age anyway. Though the party proved to be a largish group of underclassmen guzzling punch in the hostess's parents' overheated Upper East Side apartment, my mother was dazzled. She delighted in the crackers and wore a tasselled party hat. Then, shortly before midnight, she froze mid-step. 'Who's that?' she whispered, perfectly still. That was the boy, Claire told her, the one who'd been trying to get her to meet him for coffee. His eyes met hers then and they floated across the room to each other. Many hours later, Claire found them huddled together on the icy balcony each with one arm through a sleeve of Ahmed's overcoat.

'Have you met him before?' she asked my mother on the train back.

'In a dream or something like it,' my mother replied.

'After that, they were seldom apart,' Claire tells me. 'Ahmed was in New York for only a week, but once we got back to school they found each other at once. They studied together. They ate together. They fell asleep together watching artsy movies we all, at that age, thought we ought to like. They even read books for each other's classes so they could discuss them. And believe me, our workload wasn't light.

'Ahmed would rest his head on Yasi's chest and she'd hold the book. They read that way for hours. Sometimes they'd both begin reading the same sentence aloud in one voice if it struck them particularly. It was amazing to watch, like their minds were perfectly aligned.'

'Didn't you feel left out?' I ask, thinking more of myself than of Claire.

'No.' She smiles. 'Well, maybe a little at first. I missed your mother. But they always made an effort to include me. For years, they tried to set me up with Ahmed's best friend, Mustapha.'

'You know Mustapha?'

'Quite well, actually. He was at Cornell and he often came down for weekends. I don't think he had many friends. He was a lovely young man, just very shy. I probably would have dated him if it wasn't painfully obvious he was in love with your mother.'

'Is that why she and Ahmed broke up?'

'Of course not.' She laughs. 'Yasi had no idea. Neither did your father—I'm sorry, Ahmed. Your mother thought Mustapha hated her. He barely spoke to her and wouldn't meet her eye. It was just his way of protecting himself. I don't know if they ever had a conversation until Ahmed sent him to check on your mother after they split up. Mustapha was at Yale Law by then, you see, and Crawford wasn't far away. Ahmed was in London, of course. I don't think they ever stopped loving each other, although I got the impression that they were doing their utmost to make the other pay for whatever went wrong between them in Pakistan.'

'You don't know what happened?'

'No. I know your mother was annoyed with Ahmed for going to Europe without her, but I don't know much else. They never talked about their arguments.'

'But then why …' a realization begins to dawn, 'did my mother use Mustapha to get back at Ahmed?'

Claire looks taken aback. 'I don't think it was anything quite so calculating as that. I never knew the details, I confess. By the time your mother told me what happened, she was happily married with you on the way. She and Mustapha became close after college, it seemed. It was a bad time for her. She was more than making up for all the mistakes she never made when she was with Ahmed and Mustapha was there for her. At first, she'd hound the poor man for information about Ahmed, but eventually she came to know him, to like him. I expect his presence reminded her of how life was before, her life with Ahmed. She grew to anticipate his visits and he, of course, was smitten with her. For a short while, it seemed they might make each other happy. Then your mother found him rifling through Ahmed's letters—she kept them in this painted metal box—the very box,' she interrupts herself to add, 'that I imagine has inspired all these questions of yours?'

I nod. 'How did he …?'

'Evidently, he had broken off the latch. After that, it became clear he'd been tormented by uncontrollable jealousy the entire time. The whole thing lasted a week or two at most.'

'So what happened?' I ask, feeling a little sorry for him.

'He married the girl his parents had picked out for him. They've settled in the UAE, I think.'

'And my mother never saw either of them again?'

Claire offers iced tea, which I accept to be polite. The contents of her refrigerator are ordered by height and type and size. Her face is hidden by the beverages when she tells me, no, she never did. Something about the stiffening of her posture tells me she isn't certain this is so.

I stay out the weekend with the Secks. Etienne is even more beautiful than his photographs suggest. On Easter Sunday, they take me to their church with them and everybody stares. Neither seems to notice. I suppose they must be used to it by now. We play gin rummy in the evenings or sit and watch TV. They are the first married couple I've ever met who seem to be in love. It isn't that they fawn over each other all the time, it's just the small things they do: the way Etienne pulls out Claire's chair at the dining table, the tone in which she asks him to hand her the salt. I begin to see what she meant about the way Ahmed and my mother used to read.

All weekend, she offers up anecdotes about my mother. I sheepishly drag out the sheet in which the letters were wrapped Saturday night, but she does not seem to recognize it nor does she make much of the fact that it does not match any we own. Always, our conversation stays safely in the past. When I broach the topic of my mother and Ahmed's last meeting, she claims she does not know. We do not speak of my mother's disappearance, of which I'm fairly certain Claire is aware, nor do we speculate about her whereabouts. Neither Claire nor Etienne ever expresses the least bit of surprise at my visit. Claire even takes me to Sun Valley Tanning Salon when I tell her my father believes me to be in Florida with Celeste.

'Your father,' Claire often says when referring to Ahmed. I feel as though I've entered a parallel universe where everything went as it was planned.

'Was he?' I finally ask in a whisper from within the tanning bed.

Claire is silent for a time and I wonder if she's heard. 'I doubt it,' she says, but the length of her pause has meaning I cannot parse. On Monday morning, I find I am reluctant to leave.

'Come back anytime,' they both say outside the Greyhound terminal, and I know they really mean it. For days afterward, I approach our cheery-looking yellow house with dread. More than ever the silence echoes and the whole place seems the domain of ghosts.

18

I spent an hour in the park today amidst all the trees in bloom. I could not say what colour they were, my love, because I thought only of you. I've read two thousand pages this month, but I could not say by whom. I thought only of you. I lead a life from day to day but late at night, when I lie down to sleep, my thoughts are of only you.

When Yasmeen told James she was pregnant, the first thing he did was call a realtor. She meant to wait, to tell him later at home, but when a kindly nurse offered up the telephone she couldn't help but avail. Although Yasmeen had moved uncomplainingly into the gloomy cinderblock duplex, which had been allotted to him by faculty housing almost twenty years ago, even James knew it was no place to begin a family. He found Kerry Williams, a smiling sales associate for Biltmore Callahan, in the creased and stained phonebook he'd been using as a stand for the spider plant Yasmeen had brought in some weeks ago to enliven his rather drab office. She was delighted to schedule a few impromptu viewings that very morning once he explained the circumstances of his sudden desire for a home of his own. She was all the more obliging when he confided that he'd been surviving off the dividends of a modest inheritance for the past few decades while the bulk of his earnings lay in the bank, gradually garnering interest.

Mrs Williams, the unflappable working mother of three preteen boys, pulled up outside his office in a spluttering station wagon hardly an hour after he'd phoned. Her husband had the Volvo, she explained apologetically, gesturing to the chaos of the backseat. James squeezed into the front seat, regarding the clutter of juice boxes, used tissues and PTA fliers with a wary eye. Yasmeen wanted children, he knew, but all that seemed centuries away when they married. They hadn't planned on a baby, hadn't even discussed it yet. There was an unstated assumption that they would wait a few years before broaching the subject. Some combination of his influence and her charm had won Yasmeen a part-time position as a writing tutor at the college, and they were in tacit agreement that she would see what came of it before they made any plans. Perhaps she'd enjoy teaching and apply for an advanced degree. Perhaps she'd find something new. The first semester was barely halfway through, and already everything had been flipped on its head.

When her firstborn came along, Mrs Williams told him, she and her husband fled the city. It was important to settle down with a child in the picture, didn't he agree? He supposed so. The first house she was taking him to was a refurbished bungalow on the far side of town. Did he have a car? He might want one to get to the campus in winter. It would be a good place for a baby: no stairs to fall off. Mrs Williams was a cautious driver, stopping for extended seconds at empty crosswalks and flashing lights. The car seemed powered by her ceaseless chatter. It shuddered and lurched when she paused to allow him an answer and she'd stomp at the clutch in her polished, middle-aged pumps. Yasmeen would never wear shoes like that, he thought gloomily.

The bungalow was spacious and cold. The hospital-white of the walls appealed to him, but he knew Yasmeen would hate the grey expanse of industrial carpeting and the uniform squareness of each room. She would be swallowed by so much nondescriptness. He was quiet through that tour, and during the next two through a crumbling fixer-up saltbox and a characterless colonial. Though it was almost lunchtime, Mrs Williams showed no sign of losing patience with his reticence. Outside the third, she quickly consulted a disordered box of files in the backseat. She shuffled the papers like a pro, thick fingers and heavy rings somehow gracefully restraining the world she had mastered. They would look at one final house before lunch, she told him. It was a bit of a stretch, but she could clear her Thursday and show him some more.

As they drove back in the direction of the college, Mrs Williams told him about the house. It was listed as a restored Victorian, restored being the operative word. The previous owner had been an unpublished author and a noted eccentric. Her agency had for a while considered restoring the house to its original layout, but had just recently decided to cut their losses and sell it off cheap. It was right off campus, so perhaps James would find the fixing worth trying. She smiled weakly as the car rolled to a stop before a turreted egg-yolk affair.

James had expected the house to be ramshackle and in need of many years of work, but the paint looked crisp and the cream-coloured wraparound porch clung solidly to the sides of the house. The crooked stairs creaked welcome as they climbed and sunlight filtered through the elaborate wrought-iron trellis. The previous owner had discovered a talent for welding when his third novel fell through, Mrs Williams explained. This was his last project. Delicate curlicues glowed over the narrow porch, driving out shadows that once might have lurked and infusing the whole place with a muted brightness. James wondered at the soft, almost syrupy light that came through, and thought the disappointed writer should sooner have tried his hand as an artist. Mistaking his gaze for misgiving, Mrs Williams assured him that the whole house was structurally sound. She seemed to regard it as a beloved though troublesome child, ever in need of defence. James was pleased she was so fond of it despite the outlandish amendments that had left it thus far unmarketable. He was flattered that she had elected to show him this, her handicapped favourite.

'Can we go in?' he asked.

She beamed at him then, young and happy through her greying business-suit disguise. He thought she must be a wonderful mother, always able to keep her young sons in line yet attuned to the childhood delights he knew a man like himself was quite likely to miss. She pulled a vast, jangling ring of keys from her handbag and sifted through the lot, sighing that she really ought to get bifocals but just couldn't bear to think she was that old.

Except for the lion doorknocker suspended anachronistically to the left, the original front of the first storey had been replaced entirely with plate glass. The front door opened into a large, bright room spanning the whole front of the house. Studio, should Yasmeen begin painting again, James thought. There was a grand fireplace along the back wall with a mantle so high it came almost to James's nose. A largish arch opened up to the kitchen and James saw that it had been left unchanged. It seemed the house was considerably longer than it was wide. From where he stood, the kitchen looked almost as large as the front room. Mrs Williams proudly showed him the spacious pantry to the left of it, though she had no doubt guessed that pantries were hardly within the realm of his interest. She seemed anxious and even a bit fidgety as she pointed out how it had been modified to double as a laundry room with connections at hand for both washer and dryer. James began to get the distinct impression that she was, for some reason, trying to put off showing him the upstairs. Grimly, he imagined tiny dark rooms and irreparable plumbing.

Having at last exhausted the topic of cloth diapers and the convenience of washing machines in such close proximity to the rest of the house, Mrs Williams reluctantly asked if he'd like to head up. And there, in the front right corner of the kitchen, was the enormous circular stair.

James didn't quite know how he missed it when she'd led him through to the pantry, though he guessed anyone in Mrs Williams's line of work had to be fairly good at subterfuge. Still, it alarmed him to think he was unobservant enough to have glanced past the huge ornate thing occupying almost a fifth of the kitchen.

'He got it at an estate sale,' Mrs Williams sighed. The space was large enough so that it wasn't in the way, but the staircase looked absurdly out of place spiralling over the refrigerator in all its caryatid bedecked glory. Somehow though, the blue and white tiles of the floor, which Mrs Williams informed him had been imported from Italy to outfit the kitchen, seemed to him a natural place for such a staircase to begin. He liked the bedrooms upstairs and the wide, round washroom that had been installed in what once was the turret. He liked the thought of Yasmeen lying back in the claw-footed tub and of their unknown child riding wildly down the banister. They could paint over the yellow and begin in a house made as though just for them.

James took Mrs Williams to lunch that day at Il Bello Canario, where he would one day take Irenie every birthday once her mother went away. Mrs Williams had tagliatelle with sage and pancetta and exclaimed over the freshness of the homemade pasta. He was surprised by the pleasure she took in something that was, for him, simply routine. Since the children were born, she confided, she and her husband had subsisted largely on sandwiches and things left behind: a twice-bitten drumstick, the bits of spaghetti deemed insufficiently sauced. He paled slightly and savoured the al dente bite of his bucatini as never before.

It took less than a month to negotiate the sale of the house. Yasmeen wasn't yet showing when James first took her to see it. All its oddities delighted her. She slid down the staircase and found a prism to fill the front room with rainbows. She hugged him like a Hollywood starlet and left a scarlet kiss on his cold nose. When Mrs Williams stopped by to congratulate them some months later, she seemed startled to see Yasmeen was so young. Clothes and cutlery were everywhere and half-alphabetized books swayed in precarious towers along the edges of both rooms. Bach blared from a phonograph under the stairs as James's young wife stirred a curry, conducting by spoon. She wore a childish plaid jumper and her stomach poked strangely round and adult through the straps. When James rested his hands on her shoulders in introduction, she flushed so bright that Mrs Williams thought she might almost be his daughter. She masked her surprise well though. In fact, she remained impressively unruffled until the animated young woman announced over tea that she would not be repainting the house. To the Homeowners' Union's chagrin, it would continue to stand in garish goldenrod contrast to the subdued blues and greys of the street.

'It looks like a place to be happy,' Mrs Eccles had said. Whenever Mrs Williams drove by, she wondered if she was.

For the first few years, all the oddities of their new home delighted Yasmeen. She arranged housewarmings and dinner parties to show it off. When strangers slowed their cars in the street to take it all in, she beamed like a child showing off a praised piece of artwork. Sometimes people stopped just to gawk. She'd invite them to photograph the house and if they looked harmless enough she might even ask them in for a cup of tea. James was always surprised to find Yasmeen happily bantering with women she'd never met about her love of the trellis or the view from the back porch. His taciturn daughter would giggle for these strangers and sweetly offer the biscuit tin. Once, he came home to find one of his worst pupils elbow deep in the oven, explaining to Irenie that gold sugar sprinkles could make cookies look almost like stars if you squinted hard enough. She'd straightened up sharply, wiping flour dust from Yasmeen's favourite apron when he appeared in the arch.

'I didn't know you lived here, Professor,' she had said quite incredulously on her way out, surprised, he was sure, by her dry professor's bright family and avant-garde house. She came back often and when she graduated, Yasmeen was sad to see her go. James was unendingly perplexed by his wife's fleeting friendships with all the colourless women that passed through their house. They'd chatter and laugh until all trivialities ran out, then quietly fade away to be replaced by nameless, faceless others.

'It's the magic of the house,' Yasmeen would tell him when he asked how all these people slipped in and out. It was her magic though, he'd think to himself. Even before, strangers had swarmed Yasmeen and then slowly slid off. Möbius-like, she eluded them. James sometimes suspected that he was no closer to the beginning or the end than any of them; he'd simply stapled himself on somewhere around the middle and there he hung for dear life. He was always pleased when the ten-minute friends left and he remained. He was pleased too when Yasmeen incredulously asked how it was that none of the whimsical academics in the small college town had snapped up the house in all the time it had been around. Indeed, dinner guests from the college did seem to regard it in unstated awe. Delivery men peered in through the doorway and newspaper boys often walked all the way up to the porch. Even if he wasn't the perfect man for her, for a time it seemed that James had bought Yasmeen the perfect house.

It wasn't long before he began to see just why no one else had been all that interested in 437 Chestnut Hill Lane: chunks of plaster rained downstairs if anyone stomped and the staircase was unsteady. The trellis turned grey with no one to polish it and the grand turret washroom was irreconcilably labyrinthine. The claw-footed tub that he'd once found so charming made late-night visits the stuff of nightmare, necessitating as it did that one navigate around it, then back again just to go from toilet to sink. The front room with its great wall of glass was stifling in summer and icy in winter. None of this seemed to matter to Yasmeen in their first years there though. When James muttered complaints, she'd laugh and call him olden-golden, fuddy-duddy, ancient-buddy. She thought baths more thorough than showers and sniffed at what she deemed an absurd Western fixation with keeping temperatures steady all year around. As far as she was

concerned, New York State was only ever warm enough to shed
sweaters when the mid-summer sun turned their front room to a
greenhouse. Before they were married, she'd unearthed a decaying
mink coat from a Salvation Army bargain bin and was pleased
by the chance to parade around inside all day like a dark Frances
Farmer from before fur was murder. If anything, Yasmeen relished
the minor irritations of the house for all the peculiarities they
afforded her. Until Archibald Crowe, James worried she might
love it more than she loved him.

19

I am so lonely without you. I feel so empty. My mind is blank. My body, heavy. My soul, long lost. Some days I wake up and wonder if I am dead and if they'd tell me and how I'd know. Would it even matter? I don't think so.

I'm not sure when I first found out I lived in a haunted house, but it was when I was young enough to not think about it much. Someone must have sneered it at me one recess. Or perhaps it was Halloween: despite the sunny yellow colour of our house, children seemed frightened by more than just the marshmallow spiders my mother hung from the trellis. I remember liking the idea of a ghost of our very own and visiting the basement often in hopes of finding Mr Crowe. My mother abhorred it down there. She was haunted enough, I think, but—it's taken me until now to realize—not by ghosts.

As my seventh year approached, I began to come home quite often to find my mother staring blankly at the kitchen wall with a mug of what I knew even then smelled quite unlike any tea. At first I tried to cheer her up, distract her, tell her about my day. 'Run and play,' she'd say and gesture vaguely. It was freedom unlike any I'd ever had. I spent hours in the basement. It felt far away but close enough. I ran my fingers over tools Archibald Crowe left behind and used the water heater as a drum. When none of this attracted my mother's notice, I took to perching at the top of the basement stairs, just to make sure she was still there. I watched her sit there at the kitchen table, incognizant as her cigarettes burned down to the filter. When she went to the washroom, I'd creep out and stare in fascination at the exquisite worms she'd left in her wake, 'Turkish Gold' tattooed along their backs. I tried to collect them for a while, but they crumbled to nothing the instant I touched.

Until I read her old letters, I'd forgotten those times. Memory retouched all my mother's greys and browns with technicolour brilliance. In the letters, there is a sudden incursion of hospitals and tests and concerns for Ahmed's health. There's a sense of the unsaid, each one an elaborate evasion of something too terrible to fully address. The writing grows strained there, as though the lives they once described with such flair have been revealed as a hoax, a many-act play they forgot wasn't real. When my mother painted on smiles and hung up her dressing gown, I let her act stand in for truth. She didn't bother often, though on days she drank enough in the morning for my father to notice, she'd pull herself together by afternoon.

'Irenie,' she'd call, even though I was always there, 'let's get ready. We're going downtown.'

She'd run herself a scalding bath, and by the time it grew cold she was ready to pretend everything was all right. Often, she let me pick out her outfit while she soaked her way to sobriety. As I lay out her dresses and smoothed the kinks from her tightly balled stockings, I imagined she was entrusting me with a grand privilege. I made sure the panties I selected were a perfect match for the dress, just in case she should fall and her skirt should fly up. I held options up to my chest in the mirror as I clomped around in her shoes, just so I might be certain that the styles looked perfectly right. It didn't occur to me that she no longer cared what she looked like. On occasions she'd sigh when I would select one of the flounced and ruffled affairs she'd saved from her college dance days, but she'd put them on anyway and we'd be off for the day. If people in the supermarket stared at her, I was sure it was because she was the most beautiful sight they'd ever seen in their whole lives. I would notice other little girls looking at me enviously, wishing their mothers would dress up like princesses just to buy yogurt.

These trips to the supermarket were invariably rushed. Making difficult things for dinner was my mother's chief mode of penance, and there was never enough time to have everything comfortably done by the time my father came home.

'What shall we make, Irenie?' she'd ask, as we ran to the supermarket with the rickety old shopping cart clattering behind us. Even at the best of times, my mother was so terrible a driver that she'd walk miles in winter to avoid taking the wheel. When we got there, I'd install myself at the front of the cart, pointing out possibilities as we sailed through the aisles.

'Hamburger helper? Boxed mac 'n' cheese? Tinned ravioli in sauce?'

I knew my mother would never buy any of these things. The only things she could cook were Pakistani dishes from the recipe file Nani had sent her when she was in college. Claire told me that my grandmother was delighted when my mother finally expressed an interest in cooking. Had she known it was an interest born of necessity after my mother moved into Ahmed's apartment, she might have been somewhat less than pleased. Within a few months of my mother's request for instructions on rice-steaming and daal, a file arrived, full of culinary direction so detailed that when I went about mastering each recipe I often thought Nani's true calling might have been as a drafter of instructional pamphlets for complex electronics. My mother never really developed any interest in cooking, though by the time I came along she could execute each dish in the file with surgical precision. If she strayed in the least from those tidy yellow pages, any hope for a decent meal had to be given up for lost. Her rare forays into Western cooking were especially disastrous. Roasts for my father's birthday or Christmas dinner were invariably charred on the outside and still bloody within. Mashed potatoes arrived at the table suspiciously yellow and full of raw chunks. Even the coveted boxes of instant macaroni and cheese I occasionally convinced her to buy would wind up swimming in grease, tomato-garlic-onion overwhelming the plastic taste I found so appealing.

'Be serious, jaani,' she'd scold when I suggested such items on our high-speed afternoon trips.

'Chicken qorma,' I would decree. 'Aloo gobi and peas pullao. Masoor daal. Cucumber raita. Kachoomar, mango chutney on the side,' I'd chide, as we zoomed through the vegetables, 'we'll need ginger for the qorma and that's not enough tomato.'

The recipe file was my favourite book of nursery rhymes, the first fairy-tales I'd learned. Before I'd ever touched the stove, I knew how each dish was cooked. My mother always watched in awe as I diced onions without shedding any tears. She was grateful, if perplexed, when I smelled the spices almost burning and pushed them off the flame. Between us, we'd have the counter spread with our own at-home restaurant buffet by the time my father walked in the door. When he praised the chef, my mother would beam and say the credit went to me. He'd humour me with compliments, and I'd be irritated knowing he thought I'd done little more than watch. I suppose he must know now that that hadn't been the case, though it hardly matters anymore. With just the two of us to eat them, we no longer bother to enjoy. My mother rarely ate the meals we cooked, but she loved to watch us as we did. She'd pour herself a splash of scotch with soda and some ice, smiling through her cloud of smoke as we stuffed ourselves. For days we'd eat the leftovers, leaving her the afternoons to dream. Three minutes through the microwave was all it took to convince my father everything was fine.

If I truly worried for my mother, it was only deep in basement dark that I admitted it to myself. In the bright light of day, it would have struck me as blasphemous to suggest she was anything less than perfect. I never asked her what was wrong or told my father what he didn't see. Instead, I kept a careful balance so as not to upset her. When things were getting out of hand, I'd whine I was bored. She'd snap right out of it and take us to the store. I tried to let her be until she called, but when I saw my father watching her carefully over his plate of four-day-old daal I would know the time to step in had arrived. It went on like this until the start of spring. If she hadn't felt the need to see the flowers, perhaps it all would have been all right.

My mother never liked the neighbourhood playground: the playground where I lost my first tooth plummeting headfirst from a monkey bar; the playground where Celeste and I spent a whole summer of midnights trying to summon spirits with a cracked scrabble tile and Pepsi-cap Ouija board; the playground where I often waited all afternoon before it occurred to either my father or me that I should have a key. My mother thought this playground was gaudy and cheap. She saw infection emanating from the bright, chipping metal and injury affirmed by the ungiving blacktop. When I allowed it, she preferred to take me to the park in Town Square, where babies prowled through grass, and the slide was so low that the only way to enjoy it was to leap off the top. There were flowerbeds in this park that reminded her of home. In spring, they bloomed in splendid stripes and complex configurations.

'The soil here is so good,' my mother would sigh, 'but there's hardly anyone who puts in time.'

Our own front walk was lined with ragged pink rosebushes that seemed to flinch when my mother approached with her clippers. She stifled our plants with profound expectation. At the park, she would exclaim over asters and rhapsodize about daisies, keeping enough distance so that her élan wouldn't shrivel them up. In springtime, she loved to watch the flowers and me in the sun. Sometimes, she went to see them before I came home. Such visits were surreptitious. I guess she felt guilty doing these things without me, though I didn't mind. When I saw the tell-tale grass stains on the back of her skirt, it was much easier to extract playground trips to the park she disliked.

The one thing my mother did not like about the park in Town Square was the elaborate pavilion designed and constructed by none other than Archibald Crowe. I felt famous by association seeing it there, a close cousin to the trellis at our house. I have one just like it at home, I would sometimes tell other children as I lovingly stroked its iron sides. No wonder I didn't have any friends. The day my mother gave herself away was a spring day like any other: the wind was brisk, the sky was bright, the flowers bloomed brightly in their beds.

In the end, she betrayed herself. I could have maintained the façade of normalcy indefinitely if she hadn't gone completely off of the rails. It must have been a Thursday when it happened, because I wasn't at home when it began. My mother had talked me into tennis lessons on Thursdays and my father always picked me up from Crawford gym on his way home. He was late that day, as he often was, and I was in a foul mood because the instructor had accused me of having two left feet. Instead of sympathizing, my father embarked on a lengthy reminiscence about his glory days on the court. I stalked home in silence. By the time we got there, I was in no mood to deal with any further upsets.

The minute my father opened the door, I knew the day was only going to get worse. We heard her weeping from the porch. I had seen her cry many times before, but it was nothing like this. It was as though all the blankness of the past few months was flying out of her in one great waling gust. She didn't have any tears left by the time we got there, but she was choking out sobs like some ancient motor, determined to start. The heels of her hands were dug hard into her eye sockets so she didn't realize we were home until my father was at her side. She paused for a moment, looking a bit like a criminal seeking escape. Stop, stop, stop, I pleaded silently. Just go take a bath. On another day, I might have gone up to her and whispered this aloud, but I felt too miserable and defeated. She didn't hear my silent pleas. She didn't even seem to know I was there. She just let her head fall to the table and kept weeping. In truth, I was glad not to see her face anymore. She was crying so hard her lips were all puffy and her eyes had swelled shut. She didn't look like my mother then; she looked like a plasticine model made by a child or one of the rubber baby dolls I'd put to bed too close to the fire. It took my father a good ten minutes to order me out of the kitchen. I was glad when he did because I could never have left on my own.

When I did leave, I suppose my father thought I'd gone to my room. His back was towards me and the stairs were far to his right. I didn't want to go to my room all alone though. Instead, I slipped into the basement to seek out signs of Archibald Crowe. It was pitch black, but I was more afraid of the kitchen than I was of the dark. When I couldn't hear my mother sobbing anymore, I crept back up to the top step, thinking I could slip out unseen. I didn't expect that my parents would still be sitting at the table. 'Death is everywhere,' I seem to recall my mother saying. 'It's followed me back home.' I remember perhaps because I thought I understood it, because it made sense to me when I was a child: my mother had finally read the plaque beneath the trellis. She had found out what every schoolchild knew: Archibald Crowe had breathed his last in our basement. He'd hung himself from the beams beneath the stairs.

20

If you could edit your memories what would you do? Would you ink out the unpleasantness? Would you erase all the pain that has made you you? Would you elect to forget me? Would you stamp me out through and through?

James had slept with four women other than his wife over the course of his marriage. The first was an old girlfriend who stopped by his office shortly after the wedding, shocked by the rumour that he'd finally settled down. He didn't really like Ivana, but he wasn't yet used to having a reason to say no. So when she locked the door behind her and trapped him in his chair between her powerful thighs, just like the old times, he let it happen. Afterwards, she patted his bald patch and left without a word. They had not spoken since.

The second infidelity was similarly fleeting. Missing Yasmeen, he'd had too much to drink after a conference on Sappho held in a mid-range Boston hotel. A busty redhead who had been eyeing him all through his talk cornered him at the bar. She was an intern from some California college and seemed surprisingly knowledgeable about the subjects being discussed that particular year. If she noticed his wedding band, she said nothing about it as she pulled him out of the back entrance by the tie and proceeded to have him quite efficiently against the wall although he was, by then, stumbling drunk. He woke up from dreams of being buried alive in a field full of decaying lilies with the second-worst hangover of his life. It was several years before he realized he'd never got her name.

His third slip-up had been more complicated. The woman was an infatuated student who'd hid her feelings superbly for the first three years he had known her. She was one of the increasingly rare Crawford students who actually cared about graduating with anything resembling an education. For three years, he laboured with her over thorny declensions, and by the time she mastered the third, he felt he owed it to her that she should graduate with something more than simply a supreme grasp of grammar. So he suggested an independent study. For her senior project, she would read *The Odyssey* as the story it was, not as a sequence of complex linguistic codes to be broken and parsed. She jumped at the chance, badgered her disinterested dean of studies until he agreed, and reordered her credits so she could spend the year doing nothing but Greek.

At first, James encouraged her to take other courses in classics. He tried to pitch his seminar on the history of the hero cult high enough that it would be of interest to her and even recommended she enrol in a course taught so long by Faber that Aristotelian poetics seemed somehow like reruns even to fresh-faced first-years. Neither had agreed with her. Classics majors at Crawford were stoners and slackers, attracted by the irrelevance, and by the mimeographed answer sheets that seemed always to circulate during finals week no matter how hard James tried to keep his exams under wraps. They declined nouns like robots, enjoying the strange twisty scripts that meant no more to them than abstracts in an art class and turned in crabbed homework sheets, embellished with chocolate smears and improvised curlicues. Discussions, when they happened at all, quickly degenerated to exclamations on 'how awesome those Homeric dudes' were. It was no place for a serious scholar.

So James allowed her to drop out of these classes. He cancelled his office hours, knowing no one would ever show, and dedicated his afternoons solely to educating her. It had been so long since he had intellectual stimulation of any sort. She was eager to learn and easy to teach; it was as though his dehydrated mind came alive again. He abandoned work on his book altogether to better focus on her work. For months, she hung on his every word. He loved to watch the muscles of her neck strain when his voice fell a decibel and she had to lean forward. He loved to see her suddenly grasp something and then light up like a flare—and that look she gave him afterwards, as though it would never have happened if he hadn't been there.

Her progress was impressive, alarming even. By the second semester, she really didn't need him anymore, but she came anyway. Every day after lunch she was there at his door with coffee for both of them and questions he knew she could answer without any help. They never spoke of anything but her project. She did not tell him about herself or ask about him. When she leant over him as he read through her latest discovery, her soft hair brushed his cheek and her hand came to rest, ever so softly, on his shoulder. She wasn't an especially pretty girl but there was something pleasant about her all the same. She was soft and beige like a favourite duvet. He registered this only vaguely though, as her intelligence impressed him more with each month that went by. And then one day she kissed him.

She told him later that she hadn't planned it; it was just something that happened. She was particularly excited about finally deciphering a passage that had plagued her for weeks, and when she saw how his eyes reflected the shine from her own, she couldn't resist. That first time, she left quickly, awkwardly adolescent in a flutter of papers. But she came back. She knew he had a wife and a daughter, but she kissed him again anyway. They began to spend afternoons in her small off-campus apartment. She made love to him gently, as though it was he who was young and tender and easy to hurt. It was seldom she needed his help anymore, but when she did, the discussions transpired in bed.

She kept notebooks everywhere so anytime an idea came to her she could jot it down without worrying it might escape her over the course of some trivial search. Years after she graduated, James would remember the feel of a pencil scratching across paper as she balanced notebooks on his head to take down the dictation he murmured into her breasts.

It ended when she left Crawford. They both knew she would be going on to bigger and better things. She loved him, she said, as she wept her farewell, but he hadn't loved her, at least he didn't think so. Clichéd emotions had fled with his youth, leaving behind a dense emptiness which floated somewhere between his chest and throat. For a time Yasmeen lifted it, but this student of his only obscured its presence for an instant. That summer, he immersed himself entirely in his own long-neglected work, emerging in autumn with a chapter that was finally worth publishing. When Yasmeen came back from Pakistan with sullen Irenie in tow, she threw a dinner party to celebrate and nailed framed copies of the journal, his name so small on the front, across the living-room wall. He had never been happier to see her. Cold, alone in the college library all summer, he almost wished he'd gone with her that year. When, nearly a decade later, a copy of the *New England Classical Journal* materialized on his desk with an article by a Hilary Maythorpe circled in red, it took him several minutes to recognize the name.

Though Hilary herself flew fast from his mind, a new sense of disappointment beset James once she left. After having held the undivided attention of a single rapt student, lecturing rows upon rows of blank faces began to unsettle him. He lost track of names and returned tests to the wrong students. He berated classes for their poor grasp of the dative when all they'd done thus far in the semester was copy declensions from the board. For the first time, his reviews came back negative at the end of the semester. 'Grades way too harshly,' one student wrote. 'Seems to expect us to know things he's never explained,' wrote another. Faber, who had been elected the head of the department again that year, told him to rest over Christmas and come back his old self.

'You're the only one in the department who's ever managed to teach these idiots anything,' he told James. 'I know it must be tiring to drill away at them year after year, but sometimes one actually cares and then isn't it worth it?'

James wondered then if Faber knew about Hilary. He had an uncanny way of ferreting out secrets, no matter how well they were kept. But on that last day of term he just looked tired and old. James surprised himself by inviting him for dinner and over Yasmeen's ras malai he had advised, 'Just give them B minuses. It isn't like any of these students actually need educations to succeed.'

This depressed James all the more and affecting dedication the following semester was a terrible struggle. If he sometimes came home to find Yasmeen unnaturally bright-eyed or flying frenetic through a food-bedecked kitchen he just assumed she was in one of her moods. If he noticed Irenie eyeing them both calculatingly, he put it down to her general detachment and un-childlike nature. He sometimes suspected she could see right through him, read his bones as though they were words. She read her mother too, he knew, though not with the same cold, medical gaze. Perhaps he should have asked what she saw. Perhaps he should have known that when she was watching so closely there was something afoot. But as she'd marched home behind him after her tennis lesson that day, so pointedly ignoring each thing he said, Irenie just seemed a petulant child. When they found Yasmeen in the kitchen, James simply had no idea what to do.

After that one transatlantic tell-all so many years ago when Yasmeen had confessed her lifelong love for Ahmed, she had rarely mentioned him. James knew they sent letters back and forth and that they telephoned sometimes. He did not know whether they had seen each other since Ahmed married. He did not know if he was there every summer when Yasmeen went back to Pakistan. He did not want to know. She did not tell him. When he stroked thighs that weren't hers, nibbled necks, kissed ears, he never thought she might do the same. Yasmeen had a strange sense of honour, and she would think adultery profane. James had come to see Ahmed almost as a weekly column his wife read in the newspaper, something that piqued her interest but had no bearing on him. He had reduced their whole history to a passing romance, no more significant than his with Ivana or Agnes or the bank teller who'd once made him doughnuts from scratch. To him, it was all dust-laden prelude to when they first met. Even then though, he preferred not to think of Ahmed. That day in the kitchen, though, he knew that he'd have to.

It had taken him almost an hour to calm Yasmeen down. She would wail that she was haunted, she found death even at the park, and then burst into tears when he asked what was wrong. Everything he said seemed to make her sob harder, so finally he just held her hand over the table until she was quiet, catching her breath. She was drunk, but drunkenness made her unusually lucent when she stopped crying enough to speak.

'Ahmed is dying,' was all she said. James saw then that Ahmed had been beside them since the very beginning. Their marriage had grown not outside him or over the wreckage, but around a bright, shining spectre that was solid and real to Yasmeen. Ahmed was as concrete to her as James was, perhaps even more so. He had grown no less important in all the years she spent never saying his name. Her rare fits of melancholy were no doubt over him; her occasional elation must have been because of something he'd said. And now he was dying.

For half a second James was happy. With Ahmed gone, perhaps Yasmeen would finally belong only to him. Then he saw the circles under her eyes and the bones poking through where there had once been more flesh. Her neck looked too thin to hold up her head and her lower lip was blistered where she balanced her cigarettes, too many, too hot. Her hair had grown dull and her eyes even more so. He reached across the table to brush ash off her hand and was alarmed to find that what he brushed away was dry skin. His wife was an ashen dust doll, held together by tears.

All at once, James hoped Ahmed wasn't dying at all, that it was just a misunderstanding and he could set Yasmeen straight. He pressed her for detail, as though knowing would somehow make everything fine.

'What exactly is wrong with him? How long has it been? Has he sought a second opinion? What about a third?'

So she told him: Ahmed had lymphoma, he'd had it for months. The prognosis was poor. That morning his doctors had said they doubted he'd live through the winter, if he lived that long at all. He was in terrible pain. He could no longer get out of bed. His hair had fallen out and radiation had given him an incurable rash.

'Has he tried acupuncture? Or eating organic? Sometimes people recover quite out of the blue. One day they're dying and the next they're up on their feet.'

He hectored her like an anxious relative berating the doctor for a mean shred of hope—as if a verbal concession might buy the patient more time. He wanted her to believe that Ahmed might still recover. He wanted to go back to ignoring the letters and adoring his wife from whatever small distance there was between them. If this was what Yasmeen was like with Ahmed still there albeit ill, maybe she wouldn't be anything once he was gone. Maybe she would curl into a tiny pile of nothingness and blow off the kitchen table in a brisk gust of wind. It was awful to watch her sit so expressionless as he asked his empty questions. He was running out of things to say, grasping at straws. Heartfelt conversation had never quite been his forte. Trying to comfort people made him incredibly uneasy. It was probably one of the reasons he and his daughter were never close: children required all sorts of intimacy and James was poorly equipped. They wanted you to watch them, listen to them, to kiss them spontaneously and say they were great.

And you always had to take care that they wouldn't cut themselves on a tetanus-stained fence or jump twenty feet out of a tree just to see if they could fly. One had to constantly rescue them from invisible peril. As it happened though, it was Irenie who saved James that particular night.

21

To me, you are perfect. You make my world whole. You are my first thought in the morning, my last sigh at night. You are the star of my every dream, the subject of my every wish. There is nothing in the universe I wouldn't trade for one last kiss. You are the sun of my solar system, the moon to my tides. And yet I must somehow navigate life without you, all alone through the night.

As a six-year-old, I was spectacularly good at sitting still for long periods of time, even when I was bored. Strangers at the dentists' office or the bank were always complimenting my mother on how well behaved I was. Of all my many efforts to be a perfect child, learning to keep quiet was both the most sure-fire and the easiest. I could make up stories to keep myself entertained. I didn't even have to touch; all I needed was to see. Staplers rescued wads of blue tack from electric pencil sharpeners and knives danced illicit rumbas with spoons when forks had their backs turned. In the basement stairwell that night, however, there was nothing to look at. When I felt the sneeze coming, I simply let it escape.

What followed takes divergent roads in my memory. Before I found the box, I vaguely recalled having been trapped in the stairwell without any lights as a child. This scenario is in keeping with my mother's hysteria and my subsequent trepidation regarding the basement. I remember being suddenly blinded and bursting into tears when the screaming began. I remember also that it was my father who made me toast and took me to bed. I'd always assumed my mother had been too overwrought over my temporary disappearance to do these things, but it seems to me now that I was only the epilogue to the events of that day. When I put together the dates on the letters, my mother's forgotten depressions, and the scarring memory of those dreadful tennis lessons, I remembered things quite differently. I had forgotten my mother was crying before I was found in the basement. I had forgotten I hadn't been stuck, that I was hiding. I'd even forgotten why.

Since all this came back to me, I've begun to remember what the screaming was about. When my father opened the basement door to find me perched atop the stair, I had a length of rope wrapped over my throat. You see, in my search for Archibald Crowe, I'd found a rope and draped it around my neck for later use. To my overwrought mother, it would have been an eerie sight. She screamed and wailed that death would steal everything from her and hugged me so tightly I thought my ribs might break. The whole thing set off her crying again, and she'd gone on for days. I stopped going down to the basement, but it made little difference. My mother no longer bothered to change out of her robe, and when I said I was bored she just stared at me blankly. She swallowed so painfully before even the smallest response that I soon gave up talking and just sat across from her, watching the smoke. Now and again, a tear would leak down her cheek, but mostly she just sat. When my father came home she'd still be at the kitchen table with her mug and her ash snakes. He began coming back earlier to fix the two of us dinner, but I could barely swallow food anymore. All he'd ever learned to make was eggs. So my mother and I just sat hollow-eyed at the table while my father had dinner. He knew enough not to try talking to her, but not enough not to try talking to me. He never knew what to say and I could never think how to answer.

Each night, my mother saved the artless exchange. Somewhere between dinner and dishes, all the alcohol would finally catch up with her and she would begin to weep. My father would carry her upstairs to the bath while I finished tidying the kitchen. I could hear them murmuring in there sometimes, but I never went in. My father didn't even have to say it for me to know I wasn't allowed. More than anything, I wanted to know what was going on in there, though after I found her in the tub that day I wished I could un-know.

22

Without you, there is nothing.

Shortly before Yasmeen first attempted suicide, he began to notice couples arguing in cars. Every time he drove somewhere, he'd stop at lights or pause at signs to notice tightly sealed cars aflurry with curses and wildly gesticulating fingers. Sometimes, he could even catch a sense of what the arguments were about. To his mind, it was never anything worth all that trouble.

23

Why is it that mistakes are so easy to make? Mistakes are easier than sleeping, more natural than breathing. 'I didn't mean to' must be the words that spring most often from our lips. You and I, my beloved, are rich in love and accidents.

James knew something terrible had happened when he heard Irenie's voice, tinny over the telephone. His daughter never called him at work, not when she snapped her wrist in kindergarten and her mother was at Claire's wedding, far from the phone, not when Yasmeen was lunching with painting class friends and he was three hours late to collect her from school, not even on god-only-knows how many afternoons when Yasmeen had drunk herself senseless by mid-afternoon and then insisted upon intricate operations with sharp knives and hot stoves. It was the first time James had spoken to his daughter on the phone; he didn't even know she was old enough to operate the device.

He found her wavering over the bathtub, desperately clutching dark handfuls of her mother's damp hair. 'I'm sorry,' she kept whispering, 'it's all my fault.' In the seconds it took him to make out her refrain, to realize that his daughter's firm fistfuls were all that kept Yasi's head above water, the paramedics had arrived and pulled her out of the tub. Irenie had a good grasp of telephone protocols after all. And then there had been so many forms to fill out, so many papers to sign. He didn't think about his daughter until over five hours later, when he was heading out through the

door, and a nurse had pointed her out: asleep, braids undone, tiny
glasses fallen to her chest, in a waiting-room chair.

'Were you just going to leave her here all night by herself?' the
nurse asked sharply. James blushed. He probably would have.

He tried to pick her up as Yasmeen often did, without
disturbing her sleep, but her eyes snapped open the instant he
touched her. 'I didn't mean to,' she whispered. 'Tell Mamma I'm
sorry.' He hushed her gently, too tired to do much more than
assure her it was not her fault.

She insisted he take her with him when he went back to the
hospital even though he warned her that she'd probably have to
sit in the waiting room by herself the whole day. Irenie didn't care.
All day, she just stared at a poster of Belize on the waiting-room
wall, her mother in miniature. He forgot to feed her lunch but she
seemed unperturbed. Finally, James found Dr Zimmerman and
settled on him. Unlike the others, he seemed willing to believe
there was nothing more wrong with Yasmeen than a tough couple
of months. His wife, James knew, would refuse to put up with
being treated like someone insane. Dr Zimmerman thought it
important to meet Irenie, so towards the end of their consult a
nurse brought her in.

James wasn't sure how much of what Dr Zimmerman said got
through to his daughter. She stared him in the face the whole
time he spoke, as though memorizing his words so she would have
them on hand whenever she found she had grown old enough to
fully understand. Only twice had she spoken over the course of
the interview: first to tell Dr Zimmerman no thank you, when he
said she could come speak to him anytime she felt sad, and second
when they were saying goodbye and he told her she'd have her
mother back in just a few short weeks.

'I'm sorry,' she wailed. 'It's all my fault.' It was hard to say
whether she believed their insistences to the contrary. She
wouldn't say a word about it; she just wanted to know why they
were sending her mother away. Just for a while, they tried to

explain. Just for the drinking, and then Yasmeen would come home. But Irenie's face was closed as a stone.

'How about an ice cream?' he asked, glancing at her in the rear-view mirror on their way home. All children liked ice cream, didn't they?

She regarded him blankly in the mirror and he realized with a start that, framed by her mother's dark lashes, her cold grey gaze was his.

He remembered going to parties years ago, when Yasmeen still had the will to drag him, and occasionally overhearing snide comments about those lashes. They're fake. Yes, they must be. Who wears fake lashes in this day and age? Does he think she's at Studio 54 or something? They weren't, of course. They were real. Long and black, they curled upward and to the sides in a way such that when she looked at you from beneath them it was as though there was no one else in the room. Bartenders slipped her free drinks and airline attendants bumped her up to first class when she peered at them from under those lashes.

'Raspberry,' said his daughter, looking down suddenly. 'With almonds.'

Her mother's favourite. Irenie hated nuts.

When James took his first stumbling steps into adultery, he'd waited for the guilt like a lackadaisical patient who's held out so long he has to have eight root canals all at once. But it never arrived. He stumbled again, and yet again, and then straight onto Hilary Maythorpe, and not even then had he felt anything more than a vague sense of regret. Sometimes, he even found himself irritated at Yasmeen for not noticing his lapses. He would have noticed if she had an affair. He would have seen the signs had she been with anyone else. And he would have been jealous, furious, hurt. But if Yasmeen ever noticed anything, she did not say a word. With no one to exact confession or penance, the guilt he ought to have felt translated into anger. It was a benign anger which flared up rarely, and never at her, but it lurked there all the same. The glare Irenie held fixed upon him the whole time Yasmeen was gone weighed James down with guilt far heavier than either his Catholic upbringing or his brief infidelities had led him to expect.

Which, funnily enough, led directly to his fourth affair.

Jo Anne the Sports Fan, as James referred to her in his mind long before he ever thought he might one day find himself weeping in her arms, was the associate director of financial aid at Crawford. As the associate director of financial aid at a college attended almost exclusively by legacies, Jo Anne didn't have much to occupy her time. Occasionally, she forwarded appeals for aid to the director, but mostly she sat in her office and watched sports on her small black and white television. In fall it was football, in winter, basketball or ice hockey, in spring, baseball. Between times, there were reruns, wrestling, even men's swimming in Olympics years. The mass of acronyms that was her day planner—NFL, NBA, MLB, NHL— was mistakenly believed by the director of financial aid, a man much more familiar with the acronyms BSc, BA, BFA and MBA, to represent her diligent research into obscure scholarships. Jo Anne did excel at cobbling together grants for both students and recent graduates, usually Crawford-funded, which would allow these disillusioned bright sparks to study Sognamål in Gjøvik or Whooper Swans on Surtsey or whatever abstruse discipline they thought might distinguish them upon their entrance into the real world. Given the ratio of bright sparks to dullards, scholars to socialites, this cost Jo Anne roughly eleven man hours each year, leaving her the other eight thousand seven hundred and fifty-five to carefully calibrate her sports-watching schedule.

James first encountered Jo Anne shortly after he got married, when Yasmeen received a letter claiming she had loans outstanding, though she was certain her tuition had been covered by the terms of her work-study. Jo Anne's TV was on the fritz that day, and she clutched a transistor radio in one great, hammy fist.

'Run, numb-nuts, run,' she was trying hard not to yell. Displeased by the interruption, she settled the matter in seconds flat. Though grateful for her efficiency, James henceforth went out of his way to avoid her at all college events. Her fervour frightened him; her devotion to something he considered entirely inconsequential alarmed, almost offended him. It wasn't for almost another seven years that James felt the need for her fierce brand of competency once again.

Irenie was asleep in the backseat, her ice cream melting, almost untouched, down her front. It had been a tough couple of days for them. James would have liked to take a quick nap at one of the five stoplights between Mr Fripp's Frozen Delights and home, but of course, he couldn't. He couldn't immediately fall into the welcome oblivion of dreamless sleep even after they got home. Irenie could have, but she didn't. She protested when he tried to clean her up, rebuked him for his attempts to help her brush her teeth.

'Get out,' she'd screeched when she awoke slumped against the toilet, her dress a sticky mess in James's hands.

He found her asleep again in the half-filled tub two hours later, two hours after he went downstairs to check the messages and learned that Yasmeen had disappeared. She had flattered a young orderly into releasing her and promptly walked right out of the front door. Dr Zimmerman apologized profusely; it wasn't often patients escaped. Did James think, he wanted to know, that his wife could have taken off to finish the job? James didn't think so. Yasmeen was never much for second attempts. He wasn't worried his wife was dead. He wasn't worried she wouldn't come back. True, she had taken the suitcase their daughter had packed for her the night before, the suitcase James himself had dropped off in her room. She had her handbag, which, he knew, always held her passport, her wallet, her credit cards. He didn't even have to wait till business hours to know their bank would report a ticket on a transatlantic flight had been bought the night before. But James knew she would return.

'She'll be back,' he told Dr Zimmerman, certain she would.

But when, he wondered, feeling the first stirrings of panic as he watched his small daughter twitch and turn in the cold water of the tub. She looked to him like a specimen, a half-formed foetus in a lab. Her thin limbs floated ghostly grey, something cold and dead one wouldn't want to touch. Her hair was like strange seaweed, fingerlings reaching out to analyse the nutritive possibilities of the bath. It would be hellish to disentangle the next morning, James knew. What was his wife thinking, letting a little girl's hair grow so very long?

He sat down on the edge of the tub, hoping his presence would wake her up. It didn't. For a few moments more, James regarded the blurred body of his daughter. Bending to retie one of his shoelaces, his hand grazed her bare shoulder. It was cold. Freezing. He pulled away as though shocked, crumpling on the bathroom floor. It didn't wake her up. Yasmeen's skin had still been warm, her cheeks a rosy pink. Even intent on death as their daughter now was not, she seemed somehow more alive.

Steeling himself, James let his hand come to rest on Irenie's shoulder once again. It was the cold of a water pump in the New England winter, the cold of an antique army pistol found in your father's desk after his death. James didn't want to touch her. He didn't want to lift her out and wrap her in a towel. But he couldn't leave her all night alone, sleeping in the tub. Could he?

'I didn't mean to,' she whimpered, catching him unawares. She held her arms up for him to lift her, as she hadn't since she was a tiny child. 'Uppy,' she sighed, and he realized she wasn't quite awake. He got her out of the tub and into her bed as best as he could, determined even before he laid her down to find someone other than himself to take care of her for the time his wife was gone.

The most obvious candidate for the task would have been one of the flighty co-eds Yasmeen enlisted on the rare occasions they needed someone to babysit: Cindy Marlowe with her nail file or Abigail Comte with the piles of reading she never did. But, intuitively, James knew girls like them would be no help at all. Irenie needed someone sensible, someone competent, someone who would make sure she didn't spend the next month in a sulk, a Mary Poppins or Nurse Matilda who would take the girl in hand. A Jo Anne the Sports Fan, perhaps.

Over the course of her tenure as associate director of financial aid, Jo Anne had, at least once, babysat every last one of the faculty brats. Had she ever been interested in painting lessons, she would no doubt have babysat Irenie long before Yasmeen left. But Jo Anne had no interest in art and Yasmeen would never have hired a woman she hadn't met. It wouldn't have mattered that Jo Anne came highly recommended, that she had a certification in CPR: Yasmeen Eccles only left her child alone with women she knew. None of these women, however, were known to James.

When word spread, as it quickly did, that Professor Eccles was looking for someone to watch his daughter after school, Jo Anne was one of the first candidates suggested. She had got the Patel twins in bed by eight, he heard, had dissuaded Candace Folcroft from publicly spewing profanities at her imaginary friend. She had taught Faber's youngest grandchild to read at three, convinced young Janine McClintock to take a bath. Jo Anne was the sort of woman who regarded children as indulgences of the very self-involved. Like porcelain and Persian rugs, they demanded careful maintenance, though, unlike such heirlooms, it was debatable whether they would appreciate with age. Accordingly, she treated them with the brusque assiduity of a good dog trainer. It was an attitude to which children, particularly the most petted and pampered of the lot, responded well. So well, in fact, that grateful parents had often suggested Jo Anne give up her part-time position altogether and open up a day care. Childcare, however, was only a side venture for her. Having grown up poor in Minnesota, Jo Anne enjoyed helping ambitious young people achieve their dreams.

She also enjoyed health insurance and charges who understood not to interrupt her when a particularly important game was on TV. Her babysitting jobs, though lucrative, were not something Jo Anne actively sought out.

It was thus that James spent two full afternoons interviewing students before he threw his hands up in frustration and approached her himself. The last girl he had interviewed had been a classics major, blatantly flirtatious and after an A any way it could be got. One thing James was sure he *didn't* want was another avenue to go astray. Where, ordinarily, he might have sought out a young slip of a thing, a pretty girl whose inane banter he could enjoy for a few minutes as she poured him coffee after work, he was now determined to hire someone who would pose no temptation at all. The glare his daughter had fixed upon him in the car was not one he wanted to be reminded he deserved.

Jo Anne agreed to watch Irenie weekdays after school. After hearing how his sudden need for extensive childcare had come about, she agreed also to attend to the girl on weekends when James couldn't stand to be around. She would draw his daughter out, she promised, refuse to let her retreat into a shell.

James had expected Irenie wouldn't like Jo Anne. He'd expected tantrums and silent pouts. His daughter liked the silly, substanceless girls her mother appointed to paint her nails when they went out; Jo Anne was hardly the type for things like that. But to his surprise, they got along brilliantly. Irenie often begged her babysitter to stay even after her father had come home. To his relief, she never again mentioned it having been all her fault. Nor did she state outright that sending Yasmeen away was his. He found it easy enough to ignore the accusation in her eyes.

Without deferring to him, Jo Anne began to join them for the simple meals she prepared—bean soup boiled all day or pilaf from a box; nothing like the grand events that were dinnertimes when Yasmeen was around—often staying long enough to put Irenie to bed. When, as James had known she would, his wife

rematerialized a few days after she'd taken off, it was Jo Anne
who consoled their daughter when they found at the rehab centre
that children weren't allowed. She engaged her charge in rowdy
outdoor games that left her too tired to think long and late of
Yasmeen when it was time to go to bed. She arranged outings to
the park, the library, the college grounds. Most importantly, she
never let Irenie clam up. She'd ignore her on her sullen days, draw
her out when she was sad. To James, the woman was nothing short
of a godsend.

Sometimes, after Irenie had been put to bed, Jo Anne lingered
over the dishes, watching athletic feats of one sort or the other
on her portable TV which, James soon learned, accompanied her
everywhere she went. Though sports held even less appeal for
James than Jo Anne herself, he found the quiet noise of her in
his kitchen comforting. They stayed up late together, watching
baseball, sometimes popping corn. It wasn't long before he was
confiding in her, telling her how guilty he now so often felt.
Though Irenie, it seemed, behaved impeccably for Jo Anne, she
never so much as looked at James unless it was to glare.

'My own daughter *hates* me,' he would self-pityingly proclaim.
Unlike Yasmeen, Jo Anne never tried to assure him that she didn't.
She just told him to pull himself together; his daughter didn't need
two parents who'd fallen completely apart. Though Jo Anne was
younger than James by a decade or more, he often felt she was his
elder, a woman well-versed in all the ways of the world. There was
something infinitely reassuring about her phlegmatic approach to
everything but sports, something marvellously stilling about the
way she sat there at the kitchen table, perdurable as a boulder.
Sometimes she seemed less a person than a life-form that would
eternally endure, a life-form bearing semblance to humanity only
in her inexhaustible capacity to make her fellow humans feel that,
with her, everything would be all right. It was little wonder she'd
ended up alone. Though Jo Anne made no secret of how much she
enjoyed the broad shoulders and pert buttocks of the sportsmen she

watched on TV, decades as a sports fan had left her irreconcilably disappointed in the lesser specimens she encountered from day to day. She had never married, nor did she wish to. James thought she might once have been attractive had she not so ruthlessly adopted the style of sexless English sportswomen who delight in nothing more than the running of the hounds. With her close-cropped hair and muscled thighs, she was no more his type than one of the hulking athletes she so liked to watch. He simply enjoyed her solid, stolid company on the nights she chose to stick around.

A few days before Yasmeen was to be released, she admitted to Dr Zimmerman that she had, in fact, been trying to kill herself that day in the tub. Up until then, she had maintained that it had been an accident: having had too much to drink she'd swallowed a handful of painkillers with the idea that if one would cure her headache in half an hour, twenty would cure it in just over a minute. Dr Zimmerman deemed the admission a prodigious breakthrough. He told James that Yasmeen would need at least another two weeks of in-patient care before they worked the whole thing out. James had been devastated, his daughter even more so. At least *he* got to go to the hospital and see her, Irenie accused when he tried to convince her that he didn't want Yasmeen to stay away any more than she did. Not surprisingly, it was Jo Anne who got her to calm down. There was nothing like a little mass enthusiasm to cheer a person up, she told James later. The Yankees were playing the Orioles that Tuesday, a home game. Jo Anne herself had already made arrangements to take a personal day. Why didn't the two of them take one as well? Though Irenie was, if possible, even less interested in sports than her father, the promise of a day off school and all the hotdogs she could eat was appealing nonetheless.

To James's surprise, they had a box all to themselves. Jo Anne alluded to a strategic dalliance with a certain married player, which made both of them blush. He hadn't seen her look even remotely girlish ever before.

As Jo Anne had predicted, the crowd's energy was contagious. James found himself grinning like an idiot when the camera zoomed in on couples kissing and Irenie leapt up to cheer even when the batsman didn't make it to first base. She threw up in the fifth inning—too much excitement, too many hotdogs—and fell asleep just as the seventh began. By this point, James was beginning to feel rather tired himself. Neither team had yet scored and both seemed determined not to all night long. He was just beginning to nod off when the Yankees finally scored a run. They had won. Far below them, the whole crowd erupted in a cheer so earth-shaking that for a moment James mistook it for the roar of an approaching train. Jo Anne jumped up and down like a child, her mountainous bosom bouncing so extravagantly it could have knocked a small child out. Tears streaming down her face, she pulled James to her chest and pounded him on the back as he imagined a man might have done, if he'd ever known a man prone to hugging. Momentarily, James considered following athletic events himself.

Back at 437 Chestnut Hill Lane, they watched the replay on Jo Anne's TV. She was there so often that she'd taken to leaving it on the kitchen counter, making due with the transistor during the hours she was at work. Though James's interest in sport evaporated as quickly as it had come upon him, he wanted to relive the excitement, the elation, the unadulterated joy that had made plain Jo Anne almost pretty. Quite unexpectedly, he found he was overcome with disappointment when the last commentator commentated his last on the night's game. It was as though he'd passed through an enchanted wardrobe or down a rabbit hole only to be cruelly dragged back out. To his horror, James began to cry, to weep as he had not since the day Irene had died.

'What am I going to do?' he wondered aloud. It was a question he'd been trying hard not even to consider for almost an entire month. What he was going to do was something James did not know. He was a man used to being cared for. After Irene, there had been all the girls, after the girls, the women, after the women, Yasmeen. He had yet to master the delicate art of taking care of himself; how he was to take care of two other human beings was quite beyond his comprehension.

For the second time that night, James found himself pulled into the mountainous bosom. Jo Anne let him exhaust his pity for himself as she never had before. If James had been a more cynical man, it would have occurred to him decades ago that crying was a fail-safe way to women's hearts. The urge to look after him, which his very presence inspired, inevitably translated itself into something overtly sexual anytime he so much as looked sad. But James was not a cynical man, not really. That night he was grateful only that Jo Anne was there to hold him, that she didn't pull back when he kissed her softly on the mouth. He didn't sleep with her that night nor did he on the next. It was three nights later that he did, after he came home to find her painting her toenails, her muscular legs straining the seams of a pair of purple pedal pushers. It was, he felt, as though they were acting out an inevitability established long ago. It was a pleasant inevitability nonetheless.

The whole thing might have faded into hazy half-forgotten history, as James's love affairs were wont to, had not Irenie stumbled across them on the couch a few days before her mother was to return.

So this is why Mamma left, her eyes accused as she glared down at them from the stairs. James hadn't it in him to contradict her.

'Nothing, nothing,' he whispered to Jo Anne when she asked why he'd gone still. The next time he looked up, Irenie was gone. It was another two days, as they were driving to the Fairview Centre to collect Yasmeen, before he could bring himself to say anything at all.

'Don't mention Jo Anne to your mother?' he suggested, catching her eye in the mirror as she bounced over the backseat. She hadn't said anything. The ferocity of her glare had been enough to confirm that she knew just what he meant. Nevertheless, James had expected that it wouldn't be long before Yasmeen learned all about what he'd been doing with Jo Anne. He hadn't counted on how far Irenie would go to spare her mother any hurt. Sometimes, he wondered if she'd told her and Yasmeen just hadn't cared, but when he saw how hard his wife worked to resurrect the normalcy of their former lives he was sure she hadn't heard. What James was going to do turned out to be simply this: leave everything to Yasmeen, just as he always had. Years later, he would learn that her miraculous recovery had coincided nicely with Ahmed's, but at the time he'd admired her for her will to carry on—if not for him then for their daughter, who'd been devastated the whole time she was gone.

Almost immediately, James went back to his old habit of avoiding Jo Anne at college events. She made no move to speak with him and continued to offer her babysitting services only when she was solicited. Irenie refused to be left alone with *any* babysitter; she never once mentioned Jo Anne. Occasionally, James would let himself hope that she'd forgotten—children that age often did, didn't they?—but then he'd catch her watching him when she thought he couldn't see, watching him with a look that plainly said, I know your game. A few years later, Jo Anne moved to Michigan. James didn't stop by to say goodbye. Neither, as far as he knew, did his daughter. Though he didn't know it then, she was already busy holding up her mother for the second time.

24

Do you remember that fishing trip in Hunza? The trout I caught and lost? An instant before it flipped back into the river I knew that it was gone. Even as I held it, I felt it slipping from my hands. And then you dove in, headfirst, heavy-clothes, and snatched it from the depths. Sometimes I feel my life is like that fish and there is no one to get it back.

The school year draws to a close quite without my noticing. Since my visit to Claire, I have been so wrapped up in the past I've scarcely noted the passage of time. I read the letters twice more, each time inferring more from things not said. Ahmed Kakkezai is my true father, I'm sure of it, despite what Claire and Mrs Winterbourne have said. His penmanship is not unlike mine, his letter P a perfect match. He loved oranges and so do I. Though I've yet to find a photograph, I deduce he wore glasses and his hair was curly just like mine. I have seen little of my father since Professor Faber's funeral—for all his protestations that he never liked the man, he seems unusually withdrawn—but when I do see him I study his face closely, searching for traces of mine. So far I see none.

Until the day school ends, I'm uncertain as to what to do with the information I've unearthed. Do I confront my so-called father? Do I ask Nani for the truth? Then one day, as I'm trimming the roses along the walk, I'm nearly trampled by Dionysius bolting across the yard. The cause of distress is, inevitably, Celeste.

'She's leaving me,' he tells me, before I can even inquire. There are the beginnings of tears in his eyes. He rubs at them fiercely. I learn Celeste is being dispatched to Florida post-haste to care for the Grandmother, who has cracked her hip. She's decided to end it with Dionysius before she goes because by the time she returns he'll have left for college anyway. I try my best to comfort him, but I fear it's something for which I haven't any skill.

'Take this,' he says, handing me a bottle. Inside it is the ship. In the end, he somehow managed the sails himself. They're a little crooked and there's what appears to be a drop of blood on one, but he managed nevertheless. I feel terrible I didn't help.

'I can't,' I protest, trying to hand it back. 'You worked so hard on this.'

He shrugs. 'It was for Celeste. She said ships go on seas, not shelves, and it's the most depressing thing she's ever seen.'

And since the ship has nowhere else to go, I accept it from Dionysius. Celeste looks at it and shudders when I go over to ask her what she's thinking. 'It's for his own good,' she tells me. 'I've set him free.' She snatches the ship from me then and smashes the bottle against her desk. 'Here,' she says, and hands me the little vessel. 'Now it's the way it ought to be.'

For a moment, I think I might hit her. So much work went into keeping it there in the bottle and she's destroyed it in a second. Instead, I burst into tears. 'I should've helped him,' I sob. 'I promised I would.' She looks at me oddly. It's then I confess the thought I've repressed since I had it all those months ago: James Eccles is not my father.

Celeste doesn't laugh or question this. She hugs me tightly and tells me ships are meant to sail the seas.

For the next few days, I mope around the house. At the library, I'm so morose Mrs Winterbourne sends me home. I'm depressing the patrons, she says. When Friday arrives, I'm not even excited about speaking to Nani, though she's been obliging me with stories of my mother's youth each week. They're never what I wish to hear. Ahmed hasn't been mentioned even once. I bring up the love stories my mother used to tell me: the tragic tales of Sassi and Pannu, Sohni and Mahiwal, Tristan and Isolde, stories ending in separation, death. I even go so far as to ask what could have drawn my mother to such sagas, but Nani just sighs and says her daughter was always a romantic of gloomy bent. Towards the end of the conversation she asks me, as she always does, when I'm coming to visit.

'Soon, Nani,' I tell her. 'Very soon, I hope.'

'Inshallah,' she says.

It is to my credit, I believe, that I bring up my plans with my father before taking further action. I serve him an insipid dinner of roasted lamb and minted peas so bland it might hasten an invalid's death (through the boredom it inspired alone), which he devours happily. When he's on his third serving and I've managed to choke down a few mouthfuls with the aid of mango achar, I bring up Nani's invitation, the one she issues every week.

'It seems a bit rude, don't you think, to keep promising to go and then never doing so?'

My father, who has surprisingly immaculate table manners when not eating alone, dabs delicately at his mouth with his napkin. 'She understands,' he says, taking his plate over to the sink. He opens the freezer and stares into it for a long while. 'Is the ice cream downstairs?'

'I'll get it,' I cry, leaping for the stairs. The last thing I want is for him to open the deep freeze to find the stacks of neatly labelled frozen dinners I've been steadily preparing. 'Chocolate or butter pecan?' I call from the bottom of the stairs. A few years ago, Professor Faber thought he might enjoy welding and my father gave him use of the basement. He discovered he did not enjoy it after all, but not before he redid all the lighting in the basement so he could see. The dark corners are gone now; the ghosts or figments fled.

He selects the chocolate, but I'm too on edge for either. 'So I was thinking, maybe I should go this summer...'

He doesn't even look up from his ice cream. 'I don't think so, Irenie.'

I protest and question, but he will not budge. If I didn't know better, I'd think he doesn't want to be left alone. Given his initial bullishness about my proposed trip to 'Florida' over Easter, however, I have a watertight plan B. Mrs Winterbourne has agreed, reluctantly, to help me get my documents in order. She is retiring after the summer and she says it is her parting gift to me. Nani agrees, also reluctantly, to make arrangements for me without telling my father. I assure both of them he will come around if I approach him again with the legwork already done. I hope this is not a lie.

By the first week of July, everything is in order. The freezer is stocked and gifts have been bought. I call my grandparents to confirm I'll be arriving on the eighth at five a.m. and Shamim answers on the second ring.

'Oh, it's you,' says my cousin, as though I'm calling from two streets away. 'Hello Irenie.' Shamim has disliked me, quite literally, from the day we were born. Though she came late, she blames our shared birthday on my early arrival. Our grandparents spent those first few hours of her life that should rightfully have been her time in the limelight conferring anxiously with my father over the phone as my mother squeezed me out continents away. Shamim was born first, but I spoke first. She walked first and I smiled first. Our lives have been a low-stakes greyhound race over the phone and Shamim is the only one who makes any bets. 'I suppose you want to speak to Nani?'

'Yes, please.'

'She's not here, I'm afraid.'

Though she does not offer to take a message, I leave one anyway and hope it will be passed on. I'll email Naaz later just in case. As we hang up, I'm startled by a crash from the basement.

For a moment I think: Archibald. But of course it isn't. The shelf
over the sink has come down in a cloud of cleaning supplies. The
shelf was huge and high and deep and I see ice skates and model
airplanes which were never ours have fallen to the floor as well.
There are Christmas lights and broken glass and a tiny box of baby
teeth. I sweep up the mess, putting aside things my father might
like to keep. Underneath a wreath, I find a cardboard box labelled
'Irenie'. The writing is in his hand. I peel away the tape and find it
full of baby photos I've never seen. My mother, ever camera shy, is
featured only from the back, bending over me, but there are many
pictures of my father holding me up awkwardly for the camera.
There are a number of photographs of three girl babies seated in a
row: me looking bewildered, Naaz with biscuit or a binkie always
in her mouth, and Shamim glowering beneath brows that were
Marx-esque even then. There's me on my first birthday, me eating
a snowball, me splashing in the bath. They're all labelled and dated
in my father's hand. At the bottom of the box, there is a small pile
of albums: it was my mother's job, I gather, to put the photos in.
They're arranged artfully for the first few pages of the first album,
accompanied by sketches and little notes. The second album is
empty. It is on the first page of the third album that I find my birth
certificate. Irenie Eccles. Six pounds, eleven ounces. Born 8 April
1986 to James and Yasmeen Eccles in Crawford, New York. For a
long time, I sit motionless. All this while, I was sure someone had
destroyed it to somehow hide the evidence, but it was just here
in the basement, forgotten in a box of familial filing my mother
never did.

I look down at it again. Though it bears the name James Eccles,
my mother could hardly have demanded Ahmed's name be put on
the birth certificate with her husband right there even if Ahmed
was my real father. The piece of paper before me is badly damaged.
Does the damage look intentional though? I cannot tell. Is what
it says the truth? I carefully pry it from the album and tuck it into
the waistband of my skirt. I leave the box of photos in the 'keep'

pile, unsure what I should do with it, and push all the detritus of other families into a heap beside the freezer.

When I emerge into the kitchen, my clothing covered with dust, glitter in my hair, I'm startled to see my father standing there. He is at the table, by the phone, my ticket in his hand. Slowly, oh so slowly, he looks up and meets my eye. 'What. Is. This?'

I shrug and move towards him, my hand outstretched. He snatches it away, as though I might leap for it, as though I might tackle him from across the room.

'This appears to be a ticket to Islamabad, Irenie.'

'Yes.' I pause in the middle of the floor.

'We discussed this.'

'We didn't discuss it. You refused to discuss it. You just sat there and shook your head without listening to anything I said.'

'Please, Irenie,' he says, holding up a hand. 'It isn't safe. I can't let you go.'

'I always went, every summer. You just don't want me to be close to Mamma in a way you refuse to share. You just want to keep all the memories of her to yourself. Just like you keep that photo of her in your study to yourself, the one of her in the snow.'

'You can have it,' he says. 'It's all yours. I'll give it to you right now, Irenie. Just … you cannot go.'

'I can and I am. I want more than an old photo now.'

'Well, it will have to do,' he says, and rips the ticket into bits. I lunge for it, but I'm too late and he's too tall.

'What have you done?' I shout. 'I spent all my money on that!' Well, all my mother's money, but it's not as though I have more. 'I can't get another. How *could* you?' I fall to my knees and begin collecting the tiny pieces of the ticket. To my horror, I begin to cry.

'Irenie,' he says quietly, kneeling to put his hand on my shoulder. 'I'm sorry, Irenie, but I just can't. I can't let you go.' His eyes are filled with panic now, almost as though he wants to cry, but I don't care. He has stolen my mother from me in every way he can.

'Get away from me,' I sob, shoving his hand away. 'I *hate* you.'

'What has got into you? When your mother was around, you never behaved like this ...'

'Well, if she were here maybe I wouldn't now.'

'What is that supposed to mean?' he asks, his voice louder than I've ever heard it rise before.

'If *you* hadn't let her go, maybe she would still *be* here.'

'I didn't let her go,' he yells. 'She left. She didn't even tell me she was going. She just *left*.'

'If I had been here, I wouldn't have let her leave,' I scream back just as loud.

'She was an adult, a grown woman, I couldn't stop her.'

'I *would* have stopped her.' And we're yelling, both unheard, about where the fault ought best to fall.

'She left you too, Irenie,' he finally roars, slamming the door.

PART II

Islamabad, Pakistan 2001

Khalil Family Tree

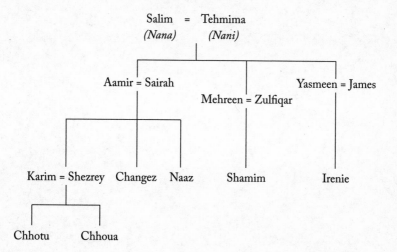

1

I have spent months, maybe years, of my life in airports, bus depots, train stations. Sometimes I travel towards you, sometimes away from you, and always with you in my heart. How is it then that after all these hundreds of thousands of miles we are still apart? How is it that, for all my travels, I have yet to reach you?

Peering past the smudges left on the glass by other, more avid, lookers I squint at the horizon, blurring bright scenery to an indistinct grey. Occasionally, my eyes close out the world entirely and install in its place a blank sheet of red far too deep for my taste. Lately, my shades of choice have been muted non-colours, hues that usually exist only to be coloured in, embroidered, dyed; emptiness colours that primary school teachers penalize schoolchildren for leaving patches of in their drawings. The colours of letters, say, left to yellow in a locked-up box. Letters, which I may never see again. They are gone, along with Nana's Mont Blanc cartridges, Sairah Mumani's rum truffles, my red corduroy trousers and an assortment of t-shirts. My small suitcase never came.

The light hurts my eyes but I force them open anyway. This was my mother's favourite part of the drive. Will they bring her up? I wonder. Or will I have to? UNITY FAITH DISCIPLINE proclaims the hillside whitely in the morning glare. As far as I remember, this is the only landmark to be found along airport road. Now and again we pass a tent or a goat, but there's little else to suggest this semi-tamed in-between land is inhabited. Trees grow haphazard and bushes flower brightly in no apparent order. The median, encased in its concrete sleeve of black and white checker, looks alarmingly subdued in the midst of all this. Roses struggle valiantly in the already mounting heat and a fuzz of green battles the encroaching brown baldness that spreads from the edges. Battered black taxis fight their way through traffic, avoiding being flattened by the much larger disco-painted trucks. Now and again an overloaded white van passes by, undecorated but for a decal on the back window depicting a female eye peering seductively through a plastic shade. My mother would always open the windows as we travelled this road. I toy with the little plastic button on my armrest, but Nana is so proud of his new car's powerful AC, he keeps adjusting the vent so the air reaches Naaz and me in the backseat. I haven't the heart to tell him I'm cold.

My plump cousin clutches my hand and prattles earnestly and without pause. I see Nana's cheeks curving into a smile now and again. I do my best to answer Naaz's questions but I fear, in my exhaustion, I am failing her. When we turn onto the double road through Blue Area, she proudly points out the Saudi Pak Tower, the prime minister's house, a garish new skyscraper she believes is a bank. I close my eyes and wonder whether I truly remember all of this or if it's merely tinged with a familiarity that sparks off vague recollections of long-ago drives up the same road.

It was Nani who fixed everything in the end. She called back after Shamim forgot when I was to arrive and got my father on the line. I was in the crawlspace, crying into the insulation, and I didn't even hear the phone ring. The next morning, my father slid a ticket under my door. Somehow, Nani had convinced the airline to reissue it. I avoided him diligently until I left. As the taxi driver slammed the trunk shut, I thought I saw him mouth 'I'm sorry' from the porch, but I did not turn back to see for sure.

In the dining room, Nani and Naaz's mother linger over eggshells and toast crusts. They leap to their feet and I'm pulled into bosoms and clenched against cheeks, flagged with bright lipstick, then pinched pink and clean. They'll get my suitcase back, they assure me, they'll call the airport every day. Finally, Nana pats me brusquely on the head, putting an end to it all.

'Come, sit. Have some breakfast. You're looking too thin,' Nani says. She's looking rather thin herself, and her plate bears evidence that she still leaves half the single toast she has for breakfast.

'What will you have, hmm?' my aunt asks. She herself only ever has tea.

'An egg?' suggests Nani. 'We'll have Makarram Khan make whatever kind you like.' She always tries to force eggs upon me. Before, I hid behind Mamma and shook my head shyly. Year after year, she'd patiently explain to my incredulous grandmother that I just didn't like eggs.

'Rubbish!' Nani would trumpet, 'everybody likes eggs. Even mongooses like eggs. Salim, please just tell me, who doesn't like eggs?'

'Irenie?' my grandfather would ask, fumbling with the newspaper. He never paid me much attention, but I loved him anyway for the acknowledgement that it was indeed possible to not like eggs.

This year, though, I'm on my own. 'Hard-boiled?' I say tentatively, thinking I'll at least pick out the yolk.

'Nani,' chides Naaz, 'Irenie doesn't like eggs.' I look at my cousin gratefully, surprised she still remembers. 'I'll have an omelette though?' She smiles hopefully.

'Omelette, indeed,' snorts her mother. 'You can have wheat toast and tea.'

'Oh yes,' sighs Nani. 'Sorry, jaani, shall we have a paratha made for you, a nice hot aloo paratha?'

'I'll have wheat toast and tea,' I tell her, relieved.

'Your Mehreen Khala had to go to office,' she tells me. She

wanted to meet you first thing of course, but then your flight was late and the bags took so long.'

'She'll see her in the evening,' consoles Sairah Mumani, patting her hand. 'I've also told Aamir to come back by dinner, but with him, tau, you just can't say anything.'

'Aamir's not coming?' Nani asks, looking upset.

'She's asked him to come, Tehmina,' Nana tells her. 'We'll just have to see if he does.'

'See if he does? I have to see if my own son comes? Just give me the phone and I'll call him right now!'

'No, no,' interrupts Sairah Mumani, having, I expect, been warned repeatedly by her husband to keep his mother away while he works. 'I'll see that he does.'

'And where is Shamim?' Nani demands suddenly.

Naaz mutters something about having tried to wake her up. She's emptied half a jar of marmalade onto her toast and is struggling to stuff it into her mouth before her mother spies it and insists she eat it plain.

'Really, Naazie,' says her mother, lighting a cigarette, 'always you're trying to get your cousin in trouble. So rude.'

Naaz rolls her eyes at me and I smile back at her. Pretending her daughter is often an instigator of mischief is one of Sairah Mumani's strange forms of domestic diplomacy.

'It's all right,' I say. 'She can sleep. I don't mind.'

'What a lazy girl she is,' sighs Nani, ignoring me. 'Tell her I'm saying to come down this instant. What kind of girl doesn't bother to get up to see her own cousin?'

I smile weakly. Naaz looks like a gravedigger who's just been told the pit she's dug is for her, but she goes to wake up Shamim anyway. As I finish choking down my toast, Nana asks about school and what I've been reading. Nani asks about my father and what I've been cooking. Sairah Mumani asks about high school and what top American designers are doing. I always forget that she lived in America until she was older than I am. She seems as

though she was born in a sari, with a cigarette wand, and a knot
bound in jasmine. We discuss everything and nothing, avoiding
the one subject that is on all our minds.

'Give one here,' says Nani as she reaches across the table for
Sairah Mumani's menthols. She claims not to smoke, but it
seems the crushed mountain of lipsticked cigarettes has become
too much to bear. Nana gives her a disapproving look, which she
pretends not to see. My grandfather does not approve of women
smoking in public, and puts up with it from his daughter-in-law
only because he disapproves more of confrontation. I remember
many washroom afternoons at other people's tea parties with my
mother, Mehreen Khala, Sairah Mumani and Nani puffing away
over swatches of pink toilet roll for fear the water would not come
when the time came to flush. They'd mince out into unfamiliar
guestrooms with smoke in their eyes and sprays of perfume. I
always went with them in hope of a piece of gum.

Naaz returns with a sullen Shamim. She gives me a perfunctory
hug, and slumps down at the foot of the table. Everyone says the
two of us look like twins, though Shamim is taller and thinner.
Her hair is shorter and curlier and her glasses are much cooler.
Briefly, I wonder how I would look with Buddy Holly frames.

Nana clears his throat and folds up the newspaper. Sairah
Mumani upsets her empty teacup. Naaz watches as Shamim sets
up toast soldiers in someone else's eggcup and Nani takes a drag
on her borrowed cigarette like a woman resigned to waiting days
at the terminal for the right train to come.

Dishes clatter in the kitchen and a pair of cats quibble over
some distant prize. In the dining room, the silence is probing. Now
that all relatives have been accounted for, breakfast has been eaten
and teacups drained, unspoken questions whiz through the air.
Why didn't I come earlier? Why have I come now? I wonder if we
will sit here forever, a crumbling tableau of our final fairy-tale meal.

On the plane, I'd planned what to say, but in my tired mind
it all seems cleared away, discarded with the remains of my last

compartmentalized meal. So I simply blurt out the truth. I know my mother is dead. There's no need to tell them I've finally stopped waiting for her to return. They already know. They stopped waiting long ago.

'God rest her soul.' Nana shuffles from the table, suddenly ancient mariner old in his checked slippers. Sairah Mumani quietly gathers her shawl and her daughter and heads back next door. Shamim looks interested for the first time that day, but Nani scowls at her so fiercely she quickly flees the scene. I gather I have brought up a topic quite unsuited to the breakfast table.

Nani comes to sit beside me in Sairah Mumani's cigarette-ringed throne. I expect her to admonish me in her ineffectual grandmother way, but she just puts her hand over mine. We watch them in silence for a while, inanimate hands piled up perhaps for an answer: hers velvet-soft over bones, under rings; mine lighter though rough, irregularly punctuating the geisha fan of her fingers in ragged-nailed points.

'We always told James he should tell you,' she says finally. 'It's been terribly hard for him, you know.' She says she will do her best to tell me all I want to know as long as I promise not to bring it up in front of my grandfather again. He does not speak of my mother. A piece of him died the day she did. A tear rolls down Nani's cheek. This is the first time I have ever heard anyone say that my mother is dead. I have known for months, suspected for years, but no one has ever said aloud to me that she is.

'My mother is dead,' I say again. For the first time, I realize it has always been a question. Now, it won't be ever again.

2

I wish I could take things back. I worry for my soul. When I die I'll leave behind a sad and restless ghost. I wish I could save our love. I wish I'd sacrificed my pride. I wish all this even now, knowing as I do that wishes don't come true.

After Irenie left for Pakistan, a strange thing happened to James: he began to develop a certain sympathy for their prank caller. In the first few days without her, he must have picked up the phone to call the house in Islamabad a dozen times. He found he couldn't bring himself to dial. What did he imagine he would say? He'd been making mistakes with Irenie for so long now that 'I'm sorry' would have been a strange and ineffective palliative, a wisp of tissue stuck into a wound wrought with a kitchen knife.

Fatherhood did not come naturally to James. He never wanted to have kids. Though he was swept up in his wife's excitement while she was pregnant, he scarcely paused a moment to consider where that pregnancy would lead. Then, at half past two on 8 April, a grinning Gollum nurse dropped a child into his arm. The thing was red and wet, covered in slime, and squalling so loudly it hurt his ears. The great, benign bump of Yasmeen's stomach, which he'd lately come to love, had disgorged some strange monster.

'Isn't she beautiful?' his wife asked.

'Er, lovely,' he agreed, wiping his hands discreetly on his trousers.

'She's so tiny, so perfect,' his wife sighed, holding her finger for the child to grasp. 'Look, look, see how small her fingers are? They're reaching for me! She knows who I am!'

They did indeed appear to be reaching for Yasmeen. The bundle had quieted as soon as she held it. Someone had cleaned the infant's face and it was no longer so red. It's not so bad when it's quiet, James thought hopefully, perhaps I'll love it too when the shock has worn off.

But the shock didn't wear off. He was terrified he would drop her or drown her and Yasmeen would never forgive him. When it was his turn to bathe her, he'd turn for the towel and find her face under water. When Yasmeen asked him to dress her, her flailing limbs would catch in the tiny armholes and refuse to pass through. Her head got stuck in every sweater he tried to put on, and her fingernails left bright, bleeding streaks down her face whenever he was on watch. Even the standard diapers would fall off or leak if James had pinned them. It all reminded him of cutting out paper dolls as a boy with her namesake. Try as he might, James had never been good at the intricate work his sister demanded. Untangling stubborn barrettes from his young daughter's hair, he often felt that this second Irene, this Irenie, expected far too much of him, just as his sister once had.

At first, his daughter bore his fumbling attempts with stolid goodwill. But before long, she learnt that James would harm and her mother would help. The more he tried to love her, the more he worried he would hurt her. Any time he tried to touch her, hopeless panic would assail him. She'd slip from his grasp or knock her head on a corner. Her hands would twitch as he trimmed the tiny, soft nails and he'd cut through her skin. By the time she was one, Irenie had begun to wail inconsolably any time he picked her up.

'It's because you hold her like she's an explosive bag of dung,' Yasmeen once snapped when he remarked upon this.

But wasn't she an explosive bag of dung?

When she's older, he consoled himself, I'll be much better. She won't be so breakable and we'll have all sorts of fun. He thought back to his days sledding with Irene and chasing their dog. He had known what to do then, when she was a child. That he had been one too somehow slipped his mind.

When Irenie was five, he took her to see *Home Alone 2*, which gave her nightmares for weeks. When she was six, he signed her up for tennis lessons, thinking they would some day play, but she loathed the sport. For her eighth birthday, he'd brought home a pink bicycle with pink streamers, pink training wheels and pink flowers on the pink basket—a vehicle any little girl would love, the salesman had assured him. She'd looked upon the thing with horror, but James assured her riding wasn't hard. For weeks after work, they practised in the drive. Then one day, he came upon Yasmeen in the garden shed, readjusting an old tarp over a shiny red bicycle with a wicker basket at the front. 'We didn't want to disappoint you,' she said guiltily. Not long after, he spotted Irenie and Celeste soaring down Macon's Hill, his daughter on the red bike, Celeste on the pink. It seemed whatever he did with regard to Irenie, he always did it wrong.

He didn't intend to tear up the ticket when he found it. He should have expected this, he told himself. She'd tried to tell him what she wanted but he hadn't even let her talk. When he saw her atop the stairs, the thought of her leaving was suddenly too much. Please, he wanted to say, don't leave me like all the rest. I'll get it right eventually. I know some day I will. But instead he tore up her ticket and told her Yasmeen had left her too. And now his daughter was gone. Who knew if she'd return?

3

Do you remember our trip to Niagara Falls, how we had to turn around midway because I suddenly remembered there was a paper I had yet to do? 'Life goes on,' you told me then. As many times as I've said so to myself in the years I've spent without you, I sometimes still have trouble believing it is true.

Despite my intention to investigate, my focus seems to have been lost with the letters. Though we've called the airport daily for the past week, there's been no sign of my suitcase and I'm running out of clothes. It has been easy to fall into a routine here. Nani runs a tight ship, meals served on military time. We're permitted to sleep through breakfast, but lunch is a must. Naaz stays the night when her mother allows and we stay up until Fajr draws day across the sky, falling asleep to the cacophony of rooster calls that rouses Nana every morning. While the adults are safely cloistered in the air-conditioned lull of their bedrooms, we watch R-rated films in the lounge, squinting so as not to miss good bits while the camera-print tapes jostle images blearily over the screen. Now and again, a silhouette head blocks out the whole picture, and we know Shamim will wreak havoc the next day.

The videos are just part of a ritual though. They are the nervous first drinks and inevitable pleasantries that precede a new couple's night on the town. We begin our trek towards dawn with them and talk our way through. The first tentative minutes are passed critiquing what we can't even see, but by the time they are through,

172

the conversation has segued into something quite new. I know I am on trial here, by Shamim if not by Naaz. We dance a jolting polka through the dark and as we lie on the roof late at night, I worry one misstep might send me spiralling off. I did not come here to infiltrate my cousins' schemes or to win over their confidence, but our age has made it almost inevitable. Since they are stuck with me all summer, they want sound insurance I won't give even the barest triviality away. Though I would never tell Sairah Mumani that Naaz skims two cigarettes from each pack of her menthols, they're now sure I won't because I've told them how I haunt my father with cigarettes. I can't imagine letting slip that Shamim pierced her navel last year on a whim, though if I did she could mention the frat party fiasco compelled by Celeste.

I imagine my mother up there with her best friend Shireen and maybe even serious Mehreen. Now and again, I ask my cousins if they remember her, if they've heard anything about her they're not meant to hear. Naaz's eyes widen and she asks, 'Like what?' but Shamim seems entirely uninterested.

As the days pass, Shamim grows less suspicious. We spend the stuffy hours reading in languid silence. Naaz passes the time click-clacking away on the family computer, which has been installed in Shamim's bedroom. I have no idea what she's doing, though I suspect it has something to do with the pile of records I brought for her, recordings by bands with names like The Corrugated Roofs and The Lycanthropic Legionnaires, whose purchase earned me the incredulous respect of the tattooed vinyl store clerk.

When I exhaust the small store of novels I've brought with me, Shamim offers to bring me something from Nana's study. She has had unlimited borrowing privileges since she turned ten. Nana is a firm believer in Literature spelled with a capital L. On Sundays, he trawls used bookshops for the classics he never had time for during all his years as a judge.

Like many men with lingering memories of the British Raj, Nana has an unshakable belief in the Western intellect of centuries past. With the fortitude of advancing old age, he rails against the contemporary drivel passed off as literature. All these brainless adventures, he often intones over dinner, are both source and symptom of a worldwide trend towards intellectual degradation. Since his retirement, he's written several mysteries under the name Geoffrey Chance, which he believes are subversions of the prevailing depravity. They feature an Anglo-Indian detective named Alistair Farouq who elegantly infiltrates the upper echelons of 1850s Indian society to expose intrigue and insidious vice. Though the novels are intricately plotted and historically apt, the moralizing tone and the outdated novelistic tricks Nana has picked up from his readings has prevented them from generating anything beyond a measure of bemused fascination amongst critics. He swears they're missing the irony, which might well be true, only I've never managed to plod all the way through any of his sinuous seven-hundred-page epics.

'I haven't either,' Shamim confesses one night on the roof. 'I got almost halfway through the *Vicar of Northridge*, but the first paragraph of chapter thirty-one kept putting me to sleep.'

I am impressed. 'I got to chapter nine of *Arise, Alistair!*,' I tell her. 'The description of all the riding paraphernalia threw me off though.'

'I read the dedication of that one!' Naaz chimes in. 'Did you know it's to my family?'

Shamim regards her condescendingly. 'Nana prefers I read the greats anyway. They're his inspiration.'

'I did see that,' I tell Naaz. 'Shamim is just jealous because neither of our names has ever been in a book.'

Shamim sniffs and mutters something about the insignificance of such things, but Naaz puts her arm around my shoulder and asks me to stay forever.

Shamim turns out to be a competitive reader. When I ask for *The Inferno*, she begins *Paradise Lost*. When I take a stab at *Endgame*, she turns up with *No Exit*. Her brow furrows over these books and she takes conspicuous notes. The 1954 *Oxford English Dictionary* on her night table comes to frequent use, not only when she encounters a new word, but also when she finds one of which she's not entirely sure. Now and again, she'll look up from what she's reading and ask 'What does anfractuous mean?' or 'What's an ushanka?' When I admit I don't know, her retorts are cruel, possessed of a scholar's cold contempt for my plebeian enjoyment of unexplored depths. When I do know a definition though, she gives me my due. I make the mistake of finishing *Crime and Punishment* before she's through with *The Idiot*, and she purposely makes me wait days for a new book as she checks and rechecks her lists of characters' names and defining traits. We read *The Canterbury Tales* in tandem and she spends half an afternoon with her nose in an atlas, mapping the pilgrims' path, and then refuses to share. She claims she can't find a copy of *War and Peace* when I ask for it, just out of spite, and she won't let me get at *The Wasteland* even after she is through. I wonder if she enjoyed her library privileges quite so much before I arrived. The pleasure she takes from reading is that of bloody conquest, and what's a victory with no one to watch?

When Mehreen Khala gets home from work, we're both forced to put aside our reading and go down to tea. Often there are guests and often they knew my mother. It's an informal hour and if I angle my questions correctly it's easy to elicit tales.

Nani remains fretful about the past, but Sairah Mumani and Mehreen Khala prove obliging. They offer up anecdotes with long-suppressed candour. I begin to suspect that Nana's moratorium on talk of my mother has impacted the family more than they might know.

'She was his little princess,' Mehreen Khala explains one morning when we're out shopping. 'Your mother could do no wrong, as far as he was concerned.' Until she died and wronged us all.

My mother was unhappy from the day she was born, Mehreen
Khala tells me. This is one of the many things I know Nani would
prefer I not hear. As a baby, she cried and cried for no reason. Her
wailing drove Nana mad. He did all he could to stay away from the
house, and when he was there he rarely took time to see his young
daughters. Mehreen was quiet and obedient, never getting in his
way, but as Yasmeen grew older she was resolutely affectionate,
taking no heed whatsoever of her stern father's distance. She would
crawl into his lap while he worked and pull at his moustache or
play with his ears. On the rare occasions he came home for lunch,
she'd slip her best bits of meat onto his plate. Gradually, he found
himself giving in to her charm in ways he never had with his first
two children. Aamir Maamu was sent off to Aitchison as soon
as he was old enough and Mehreen Khala's upbringing, when
she was not away at school, was put exclusively into the hands
of her mother. By the time Yasmeen was three though, the judge
would come home from work calling out 'now where is my Yasi-
masi?' and then tossing her up in the air despite his wife's protests.
Although he tried to pay Mehreen equal attention, she was shy
around him. Having spent the first six years of her life learning to
make herself invisible, Mehreen preferred to be left alone.

As the girls grew older, Mehreen started to suspect that fate
always aligned itself for Yasmeen. When her sister went to the
market, the candy floss man would just have spun a new batch;
when she took pity on kitchen mice, they'd figure out some
secret way of evading their traps; when she wished it would rain,
clouds would sweep down from the mountains. While Mehreen
studied hard and brought home top marks at the end of each
term, Yasmeen spent the whole year skipping homework and then
got one hundred in science when she decided she wanted to go
to the moon. Everywhere they went, people would exclaim over
how cute and clever she was. As Mehreen's eyes settled into a
permanent squint that required she be outfitted with thick plastic
glasses, Yasmeen's hair grew into long, shiny waves admired at the

hairdresser's even before she could brush it herself. There were times she was so jealous of her little sister that she wanted to pinch her when she offered her last toffee or begged for help with some simple division. There were other times though, when she was grateful above all that she wasn't Yasmeen.

'Why?' I ask, so caught up in the story that it doesn't occur to me how very rude it is. Mehreen Khala looks amused though.

'Well, would you want to be her?' she asks.

'Of course,' I say quickly. She turns off the car but doesn't get out. As I sit beside her, I try to decide if what I've said is true. Though saying I don't want to be my mother seems like a betrayal, I'm no longer sure that I really do want to be her.

'I was glad not to be her because she was inclined always towards unhappiness,' Mehreen Khala says finally, rolling down her window.

Whatever had caused my mother to cry ceaselessly as an infant lingered as she grew older. She tried very hard to keep it in check but occasionally it would rip free. Mehreen learned early to tell it was coming. Her sister would grow silent, looking at them as though she was seeing them from under water. Her eyes seemed to give up reflecting light and when you looked into them it was like peering into some ancient, unending well. She would stop eating and when she endeavoured to smile, her eyes would crinkle around the edges as if someone was carving out her grin with a knife. Then something small would happen and Yasmeen would sob grievously. Her despair was desperate and irrepressible, leaving her unable to breathe even as she choked out 'I can't' when they begged her to stop. She remained inconsolable even after she ran out of tears. Dry sobs would resound through the house, often for hours, before she slid off into deep, empty sleep.

'Come, Irenie,' Mehreen Khala says. 'It's getting hot, no?'

I get out of the car reluctantly and follow her to the small market. Though I expect her to divert her attention to the task at hand, she buys me a Coke and continues her story between sips and feels of fabric. She makes a face when I point to the colours I like and says even Nani doesn't wear shades so drab.

When my mother was very young, she tells me, she would say that she was sad because she'd seen a dead dog in the road or because a girl at school had dipped her pigtails in ink. By the time she was six or seven, however, she simply began to say 'I don't know'. She once told Mehreen Khala that she'd been sad all those years because she missed Ahmed. Mehreen Khala, ever the practical one, told her not to be ridiculous; it was impossible to miss someone you hadn't yet met. Still, it was often said that the child Yasmeen wailed like Sassi through the desert. The judge, thinking his own heart might splinter each time hers seemed to break, dragged her to a slew of specialists, none of whom found anything wrong. He located a child psychiatrist of dubious distinction, but caved in to Yasmeen's promises that she'd never cry again just as long as she didn't have to go back. She had learned to keep her grief quiet. Whenever she sensed its approach, she'd draw a hot bath and wail underwater. Mehreen always knew, but she kept it to herself. Yasmeen's moods, despite her apparent perfection, somehow balanced out the careful correctness Mehreen managed despite her imperfection. They grew up on either side of this fundamental divide, not hating each other, surprisingly, but never quite knowing each other either.

'Sometimes I used to think her life was like a fairy-tale,' Mehreen Khala says as she pays for the fabric we've selected and tucks a few stray hairs away. 'The beautiful, sad princess whose father will do anything in hopes of a smile. The gallant prince who chases all her sorrows away. If Papa had had a kingdom on hand, I'm sure he would have given it over without a second thought.'

In this story though, the prince and the princess didn't live happily ever after. 'What happened in the end?' I ask, as we barrel through the gates of the Naval Colony in her Suzuki Mehran. Mehreen Khala rolls down her window further and pretends she doesn't hear.

4

*In the years since I last saw you, I have become intimately
acquainted with a strange sort of aloneness. It overwhelms me
at parties and on busy streets. It drowns out rush-hour crowds
and accompanies me even in sleep.*

'You are losing your mind,' James tells his reflection in the
bathroom mirror. 'And also a rather large amount of your
hair.' He thinks he hears a snicker, but the bathroom is empty
except for him. Ghosts follow him everywhere, he thinks.

His dead wife has been haunting him for the past several years.
When he's sitting alone he can sometimes smell Chanel; cigarette
smoke lingers in the house although it's been years since she's
been here. On quiet nights, the songs she loved play through his
head and he swears he hears stanzas from her favourite poems
echoing through empty rooms. Many times, he's wanted to ask
his daughter if she senses it as well, but how can he ask Irenie if
she sees her mother's ghost when she doesn't know her to be dead?

He hadn't meant to deceive her, but he couldn't bear to tell
her the truth. When Yasmeen vanished that last time, he was
beside himself with worry. He hadn't had any news of her until
the day before Irenie came back from Florida, and when she
turned up on the porch all sun-tanned and happy with a bag full
of seashells to give to her mother he simply hadn't known how
to tell her.

'Where's Mamma?' she demanded the instant she came in.

The possibilities ricocheted round his head. Your mother is dead; your mother has died; Yasmeen, I'm afraid, is no longer with us. He couldn't even say any of these things to himself yet; it seemed too terrible to say them to her.

'She's gone,' he said slowly, clearing his throat and hoping that she knew what he meant. She hadn't though. Irenie was only ten when it happened. She wanted to know where Yasmeen had gone and when she'd be back. All James could think to say at the time was, 'I don't know.'

'Make her come back,' Irenie begged him desperately a few days later. It was the one thing she'd ever asked of him, the only thing she needed from him, but all he could say was, 'I can't.'

Irenie shut herself in then, silent for two terrible years. He saw her only in the plates she left on the kitchen table for his dinner. A far more careful cook than her mother, she left meticulous lists on the freezer for him to fill: 500 grams boneless roast, three kilos russet potatoes, four ten-centimetre tamarind pods. The quietly refurbished cupboards went unremarked upon. When he tried to compliment her meals, she just looked at the floor and mumbled indifferent courtesies. James wondered if he was any more capable of grasping the magnitude of sudden emptiness than his daughter. The unspoken absence was everywhere, in every way stifling, until Yasmeen slipped back in her quiet scents and sounds.

Then everything was always all right. Baths were tepid and the many bottles of nail-polish which accessorized his daughter's now-adolescently equipped shelves were uniformed in dull and neutral colours. Tea was always lukewarm to spare the drinker the trouble of deciding between iced or hot and nobody really cared what was to be had for dinner. Though nothing was unhappy, nothing was ever quite happy either. In fact, it could be said that a general air of melancholy hung over everything.

It was long past time to tell her now, but he'd let the lie go on for so long he didn't know how to begin. This was why Yasmeen was haunting him, he was fairly certain. It wasn't so bad when her ghost lingered just at home, but things were beginning to get out of hand. Shortly after Irenie left for Pakistan, he began receiving parcels of the sort of travel brochures Yasmeen liked to read. They arrived unaddressed; even though he'd got into a rather dramatic altercation with the post office over it, they'd continued to come. It was distracting him from his work and making his life miserable. His wife was trying to tell him something, he was sure of it. He knew it had something to do with their daughter, something to do with apologizing to her. He'd called Islamabad thrice already, but each time she'd been out.

5

*Last night I met you in my dream, in a glade, beside a brook.
We sprouted wings and flew then, across the wood and world.
You led me through the Milky Way and danced beside me on the
moon. And then I woke, alone, to winter light and I wanted
only to be dead. Return to me tonight, my midnight Magellan,
and all will be well again.*

A few days after my talk with Mehreen Khala, I remember
something interesting: Claire mentioned Ahmed was the
son of 'some relative of my mother's brother's through marriage'.
I want to kick myself when I realize what this means. Ahmed
was related to Sairah Mumani! She must know what happened
between him and my mother, how he came to marry this
Mehrunissa woman instead. Perhaps she's even met her! I ask
Naaz whether she remembers them, but she confesses she has a
terrible memory. They rarely see the Chicago side of the family
except for at weddings and funerals. Shamim, who is pretending
to read *Ulysses*, looks up calculatingly.

'This wouldn't be Mehrunissa Shabaz you're talking about,
would it be?'

'I think so.'

'The one with the two sons?'

'Do *you* know her?'

Shamim looks smug, Naaz confused. 'No. But I heard Nani
talking about her to Shireen Auntie on the phone—Shireen

Auntie was your mother's best friend when they were kids you know—'

'I know,' I say impatiently. 'I'm going over to talk to her next weekend. She's busy with her daughter's wedding and she can't see me till then.'

'Do you want to hear or not?' she asks, making as though to return to her reading.

'I do. I'm sorry,' I say, and gently push the book down. Shamim looks very pleased.

'Well, Nani and Shireen Auntie were arguing. Apparently, Mehrunissa was somehow related to Shireen Auntie's husband and, since she's in town with her sons, Shireen Auntie had to invite them to Shezzie's wedding. Nani was saying that's all well and good, but we're not going if that woman will be there. I think Shireen Auntie was trying to persuade her.'

'She's *here*? Mehrunissa is *here*?'

Shamim shrugs her thin shoulders. 'Don't get your knickers in a twist. You'll never get a chance to meet her, and even if you did, what exactly would you say to her? Hi, I'm Irenie, it's all your fault my mother's dead.'

'Now, Shamim, that isn't nice,' says Naaz.

'What do you mean?' I ask. 'How is it her fault?'

Shamim shrugs. 'It isn't. That's just what everyone wants to think: that if she'd let your mother say goodbye to Ahmed they wouldn't have run off together and Yasi Khala, at least, wouldn't have died.' Seeing my expression, she nudges me with her foot. 'It's *not* her fault, Irenie. You can't live your life in what-ifs. Nani and all are old, so if it makes them feel better, let them believe what they like.'

I regard her stubbornly. 'Nani said she stole Ahmed from my mother. Seduced him.'

'Oh please. What else was she supposed to do after he knocked her up?'

'Shamim!' cries Naaz.

'He *what?*'

'You didn't know?'

'*You* don't know,' says Naaz.

'If the two of you would pull your heads out of the sand it would be perfectly obvious to you as well. Why else would Ahmed have married her? If you ever get the letters back, I guarantee you it will be right there between the lines. Any word yet, by the way?'

I shake my head.

She nods. 'Good. It sounds to me like it was all a total mess. You should stop wasting your time.'

'*Shamim,*' Naaz cries again. 'I think it was very romantic,' she says, turning to me, 'Yasi Khala and this Ahmed. Shamim doesn't know what she's talking about. Let's go find my mother, Irenie. At least *she* has some sense of romance.'

At Sairah Mumani's, pandemonium abounds. The maid rushes in and out with lengths of crisply ironed saris still emanating heat despite the determinedly air-conditioned room. Petticoats of six different colours adorn every surface and blouses loiter adulterously over petticoats they don't belong with. Jewellery cases spill over on the dressing table, gold lengths a gleaming mess around stern, solid bits of stone. A clutter of half-filled perfume bottles march over the bureau and cosmetic implements of every type are scattered to and fro. Ashtrays and undergarments lie forgotten on the floor where stiletto heels with sharp, cruel points endanger every step. In the middle of it all stands Sairah Mumani, still in her dressing gown. One eye is decorated splendidly with gold shadow and dark lashes while the other one is bare. She's stuck two earrings through each hole and is trying hard to choose.

'Girls!' she exclaims when she finally spies us through the mess. 'Come, come, tell me quickly, which one do you think is best?'

'The green, the green,' I tell her hastily, fearing both her ears will soon tear off.

'Haan, that's what I was thinking too.' She smiles and heads towards the bureau without taking any out. 'We're going to Maliha's house,' she says, as though the name should ring a bell. 'That woman is always just too well dressed. Always trying to show everyone up. Well, I'll just show her, if only that man would ...'

'Aamir,' she bellows, banging on the bathroom door. 'Kindly come out of there right now. You're going to get piles sitting on the pot so long. He's been there for an hour,' she says in an aside to me, 'reading those bloody *Reader's Digest*s again, no doubt. Put that samosa *down*, Naazie!' Naaz, startled, drops the savoury pastry on the carpet.

'I told you, na,' she yells again, banging on the door, 'what happened with Namoose's husband? He also loved spending ten hours a day in the loo. His piles became so bad the doctor had to insert a flashlight up there. *A flashlight!* Do you hear?'

Aamir Maamu's response is too muffled to make out.

'Don't marry a man who's irregular,' Sairah Mumani tells me sadly. 'You'll never get anywhere in time. Just look, it's almost half past eight. By the time he comes out of there, it will be smelling so much I won't even be able to wash my face till nine.'

There are four other washrooms in this house. Naaz suggests she use the guest one, but she just sighs and shakes her head.

'My lotions are there. My creams are there. How can I wash my face somewhere else?'

'What are you wearing?' I ask, hoping that might cheer her up a bit.

It does.

'It's the question of the evening, darling,' she says, gesturing to the chaos all around. She pulls two saris from their wrapping: a faded and very familiar pillowcase decorated with delicate embroidery. 'What do you think, should I go with the green or with the rose?'

'What a pretty case,' I say, trying to hide the tremble in my voice. 'It looks like it was hand done. Do you remember where it's from?'

'Oh that …' She waves indifferently. 'Some village acquaintance of your maamu's. Apparently his wife embroidered them for us, but she didn't bother to give a bedsheet. We never did find anything to match. Now tell me, which one shall I wear?'

Why on earth would my mother have pilfered a part of Sairah Mumani's trousseau, I wonder. 'I like the rose,' I tell her, still intent upon the pillowcase. 'But the green will match your earrings.'

'Oh, the earrings!' she exclaims, beginning to pull them from her ears. 'Ow, ow, ow,' she moans as a tiny stream of bright blood trickles down the right side of her neck. I evict a samosa from the tea tray on the floor and hand her the napkin folded underneath.

'Thanks, sweetie,' she begins, then all at once cuts herself off. '*Oh no,*' she wails, 'now I smell of old samosa.' She counters it quickly with a liberal douse of flowery perfume.

'Am I stinking?' she asks, pulling Naaz's into her neck.

'You smell delicious.'

'Cheeky, cheeky. The green then? I've already worn the blouse, just look?' She lets her dressing gown slip open, and indeed she's wearing the green blouse. 'Am I looking very fat in it? I like the rose also actually, but rose looks better in the afternoon, doesn't it?'

She's swaddling herself in yards upon yards of viridian silk before I can answer. It looks almost easy as she quickly folds the pleats, one-two, back-forth, though I know how hard it is to make them even from long-ago experiments with bedsheets and bath towels.

'So then, jaani,' she says as she lights the cigarette I fear may well be her last with all the delicate fabrics floating around, 'don't tell me you've come just to visit with your old auntie at this time on a Saturday night?'

'You're not old,' I demur, 'but you're right actually, I wanted to ask you about your cousin? The one who was to look after my mother when she went to college?'

'Ahmed,' offers Naaz obliviously through a mouthful of samosa.

'Ahmed?' says Sairah Mumani, scowling. 'I can't say I knew him too well. He was a *distant* cousin. He seemed like a sweet boy, but …'

'But?'

'But, never mind. It didn't work out between them. These things happen sometimes with young people. Tragic, really. They seemed so in love.'

'Why didn't it work out?' Naaz asks. I shoot her a grateful look.

'It's really not for me to say, darling.'

'You have no idea?' I say desperately. 'What about Mehrunissa? Is it true that she was pregnant?'

Naaz chokes on her samosa. Her mother looks surprised, but does not deny it. 'I'm sorry, Irenie. I have nothing to say about that woman. And after what she's done to this family, I'm surprised you'd be interested,' she says as the bathroom door begins to open. 'Oh thank god, Aamir, finally you've come out. Listen, I have to get ready.'

'But why did they split up?' I plead. 'What happened with Mehrunissa?'

'Nani won't even say her name,' adds Naaz. 'She calls her *that woman*.'

'It's not my business, darlings,' she says. 'Though if you're determined to dig into it you should go speak to Baby Tamasha. The woman knows everything about everyone.'

And with that she closes the door in our faces.

6

I am like a ghost ship. I sail unmanned upon the sea. Stripped by mutineers and profiteers I feel I will soon sink. The shipboy and the boatswain took their chances with the drink, but an obsolete old thing like me is useless as a pole-less skiff. I did not see it coming; what was there for me to do? I had no past to learn from because my past was only you.

'Why do I bother going to these things?' James sighed. It was after six, though still bright as noon, and he'd just come in from a guest lecture, 'Mimicry and Metronomes: Metrical Iterativity in the English Ghazal'. He and Faber used to attend these lectures together. Now, James went alone. Since Irenie left, he'd gone to all of them, even those so far outside his field he barely understood a thing. The prospect of returning to the empty house and microwaving one of the frozen meals his daughter had left for him was more depressing than even stale bruschetta. She still wasn't speaking to him. 'Give her time,' TM had said, and so he did.

Tonight's lecturer was a PhD candidate whose thesis was ambitious, if irreparably convoluted. Watching the young man compulsively run his hands through his orange hair, James felt old. He remembered when he first came to Crawford as a guest lecturer: 1971. OPEC negotiations were beginning in the Middle East and the NASDAQ had just been launched. The Weather Underground set off a bomb in the Capitol, Jim Morrison died, there were riots in Attica. Apollo 15 left and returned. *The Ed Sullivan Show* ended. Rolls Royce was nationalized, the Vietnam War went on, and Charles Manson was sentenced to death. Far away, eleven-year-old Yasmeen watched as East Pakistan became Bangladesh and the world condemned her country. James had barely been aware of any of it. For five years, he had been living hand to mouth in a Pittsburgh basement, working frenetically on his dissertation. His hair grew long he seldom took the time to shave. Sometimes, leonine young men would nod at him knowingly in the street and dream-eyed girls would approach to stroke his arm. He'd later suspect they'd all been stoned.

It had been nearly a decade since his father died and his mother moved back to the Old County. He cashed the yearly cheques she sent and wrote terse thank-you notes in response. The handkerchiefs were especially welcome then, when the draughty basement afflicted him with a perpetually runny nose. His landlady, whose name he'd long since forgotten if indeed he'd ever known, had worn nothing but pink pedal pushers. Pink pedal pushers with flowered blouses, pink pedal pushers with her dead husband's sweaters, sometimes, on the hottest days of summer, pink pedal pushers with halter tops that showed her stomach when she stretched. Occasionally, she'd catch him en route from the library and lure him into her sitting room to chat. She'd serve him stale cheese straws and Whiskey Sours that reminded him of his father. And she'd talk about her cats. How she could talk about those cats! They weren't real cats, just feline figurines. She'd even had kittens woven into her rugs. Once, when James asked why she didn't just get a pet cat, she wept. Her last one had died the same day her husband had: he'd flattened poor Ginger falling off a ladder. It was the most meaningful conversation James had had for several years.

Late at night, James often felt at edge in the dreary basement. The click-clack of his typewriter distracted him and the single swinging bulb made him faintly seasick. He'd pace the narrow basement then, willing himself back to his work. Nothing else seemed to matter. He chewed coffee grounds to stave off sleep until his traitorous eyelids drooped and he sometimes woke to find nonsense sentences trailing off amidst ideas he liked the night before: certain illocutionary acts of antediluvian time are infinitely significant for how they gesture, in their minutia, to perlocutionary effects beyond the psyche of each toothbrush. James viciously eradicated such missteps. Whenever he deemed a page complete, he typed it out afresh. Sometimes it took him several tries, his hands trembling with the excitement of a new father who has just counted his son's ten perfect toes. His dissertation would be revolutionary; he'd had no doubt about it then. He often found himself in a similar sort of fugue state alone in the house, only now there was nothing on which he was so intently focused, nothing that struck him as so earth-shatteringly important. I'll see if the others want to get a drink after the talk, he resolved. Perhaps it will shake me out of the past.

As the candidate droned on about metre, however, his mind continued to wander. His landlady's face rose up before him for the first time in decades. Absently, he touched the dent on the back of his head: she'd whacked him with a hand-carved cane when he returned from his thesis defence, his beard shaved and his hair closely cropped. His paper, 'A Study in the History of Intimate Theory: the Scatological Hermeneutics of Internal Terminologies', had been deemed the irreverent insight of an emerging intellect. He came home whistling, almost skipping.

She hadn't recognized him, she'd apologized. She defrosted a bag of baby peas on the bump and then served them sautéed in butter once he agreed to stay for dinner. There was also meatloaf with mashed potatoes from a box and leftover cherry pie. It was the best meal James had had in years.

That night, for the first time, James accepted the offer of a proper bath upstairs. Though the tub was small and James was long, he lay there for what felt like several years. Afterward, he stood watching steam drip from the full-length mirror until there was nothing left to look at but himself. Somewhere in the years beneath the beard, his jaw had lost its roundness and reconfigured itself in sleek, straight lines. The minimal muscle tone he'd proudly cultivated over his many years of rowing crew had long disappeared. Without even sucking in his stomach, he could count each one of his ribs. Chest hair had finally sprouted thin across his breast. When he stroked it, he was surprised to find that it was soft. For a moment, his gaze grazed his genitals, then shot, embarrassed, to his face. There were wrinkles now, small crow's feet spreading from his eyes, though smiles had yet to gouge trajectories on either side of his mouth. He bared his teeth at his reflection and was pleased to find they all seemed to be there. His hair, which had once been blonde, had faded to light brown. Already, there was a hint of salt and pepper where the hairline met his neck.

James was so intent upon the mirror that he didn't immediately notice his landlady had slipped in undressed. It wasn't until he saw her reflection. It was the first time he'd seen her not wearing the pink pedal pushers. For a moment, he thought she had come in to rebuke him for having tied up her bathroom for so long. When she didn't say anything, James wondered if he should move to cover himself or bend down for his towel, but he figured she'd had long enough to see him in his entirety so he just stood there, still and silent. Gulping down the great lump that had risen in his throat, he slowly shifted his gaze from his reflected feet to hers. Her toenails were unpainted, clipped short except the smallest one, which was growing at an uneven, jagged angle. He could see that her soles were cracked and tough, the whiteness spreading up either side of her foot. It alarmed him that he couldn't see her right foot, blocked as it was by his left. What if it was something else entirely, long-toenailed, painted pink? Why, in all these years, had he never thought to check? Suddenly, ensuring both her feet were alike was the most important thing to him in the world.

But five years had taught James tremendous discipline. He glanced quickly up her leg to the curve of her hip. Her waist was slim but soft; he could see the beginnings of a belly. To him it looked inviting, like a nice place to rest one's head. More so than the breast before him, which struck him as too large. It hung heavy on her chest, facing out. The areola was wide and brown, the nipple large enough to nurse a calf. James wondered if it was uncomfortable to go around all day with such things hanging off one's chest. He supposed a brassiere might help. He saw the straps of hers had dug deep grooves into the softness of her shoulder. They looked like something he would rub at, were they on his body, but her hand hung to her side. He paused a moment to consider it before moving up her neck: small and flat turned inward with the lifeline extra-long. Having heard somewhere that a woman's age is most apparent on her neck, James had been hesitant to move upward once he got beyond her chest. But his landlady's neck looked quite all right to him. A little wrinkled perhaps, and lined much more than his, but not at all shameful for a woman of perhaps forty-five. It was her face that shocked him the most. All the while his eyes travelled up her side, she'd watched his face reflected in the mirror. It was as though she was looking through his face to something in his head.

After so many years spent sleeping in the basement, James found it odd to awaken in sunlight. His landlady was sleeping still, spread flat upon her back. It was the first time James had seen a naked woman. He was tempted to rest his head gently on her stomach, but instead he stroked her neck. In the bright light, he noticed a long scar down the right side of her abdomen that he hadn't seen before. A child she'd had? A child she'd lost? Some terrible event she hadn't mentioned? James was never to find out.

'What are you doing?' she demanded, opening an eye. 'Why are you here?' She lumbered to her feet, an aging naiad in the sheet. 'Who told you to come?'

To James, she was spectacular. Her stance was like a Valkyrie's; the sun glinted off her skin. He hadn't noticed the hint of auburn in her hair till then. 'Come back,' he murmured drowsily, patting the space still warm from where she'd slept. He hadn't yet learnt to tell when a woman was through with him. When it came to his wife and daughter, it was something he would never accept.

'Get out,' she ordered. 'Collect your things and go.'

Still sun-drunk, maybe love-drunk, James gathered up his clothes. Women were strange creatures, he mused, or maybe she just didn't want him to see her without clothes or make-up in the morning light.

James passed the afternoon doing nothing. He bought a ticket for *A Clockwork Orange*, but then didn't go in. It was too nice a day to spend sitting in the dark. Perhaps his landlady might like to go out some night to see a film. What kind of movies did she like? James wasn't sure what he liked himself.

He walked half a mile along a river before realizing he didn't know which one it was. There were three, he believed, but he could only come up with the name of one: the Ohio. The others had more syllables in their names, he knew. He walked down streets he'd never seen though he'd walked them every day. He greeted shopkeepers sweeping trash into the streets. Perhaps he'd come to know their names in time; perhaps he'd even learn the names of all the streets. Perhaps Pittsburgh would some day become home to him as no place had been since Irene died. He would make an honest woman of his landlady and they'd memorize the town together, they'd make this sprawling city of three rivers theirs in secret demarcations.

At half past six, James paid too much for a dying bunch of pink carnations and made his way back home. Perhaps his landlady would make him dinner again; perhaps this time she'd let him take her out.

But when he got back to the house, her windows were all dark.

James pounded relentlessly at the door. Just as he was about to give up, he saw something shift behind the curtains.

'Open up,' he cried, brandishing the flowers and redoubling his efforts with the other hand. 'I've been thinking about you all day long.'

'Clear off kid,' barked a neighbour, coming out to see what all the fracas was about. 'Can't you see she ain't interested?'

'But …' James stammered. 'But she is. She was.'

'Just go away,' whispered his landlady. He could only see a sliver of her face: an eye, a cheek, a bit of chin. James would later come to feel a great wariness for things he couldn't fully see. He would use it as an excuse for everything from his dogged avoidance of Crawford's faculty masquerade to his inability to relinquish any bit of scholarship before checking many times to see that everything was there. What James had yet to learn, however, was that what you see only in part is most pernicious when you believe that part's a whole.

'Leave me alone,' the sliver of his landlady hissed that night through the door.

And so that is what he did.

Later that week, James packed his few possessions into an old suitcase of his mother's, left another overpriced bouquet on his landlady's doorstep, and set off to deliver a guest lecture at Crawford. The lecture became an extended interview, which in turn became a job. He was allotted a sunny third-floor apartment and a bed with unbroken springs. He bought a coffee pot, kitchen wares, and a matching set of towels. He never went back to Pittsburgh.

'James?' whispered someone. 'Are you asleep?' His eyes flew open. Had he been?

'Thanks, Doris,' he said to the department secretary, who'd just sat down beside him.

She smiled. 'Dreaming of a different talk, are you?'

For a moment, he had no idea what she was talking about. Then, recalling her role in the genesis of his relationship with Yasmeen, he smiled slightly. He'd ask Doris along for this drink as well.

Sixteen years ago, James had burst into the office utterly entranced after a lecture, which in all likelihood had been no better than this one. It had been a January evening, so different from this one now. The sun in Doris's hair had made a halo; dust had floated gold throughout the room. Outside, the snow had seemed a splendid stole, sparkling over the shoulders of a woman of infinite grace. A woman like Yasmeen. James had come in singing that day—or if not singing exactly, humming unmistakably.

'Interesting lecture?' Doris had asked, bemused.

'Fantastic,' James responded, though, in truth, he hadn't heard a word. The woman with the high-heeled shoes was there. She sat down right next to him. Yasmeen Khalil, he hummed the cadence of her name quite without tune. He hadn't seen Yasmeen Khalil since December.

'Dr Eccles,' she'd nodded pleasantly.

'James. Please, call me James.'

She'd smiled and said, 'Yasmeen.'

And that was it for James. All through the lecture, he'd thought of nothing but the three inches between his leg and hers. So bowled over by the scent of her perfume was he that the candidate could have announced the existence of an undiscovered Homeric epic and James wouldn't have cared. Even after forty-five minutes by her side and an excruciating question-answer session he'd feared would never end, he was still too overcome to speak a single word.

'Have dinner with me,' he spluttered, just as she was about to leave the room.

Yasmeen Khalil spun on one magnificent heel and regarded

him consideringly. 'All right,' she agreed, as though, in her mouth, consent had a certain taste.

James had been on many dates in Crawford. He had taken Sarah Milburn to Fabrizio's Bar & Grill on Market Street, Melinda Fischer to The Taproom downtown, Clarice Waldorf to a portraiture exhibition at the town's one gallery: a poorly lit converted warehouse down by Hannameyer Creek. He had picnicked in the square with Philippa Macintyre, been bullied into bowling by Christine Woo at Al's Amazing Lanes, spent a Sunday sailing down the river with Milla Yanowitz. Then there were the evenings in the city: a series of inane off-Broadway musicals with Mary Jane Ostroeff, trips to the Met, the MoMA, museums of everything, from television to sex, with women whose names he could no longer quite remember, meals and movies and slow walks through Central Park. James could scarcely keep track of all the things he'd done on dates. But for Yasmeen he wanted to do something special, something he'd never done with anyone before. In desperation, he'd finally gone to Doris and asked her what she thought.

Doris, of course, was delighted to be consulted on matters more significant than where to find spare toner when the photocopier ran out or how to kick start the coffee maker.

'Ice skating on the pond,' she'd said at once. In wintertime, the town decked out the square in fairy lights and lent out skates for free. There was a stand that sold hot cider and an enterprising freelance photographer who offered couples candid snapshots. In a word, the whole thing was the very pinnacle of small-town romance. The thought of it left James pale and weak.

'Anything else?' he'd asked, trying not to remember red hats, red gloves, two red scarves tied end to end.

'If you really want to treat the woman like a queen, you could make dinner for her yourself,' Doris suggested.

Though James had little confidence in his cooking skills, that's precisely what he set out to do. It was different and it wouldn't

be expected. Armed with a detailed list of instructions, he set out
for the store. For the first time in his life, he used a shopping
cart rather than the pink plastic baskets, so perfectly sized for the
grocery needs of one. He filled it with all manner of eccentricities:
whole artichokes, morels, a standing rack which even he realized
was a particularly attractive cut of meat. But when James left the
supermarket, these ingredients turned strange. The artichoke was
unwieldy and the standing rack refused to stand. Hurriedly, he
scraped the whole mess of a meal into the trash. When Yasmeen
arrived, she was greeted with half a ready-made apple pie and the
moulding remains of a wheel of Emmentaler cheese. Taking in
the chaos of the kitchen, she'd suggested they go out for Chinese.

At Yeung Ching's House of Noodles that night, James
discovered something about dating he'd never guessed: if the
company was pleasant enough it didn't matter where the date
was set.

Yasmeen Khalil was charming and vivacious. She made him
laugh more than he'd thought was possible and drew animated
anecdotes from him. Catching a glimpse of himself in the
window, James thought he was watching someone else. As they
were splitting open fortune cookies, Yasmeen quietly apologized
for her outburst earlier in winter, an event that James had by then
been sure she'd long forgotten. It had been a terrible morning, she
explained. She'd fallen into a puddle on the way to the bus and
the driver had yelled at her because she'd made him wait. A group
of schoolchildren had snickered at her mud-covered coat and a
teenage boy had hissed 'go back to India where you belong' as
she'd passed him in the aisle.

'Brighter times await you,' James said, handing her his fortune
when she looked at him askance.

'Of that, one can only hope.' He didn't notice she sounded sad.

When they had lingered over fortune cookies for as long as was
possible in the restaurant, James suggested they walk down Main

Street, in the direction of the square. He wanted to offer Yasmeen his hand, but the words sounded too old-fashioned to his mind, as if he were some sort of Venetian courtier offering a concubine his pledge. Then, as though the gods he'd long since ceased to believe in had ordained it, she went skidding over a patch of ice in her ubiquitous high heels.

'Oh no,' she'd cried, linking her arm through his.

They'd walked down the street arm in arm, talking about nothing in particular. Even in her high heels, James saw that Yasmeen was at least a whole foot shorter. Funny how she'd never looked so small when he'd seen her from a distance. Taking this opportunity to examine the top of her head, James noticed that the pins with which she bound her hair were ornate, old-fashioned things with pretty pendants on their tails. It hadn't ever occurred to him to notice how a woman did her hair. Every second step or so, she slipped a little bit and skidded into his side. When she did, she looked up at him laughingly, more beautiful in these brief glimpses than she'd been all night. James couldn't remember a time when he'd been happier.

As they approached the square, however, he found himself growing more and more on edge. Surely she would see the other couples on the pond and want to skate as well.

'Oh look, ice skaters,' she'd exclaimed, delighted. James's heart began to sink. 'I don't know how they do it—I'd be so scared.'

It was then that James knew he loved her.

He bore the burden of unconfessed ardour for months. I love you, he thought, watching her laugh at movies, the plots of which he'd never remember. I love you, he mouthed into the bathroom mirror when he took her to the symphony. I love you, he murmured into her hair when he was certain she was asleep.

'ThankyouIloveyou,' he finally blurted out one morning as she set his coffee before him and kissed him on the head. Then, he knocked his cup over so violently it smashed onto the tiles.

She regarded him uncertainly, as one regards a sneezing stranger before wishing him 'gesundheit'.

'I suppose we should get the coffee off your trousers,' she finally said.

Doris poked him. 'It's over,' she said, looking amused. He realized he had been staring off into space again.

'Would you care for a drink?' he asked her.

'A drink?' she repeated, looking surprised. 'I'm afraid I can't. A few of us are going to the Taproom.' And then, after a pause only fractionally too long, 'Care to join us?'

'Don't mind if I do,' he replied, surprising them both.

A few drinks later, he surprised himself again when he realized he was having fun. The only low point of the evening occurred when he overheard a member of the English department explaining to a man who looked remarkably like Timofey Pavlovich Pnin that James, actually, had been at Crawford 'forever', but hadn't come out much since his wife 'ran off with her childhood sweetheart', leaving him and his teenage daughter behind.

'What's the daughter like?' asked the bald man, regarding James curiously over his perfectly circular spectacles.

'Sweet kid. A bit creepy though. Been wearing the same outfit since her mother left.'

James slipped out without saying goodbye.

A few days later, he found himself passing a shop full of mannequins dressed like Celeste St Clare. When he explained that he wanted to surprise his fifteen-year-old daughter, the bubbly sales associate helped him spend far too much on outfits that any teenage girl would 'totally love'.

'They're all returnable, unworn,' she told him, handing him the lengthy receipt. He sorely hoped the raggedy-looking denim miniskirt the girl had insisted was a wardrobe essential would not meet with Irenie's approval.

7

It rained today, my darling; I thought of you. It snowed last week, my darling; I thought of you. A leaf turned green, my darling, and, again, I thought of you. I thought of you when the sun rose and then when it set. I thought of you on Eid, on New Year's Day, on Kwanza, uncertain as I am just what it is.

The acquisition of an AC some years back had infused the house with a modern chill, but one which has not quite overcome the heavy nostalgia of the air. Smoke and high spirits of soirees decades past linger in the dark velvet drapes and the ghost of jejune merriments remains long after its enactors have died or drifted far away. A relic of the rousing nights and cut crystal snifters, Baby Tamasha reigns alone now that all her court has faded into old age.

'Come, darling, sit,' she bids with aristocratic grace. I half expect billows of memory, dancing as dust, to arise from the settee she pats. 'Tea?'

I nod.

'What a start I had when you came in, my dear. I almost shot through the roof!'

I suppress a smile at the thought of Baby Tamasha shooting anywhere. She seems as fixed an aspect of the room as the heavy teak settee, both upholstered in silk and nearing a metre in width. I don't believe I've ever seen a woman quite so wide. Her hands flutter gracefully as she pours us the tea. Aside from them and her head, which is anchored to her body by a surprisingly slim neck, her whole person seems as inert as an armchair.

'Of course I was expecting you,' she goes on, 'but nobody told me how like your mother you have become. Why, the last time I saw you, you were too small to be considered a person at all. It was lifetimes ago, darling,' she assures me, evidently seeing the lack of recognition on my face. 'Beauty and Bubbly were still with me then. It must have been twelve years now. Thirteen. You were just a tiny little baby, staring silently at everything with those big eyes of yours. Biscuit?' They're the imported kind, jam filled and chocolate coated. I take a broken one and then, when pressed, two more. 'I hardly ever have an excuse to get out the good ones anymore.' She regards the tin mournfully, then extends a tiny hand. I take it gently.

'She's very fragile,' Nani had warned before I left. 'Since her sisters died she sees almost no one besides Shireen.' It's been over a decade since Beauty died of a heart attack and Bubbly, three months later, of a stroke. No one thought Baby would go on so long alone. The sisters were inseparable, right from the start. Six-year-old Beauty and four-year-old Bubbly practically raised Baby after her birth proved too much for their mother's weak heart. Though it was expected that cross-eyed Beauty and cleft-lipped Bubbly might never find husbands, beautiful Baby was held back by only her fat. As most children grow taller, Baby grew rounder. By late adolescence, she weighed three hundred pounds. Even then, beatific Baby might have married had she not been determined never to leave Bubbly and Beauty. The sisters spent all night at parties and slipped washing detergent into potential in-laws' cups of tea. They danced on tables. They composed profane qawwalis. They dressed Baby in the most outlandish outfits and stuffed her full of foods that forced her to pass gas.

'What tamasha, those sisters,' the rebuffed suitors and their families sniffed, which is how the sisters got their name.

Throwing up his hands in defeat after his youngest daughter

reached the marital benchmark that was then only twenty-two,
the old colonel abandoned his efforts altogether. When, three
years later, he quietly passed away in his sleep, the sisters were
left in the care of their elder brother. Sheryar, whom they all
called Pinky, built them a house across from his own in the new
capital, making sure they had views of the hills from every room.
He imported flowers for their garden and had a fountain dug.
When the sisters, who had been educated in Lausanne, expressed
nostalgia for snowfall and winter nights by the fire, he had a house
built in Murree so they could spend their winters there. Pinky
must have spent a small fortune on devices of climate control
so his sisters could winter where others summered and summer
where others wintered.

'Why come down in summers?' he asked time and again.

'To catch up on the gossip,' his sisters would reply.

The three were soon as famous in Islamabad as they'd been in
Lahore. Baby Tamasha tells me of the parties once hosted in this
very house, the meetings, the dancing, the secrets, the passions.
She tells me of a man who would one day be dictator knocking
himself out on the chandelier and how a film star too famous to
name fell for a Pakistani playboy right here on this couch. She
spins stories of drunken congas down Constitution Avenue and
noted eccentrics with strange creatures for pets. I imagine her
visits with my mother were much the same: Baby reminiscing, my
mother listening; my mother drawn in by her confidence, Baby
then listening. As she describes all the comings and goings of
her long, eventful life, all the intrigues and affairs, I realize she is
a more expansive compendium of others people's personal lives
than even Mrs Winterbourne. If anyone knows the details of my
mother's relationship with Ahmed, it is her.

'So it was when she was at boarding school that you first met
my mother?' I prompt.

'It was.' She helps herself to another biscuit. 'She was best
friends with my grandniece, Shireen. They had special permission

to come for Sunday tea. Shireen was a quiet one, but not your Mamma. I saw the fire in her at once. "That one's the lively sort," I said to my sisters. "And my, but she was!"' Not long into their acquaintanceship, my mother began delighting the sisters Tamasha with tales of her escapades. Having once been rather mischievous boarding scholars themselves, the sisters adored it. Baby Tamasha tells me of how the young Yasmeen once decimated an obnoxious history tutor's machismo by dyeing all his blackboard chalk bright pink, how she somehow managed to send a herd of goats stampeding through the sports ground during a field hockey game just when it seemed St Mary's was sure to lose, how she convinced the entire kindergarten class to lift their skirts in unison to reveal well wishes written on improvised diapers one assembly when exams had left the older girls' morale low.

'What a character she was, your mamma,' Baby Tamasha muses, wiping her streaming eyes with a lace-edged handkerchief. It's apparent even now that she could once have been a beauty. Her earlobes are exquisite, her features daintier than those of many women less than half her weight, less than half her age. Indeed, her age is apparent only in her hair, which, though still thick and shiny, is the white to which starched school shirts can hope to aspire only after untold bleachings. It crosses my mind that at some point Baby Tamasha decided not to be beautiful, not to steal one sister's name, not to steal out ahead of both along the path down which, given their ages, they ought to lead, but, given their looks, they would never so much as follow.

'Just look at me,' she says. 'Your nani said you had questions to ask and all this while I've been talking. Here's an idea: why don't you stay for dinner? You can phone from the hall to see if it's all right.'

I do, assuring Nani that Baby Tamasha seems not to be tired. 'She's not well, you know,' Nani cautions, 'her doctors have recommended bedrest and keeping visitors to a minimum.'

Though I've only known Baby Tamasha these few hours, I

have trouble imagining she'd take kindly to such advice. I tell Nani as much.

'Well,' she concedes, 'since she seems to be having a good day, you may as well spend time with her while you can. There's no telling when she'll be well enough to make time for you again.'

When I re-enter the living room, Baby Tamasha is so still upon her settee it looks as though some sort of special remote with somatic reach has put her on pause. For the first time, it occurs to me that she's making a spectacular effort solely for me. Or for my mother; Yasmeen Khalil always did inspire such things in people.

'I wanted to ask you about Ahmed's wife,' I venture. 'In our family no one will even say her name.'

'Ah, Mehrunissa,' she snaps back to life. And to my surprise: 'Poor Mehrunissa.'

Our dinner is brought in on trays, and although it is probably the best biriyani I've ever eaten, Baby Tamasha barely touches hers. As I clear my plate of firsts, seconds, and, with great effort, thirds, she tells me what she knows about the woman who killed my mother. Mehrunissa Shabaz was born and raised in the UK, but by parents who did their best to pretend they were raising their daughter in Pakistan. An only child of aging parents, she was doted on to absurd extremes. What Mehrunissa wanted, she got. Though she was undeniably spoilt, she hadn't the imagination to be altogether impossible. Most people agreed that she was an unremarkable child, both in aspect and intellect. It is unlikely Ahmed Kakkezai would ever have paid her much attention had circumstance not been just so when she chose to act upon her affections.

I have already inferred most of what Baby Tamasha tells me from the letters and from stray comments from the older members of the family. What interests me is how freely she seems to love Ahmed. At home, his rare mention is inevitably fraught. Once loved like a brother or a son, he went terribly wrong. And though I believe even Nana has been unable to fully divest himself of the love he once felt, my family cannot quite let go of the notion that everything that happened was Ahmed's fault. Sometimes he's brought up in passing, in a slip of the tongue: 'How Ahmed loved langras raw like these ones; if Ahmed were here he'd no doubt quote something grim from Goethe in response to what you just said; Ahmed always insisted August rains are the freshest.' And then the uncomfortable pause as they remember.

But Baby Tamasha knew Ahmed's family long before mine did. His grandfather taught the Sisters Tamasha how to play backgammon and his mother kept Beauty supplied with a particular brand of talcum powder available only in the western United States for which she'd somehow developed a preference. When Baby Tamasha speaks of Ahmed, she doesn't mitigate accidental praise with insults, she doesn't utter anecdotes then clam up, embarrassed. It seems she was as fond of Ahmed as she was of my mother. Unable as ever to stay on track, she expounds upon what a bright little boy he was, how much she missed his visits when the Kakkezais moved to America, what sweet little stories he told the sisters to keep them entertained. When their beloved Yasmeen met their adored Ahmed and they fell in love, it was as though fate had intervened.

'It was like witnessing the birth of a star,' she tells me. 'Everyone was blinded by the brightness. The only trouble was, they were blinded too.'

'What do you mean?'

'They were so confident in the strength and breadth of their love that they treated it carelessly.'

Reflecting back on the cruelty of some of the early letters, I suspect I know what she means. 'How so?' I ask, nevertheless.

'Small things, really. Yasi would tell Ahmed she was unwell and then he would turn up with flowers only to hear she'd gone to the salon to have her nails done with Shireen. He would go charging right in and cause such a scene. "I just didn't feel like seeing you today," your mother would say petulantly. And he was just as bad. Maybe worse. When Ahmed wanted Yasi to do

something unpleasant, he'd never ask outright. Always there was a
dying aunt at stake or an estranged cousin or an urgent deadline. I
remember this one time in particular, Ahmed wanted your mother
to go meet an aunt of his from Riyadh with him. Yasi could be
very shy, despite what you may have heard. She didn't open up to
people until she knew what they were all about. Anyway, Ahmed
told her some nonsense story about the aunt—not even an aunt,
by the way, she turned out to be a second cousin—wanting to
meet his intended before resigning herself to a long and painful
death from cysticercosis—cysticercosis, imagine, wherever did he
come up with such a thing? So Yasi very dutifully went to meet
this aunt, who turned out to be perfectly fine except for that she
was a thoroughly unpleasant person, and Ahmed never turned up!'

'But *why*? Why would they do that sort of thing if they loved
each other so much? And what was it that broke them up?'

'That, I can't say for certain. Something came between them—'

'Mehrunissa?'

'No, not Mehrunissa. Poor Mehrunissa was never more than
anyone's afterthought. She was a complication, perhaps in a way
an inevitability, that arose in the interim,' she says, and I know
suddenly and with absolute certainty that Shamim's speculation is
correct. Poor Mehrunissa did indeed lack any other choice. 'At the
end of the day, I think Ahmed and Yasi were just too similar,' she
continues. 'Too passionate. Too dramatic. Not to mention, *much*
too stubborn.'

'But why couldn't one of them have just apologized?' I ask,
impatient with them as I've never been before.

'Some things are beyond apology. And anyway, theirs was a
relationship beyond apologies. Or so they thought. Nothing was
beyond the realm of forgiveness. Nothing could keep them from one
another. They imagined it would be impossible to lose each other.'

'No loss is impossible.'

'I know that,' she says sadly. 'You know that, young as you are.
But they hadn't learnt it yet.'

For a while I am quiet, reeling from the realization that my casting of the two of them as tragic leads in a story my mother might have told is perhaps less apt than I'd imagined. In what version of those romances does Heer take up with Ranjha's best friend after the lovers have had a falling out? In what version of those epic tales does Romeo impregnate another woman whilst in some sort of mythic sulk? 'Is he my father?' I ask, for the first time uncertain whether I hope that it is true.

'Ahmed?' She looks surprised. 'No, darling. Certainly not.'

'What about the summer of '85? He said something in a letter about meeting at the Japanese Park.'

'Have you seen the Japanese Park, Irenie?'

'Not recently.'

'It's hardly a likely site for assignations.'

'People keep saying "your father this, your father that" when they're talking about Ahmed though. Even Nani said it once.'

'Slips of tongue. Everyone thought they would get married. Everyone thought Yasmeen's children would be Ahmed's children. But that wasn't how it happened. They never did see each other that summer. Ahmed wanted to, to say goodbye, he said, but she'd just married your father and she wasn't sure if it was the right thing to do. I told her it wasn't, but the two of them hatched some plan to accidentally run into each other at the Japanese Park—'

'I told you—'

'*But*, at the last minute, Mehrunissa caught wind of it and put a dampener on the whole thing. She dragged the whole family up to Khaira Gullee without a moment's notice. A few days later, your parents left. There wouldn't have been any other opportunity for Yasi and Ahmed to meet. Mehrunissa had had him on a particularly tight leash because of what had happened the summer before.'

'The summer before?'

'Oh dear. I was sure you already knew. You seem so well versed on all this ancient history.'

'Already knew what?'

She sighs deeply. 'Well, now that I've given it away I suppose you'll find out somehow or the other. Supposedly, Ahmed ran off to America so he could be with your mamma.'

'Supposedly?'

'Supposedly. Neither of them ever breathed a word of it to me, but that's how the rumour mill ran.'

'So you don't know for sure?'

'I don't know for sure. Shireen doesn't know for sure. The only one who thinks she knows for sure is Mehrunissa.'

'Does she?'

'I really couldn't say, darling. But I certainly doubt it. She doesn't strike me as all that bright.'

'I have just one more question,' I say tentatively. 'If you're not too tired?' She promises she's not though I'm sure she is. 'Do you know anything about an embroidered sheet? It was a wedding gift for my uncle.'

At this, Baby Tamasha laughs. She tells me it's the strangest thing anyone has asked her yet. If she knows nothing about it, no one does. No one alive, at any rate.

'I almost forgot,' she exclaims as I kiss her goodbye. 'I have something to give you. I believe it's your mother's diary. Yasi gave it to me the last time she was here. She wanted me to give it to Ahmed when I saw him, said to tell him "this isn't right". What wasn't right, I have no idea, but that's what she said. Of course, I never did see him again. Poor thing passed away before I could give it to him. Now if only I could remember where I put it ...'

She'll have it sent, she promises, sinking further into the settee. She seems utterly drained. When I turn back to wave I see her eyes have slid shut. She sits perfectly still in the gloom, shoulders bowed beneath the weight of so much memory. For a fraction of a second I see my father in her place, shrunken, almost swallowed, by the spectre of the past. For once, I do not turn away.

8

*I first saw your face in moonlight; first felt your skin beneath
the stars. I first yearned for you while flying, first heard about
you from a confidante. To graze your arm while reaching for
the newspaper would be more rare and wonderful, seeing you
as you brushed your teeth a dream come true. And to call your
name each day at half past five—well, that is something I hope
and pray even now to one day do.*

There are men who forge their destinies, persevering against
the odds, as though they know their efforts will ultimately
lead them to the particular future fate surely has in store. Their
dedication is single-minded, their enterprise unflagging. Their
lives are complicated board games along a course they have set.
And then there are men who only observe such struggles. Like
stowaways on cruise ships, they enjoy the occasional windfall:
slightly scorched French pastries thrown out by the tray or polka
music filtering through the hull as paying passengers dance
upstairs. They do not determine where the ship will take them, nor
do they have any say along the way. They do not consult maritime
maps or star charts—though on occasion the opportunity to do
so might arise—for, considering a course in which they have
no say is as futile as a deaf man reading biographies of dead
composers in the hope that he might one day hear a symphony.
Watching the woman he loved blot coffee from his trousers,
James was more certain than ever that he was this second kind

of man. Twenty years later, drinking coffee at the kitchen table in his undershorts because there was no one there to care, he knew he had been correct.

Since the talk, he'd been dividing his time between picking up the phone to ensure there was a dial tone, peering into Irenie's bedroom to see that the neat stacks of clothing were still there, and mulling over the details of the past. He'd been thinking all morning of how soft Yasmeen's hands had been. He remembered what a relief it had been when she finally touched him, that terrible, wonderful day when he told her how he felt.

He still remembered how cold Yasmeen's kitchen chair had been beneath his legs. He crossed and re-crossed them to minimize exposure, spread his hands under his thighs. She didn't seem to notice. Her back was to him as she bent over the sink. Neither of them said a thing. She dabbed at the coffee spot with a patterned paper towel, a second tucked into the leg so the stain remover wouldn't seep through. Yasmeen was meticulous when it came to matters like this, peculiarly so, as though she was following a step-by-step manual in her head. James himself had never been much for such definitude, in small matters or large. His life had been amorphous, as vacant of agency as a piece of fluff on a spring wind. There was the scholarship to Yale, which he hadn't expected or worked for but which, of course, he accepted. Then there was Dr Oliver Theuriau with his unanticipated conviction that James had a true flair for the classics, the offer from Pittsburgh that Dr Oliver Theuriau made sure he accepted, the almost immediate appointment at Crawford James could not have predicted. He knew now that Crawford had hired him on a complete misassumption, that his tenure had been as much a result of chance as every other event in his life.

On the basis of his dissertation topic, Crawford's hiring committee had mistakenly identified in James an irreverent wit. They had offered him a position with the idea that his subversive brand of scholarship would shake up the ageing department. But James Eccles was not subversive. Nor had he intended to be witty. In truth, James Eccles was not even very much of a scholar. Academia was simply something he slipped into after having been sidelined early into a thoroughly impractical discipline. A college more esteemed than Crawford might have recognized this sooner, but 'publish or perish' was not a particularly popular maxim in its classics department. Its most prolific member was a woman named Charlene Weber, the rather transparent nom de plume under which Dr Charles Faber published his popular, if alarmingly inaccurate, historical romances. At the time of James's appointment, the other eleven members of the department had been struggling with their own unpublished manuscripts for so long that the minor achievement of his dissertation's publication by the *Bridgeport Free Press* allowed him to proceed without scrutiny for several years.

Over the course of these years, James learned something about himself that neither he nor anyone else would have guessed: he was actually good at teaching. He had a way of making the abstruse apparent, of transplanting precision with predictability. His natural tendency to be pedantic had the unforeseeable effect of making his students feel that they and he were in some special clique. His general inaccessibility and impersonal demeanour only furthered this. Enrolment in first-year romance-language courses flagged as more and more students elected to fulfil their language requirement with a semester or two of ancient Greek. 'The man is brilliant,' James's evaluations typically read. 'Makes the impossible almost easy.'

But not too easy. Though he wasn't consciously aware of it, that was James's secret: he made the avenue to the esoteric accessible enough that any idiot could peer down it, yet somehow maintained its loftiness. It was thus that, year after year, former French students and disinterested Spanish students registered for

Dr Eccles's Fundamentals class in order that they might be near the possibility of enlightenment even if they hadn't the dedication or the desire to work towards it very hard at all.

So, during the years that James's lack of scholarship was being overlooked, he quite accidentally established himself as an indispensable member of the classics department. Instead of being booted after four years without a single article in the works, he was made aware that he might be up for tenure soon if only he would publish something. It could be anything, the dean told him: an essay, an article, a comment on a seldom-used quotation. If James could have obliged him, he would have, but he simply wasn't up to task. Every sentence he wrote lacked direction; his arguments meandered and made no sense. In despair, he turned his attention to his class notes—maybe if he could profess well enough they'd make him a full professor anyway. There was order to these notes, he realized, a synchronicity he hadn't seen before. In his lesson plans was the tight, well-ordered cohesiveness of a good work of scholarship. This might have remained just a source of minor irritation had James been the helmsman of his own existence, but, fortunately, he was not.

The semester James was told to publish something or else was an especially busy one. He was teaching three courses—none of them at the introductory level, co-chairing a visiting scholars' committee, and leading an elective seminar on early Minoan art forms in the hope that the entirely non-mandatory commitment would garner favour. For the first and only time, he'd felt it prudent to apply for a TA. The TA was a young-ish man named Wilton, who was passed listlessly between members of the humanities faculty like a baton in a relay race no one really wants to run. James was unaware of his reputation when he asked his TA to send off the handful of first drafts he'd cobbled together a few weeks before his fateful meeting with the dean. He was so caught up in all his classes and extracurricular commitments that he failed to notice the stack of his lecture notes missing in their stead. He did not register just what it was a fairly prominent publisher was eager to purchase the rights for when he received the congratulatory letter. He was too busy even to note the caveat that his 'teaching book' was expected to be the first in a set of three. He'd simply signed off on their offer and taken off to tell the dean.

And so it was that the most ineffective TA in Crawford's history secured tenure for James. The teaching books did shockingly well. For years, they were set texts for first-year Greek students in institutions of higher education across the nation. The final instalment was published a few months before he first encountered Yasmeen Khalil. Without his having plotted it, life had taken him where he was meant to be. As he sat there, trying to spare his thighs the coldness of the chair, it occurred to James that life could, in fact, be plotted, that most people probably did plot theirs to some degree. Up until that moment, the course of his relationship with Yasmeen had been charted quite without deliberations on his part. He told Yasmeen he loved her because he did. Some vague awareness had alerted him to the fact that when you loved a woman, telling her was what you did. Doing all you could so you might possess her was what instinct told him you did next. But, for once, James resisted the natural progression. He did not repeat what he had said, nor did he try to take it back. He did not ask Yasmeen what she thought. He simply sat there in his undershorts as she ironed his trousers dry. She didn't love him then, he understood, but, if he waited, perhaps some day she would. It would be a quiet kind of love, a love born of familiarity, solidity, security, something she could grow into when she realized it would always be there.

'All done,' she said, smiling at the squelch of sweaty leg peeled from sticky chair. Struggling into his trousers, James knew the smile was not at his awkwardness but about an aspect of it she found endearing. He had set sail for a certain future. Though neither he nor Yasmeen ever brought up the declaration he'd made that afternoon, something in the subsequent silence crystallized it.

A few days later, she accompanied him to the classics department's half-term tea. It was their first official appearance as a couple. Two months later, she agreed to be his wife.

He drank the last of his coffee, not tasting the bitter grounds. TM's call was late again. She'd promised that Irenie would speak to him this week. James was prepared to wait. He was good at waiting. It was his forte. Though his mother-in-law was appalled by his outburst with the ticket, she seemed to understand why he'd done what he'd done. She knew what it was to lose a child.

9

*Lying under stars and sheets we loved each other. People were
pieces of sand, like diamonds in water down there. In minutes,
our universes expanded beyond the realms of comprehension.
And in that strangeness, we hadn't a care.*

For days, I wait on edge for the telephone to ring. The airport
does not call nor does Baby Tamasha, but on Saturday
morning James Eccles does. Nani 'forgets' to mention he will be
calling when she asks me to answer the phone while she is out.

'Irenie!' he exclaims.

I almost hang up. 'Father,' I say. Father, father, father. It seems
to echo over the line.

'How are you?' He sounds so utterly miserable I feel compelled
to ask him in return. I wonder what he does on weekends now
that Dr Faber isn't there. Instead of the perfunctory 'fine thanks'
with which he usually responds, he tells me, not so well. He's had
a cold, he says, and summer colds are so much worse. Work on
the new book isn't going well. He has been spending a lot of time
in the library and still finds that he is blocked. The frozen meals,
he says, have been his saving grace. I realize I forgot to tell him
they were there. He's chattier than I've ever seen him and seems
desperate to stay on the line so I grudgingly tell him about my
cousins, how Shamim is reading *Beowulf* while Naaz spends all
her time online. I tell him about meeting Baby Tamasha, though

of course not everything she said, about how Shireen Amin is expecting me for tea.

'Shireen!' he exclaims, 'tell me how is she?' It turns out my father has a soft spot for my mother's best friend. He tells me she's the warmest person he's ever met. We talk for a while about the old days, when he visited with my mother. Half an hour flies by. I've never heard about all this before. In fact, I cannot remember him ever discussing her with me. When he says her name, it's as though his voice is filled with light. In an instant, I forgive him for the ticket. For the first time, I realize he lost her too.

Before we say goodbye, he tells me Shireen will like me, I shouldn't worry. I wonder how he knows.

Shireen Khala, as I've been instructed to call her, is older than I expect. I'd imagined she'd be the same girl who pulls at my mother's arm in the silver-framed photo on my grandparents' mantle, only taller now and maybe with one braid instead of two. This woman looks nothing like that girl. I discreetly scrutinize her for a trace of her girlhood self as I often did with my mother, but neither girl is there anymore, one grown, one just gone.

I want to ask her a million questions all at once, but I don't know where to begin. Her kind eyes seem to read my mind. She regales me with tales of my mother for an hour before we're interrupted by the phone. Her daughter Shezzie is on the line: it seems there's been some sort of mix-up with the groom's shoes.

'I'm afraid I'm going to have to go see to this,' she apologizes. 'The wedding's on the seventh and we're all going a bit mad.'

'Of August?'

'September. I do hope you'll be there.' Before I can explain the impossibility of this, she begins rummaging around behind the sofa. 'Oh! I almost forgot! Look what I found!' She hands me a battered cardboard box.

Inside is a stack of old photographs. The one on top is of two girls about my age dressed up in saris. One has wound her pallu conservatively around her middle while the other jauntily cocks a hip and lets it hang free.

'Aamir's wedding,' Shireen Khala says, peering over my shoulder. 'We imagined we were the very picture of sophistication in those saris. I thought you might like to keep these ones. I've framed my favourites already.'

I thank her effusively, not believing my good luck. There are photos of both girls arm in arm at every age since they met, sometimes decked out in fake moustaches, other times just lying under trees. There's my mother on horseback, Shireen knitting a scarf, both of them dipping their toes in a stream. I'm particularly taken by one of them in what appears to be their school uniform. In their dark starched tunics, they look like the little girls my mother berated me for drawing. The white of their shirts glows brightly in black and white. Some sort of badge adorns each of their chests with military precision. Their Mary Janes glimmer in the sunlight. This was the sort of little girl I wanted to be.

'That was the day we first started at Saint Mary's,' Shireen Khala tells me. 'I met your mother all of five minutes before that photo was taken.'

I'm surprised. It looks there like they've known each other a lifetime.

'I was so nervous about meeting the headmistress,' she continues, leaning towards the mirror to touch up her lipstick. 'I remember I was sitting on this stump with my head in my hands while my parents talked to the other adults. Out of nowhere, Yasi pops up and tugs on one of my pigtails. At first I thought she was teasing me and I almost started crying, but then she told me not to be scared. I guess she just knew. Then she started telling me this hilarious story about the headmistress's moustache. Mehreen had told her about it. I was laughing so hard by the time my parents came to find me that they had to beg me to calm down. That was when they took the photo. "Best friends forever," said my mother, and she was right. You were named after me, you know.'

'I thought I was named after Irene, my father's sister?' We're in the foyer now, headed for the door.

'You were. After Irene but also after Reenie, me!'

'I'm glad,' I say slowly. 'To be named after you. I don't know anything about Irene except that she's dead.'

'Well, perhaps one day your father will tell you about her. Your mother seemed to think he never got over what happened.'

'I found a photo of the two of them in his study. I don't think she was like me—or rather, that I'm like her. I think my father wishes I was.' Embarrassed, I blurt, 'This is Ahmed, isn't it?' and brandish the photograph of my mother casually resting her hand on the chest of a young man with the thick, wavy hair of a shaving foam model. She's looking up at him, laughing, clearly in the middle of a joke. He pushes his glasses further up his nose and beams down at her. They're both dressed up for a formal occasion of some sort—my mother in the same sari she wore at her brother's wedding and Ahmed in a suit.

Shireen Khala looks startled. 'I forgot that was in there. Yasi came over and tore up all the photos of them together after—'

'After?'

'It's really not for me to say.'

'Are they dressed up for a wedding?' I persist.

'In a sense. They were dressed up in memory of a wedding—of the night they met.'

'I thought they met in college?' But what was it Claire had said? My mother told her they'd met once before, in a dream or something like it. 'They met at Aamir Maamu's wedding, didn't they?'

'No one knows but me. And now you.' She pauses. 'I suppose I'd better call the shoemaker and tell him I'll be late.' I beam at her and she sits back down to tell me the story only she knows.

On a hot, breezy night towards the end of summer, Aamir Khalil married Sairah Kakkezai in his parents' garden and the lives of both families were forever changed, though not in the fashion anyone might have imagined. It was a grand affair, boasting attendees from as far away as Melbourne and Manhattan, caterers brought in for the occasion from Lahore. For years, the details of the evening would be referenced by brides-to-be when explaining to friends and family just what they hoped for of their weddings. For decades, the events of it would shape the lives of two young people who, as of eleven o'clock that night, had not yet met.

Yasmeen Khalil, age fifteen, adjusted her sari and sucked in her cheeks in annoyance. Would the evening never end? In less than a week, she would be back in boarding school with not a single interesting story to tell the other girls. Earlier in the evening, the boy with light eyes had accidentally grazed her hand and for an instant she had felt both known and knowing in a way she never had. He had vanished now, probably gone back to Chicago with the rest of the bride's family, never to be seen or heard from again. She was bored with her brother's wedding, bored of smiling at relatives she barely remembered or had perhaps never known. She was bored of having her cheeks pulled, her hair patted, even of having to endure treatises on how beautiful she'd grown.

'Let's slip off for a cigarette,' she whispered to Reenie as the bride readjusted her skirt for yet another round of photos.

'Are you mad?' her best friend hissed back. 'What if someone comes looking for us?' No one would come looking for them. In the hubbub, no one would even notice they were gone. And even if there had been any risk, Yasi would have insisted anyway. When she was bored, she threw caution to the winds.

The two girls backed away from the dessert table, heading for the hole they'd worn into the thorny hedge over the summer. Her brother's valima was being held in the garden of his parents' house. It was a beautiful venue, almost adjacent to the Margallas, and the newlyweds' house next door had been completed just last week. The entire wedding party would accompany the bride and groom to their new front door. A feeble white steed named Raja had been procured from somewhere for their transport and the whole street strewn with marigolds. An ill-tempered old chowkidar known to all as Kaanta had been engaged to guard the blossoms from passing vehicles and pilfering children. In his boredom, he'd begun feeding the horse flowers shortly after midnight. All the roughage had spurred Raja's rickety bowels to action, causing him to release a torrent of excrement over both his back legs. Swearing furiously, Kaanta had just embarked upon the supremely unpleasant task of picking half-digested marigolds from the bells adorning the horse's hind legs when the two girls giggled past. Unbeknownst to all but Raja, a young boy was perched atop the gatepost watching the whole tableau unfold. Tired of the wedding, the boy had decided to go for a walk along the drive. He had sought cover in the shadows at the sound of Kaanta's ferocious curses. Then, he had climbed atop the gatepost hoping to locate the source.

By the time the two girls made their approach, Ahmed was thoroughly bored of Kaanta and the horse. He watched as they tiptoed over the drive, made their way through the cactus patch, and seemed to vanish into the hedge. Had the moon been slightly fuller or the fairy lights ever-so-slightly brighter, he might have noticed that the one in lavender was the girl whose hand he'd grazed while passing her a cup of green tea, the one whose gaze had made his heart stop every time he'd looked up to find her turned in his direction. Had he known it was her, he would have frozen at his post, at most gone to peer through the opening through which they'd disappeared in hopes of another glimpse. But in the dark there is so much of which one is not aware.

When the shorter girl came hurtling back through the hedge a few minutes later, he ducked behind a large clay pot without really knowing why. Perhaps they'd had a fight. Perhaps the other girl had been hurt. He thought he might as well go check.

Getting through the opening in the hedge was more difficult than the girls had made it look. Ahmed snared his trousers on a protruding branch and sustained a stinging scratch down his left cheek. He emerged with leaves in his hair, dirt on his clothes, blood on his chin.

The house next door was lit up with fairy lights as well, but in the quiet they seemed more soothing than celebratory. Seeing no one, he decided he would skirt the house. At its back, he came upon a compact spiral staircase. Up he climbed.

He'd expected to find a servant quarter or maybe just a narrow stretch of terrace at its top, but he emerged onto a sprawling balcony. There were plants and small trees in pots around the edges and fairy lights strung from the roof. A nest-like cane swing hung from an overhang and there was a table set for two. From this height, you could see the Margallas unobstructed, the range stretching out to where the sky went black. For the first time, Ahmed experienced that lump you get in your throat when you're overcome by unexpected beauty. Seeing no sign of anyone else, he decided he'd sit for a while in the swing in order that he might enjoy the view. As he crossed the balcony, he suddenly became aware of a shadow behind one of the larger pots. It seemed to twitch as he stared at it, to retreat almost imperceptibly into deeper shadow.

'Is someone there?' he asked, a little scared.

There was no response.

Feeling foolish, he strode towards it. Probably just a crate that's been covered up, he thought. He pulled aside what he'd assumed was a tarp—it was actually a sheet, one no doubt from the trousseau—to find a young girl curled into a ball, hands clasping her knees and both eyes tightly shut. Her eyes snapped open as she felt the sheet being pulled away and he saw it was the girl with the green tea. She was even more beautiful up close.

'Are you all right?' she asked, tracing the scratch down his face as he knelt, moistening a fingertip with her tongue to scrub away the blood drying on his chin.

Are you, he wanted to reply, but he couldn't seem to find the words. Instead, he kissed her. He kissed her as though he knew what he was doing, as though they'd been kissing each other all their lives, until they were both entangled in the sheet, sprawled out across the floor. When they paused for breath, he pledged to one day marry her. She agreed without a thought. Seconds later, they heard footfalls on the steps. Soundlessly, she extricated herself from him and hid him beneath the sheet. The whole encounter had taken five minutes at the most.

'Find them?' he heard her ask. Then another girl's voice, and the striking of a match. They chatted as they smoked, but Ahmed didn't hear. He was too busy committing to memory the softness of her fingertip and the sweetness of her kiss. He stayed huddled in the shadows until long after the girls left. When he finally emerged, it was with the embroidered bedsheet tucked in his kameez. He was scolded by his parents, who feared they'd miss their flight. Their words had no impact. High in the air that night, he dreamt of fairy lights and fancy sheets and the softest lips in the whole world. As the miles lengthened between them, a girl whose name he would not learn for several years had exactly the same dream.

10

There are days I wake in Abaddon and I wonder how I'll live. Malebolge, Gehenna, Hades, all these I could bear. If only you were there. It seems a slip so simple has pitched me into this abyss. And yet when I try to trace the schism to the second, my calculations shift. Ill fate alone could have cast us down into this pit.

In August, three things happen, the first of which is that the dreaded Mehrunissa arrives en famille. Because she is staying with relatives in F-10, Nani refuses to venture west of Capital Park. She has caught wind of my questioning and takes me aside one day before tea to tell me there's no point in giving 'that dreadful woman' more importance than she deserves. When I remark that perhaps she might not have been so dreadful had anyone ever given her any importance whatsoever, she sniffs and suggests I spend more time getting to know my cousins. It is not Naaz and Shamim she means, but Naaz's brothers, whose arrivals are the second thing to happen in August.

Changez flies in from San Francisco and Karim drives up from Lahore with his wife Shezray, who appears always to have just smelled something foul, and their twin boys, Chhoua and Chhotu, who are the likeliest source of any such odour. Every day there is an outing or a picnic or a tea. We spend a weekend in the mountains and destroy Sairah Mumani's garden with games of badminton and pithu garam. We eat ice cream, often and in quantity, and spend evenings watching movies like *Mughal-e-Azam* and *The Maltese Falcon*, projected proudly by Nana on the east side of the house. Aunties and acquaintances stop by and spend countless hours telling stories of a shared past. For the first time in my life, I barely think of my mother. By the end of the two weeks, however, everyone's enthusiasm has begun to fade. The day before Karim and his family are scheduled to leave, Changez suggests we take the boys to Itwar bazaar, just for something to do. Shamim is immediately contemptuous. I think she wishes she had thought of it first. She prides herself on coming up with new entertainments in this city where there are only about four things to do, three of which involve eating. Already, she's dragged us twice to the rather wanting zoo to ride the sweating elephant and ogle the few wary apes still on display. She's instigated a rowing trip on Rawal Dam, and compelled Sairah Mumani along on hikes up Mount Happiness in the guise of getting fit. I'm fairly sure Itwar bazaar simply hasn't crossed her mind.

'Oh all right, fine,' she says when Naaz ventures that it might be fun. 'I'll come, but only because I'm embarrassed by your pleading.'

So we head out on Sunday morning. At nine o'clock it's already hot, though not as hot as it will be. We're sweating before we make our way to the not-so-secret passage through the hedge. I ignore Shamim's complaints and think of everything going to a bazaar connotes: Marrakesh and Bombay and camels pulling loads. This is the sort of thing Celeste expects I'll have stories about when I return. If not odalisques and hashish pipes, at least open-air market places full of brilliant things.

Itwar bazaar proves quite unlike the movies though. The small stream we cross to get there indeed glitters, but with broken glass and plastic bags. I suspect sewage flows beneath the trash, though once we get into the chickens I can't smell it anymore. They're stuffed into cages, feather escaping like spaghetti through a sieve. Chhoua and Chhotu demand to be bought chicks, one dyed pink, the other blue. When Karim hesitates, Shezrey surprises us all by saying, 'Oh let them have their way this once, it's a vacation after all.'

'I suppose they'll die before we have to go back anyway,' her husband concedes.

Seeing how delighted the boys are with their tiny neon pets suddenly makes me sad. Would my mother have bought me a chick if she'd brought me here? If I were ten years younger, even five, the bazaar might be a place of magic for me too. There's candyfloss and bright toys and baby booties filled with sugar-coated saunf. The goats lined up for sale are only sad if you think what's to become of them and the trinkets neatly on display are cheap looking only if you think about the delights they might bring beyond the next ten minutes. The swarms of flies over tall mango mountains simply speak to how sweet the fruit must be and the dirt still on the vegetables just means they're fresh-plucked from the ground. I buy tiny vials of coloured glitter with the excitement of a child and garish mirrors with actresses on the backs. Celeste will love them. On a whim, I buy a silver photo frame from an Afghan doing business on a sheet laid out on the ground. The picture of my mother on horseback in the mountains will fit perfectly in it. I imagine my father will enjoy that version of her. Naaz titters at my purchases and spends her money instead on hot samosas, dried apricots, balls of chalky sugar.

'Bargain na,' Shezrey urges when she catches me paying fifty rupees for a bangle made of soft metal painted gold. 'These people will rob you blind if you let them! This is my cousin from America,' she chides unsuspecting vendors, 'aren't you ashamed to make her think Pakistanis are like this?'

'She doesn't look like an American,' I hear a woman selling elastic off her head hiss suspiciously. 'She looks Pakistani.'

I am delighted to think she believes that this is where I belong. When Chhotu and Chhoua drag me to the toy stalls, I peruse their contents as delightedly as they. We see a tin fish that 'swims', a plastic bag parachutist and a garish plastic parrot that squawks 'Polly, ftt, ftt,' when squeezed.

'Why did you buy them clothes here?' Shezrey demands of Changez. I notice then that both the boys are now dressed in bright red t-shirts. 'These low-quality things will just shrink and turn everything else pink.'

'Chhoua fell in a puddle and then Chhotu wanted a new shirt too,' he protests.

'Well, let's see,' she sighs, turning her sons around. 'Hopefully they're not looking too much like the sweeper's children.' Her eyes grow wide, then narrow to a glare. 'Karim, kindly come look at this. Just look at how your brother has dressed up our children.'

'Haan, yaar,' Karim says, glancing at the gold writing on the shirts, 'a bit flamboyant, aren't they?'

'Look at what they say,' his wife says, seething.

'Champ?' he asks, puzzled. 'Oh, chump,' he realizes, laughing.

'You're a chump,' Chhoua tells Chhotu.

'And you are too!' exclaims his brother.

'It isn't funny! How can you let our sons make such a mockery of themselves?'

'It's not mockery if they're aware of it,' points out Changez.

'Do you have no shame?' Shamim screeches somewhere behind us. 'This is how you behave outside your house? You don't have a mother, a sister at home?'

'Sorry ji, sorry ji. It was my mistake,' says a man, who doesn't look sorry at all. He grins, offering up both hands.

'This man,' she informs Karim haughtily, 'grabbed me. He pulled off my dupatta and just grabbed me.'

'No ji, no,' the offender protests, at the sight of our six-foot-tall cousins. 'I fell. I promise.'

'This is my little sister!' Karim thunders. 'She is an innocent young girl, like your sister, and this is what you do?'

A crowd gathers to watch the spectacle. 'What were you

thinking, yaar?' asks a young man who might be a friend in better times. 'Can't you see this is a nice girl? How could you do such a thing?'

'It was an accident,' the man pleads. 'I slipped.'

'Should we teach this lout a lesson?' someone asks Shamim hopefully. 'Show him what happens when he puts his hands on girls.'

My cousin eyes him scornfully. 'Leave it,' she finally decides, 'what lesson can you teach a man like this?'

The crowd dissipates disappointedly. A number of women look outraged that he got off the hook so easily. The men mourn the loss of a potential punching bag. Shamim leads the way towards the parking lot with the air of a magnanimous queen wounded grievously by one of her subjects.

'So you enjoyed yourselves this morning?' asks Nani at lunch. 'It seems like you've come back with half the bazaar.'

Chhoua's chick escapes from underneath a Chump shirt and gets entangled in the grapes.

'Ugh, get rid of it,' Shamim shrieks.

'What is this thing?' Nana demands, calling for the cook.

He upends, three water glasses and assaults us all at least once with an elbow, trying to get hold of the errant chick. Chhotu climbs up on the table and promptly falls face-first into the pullao. Chhoua screams encouragement and the Khalas leap out of their seats. Nana slices a mango, ignoring the whole fracas, while Nani vainly urges him to do something. Finally Aamir Maamu manages to swat the chick off his roti with a napkin. It whizzes into a wall and lies chirping brokenly on the floor.

'You killed Night Walker,' Chhoua wails at his grandfather, rushing to its aid.

'First one down,' Karim offers grimly. 'Sixteen hours left to finish off the other.'

'It would be so nice to come from a civilized family,' Shamim complains later that afternoon. 'A family where there aren't wild creatures escaping everywhere.'

'But that would be boring,' Naaz says. She's brought over a bag of hard candies from Aamir Maamu's factory and is clacking away happily at the computer.

'Disgusting things,' Shamim sniffs when Naaz proffers the bag. They really are rather disgusting, even Naaz concurs, but I pick out all the mint ones. Sweets are a side-venture for Aamir Maamu, whose factory makes medicine.

'How can you eat so many of those, Irenie?' Shamim asks.

'The mints aren't so bad,' I tell her, extending the bag. 'Try one.'

'The mints?' Naaz looks alarmed. 'There are mints in there?'

'Quite a few.' I gesture to the pile of wrappers by my leg.

'You ate all of those?'

'Didn't you read the wrappers, you idiot?' Shamim scoffs.

I pick one up and examine it. Dr Shitz Digestive Mintz.

'They're laxative mints,' Shamim chortles.

'Like cough drops,' Naaz offers weakly. 'Baba thought people would be more inclined towards a cure if it was in the form of sweets.'

Incidentally, it's a private interest of my uncle's. Dr Shitz Digestive Mintz sell splendidly in Sweden. Though the Pakistani bowel is too stubborn for such gentle tactics, they apparently unstop the Swedes like no one's business.

'How many did you have?' Naaz asks.

'Three.' I slip the wrappers into my shoe and hope they haven't seen.

'She'll be fine,' Shamim says. 'Asif had ten that time and he didn't even get the runs.'

When she falls asleep, I go into the bathroom and count the foot-warm wrappers. Seventeen.

I wake up in the hazy grey of very early morning. For a moment I wonder what's awakened me, and then sleep's anaesthesia wears away. It doesn't creep in gradually, like wakefulness after a pleasant dream, but hits me all at once, a colossal wave of pain. My innards feel as though they've been tied up in knots. I close my eyes and when I open them it's light. The tile is cold beneath my feet. I do not remember coming into the bathroom. When finally I find the strength to leave it, my legs buckle and I almost fall.

'Loose motions, what a commotion,' I hear when I wake up next. Shamim. 'She spent all night in the loo.'

'Poor thing. God only knows what they had to eat at that bazaar,' Nani says.

'Stomach flu, food poisoning, god forbid, amoebic dysentery,' I hear next, aware that time has passed. 'Lots of fluids and bedrest, let's hope the fever breaks on its own.'

Someone, Aamir Maamu, sits heavily onto my bed. 'Naazie told me about the Mintz,' he whispers, 'you don't think they did this?'

I manage to shake my head.

'You did have the runs though, didn't you? So the Mintz might have worked a bit?'

I throw up in a basin by the bed. Aamir Maamu looks abashed and pats me on the head.

Three days pass like this, in a fever haze. It's four more before they let me out of bed. I drink orange flavoured ORS and flip through the fashion magazines Sairah Khala brings. Shamim reads by my bedside while I sleep and Naaz and I play cards. They both burst in one afternoon to tell me that Nani has declared we'll attend Shezzie's wedding even though Ahmed's family will be there, but I am too tired to muster much enthusiasm. My nights are filled with vivid dreams, images of my mother dancing ever so slightly out of reach. 'You've been calling for Yasi,' Mehreen Khala tells me when she next comes in. Later, when she thinks I'm asleep, I hear her whisper, 'We have to tell her; it's better she hears it from us.' I feel a hand in my hair. 'She always did have beautiful hair,' Nani says. 'If only we could keep her here.' When I open my eyes, the room is empty and I wonder if anyone was really there.

In the morning, though, she comes in and sits on the bed, adjusting and readjusting the counterpane. 'It's time you knew what happened between your mother and Ahmed.'

'Why they split up?'

'I'll get to that,' she says. 'It was nothing like what you've imagined, I'm fairly sure.'

The trouble all began with the engagement, she tells me. They had planned to have a small one the summer after they finished college, but as their final semester progressed, Ahmed started to have second thoughts—not about Yasmeen, of course, but about whether he wanted to spend his last summer of freedom suffering kurta fittings and guest list checks.

'Let's forget about the engagement and get married when I'm done with my master's,' he suggested. It was what they'd always planned. The engagement was a formality, an announcement to the public of intentions that everybody already knew. Ahmed didn't think Yasmeen would mind

'Fine,' she told him coldly, 'just forget the whole idea and you can go running off to England without worrying about any rings on your fingers ruining your plans.'

Ahmed thought Yasmeen was being silly. Yasmeen thought Ahmed was being selfish. They ignored each other for a week and then he came up with a plan: instead of wasting time and money on an engagement when they were sure they'd be getting married anyway, they'd spend the summer seeing Europe. They'd return with memories and photographs more valuable than any ring.

Ahmed planned the whole trip out in stealth, letting Yasmeen think he'd changed his mind. He came up with an itinerary, arranged visas and made lists of all the things he thought she might like to see. He looked up free camping grounds and festivals and even found a pair of veteran backpackers with whom they could travel. He thought Yasmeen would be delighted when the time came to present her with his plan.

She was not.

'You know Mehreen is getting married this summer,' she'd said. 'There's simply too much to do.' They sulked through finals and all the senior festivities. They even sulked through graduation. Shortly before they were due to fly back to Pakistan, Ahmed told Yasmeen he was going without her.

'Everything is booked,' he told her. 'God knows when there will be another chance like this. We can get engaged in August if you like.'

'If you're not coming now, don't bother coming at all,' Yasmeen replied.

'But why?' I ask Nani. 'Why couldn't Mamma just wait? Why did Ahmed have to go charging off to Europe without her?'

Nani sighs. 'Uff, I've never heard of two people more stubborn than the two of them. If they'd had a child, it would have been a mule. Tauba!'

'Once Yasi made up her mind, she wouldn't change it for anything,' Mehreen Khala adds. I hadn't noticed her coming in. She hands me a glass of lemon barley, at last a respite from ORS, and sits down on the other side of my bed.

'Your mamma came back in such a black mood, I can't even tell you.'

'And that summer was my wedding,' Mehreen Khala interrupts. 'I swear, I was ready to tell her, "Just stay at home."'

'Mehreen!' Nani admonishes.

'I was, Mummy. You remember how difficult she was being. I'll admit it freely: I didn't feel bad for her, not then. She and Ahmed were always doing these dramas. Then the next week they'd be fine. If we're telling Irenie about her mother, we may as well tell her the truth.'

Nani pouts. 'Are you telling this story or am I?'

'I'm not saying she was always like that, Mummy,' Mehreen

Khala persists. 'I'm just trying to make Irenie see what a state she was in. After a week or two, though, she did come around. She came to me and said, "Mehreen, I no longer give a rat's"'—she glances at her mother—'"rear end about Ahmed. Just tell me what you need done and I'll see to it." And after that she was a great help.'

'We didn't hear another word about him all summer,' Nani says.

'If he wants to be a part of our family he'll come take part in your wedding, was all she would say. Then we got busy with preparations and just assumed everything would work out. We should've noticed she'd stopped eating.'

'And that she never slept.'

'If anyone said his name she left the room.'

'She even refused to read his letters,' says Nani fretfully.

'I should have seen that things were different when she asked me to throw them away unopened.'

'Did you?' I ask.

'No.' Mehreen Khala looks uncomfortable. 'I thought a day might come when she would want them.'

'Did it?'

'I forgot to ask. First Zulfiqar and I moved to Karachi and then Yasi went to America and came back married to your father and then we had you and Shamim and there was my divorce, and I just never got around to it.'

'What did they say?' I ask.

'I haven't the foggiest notion. They're yours, if you want them.'

'When you're up and about,' Nani amends.

I nod eagerly. Of course I want them. 'So what happened then?'

Mehreen's wedding came and went. Ahmed had his passport stolen in Berlin and wasn't allowed onto his flight. 'Excuses, excuses,' said Yasmeen, and refused to speak to him when he called. They thought that she was being difficult. They thought that when he came she would relent. They never thought that all summer long she had been listening to the rumours, that she'd heard Ahmed had left her and he planned to stay away. They never guessed that a little bird had been whispering in her ear. Ahmed's travelling companions were women, wrote Mustapha. He had planned it that way to assure her comfort, but now they surely were assuring his. They'd explored Venice by gondola and spent an evening at Moulin Rouge. They'd eaten hashish brownies in Amsterdam, and after that, well, heaven knows. He didn't want to be the one to have to tell her, but since she'd asked, yes, both of them were pretty and he'd heard the blonde one was rather fast.

When Ahmed did come, Yasmeen refused to see him. She refused to meet the backpackers he brought with him, partners, she would have learned had she agreed to listen, in life as well as travel. His mother came to see her and she pretended she wasn't home. 'He won't get off that easily,' she muttered. 'He can't make her do his dirty work.' No one realized the presence of the women in the city had convinced her he had come to break things off. No one stumbled upon the letters from Mustapha until it was much too late.

'A few days after Ahmed got back, we found her curled up in bed, refusing to move or speak,' says Nani.

'She stayed like that for a good eight, nine weeks,' Mehreen Khala tells me.

'Sixty-seven days,' Nani whispers.

'What was wrong with her?'

'Nothing, so far as the doctors could tell, useless fellows that they were.'

'She was depressed,' Mehreen says. 'She couldn't face the thought of life without Ahmed.'

'She was broken,' Nani insists. 'You weren't here, darling. You didn't see how weak she was. Rashida had to carry her to the washroom by the end. She couldn't even stand.'

'Didn't he come to see her?' I ask.

'Salim wouldn't let him in. He blamed him for Yasi's falling sick. That boy used to stand outside the gate and make such a commotion, but Yasi didn't even blink. She never once asked us to let him in.'

'Do you think she even heard?' I ask, angry, but not quite sure at whom. 'And if she did, wouldn't she have been too out of it to care?'

'It's likely.'

'It might have made things even worse,' Mehreen Khala says gently. 'You must remember she was convinced he had come to break things off.'

'So then what happened?'

'So then Ahmed had to go for his degree. His khala told me much later that he never even knew Yasmeen was ill. He just thought she was being stubborn and would get over it in time.'

'When did she?'

'It was a few months after Changez was born. He was trying to eat the wire of a lamp, silly chap. Yasi jumped up and saved him.'

'And what a lecture she gave poor Aamir,' Mehreen Khala exclaims. 'Going on and on about how he almost let his son fry half his brain cells.'

'And just like that she was fine?'

'Just like that.'

My mother spent several weeks recuperating physically and then announced her intention to continue her studies in America. Funnily enough, it was because of Ahmed that she was able to do so. She had filled in the applications half-heartedly and never sent them off. It was Ahmed who did, with an American's belief that it is always best to keep one's options open. Only Crawford was persistent enough to have held her place for the winter term. They sent her off with no idea of all that would transpire once she was there. Had they guessed she and Ahmed were so inclined to vengeance they would never have let her go.

'What do you mean?' I ask, though I'm afraid I already know.

Both Nani and Mehreen Khala look uncomfortable. 'We're not sure who started it,' Nani says eventually, 'but once it started ...'

'They were untrue to each other,' says Mehreen Khala, which is the mildest way imaginable to put it. I've read the descriptions of the lovers and trysts, the lascivious behaviours. I've read their merciless depictions of what they have been doing with other people they do not love. All this while, I've imagined something terrible must have happened to inspire it. I've been wracking my mind for what could possibly be so horrendous it tore them forever apart. Nani was right: this is nothing like what I had imagined.

'Irenie?' she asks. 'Are you all right?'

I can't help myself: I begin to laugh. 'That's it?' I ask. 'It was just a misunderstanding? A *misunderstanding* is what broke them up?' They exchange a worried glance. I expect they've dreaded my finding out that my sainted mother was no such thing, but that I already knew. It's the basis of it all that shocks me: something so minor, so easily resolvable. Ahmed started it, I know. Under the not unreasonable impression that my mother had broken up with him, he sent her a letter in Crawford detailing a petty flirtation with a pretty classmate. She was quick as ever to respond. After that, each letter was an effort to outdo the other's transgressions until finally one proved undoable and their separation became their lives.

The day we first met I thought you were an angel. I thought that each breath you took turned the air sweeter, that each step you took was in a direction unexplored. I thought that when you spoke your words were empires, that when you danced the blueprint of the universe lingered in your steps. How could I have thought so simply of you: one who is ever so much more?

For some time now, James had been waiting for Irenie to ask questions. She'd been to see Shireen. Who knew what she had learnt? Who knew what she might ask? He wished he had a better story for her. He wished he had a fairy tale. Her mother would've found a way to weave a web of magic, but when Irenie asked about him and Yasmeen, all he could imagine saying was, in the end she had said yes.

James asked Yasmeen to marry him less than a year after they first officially became a couple

'You do know I'm in love with someone else?' she asked, not unkindly. 'And I always will be.'

It made sense now that he thought of it; that this beautiful young woman once rumoured so wild had settled placidly into domesticity with him. All the while he'd been falling in love with her, she had been kind but distant. She'd become a fundamental part of his existence without having really taken anything back. Now and again, she cajoled him into attending a dinner party or a cocktail hour, but other than that, she remained aloof from the life she shaped. He hadn't ever asked her why she was there, or what she was doing with him; he just accepted it as she became the central presence of his life. The fact was, he hadn't really thought much of Yasmeen beyond what she looked like in his dressing gown drinking tea on Sunday mornings while defacing the comics, how she sounded when she called out to him across a room, the sharp warmth of her elbows digging into him as she sprawled, for once unguarded, in sleep. That there was a Yasmeen beyond this hadn't occurred to him. He would occasionally overhear telephone conversations in a language he didn't understand, but he quickly pushed this to the back of his head. It disturbed him to consider that there might be a wholly different Yasmeen, a Yasmeen in a language he didn't know.

So when she told him she was in love with someone else, he simply filed it in the 'things about Yasmeen I'd rather not think about' folder at the back of his head. She might well be in love with someone else, but whoever he was, she certainly wasn't with him. For whatever reason, she was with James now, and perhaps if he asked again she would be forever.

So he did.

And she said yes.

Their wedding had been quick and quiet. Though it was preceded by a spate of increasingly frantic foreign-language telephone calls, the actual event was Yasmeen in a crimson cocktail dress he'd never seen before on a Saturday afternoon in the civil clerk's office. She asked her college roommate, Claire, to witness and he enlisted Faber. Faber seemed delighted they were getting married and Claire, though she didn't mention anything in his presence, seemed deeply surprised. She had known the man Yasmeen loved, he suspected.

They married in spring, a few months before the semester was over, and both had been far too busy to even think of a honeymoon trip. Over the next few months, he secretly scoured the travel pamphlets Yasmeen was in the peculiar habit of ordering. When he proposed the options he'd found, she surprised him by pulling two tickets to Islamabad from her night table.

'I had mine already, and I've been saving up for yours,' she said shyly. She had even scheduled a stopover in Thailand on the way back.

James did not tell her that his visions of honeymoon romance had not included a need for inoculations. 'What a surprise,' was all he said. He expected, of course, that the day would come when he'd have to go to Pakistan, to meet her family, to see her home, but he hadn't expected it would come so suddenly.

'It might take them some time to get used to the idea of you,' she warned. 'But once they get to know you I'm sure they'll love you.'

She was twenty-five. He was forty-three. She had assured him, though, that such age differences were fairly common in Pakistan. Her mother was fifteen years younger than her father, her brother was eight years his wife's senior. What would really be the problem was that she'd married a foreigner, a stranger, a man they had never met. Through the phone calls, apparently, she wrung their acceptance. It was now time to win their approval.

On the long flight overseas, the last of Yasmeen's defences collapsed. She was a terrible flyer, worse than him, but between her exhaustion, excitement, and very real terror they'd plunge into the sea, she opened up to him in a way she never had before. Almost as soon as they settled into their seats she began talking. She told him all about her family and her home, about the childhood she'd never before mentioned. By the time they touched down in Istanbul, their final layover in the two days of travel, he was exhausted. He fell into a dreamless sleep in their airport hotel, and awoke twelve hours later to find Yasmeen perched at the end of the bed, staring at him intently.

'What is it?' he'd asked, patting around for his glasses in a panic, only to find he hadn't taken them off. 'Have we missed the connection? Has there been a delay?'

She continued to evaluate him silently. The hairs on the back of his neck tingled, as he sensed something coming, something he'd much rather keep at bay.

'I want to tell you about Ahmed,' she said finally.

And so, in the few remaining hours at the hotel and over Iran and Afghanistan and across into Pakistan, he learned about Ahmed. The man she had loved. The man she still loved, whom she'd had to give up, who had given her up, but for the letters they wrote which, she warned, would continue. She thought she was doing him a favour telling him all this. He would have preferred never to have known. He was happy to love her, to have her there for him to love. He didn't need to know just why she couldn't love him too. He hoped some day Irenie would realize that not everything had to be a fairy tale.

12

*Late at nights, I admit to the impossibility of living outside
your shadow. It's the small things that do me in: a tartan scarf,
crème brûlée, the smell of burning tobacco. Everything I am,
everything I'll ever be, is because of who you are to me. And if
I'm honest, there's no other way I'd rather it be.*

On the eighth day, I wake up feeling almost fine. When I
sit up to test it, my head doesn't spin. Washing my hair
is exhausting though. No wonder my mother cut all of hers
off. I take out a pink patterned kameez, a hand-me-down from
Shamim, but then pause to regard the closet for a long moment.
There's cotton, lawn, khadi and silk, plain fabrics, fabrics printed
with abstracts, geometrics, stripes and florals. The only order is of
ownership: Shamim's clothes are on the right, my clothes, are to
the left. Over the course of the summer, I've acquired quite a few:
a sleeveless sussi one, a greenish silk one with a chunari dupatta,
an embroidered boutique one with a Nehru collar, a handful of
simple lawn ones to be worn with white, lace-trimmed shalwars.
It depresses me to think they will all be packed into a trunk
soon, layered with mothballs and tissue paper for the next time I
come back.

A few days after I arrived, Nani took me to the storeroom and
gave me the key to my mother's trunk. Most of it was saris, neat
as origami envelopes, but my mother's shalwar kameezes were
tucked away haphazardly, as though she didn't expect it would be

long till she returned. I was surprised to find a kurta that had been mine the last time I was here: an elaborately embroidered white thing I'd wanted to wear every day so my clothes would match my mother's. It seems so small to me, like clothing for a doll, but it fit just fine when I was nine. There was still a little blue stain on the collar from when Shamim tried to kill me with a pen. Even now, I don't know why she did it. It was towards the end of the last summer I spent here, the last summer I really was a child. By the following August, I cooked dinner every night. I shopped for school supplies myself and signed my own permission slips. I'd even taken myself to the dentist where I'd had my one last, obstinate baby tooth yanked out.

I'd left the kurta in the trunk but, at Nani's insistence, I'd carted out an armload of my mother's old summer suits, smelling even now of naphthalene and old perfume. All summer they've been hanging in the closet. I take out one now, a simple eggshell cotton with fine stripes of gold and red, and hold it to my chest. It will be too short, but this summer short kameezes are the style. My mother's frame was smaller, but I've lost a lot of weight this week.

I braid my hair up neatly; run a stick of kajal along the bottom of my eyelids, put my glasses in my pocket. I screw on the thick-posted earrings Nani gave just before I fell sick and spend several minutes trying to arrange my dupatta so it won't slip off when I walk. By the time I'm through, it's later than I expect. The whole family is already gathered downstairs for lunch. Silence falls when I step into the room.

'So glad to see you're feeling better, darling,' Nana finally says, his voice loud over the hush. Slowly, the family's stares fall away and a place is made for me to sit.

'Only khichdi and yogurt now, my dear,' Nani cautions. She cannot quite meet my eye. Shamim surprises me by slipping me small pieces of her parantha when she's sure Nani will not see.

'You look charming in that kameez,' Nani finally says. 'The spitting image of your mother at fifteen.'

For the first time, the comparison irritates me. I take out my glasses and put them on.

'Yasi favoured brighter colours,' Nana remarks. We all stop eating to stare. 'Irenie's tastes are far more sensible,' he continues mildly. 'In more than clothes, I hope.'

For a few moments, everyone is silent. Then we all begin to speak at once. I say I very much hope I will prove sensible in life. Nani says something about how bright colours don't match with as much and Mehreen Khala mutters something about them bleeding in the wash. Sairah Mumani goes off on a tangent about my mother dyeing her own chunari and wearing it for the first time in the rain. Nana returns to his rice, as though he hasn't just spoken of my mother for the first time since she died. The voice that finally triumphs is Shamim's, proclaiming that, speaking of sensible, thank god Nani has relented on the issue of Shezzie's wedding. Wouldn't it be nice if Irenie could come?

'She should just stay here,' Naaz chimes in. 'At least for the wedding. Irenie can't miss the wedding. You don't want to miss it, do you, Irenie?' I find that I do not. 'She can go to school with us!' Naaz gushes. 'Shamim's uniforms would fit. And if she likes it, she can stay forever!'

'Only children are inclined towards solipsism,' adds Shamim. 'Having a sibling of sorts would be beneficial to my development.'

I begin to wonder if my cousins have been planning this and, if so, for how long. 'The summer does seem to have flown by,' I say.

The table's focus then turns entirely to the possibility of my staying on. Even Nana seems enthused. 'I want to get to know my granddaughter,' he says with a shrug when he sees Nani eyeing him bemusedly after he offers his opinion on new, more girlish, curtains for the guestroom. Their excitement is contagious and I find myself losing track of my protests about school and Celeste. I forget that my father needs me and that I am Mrs Winterbourne's sole friend. When they ask if they should make arrangements I tell them, yes.

13

When you gave up on me, I was overcome with hatred. Every word that left your lips left me frustrated, every mention of you brought to mind all the terrible changes you had wrecked. Over time, all this resentment has faded. One must let go of ghosts. I now think I would not have bothered to feel so much and for so long if the love I feel for you was not so astronomical, so sacred.

The telephone ring caught James off-guard. He was putting the finishing touches on a syllabus for the new introductory-level course he would be teaching on antiquity next semester. He was trying to remember a particular aphorism of Menander's that he'd decided to use as an epigraph, something about diligent labour and despair, but all that came to mind was 'whom the gods love dies young', a maxim both irrelevant and aggravating, when the phone first began to ring. It had rung only a handful of times all summer: always wrong numbers or recordings except for Irenie's Sunday-morning phone calls, which James was fairly sure were made only at the insistence of his mother-in-law. Today was Wednesday. Now what was it? It was one of the first sentences students of ancient Greek were taught to read, perhaps pointedly. He whose labour is diligent? He who does not despair? With the telephone, he could barely think.

'Yes, hello?' he snapped, picking it up on what must have been the sixteenth ring. It had been weeks since their telephonic tormentor had phoned (James theorized it was a schoolboy aware Irenie was out of town), but who else would wait sixteen rings?

'James darling, is that you?' His mother-in-law. Only Tehmina Khalil would call him darling.

'Yes, TM, it's me.'

'I'm calling about Irenie,' she bellowed, somehow sounding refined even through the static.

James's heart rose to his throat. Irenie had been too ill to come to the phone last week. Just food poisoning, they'd assured him, she would call as soon as she was well. At first he thought she was avoiding him again, but she seemed to have forgiven him after their chat the week before, at least for the ticket. She was too polite to skirt his calls for no reason at all. 'Is she all right?' he asked, trying to sound composed. She'd been taken to the hospital. She'd died quietly in her sleep. How could you have let her go? James raged silently at himself.

'Oh she's fine,' TM assured, 'much better. She wants to stay on here is all.'

'Stay on?'

'Yes,' his mother-in-law continued vaguely. 'Shireen's daughter is getting married in September and all the girls are very keen on attending the wedding. We'll enrol her at the girls' school, of course, so her studies wouldn't suffer.'

'But when would she come back?' James asked. If they were enrolling her in school, it wasn't likely to be soon. Most definitely not next week, when he'd expected to have her home.

'Whenever she likes.' TM sounded uncomfortable. Maybe Irenie would never like. Maybe she would never even like to visit. James felt his daughter slipping away into the convoluted bureaucracies of third-world telephone connections and international airline travel.

'But she's sick,' he blurted.

'She's much better, really,' TM told him patiently. 'And now that she's won her first bout with stomach upset I'm sure she'll be more immune. Amazing isn't it, how quickly children adjust?'

But I don't want her to adjust, James thought miserably. He missed her quiet pattering about the house, her silent stares, the phone ringing off the hook. He missed her, the embodiment of all his failures though she might be, the glaring ghost of dead Yasmeen; he hadn't known how much worse it would be once he was all alone. 'It's what she wants?' he sighed.

'Perhaps the two of you should speak.' James could almost see his daughter's arms signalling no no no.

'Hello,' he heard her say. To his surprise, she sounded sheepish, even guilty.

'Irenie! How are you feeling? TM said you were terribly ill.'

'It was nothing. I'm fine. Really.' Long pause. 'So TM told you?'

'She said you were thinking of staying on …'

'If that's okay? Just for a while? To see how it goes?'

No! James wanted to shout. Come back! You are all I have and I swear I will do better. But he hadn't the right. Had he? All her life, he just sat aside and waited until the time was right and it never had been. Now perhaps it never would be. 'It's up to you, Irenie,' he said, hoping she would hear the hesitation in his voice.

'Are you sure? Will you be all right?'

He'd be fine, he assured her with false cheer. He was a grown man, after all. When they hung up, he went to her room to return the stacks of unworn clothes to their carrier bags. He found he couldn't do it. Why was it always so difficult for him to say what he meant? Cleaning his glasses on the hem of his unironed shirt, he returned to work. All at once the adage he'd been looking for came into his head: 'He who labours diligently need never despair; for all things are accomplished by diligence and labour.'

Rubbish, James thought. But he typed it across the top of the syllabus anyway.

14

*I miss you most on summer nights. I miss seeing your smile. I
miss the cadence of your sigh and even the way you roll your
eyes.*

Two weeks after my visit to Baby Tamasha's, Nani wakes me
up at seven in the morning to tell me I have a phone call. 'It's
Baby,' she whispers. 'She says it's imperative you speak.' She shakes
her head and grins.

The diary! I think. She's found it! Much to Nani's amusement,
I leap out of bed and sprint for the phone. Baby apologizes
profusely for waking me and I lie profusely about when I generally
get up. 'Irenie,' she says in a whisper, 'look around you. Tell me, is
your nani there?'

I scan the foyer and see no sign of her. She must have gone
back to the lounge.

'Are you certain?' whispers Baby, when I report as much.

I tell her I am.

'I had a most interesting visitor last night,' she whispers. 'A
young man by the name of Firdaus.' She pauses to let the gravity
of this sink in. It doesn't.

'Firdaus?' I ask.

'Ahmed's son, Irenie. The younger one!'

'Do you know him?'

'Of course I know him! He was asking all kinds of questions.
The same sort of questions you were asking. About the past.'

'Well, it's only natural he should wonder …'

'But not only about the past. He was asking about you!'

'About me?'

'If I'd met you, what you're like, do you seem happy? All manner of questions.'

'But why, Baby Auntie?' I scan my surroundings again and lower my voice. 'Why would he ask about me?'

'I think,' she says triumphantly, 'the boy must be in love. He asked about your well-being several times.'

I try to persuade her that this is absurd. He's very good looking, she assures me, as though this is the issue. He looks almost exactly like his father did when he was sixteen. And so sweet, he is. So polite. When I can get a word in, I ask if she's found the diary. 'Oh yes,' she says dismissively, 'I'll have Liaqat drop it by.'

'Could he drop it to Shireen Amin's?' I ask quickly. The other day Nana overheard Naaz, Shamim and me discussing what might have happened during the summer of 1984 when Ahmed allegedly ran away to be with my mother. Our grandfather had glared at us most ferociously. Young girls like us, he said, should have more productive things to do than dwell on the past. I can only imagine what he'd have to say if he saw the diary.

Baby Tamasha agrees; it's closer anyway. She launches back into her description of Firdaus Kakkezai then and it's almost eight before I get off the phone.

When I arrive at Shireen Khala's, ten minutes early if nearly two weeks late, the diary is waiting for me. 'Reen bibi?' the maid asks when she opens the door. I nod and she passes me a parcel wrapped in white tissue. When she goes to locate Shireen Khala, I quickly tear the paper off and tuck it into a bangle box. The diary falls open to a centre page. I see that the paper is pink and faintly perfumed; the handwriting rounded and bubbly. I flip through the slim volume thinking there must be some mistake, but each page is the same, covered in handwriting most definitely not my mother's. I turn to the first page and there it is, the owner's name: Mehrunissa Shabaz.

The maid is back, telling me to follow her. I tuck the diary hastily into my shoulder bag, though given the discord of the formerly tidy house I doubt anyone would notice me carrying it around. Fabric is strewn over the floor, shiny sleeves of bangles are stacked on every surface, and tuberoses liberally punctuate the clutter. Wedding preparations, I guess.

'Ami!' I hear a yell. 'I know what you're up to. I can smell you!' Shezzie. She sounds as I remember.

'Don't be silly, jaani,' comes Shireen Khala's muffled response. 'I'm just fixing this thing.'

'Ami, please open the door. Mariam Auntie is coming for the samples. She'll call off the whole thing if she finds you in this state.'

I look back to the maid for further instruction—Gracie, I think. Gracie giggles, shrugs. Such scenes are routine in a wedding house. I shrug back and head upstairs. Shezzie has abandoned her formal, filial politeness and is banging on her mother's washroom door. 'Ami,' she yowls. 'Now!' She tinkers at the doorknob with what appears to be a fruit knife. Just as I tap her on the shoulder to say hello, her efforts succeed and the washroom door swings open. Standing on the toilet seat with her head half out the window and what appears to be a joint just falling from her fingertips is Shireen Khala.

'Uff, that dal we had for lunch has really given me gas,' she says, not sounding in the least bit guilty. 'I was just trying to air the loo out a bit, achha?'

'Really, Ami, is now any time to behave like Pablo Escobar?'

'Please, darling, don't say such things. What will Irenie think of me after she's listened to these lies?'

'Irenie!' Shezzie cries, noticing me, apparently, for the first time. 'I'm so happy you've finally come!' She hugs me enthusiastically, then holds my chin in her hand as though to assess the changes.

'Beautiful!' she pronounces. 'Ami's being impossible. All day she's been running around and now she goes and does this right before my mother-in-law is coming.'

'Never mind, sweetie,' Shireen Khala soothes, 'we'll just offer her a special-type pastry and she'll calm down quick and fast like. Oh …' Her eyes grow wide. 'Do we still have those almond ones?'

I can't help but laugh at this. Neither, it seems, can Shezzie. 'You're a lost cause, Ami. A lost cause, I tell you.' And, with that, the doorbell rings. 'Achha listen,' she whispers urgently, 'you people stay in here. I'll tell Mariam Auntie there's been an emergency. Someone's died. Harris Chacha. You've had to go for that.'

'Arre bhai, the poor man just died last month. Do we really have to kill him off again?'

'Fine then, Masood Uncle.'

'But he's still alive.'

'Haan, so? The man is ninety-seven. It'll be true soon enough.' Ignoring the shaking of her mother's head, Shezzie quietly closes the washroom door.

'What a funny girl,' Shireen Khala says fondly, attempting to rid the room of marijuana smoke by waving her chiffon dupatta. 'You must be thinking I've gone completely off my rocker.'

I manage a vague denial.

'Nothing matters.' She giggles, perhaps sensing my insincerity. 'Once you've reached a certain age, you can get away with anything you like. Like Baby Tamasha and those biscuits, isn't it?'

'Honestly, Ami,' Shezzie sighs, re-entering the scene just in time to catch her mother getting her dupatta tangled in the exhaust. 'Sometimes you're too much.'

'Mariam's gone already? So quickly?'

'She sent Altaf. I'll have to go over there later this evening. Adnan will pick me up.'

'No muss, no fuss,' her mother mutters. 'I must go for the lights! Oh god, I told the fellow no later than four. What's the time?'

'Ten past. But you can't go anywhere in this state.'

'This state, that state. Every day I'm in every state. And anyway, I'll take Aslam. Do you want to be left with only French Colony-type lights at your Mehndi?'

'Ami ...'

'Listen, darling,' Shireen Khala says, 'make Irenie have those almond pastries. So tasty they are. In no time I'll be back, you both can catch up. You do some chilling-shilling, haina? Isn't that what you young ones are calling it these days?'

'Chilling-shilling', it turns out, means categorizing the bangles by size and colour, arranging the tuberoses in a vase, folding up the fabric samples not sent off with Altaf.

'I'm so sorry about Ami,' Shezzie says. 'I don't know what's got into her.'

'I take it this isn't one of her usual habits?'

'Oh, it is ... Don't tell her I said that. But usually she doesn't just happily decide to do it in the middle of the afternoon. It's getting ridiculous. The other day Adnan sent over some laddoos for me to try and she finished all of them before I'd even had a bite. Two kilos of laddoos! I really don't know what's gone wrong with her—she likes Adnan. For a good fifteen years she's been telling me to marry him. And now I am, and this.'

'Fifteen years? But you're only twenty-one.'

'He's been following me around since primary school. Ami's always loved him. They start early. Speaking of which,' she looks at me slyly from under her long lashes, 'I had a call from Baby Tamasha this afternoon. She says there's a certain young man who is very keen to meet you and this certain young man will be at my wedding.'

'I'm sure it's nothing like that,' I mumble. To my relief, I'm spared further discussion by Shireen Khala's clamorous return. She is laden with United Bakery bags, strung top to tip with a complicated snarl of fairy lights. Her dupatta has got entangled in the wire and, as she struggles to free herself, cellophane sachets of masala-flavoured crisps escape loudly from her shopping bags. In her tow is a harried-looking young man, perfectly pressed and dressed but for a largish chunk of blue-black hair escaping from the well-mortared mass of his heavily gelled coiffure. He carries the trailing plug of the fairy lights.

'Shazia? Where are you?' he calls, looking blindly past the mess of fabrics, flowers and the two of us. 'Jaan, we have to talk.'

Shezzie pulls lightly at his trouser leg. He bends to extricate her from the mess.

'Samples,' Shireen Khala explains breathlessly, managing to shrug the whole tangle to the floor. 'I thought Shezzie should see.'

'I'm sure whatever you've selected is perfect, Auntie,' Adnan tells her. 'You must be Irenie,' he says, spotting me for the first time. 'Shazia's told me so much about you. She said you read *Black Beauty* by yourself when you were only six.'

I blush and mumble I don't remember, pleased Shezzie has told him about me.

'She did. It was so cute. The book was bigger than she was!'

'I had to read it for school when I was eleven and I needed a dictionary even then.' He smiles sheepishly. 'Mummy's been having kittens, I'm afraid,' he apologizes. 'She says none of the dyers can find exactly the right shade of blue for the piping on your sleeves. All day, she's been rushing around trying to find someone who can find a match and nothing. She's even been to Pindi.'

'Then leave the piping off?' Shezzie suggests.

'You try telling her that. She likes you. She's been driving me mad since the morning. Is it all right if I borrow Shazia for a bit, Auntie? Irenie? I know you must have a lot of catching up to do but this shouldn't take more than an hour.'

'Of course, of course,' we say. In truth, I'm eager to speak to Shireen Auntie anyway.

Once she's disentangled herself from the lights, she leads me back upstairs. We sit on her bed like schoolgirls. Outside, the skies have broken, and it is dark as daylight can be.

'Weather like this always reminds me of Yasi and Ahmed,' she says, proffering the masala chips. 'They both adored a good storm. I remember going over to your grandparents and finding them spinning around in circles outside even though the lightning was close. Completely mad, the two of them.' She chuckles affectionately. 'They were always up to something or the other. They got so bored when they were here. If you think Islamabad is a dead city now, you should have seen it back then. If you wanted to go shopping, you only went to Aabpara and no one ever got married here if they could avoid it. We used to rent a VCR on the weekends to see Western movies and we thought that was the height of enjoyment. I told you na, that Isfandiyar and I were married before Yasi left for the States?'

I nod.

'Well, it was the five of us then, in the summers. Yasi, Sairah, Isfandiyar, Ahmed and me. Aamir was always travelling and I think Sairah got lonely. Sometimes Mehreen also would come along, but she was always such a serious type. We would sit up together all night long. Your mother and Ahmed always told the most wonderful stories. But they used to get tired of just sitting each and every day. When the lights went, Sairah used to fold us fancy newspaper punkhas, but the effort of fanning our faces just made us feel hotter. "Chalo ji, let's go for a drive," Ahmed would say, sometimes at two in the morning. We would all pile into his car and he'd race up and down the Blue Area road. So fast he used to go, sometimes aimed at the presidency, sometimes towards Capital Park. Yasi and Sairah liked hanging half out the windows and they looked like such junglees when we came back, all their hair standing up and their faces bright red.

'When he thought things were becoming very boring, Ahmed used to make Yasmeen drive. What a terror that was. I can't even tell you how bad she was at driving a car. Did she learn properly?'

I shake my head, no. 'She always hated to drive.'

'Well, she loved driving then. Uff tauba, she was so bad. She used to take all the lanes and run down the flowers. And Ahmed, he was just shameless. He was always saying "go faster, go faster". Then, for no reason, he'd scream at her to stop and we'd all go flying. All of them, even Isfandiyar, thought driving with Yasi was great excitement, just like riding the swings at a funfair. It's a miracle she didn't kill the lot of us. She never even hit anything though, I don't think. Ahmed always grabbed the wheel just before it was too late.'

Shireen Khala is decades away, flying fast through the night with a car full mostly of ghosts. She grips the edge of the coffee table; knuckles white as they must have been.

'Once, Yasi persuaded us to sneak into Islamabad Club at night so we could go for a swim. What a sight we were when the chowkidar came and caught us. We were so wet and slippery we couldn't climb back over the gate and the poor man had to unlock it in the pitch dark. By the end, even he was laughing though.

'Oh, oh, and this other time, Ahmed decided Islamabad was simply too hot so we drove all the way to Nathia Gullee at three in the morning. The roads were full of bandits then and he'd packed the boot full of Murree beer, so I was terrified we'd be thrown into jail, if not murdered and robbed. Your grandparents were so furious when we returned, but that didn't stop them; nothing ever did. We would never have guessed that before long all of it would end.' She shakes her head.

'Nani and Mehreen Khala told me what happened between them. A misunderstanding. All it would've taken to fix everything was for someone to say something.'

'Someone would've had to listen. They were never any good at that.'

'I suppose it makes sense. In a way, I knew the ending before I ever heard the story. It's how they always ended, my mother's stories.'

'Those stories seldom end in forever. It was wonderful and beautiful and they worshipped one another, but together, they were explosive.'

'It would be a different story if the ending wasn't sad.'

'But it wasn't,' she says, surprised. 'Your father was always a better match.'

'My father?'

'Your father. Why do you think your grandparents accepted the marriage, despite everything? He balanced Yasi out, calmed her down. When she and Ahmed were together, they were always delighted or furious or ecstatic or miserable. With James, especially after you were born, your mother seemed mostly content. It may sound boring, but they got along well. They enjoyed the silences they shared. The sort of love that inspires romances is not necessarily conducive to the sort of life one wants to live.'

'I'd never thought of it like that.'

She nods sagely and bites into a crisp. 'Maybe it's time you re-evaluate where the story ends.'

15

*Our lives are litanies of loss. I cannot even begin to tally up
all the things we've lost. But what I have been able to deduce
is that all this loss does not even begin to pay for our crimes.
We have forgiven each other, but I often fear there will be no
absolution, no way to cleanse our souls of all this grime.*

The woman in the coffee-coloured sari eyes me through the
melee. A dozen dancing girls sway sequined between us, but
it's me who catches her eye. Shararas and lenghas sparkle over
the stage, pallus shimmer, light chiffon held to earth, it seems, by
nothing more than the bands of dense embroidery metallic at their
ends. '*Mehndi hai rachnewali*', hennaed hands, '*haathoon mein gehri
laali*'. Graceful swoops. The girls have practised for days. Tonight,
they are perfect. Dupattas do not slip and hair somehow evades
the eyes. '*Gaaye maiya aur masi, gaaye behna aur bhabhi.*' Shireen
Khala claps, entranced. This song she's sung along to at so many
weddings is different at her daughter's. On the dais behind the
dancers, Shezzie is perfect as a painting. Bridal make-up makes
ugly girls attractive and beautiful ones someone else. You see it's
her only when she smiles, which she does often, quite in violation
of the solemnity expected of young brides. Adnan grins beside
her. Their wrists, his left, her right, disappear in whorls of red and
gold. With rings and mehndi and red nails, what Adnan holds
entangled in his wife's dupatta is more an idealized simulacrum
of a hand than the limb itself. All morning long, hopeful girls

laboured over it, smoothing and painting the palm that would soon be held tightly by a husband's. Perhaps they drew their dreams into her skin. Perhaps they pictured rings slipped forever onto their own acetone-stained digits as they perfected hers for the close-ups that might some day grace her bedroom wall. Does her palm sweat underneath all its adornments now? Are his fingers rough and dry?

'*Tere mann ko, jeevan ko, nayi khushiyaan milnewaali hain*', the dancers forecast in arabesques. The woman in the coffee-coloured sari is still watching me. She knows exactly who I am. And because I have read her diary, I know exactly who she is too.

I search her gaze for hostility, but find none. She doesn't watch with curiosity or alarm. She stands alone, her sons nowhere in sight, and watches me impartially, as one might a mountain range or an ancient oak that's entered into one's line of sight. I am simply a thing across the room to her, an object on which her eyes are affixed.

The second dance is to a song I've never heard. It's rather popular; Naaz and Shamim clap enthusiastically to either side. The woman in the coffee-coloured sari claps too, perfectly in tune, yet she continues to look at me. All these weeks I've been so eager to meet her and now I can't recall what I thought I'd say. I find I am assailed by guilt, or something resembling it, and try to avoid thinking of why that might be.

I sit up straight on the cushions, legs folded like my cousins'. I count the gold and green glass bangles running up my arm again and run my fingers over the scratch made by the twenty-eighth when I broke it careering out of the car. The heels they've put me in are far too high. The kameez is tighter than I'd like, the underside of the embroidery scratchy on my skin. The girls around me are graceful on their sparkling stilts; their wedding clothes sit just right. Their hair hangs long, undisturbed by static or humidity. On their arms bangles hardly make a sound. Their jewellery does not jangle and their heavy earrings seem to pull less painfully than mine. I feel an imposter in their midst. It is the same at my cousins' school. I know I do not fit.

Does the woman in the coffee-coloured sari see this as she stares? Does she know my feet are cold, my torso hot, my earlobes ready to fall off? Does she know I am not clapping because my hands would be out of tune? Does she know my very presence here is similarly out of tune? Surely she, of all people, knows exactly how it feels. The room seems not to touch her. It's odd her eyes touch me. And yet, if not for her, I might not even exist.

On a pleasant summer evening, the first Friday of June 1983, the woman in the coffee-coloured sari made a decision. It would not have been a decision she entered into lightly, for no one who grows up to wear saris so well starched is ever that impulsive. She would have carefully considered both the pros and cons before determining to act. And once she was determined, the preparations would have been intense. There would have been trips to boutiques, appointments booked long in advance at spas, shades of lipstick selected and discarded by the score. An air of intrigue would have entered her relationships, an almost imperceptible sense of secrecy setting her apart. Conversations would have taken on subtleties only she was able to detect. By the time she acted on her decision, she would have been so intent on it that it wouldn't have occurred to her it wasn't right. She couldn't have known that a thing so small and simple would set so many lives awry. She wouldn't have anticipated her father's outrage, her mother's stroke, and the years of embittered reticence that would henceforth characterize her life.

Eighteen years ago, the woman in the coffee-coloured sari was a lovelorn college student named Mehrunissa Shabaz. For months, she had been engaged in a benign flirtation with her father's new intern, an architecture student by the name of Ahmed Kakkezai. Ahmed was only twenty-four, five years older than Mehrunissa, but to her he seemed far worldlier than any of the silly young men she was beginning to be introduced to at parties and weddings. When he spoke to her, he looked her in the eye rather than letting his gaze run lazily over her body and on to prettier girls across the room. He discussed her plans for the future with her as though there were anything more to plan for than a parentally approved marriage and a handful of children. Sometimes he winked and called her little one when he caught her drifting off during conversations she felt were rather dry. Mehrunissa loved him with all her heart.

The problem was that Ahmed did not love Mehrunissa. Sure, they bantered wittily about this or that and Ahmed sometimes teasingly exclaimed over how pretty she was, but he didn't see her the way he did the ever-changing older girls always at his side. It broke her heart to see him out in the evening with dressed-up girls, so confident in the hold they ever-so-briefly had. Those skinny twits didn't understand him, Mehrunissa felt. There was something tragic about Ahmed, a sense that beneath all the charm a crack ran through his soul. And Mehrunissa planned to fix it. Only she was equipped to understand the intricacies of his mind. Only she could love him for who he really was.

Which is how she arrived at the decision that would change so many lives.

It was at a garden party in Knightsbridge that it happened. Delicate paper lanterns from Japan twinkled between the trees and uniformed servers circulated with trays of crystal-stemmed champagne that Mehrunissa was not supposed to touch. She was wearing her first sari that night: turquoise silk with dainty silver borders and an elaborate blouse that chafed beneath her arms. She was afraid the pleats her mother had proudly tucked into place might come undone if she moved too much, so she stood quietly in a corner, taking quick nips of champagne when her father had his back turned. She hadn't been invited to this party; it was her mother who'd meant to come, but at the last minute Mumtaz developed a splitting headache and suggested Omar take their daughter in her stead. After all, they hardly knew the hostess, a client of Omar's celebrating the completion of an exhibition space he'd designed for her somewhere by the Thames. Knowing that Ahmed would be there, Mehrunissa was delighted to comply.

All through cocktails, she watched him circulate, each minute surer of her decision. Men's faces softened when they spoke to him and women crumbled into fluff. Invisible electricity issued from his pores. He was more magnetic than she'd ever seen him, winning over stiff-lipped attendees with just a look. There was something faintly frenzied to his charm that night, she thought; as though he was desperately fighting some grave sorrow that threatened to overwhelm him. Much later, she would learn he'd just had an upsetting letter from Yasmeen, which he'd carried in his pocket all night long. Mustapha had visited again, my mother wrote, and this time she gave him what he always wanted. Mehrunissa would eventually recognize the peculiar cast Ahmed's face took when he couldn't keep Yasmeen out of his mind; she would learn to hate him when it did and, eventually, even when it didn't. That evening, however, she was overcome with love. Many times, she considered placing her hand gently on his arm in reassurance, but there was always someone else there by the time she decided her sari was secure enough for her to move. Now and again, Omar materialized by her side to tell her she was doing wonderfully. Ahmed didn't look her way at all. It wasn't until she was seated next to him at dinner that he noticed she was there.

'Mehrunissa!' he'd exclaimed, surprised. She loved the sound of her name from his mouth. 'How are you, little one?'

'I'm not a little one,' she told him coquettishly. She'd perfected the tone to such a degree that in later years Ahmed would expend pages upon pages trying to explain to my mother just what it was in her voice that night that made him do what he did. He knew she had a crush on him, he knew it would be wise to stay away, but for some reason he did not. Absently, he lavished her with the attention she'd long dreamed of, the sort he paid to all the girls that came and went. He teased her when she cut her meat into pieces too tiny for a bird and gallantly retrieved her napkin the many times it fell. Once, Mehrunissa thought she felt his knuckle graze the ankle she'd meticulously managed to extricate from the yards of cloth beneath her chair. Her father, slightly drunk, conversed quite obliviously with a yellow-toothed horsewoman across the table.

'It's so good of you to entertain her,' he said to Ahmed several times.

They discussed mutual acquaintances and the films they'd recently been to see. He made her laugh with tales of contrary clients and she forgot her shoes were quite a bit too tight. As dinner table talk crescendoed around them, it ceased to matter what they said. Ahmed had had more than a little too much to drink, but Mehrunissa didn't care. It was enough for her just that he was there. Dessert was not yet underway when the call came from Mumtaz. Her headache had worsened and she wanted her husband to come home.

'Let the little one stay for sweets,' Ahmed pleaded on Mehrunissa's behalf. The way he pronounced 'little one' this time didn't sound like he was speaking of a child.

'Please, Papa, please,' Mehrunissa begged. After cakes there would be dancing; Ahmed might want to dance with her. And after that, a tour of the new building had been promised to any of the guests who'd like to go. Which Mehrunissa would. She wanted to go anywhere with Ahmed, everywhere, see anything in which he'd ever had a hand. 'Oh do let me stay and see what you designed, Papa,' she wheedled, knowing well that appeals to her father's vanity very seldom failed. In minutes, she had her father kissed, khuda hafiz-ed, and seen smartly to the door. She sat alone with Ahmed, sipping from his wine glass as they waited for the sweet.

Dessert that night was a splendid affair: a magnificent cake with custard, cream and berries. Mehrunissa, if her account of that evening is to be believed, fed Ahmed sugared strawberries and sucked raspberries from his fingertips. The South Asian surreptitiousness she'd developed in her adolescence overseas had rendered her perpetually paranoid, though not enough to prevent her from doing exactly as she pleased. Pressed to Ahmed's chest in only the semblance of a dance, she worried word would somehow get back to her father. When the hostess's sister appeared in a crumbling pair of tap shoes and received a standing ovation for her interpretation of 'O Sole Mio', it occurred to Mehrunissa that the guests were all too drunk to pay her or Ahmed any mind. She let him lead her from the courtyard, down a stairwell, through a passage, to a tiny grove of cherry trees still in fading bloom. In the moonlight, the dying blossoms on the ground looked snow-bright and fresh. They spun slowly through the shadows, his hands tracing paisleys down her back. When he slid them to the bare skin at her waist, she shivered although she wasn't cold. Ahmed held her tighter, humming bars of a song she didn't know. Silently they swayed to this. If music still played somewhere, Mehrunissa didn't hear. She heard nothing but the measured beats of his heart, the vibration notes made as they left his chest. The sari unwound itself, slipping from her body to carpet their rather graceless dance. She ran her fingers through his hair and whispered that she loved him. Only years later would she learn he hadn't heard.

So lost was Mehrunissa in the scent of Ahmed's neck that she didn't even notice the rest of the party had slipped away. When she looked up from his kiss, there was no one left. Another girl might have worried, but Mehrunissa made a decision that had been brewing for many months. She saw it through on a sofa, in a guestroom, at a party where there was no one she knew.

Three weeks later, it occurred to her there might have been an outcome for which she wasn't prepared. Six more and she was sure. Within a month, she found herself married. Within two, she realized she'd made a terrible mistake. Her mother's chronic headaches proved precursors to a debilitating stroke. Her father refused to look her in the face for several years. The husband she'd so sought was seldom home. She swelled into a small elephant, learning how to pin a diaper on her mother. Nine months later, there were two mouths to wipe, two bottoms to clean, two bodies to give baths. Across an ocean, a woman she hadn't ever heard of wept and wept.

The woman in the coffee-coloured sari is one of the first to reach the buffet. 'That's her there, did you see?' Shamim and Naaz poke and nudge. They're more excited than I am. Nani has been sitting imperiously upon a chaise by the stage since we arrived, the two of them ferrying titbits of information to and fro across the room: Mehrunissa's sons are nowhere in sight, her sari is silk chiffon, she's going back to England on Tuesday night.

'Can you believe the sari she's wearing?' Naaz asks in an attempt at what I see is the support she thinks I need. 'It looks like she's just arrived by post. First class. No smudge, no string, just stamps.'

'Yasi Khala was much prettier,' Shamim adds.

That much is true. But I realize I like how she's dressed, benarsi beige and crisp. 'Shamim was right. It's not her fault, what happened,' I say softly.

Naaz looks at me aghast. 'How can you say it's not her fault?' she demands. 'You heard what she did to your mother, and to Ahmed, and even to her own family. You read the diary. It sounds like she had it all planned out.'

Nani railed on about the immeasurable evil of Mehrunissa Shabaz all the way to Chak Shehzad. Mehrunissa Shabaz got her claws into Ahmed and wouldn't let go. Mehrunissa Shabaz caused Ahmed's death and my own mother's as well. Mehrunissa Shabaz all but murdered her mother and then drove her father insane. There were droughts in Bangladesh and floods in the Punjab because of Mehrunissa Shabaz.

'Look at her,' I say when we've settled in a corner away from eager ears. 'No, look properly.'

'She looks like any other auntie to me,' shrugs Shamim, stealing a piece of naan off of my plate.

'Exactly. She was just a stupid little girl who fell in love with the wrong man.' As much as I hate to admit this, even to myself, it's recently occurred to me that it's true. Mehrunissa became incredibly spiteful as time went by, certainly, but she didn't start off that way. For a while at least, she really did love Ahmed. For a while, she truly wished to make him happy. And how many mocking letters did he write, belittling her attempts to win him over? How many times did he tell my mother it pained him to see her face every morning when he awoke? Mehrunissa never had a chance.

Your bhel puri bride, my mother called her: a cheap snack, picked up thoughtlessly on the street, that never stood in for a meal.

'But look how she behaved,' Naaz reminds me. 'Look how much suffering she caused. Ugh, what an ugly name it is, even: Mehrunissa.'

Coming as they did from a culture so predisposed to nicknames, I had thought it strange that Ahmed never shortened his wife's name in his letters. Yasmeen was Yasi, Shireen was Reenie, Sairah, somehow, Sissy, but Mehrunissa was always spelt out in full, four syllables, ten letters, finger strokes all across the keyboard even when Ahmed was so ill. She never became Mehr, Nissa, Mehroo, or even shorthand MN. The woman Ahmed married was not easily abbreviated, I thought. Then, just this morning, I learned what it is Mehrunissa means: benevolent.

'Why should I be Mehrunissa to Mehrunissa when the woman has never in her life been as such to anyone else?' Nani snapped when Sairah Mumani suggested it was time to let old grudges die.

It struck me then that Ahmed typed out all ten letters of his wife's name with irony, each time intending it to be a bitter curse. Benevolence was not at play when circumstance stuck him with her; she exhibited none when she realized he felt he was stuck. I

refold my napkin and picture the letter where he told my mother
about Mehrunissa, the one that broke her heart and mine.

I have read that letter so many times I know it by heart. Even
if I never get the box back, I think I'll remember it until I die.
Before me, my mother must have read it a great many times. It's
crumpled at the edges, smudged with fingerprints. When they
fell, my tears ran where someone else's used to fall. The letter is
a transmutable epiphany extending across space and time and
person. To me, it is the precise moment at which I finally grasped
that my mother existed in a capacity quite beyond what she was
to me made manifest in paper. Alarming as the explicitness of
earlier letters was, the magnitude of circumstance was lost on
me until this one. Believing my mother once had an epistolary
affair was somehow less disquieting than realizing that she loved
a man I can't even recall her having mentioned. I've perused the
letter time and time again, as though it might be a key, as though
the ancient scrap of stationary that unravelled my present might
magically ravel it back up. It gives me an uncomfortable feeling in
my stomach—something between guilt and grief and succour—to
feel my existence each time undone by the same letter that undid
my mother's.

I considered putting away the box for good after I read this
letter, but of course I couldn't. I came back to it after two bristling
weeks of abstinence to find that, for months, their correspondence
had halted altogether. My mother did not even acknowledge that
she'd received his letter. It seems whatever she was feeling then
will be unknown to me forever. That winter, she elected to stay
in America, perhaps to permit herself a greater spectrum of self-
destructivity than would have been possible in Pakistan, perhaps
just to avoid the sympathy, the spite, the eternal all-knowing
glances she'd indubitably be subject to back home.

In March, a birth announcement came: Baby Boy Kakkezai,
Khuram; 8 pounds eleven ounces, 22 inches, black hair, black
eyes, brown face. My mother didn't respond. That summer, she

stayed in America again, conducting some mysterious manner of 'research' for her dissertation. Her letters home were vague, brief notes about the weather and what she'd had for dinner. The family worried, but there was very little they could do. Neither they nor she mentioned Ahmed's marriage, though by now there was little doubt she knew. Sairah Mumani, pregnant the third time around, planned a visit after her first ultrasound, but had to cancel when she lost the baby midway through June. In July, Ahmed wrote to say he was finding marriage hellish, his son never stopped crying, his in-laws hated him, and his wife was forever on his head: he planned to ask for a divorce. And, of course, that he loved Yasmeen as much as ever. Still, she did not respond.

Let me take a moment to remark that 1984 is a lost year of mother's: no one seems to have much idea how she spent it. There are no photographs, few letters and fewer first-person accounts. She quietly turned twenty-four during the first big snowfall of January, apparently without having received any cards she found worth keeping. Her academic records reveal that she did passably, her bank statements that she held some sort of part-time teaching job at Crawford and paid $115.65 each month in rent. In February, she had a cap placed on her left lateral incisor after it sustained an irreparable chip in an unspecified accident. In October, she was prescribed amoxicillin for a persistent sore throat. Also in October, she encountered my father for the first time, though there's no evidence he made an impression of any kind. If she had friends, I have found no sign of them. If she did anything of consequence, no record of it exists.

The one thing of interest that did happen in 1984 is that Ahmed left his wife. Twice. He left her for the first time on February seventeenth, coincidently the same day my mother was having a porcelain crown cemented into her smile by one Dr Melanie Sutcliff of 42 Essington Place, Crawford, New York. On the morning of the seventeenth, Ahmed kissed his very pregnant wife goodbye, boarded an express to Edinburgh, and spent several hours eating custard

creams and contemplating the frozen countryside. He disembarked
at Newcastle for a cigarette and never got back on. His balsam-
handled umbrella, the magazine he'd pilfered from a rack just
inside the dining car, and the gray Biltmore hat his father-in-law
had given him shortly before he impregnated Mehrunissa went on
across the border without him. Of these possessions, Ahmed most
regretted losing the magazine. He had been halfway through a very
interesting article on bioluminescence which he was never again
able to locate. The only person who ever found out he'd planned
to leave his wife that day was my mother, to whom he confessed
in an intensely melodramatic letter penned on the twenty-fourth
of September, 1989, which catalogued the multitude sins he'd
committed over the course of his thirty tumultuous years of life.

The second time Ahmed left his wife, it was a well-known
affair. Everyone from estranged third cousins in Muzaffarabad
to the sweepresses of sister-in-laws settled in Kuwait heard
what happened. I'd had no idea Ahmed left her a second time
until I came to Pakistan. When he did not receive a response
to the letter he sent my mother in July, Ahmed decided that his
marital difficulties would best be resolved if he were to take off
for America without a word. Hardly had his plane left Heathrow
when his father-in-law began to lose his mind. It started with
small things, like his inability to distinguish between an apple
and an orange, or his failure to comprehend why he should not
sunbathe in his own garden, attired in an old swimming costume
of his wife's, but it was not long before it accelerated. By the time
it occurred to Mehrunissa that her husband was gone, Omar was
already beginning to converse with traffic lights and urinate on
unsuspecting dogs. A good six days had passed by then, though,
to be fair, Ahmed often stayed late at the office and left for
university the next morning before anyone had yet awakened.
When Mehrunissa realized she couldn't remember the last time
she'd seen her husband, she panicked. It didn't take much digging
for her to figure out the most likely place he would have gone.

How exactly Yasmeen and Ahmed passed that week in August isn't known. There has been all manner of sordid speculation, of course, but no one has any idea what they did. Though it is assumed they were in Crawford the whole while, they might well have gone to Mexico or Canada for all anybody knows. Did they spend their time together arguing? Did they make plans to run away? Was my mother too deeply into one of her spates of sadness to even care Ahmed had finally come? There isn't anyone who knows. I like to imagine they were happy then, spectacularly, stupendously happy, but, realistically, how happy could they possibly have been on stolen time? All I have been able to confirm is that Ahmed flew into JFK, the airport closest to my mother, on the ninth of August, 1984. Less than a week later, he was gone.

When Mehrunissa finally got a hold of Ahmed, he was in Chicago with his parents. It seems he was reluctant to come home. His wife was financially solvent, after all, and classes didn't begin again for more than a month. He had his failing in-laws to consider, however, not to mention his unwanted wife and new-born son. The general consensus on the matter is that Ahmed's sense of responsibility would in time have prevailed of its own accord had his wife not launched so underhanded an attack.

The first thing Mehrunissa did when her husband delayed leaving the States was ransack his files. Amongst them, she found an old letter to Yasmeen about their night in Knightsbridge. Though the cherry blossoms were there, the turquoise sari, the dance beneath the stars, his account was nothing like the night she remembered.

Enraged, she dug deeper into Ahmed's filing cabinets and found months of explicit letters Yasmeen had sent, which he'd intended to destroy but hadn't. She packed a suitcase, booked a flight to St Tropez, and left baby Khuram with her parents. Shortly thereafter, Ahmed received a postcard addressed to 'Sister Fucker' to which was attached a particularly graphic letter from Yasmeen. 'Your father-in-law keeps trying to sprinkle your son

with salt and put him in the oven. I suggest you go attend to that,'
read the postcard in purple cursive. And that is how Mehrunissa's
benevolence became a bitter joke.

Whether or not Ahmed truly intended to leave Mehrunissa
for Yasmeen isn't known. Whether or not he and my mother took
up right where they'd left off that week cannot be confirmed. Even
that they saw each other then cannot be confirmed beyond the
shadow of a doubt. But when questions are asked about subjects
like these, just the asking is as damning as any imagined answers
could ever be. It was observed smugly, sadly, with the indifference
of crows to the particularities of crashes producing prime carrion,
that no one would marry Yasmeen now. When, seven months
later, she announced that she'd married an aging classics professor
by the name of James Eccles, it was not without a modicum of
relief that her family received the news.

Some years later, Mehrunissa hurled the diary she'd kept as an
adolescent at her returned husband's head during a particularly
nasty fight.

'This is what you threw away,' she'd screamed.

The diary's cover was purple plastic. Inside, the pages were
pastel, perfumed, adorned all over with dreamy Ahmed Kakkezais,
Mrs Ahmed Kakkezais, Mehrunissa Kakkezais. Amongst the
lazy doodles of daisies and azaleas was Mehrunissa's defloration
in no less than six shades of neon ink. Then comes Mehrunissa's
marriage, motherhood, her many attempts to make her husband
happy. It stops abruptly when she threw it at him; before he sent
it to my mother, he inscribed on the front page that it had left a
scar. My mother adds onto his emendations, sometimes writing
perhaps it was the best she could do, other times mocking Mehrunissa
too. From the varied inks and writing styles one can infer that
she and Ahmed sent this diary back and forth for several years: a
ripping joke even when they ran out of things to comment on and
were reduced to writing brief notes on the empty pages. At first,
I thought the whole thing amusing, like something Celeste and I

might do were we to find the diary of someone who had done us ill. Only upon seeing her has it occurred to me that the woman they were making fun of was Ahmed's wife. Only upon seeing her here in her coffee-coloured sari do I consider what it was they mocked. The sins of the mother, I think. This is the source of the unsettled feeling in my stomach, the patina of guilt settling over my skin. No, says a firm voice buried deep in my mind, not only that. You've borne hatred towards the poor woman too.

16

On days I feel that I will die only the thought of you can bring me comfort. All around me, everywhere, all I see is hurt. I wonder, would it be better if we just went now, faded from this world?

Shezzie's valima is held at the Marriott, 'a much more civilized avenue' sniffs Sairah Mumani.

She lost an earring somewhere along the unpaved driveway of Shireen Khala's uncle's house and seems determined no one forget.

'I thought it was rather charming,' Mehreen Khala says mildly. 'The garden looked lovely with those diyas burning everywhere.'

'Who has diyas at the height of summer? As if it isn't hot enough.'

'Really Sairah, it wasn't as though they held the function outside.'

I wonder if Mehreen Khala and my mother used to bicker like this. I wonder if Naaz, Shamim and I some day will. I'm suddenly sad at the thought of my father and me sitting in silence in the kitchen. I'm sadder still to think of him sitting there alone. Last week, we spoke for almost an hour. He told me about Irene, something he has never done. Would it be different now, I wonder, if I were to return?

'Reenie!' Sairah Mumani exclaims, catching sight of Shireen Khala. 'You look stunning darling, absolutely stunning.'

'I'm so glad you could come,' she says, dispensing kisses and compliments. 'Tehmina Auntie's still not well?' I suspect she knows just what provoked Nani's sudden weak spell at the function night before: an aging acquaintance attempted to introduce her to Mehrunissa Shabaz. Nani dropped her handbag on the floor and demanded to be taken home. She was dizzy, or so she'd said.

'Still reeling slightly.' Shamim smiles wickedly. Mehreen Khala gives her a warning look.

'Come, come,' Shireen Khala urges, 'Shezzie said to make sure she gets photos taken with all of you.'

On stage, the whole family poses behind a smiling Shezzie. The groom joins in, along with an assortment of unknown cousins. Cameras flash, digital and analog. My grin is growing weary when I see my cousins are no longer by my side. A tall boy in a dark suit has taken their place. I didn't notice him arrive. He's my age or a little older and wears the indeterminate look of an inveterate dreamer. Eventually he might be handsome, but for now he is too thin, too vague. There's something about him, however, that makes me take a second look.

'Hello,' he whispers.

'Hi,' I reply and immediately refocus on the camera, embarrassed I've been caught.

'Irenie, isn't it?' he whispers, as the photographer exhorts us, in the name of God, to smile.

I look up at him in surprise, provoking a grumble from the photographer. 'Faces in front, please,' he says. I turn around quickly, but it's one of the children to whom he's speaking, a little boy who's tried to climb up into Shezzie's lap. 'It's fine,' she tells him, 'I'm sure we have enough.'

'You're looking gorgeous, my love,' I hear Adnan say to her as the photo shoot disassembles. Even through her thick bridal make-up, I make out a pleased blush.

The boy lingers, perhaps waiting to congratulate the couple. There is something familiar about him, but I can't quite pin it

down. Is he someone I met on a visit long ago? He catches my eye
and nods pointedly to an enormous floral display towards the back
of the stage. I look around, but there is no one near me, no one
else for whom this gesture could have been meant. He nods again.

It is not curiosity that draws me to him, nor is it recognition
or even interest. It is more a sudden clarity that causes the rest of
the crowd to blur. My cousins making mischief with the mithai
are all at once invisible. I do not see Shireen Khala settle herself
on the stage again, no doubt attending to some imagined need,
or Aamir Maamu, taking advantage of his wife having been beset
by a woman I once heard her refer to as 'that appalling creature'
in order to slip out for a smoke. I do not notice Mehreen Khala
readjusting gladiolas not far from where I stand or the bride and
groom rising to form a new tableau. Even the woman in the
coffee-coloured sari, today in grey, is no longer in my sights.

'Firdaus? I ask the boy.

'We must talk,' he says, nodding. He surveys the sequinned
aunties all around as though they're spies for the KGB. 'But not
here.'

We slip out a side door and creep down a dimly lit corridor.
'Do you know where you're going?' I ask.

'I never do around here. Do you?'

I shrug. We proceed in silence until we come upon an empty
conference room. Without speaking a word, we seat ourselves in
executive chairs at either end of the oval table. He rests his chin
upon his hands and stares. 'You're just as I'd imagined,' he finally
says.

Why has he imagined me? Then he smiles and I see I have
imagined him as well. Since Shireen Khala gave me her box of old
photographs, I've pictured his face many times, for it is an almost
perfect embodiment of an image I've only seen as flat. In three
dimensions, it is somehow less vivid, an echo of the face I know.
Do my features seem hazy to him as well, I wonder, a smudged
copy of what he had expected?

'I'm sorry to stare. It's just that I've wanted to know you for so long.' He pauses to breathe in deeply and in that breath everything is clear. 'I owe you an apology—'

'It was you, wasn't it?'

He pauses again, examines his hands. 'I didn't mean to hang up. I wanted to talk to you. I really did.'

'Why didn't you?'

'I couldn't. Every time I heard your voice on the other end, all the things I wanted to say flew out of my head.'

'Because of that one time when I shouted? I'm sorry I did that.'

'No. No, of course not. I deserved it. I should have said hello right then. It's just so difficult to know where to begin.'

'To begin?' I lean forward.

'I'm sorry … no, that's not what I mean. Well, I do mean it and I am, but, okay,' another deep breath, 'you've read the letters, right?'

'You've read the letters?' I ask. 'But how?'

He shakes his head. 'When my father wasn't well he asked me to look out for your mother's name in the post. Yasmeen. If I saw it, I was to hide the letter and give it to him when my mother wasn't around.'

'He made you smuggle love letters for him?'

He looks uncomfortable. 'It's not as bad as it sounds.'

'But you were just a child.'

'At first, I didn't even know what they were. I just knew they made him happy, that he'd feel better when he got one. That was enough for me.'

I think of the box, of how I'd both loved and loathed its incursions into my childhood. I understand then why he did it, why he would've been happy to do it.

'It wasn't as though I was lying for him, exactly,' he continues defensively. 'I just liked to see him smile. I can't remember my parents ever being happy.'

'Just because you can't remember doesn't mean they weren't,' I say, not wanting to be any more complicit in the betrayals of

Mehrunissa Shabaz than I already am. I think of all the small, unlikely evidences of my parents' affection and hope that he is wrong. As I've come to see, there are lives uncontained by our parents' writings, lives where Ahmed Kakkezai and Mehrunissa Shabaz may once have shared some joy.

He sighs. 'It's not something of which I've ever seen evidence. As far as I can tell, my mother spent her entire adult life wavering between conflicting desires for love and vengeance. Not that it's her fault, really. Or my father's, even. Imagine, Irenie, my father was trapped with a woman he didn't love, didn't even particularly like. And my mother knew how he felt.'

'May I ask you something?'

'Of course.'

'If they were so unhappy together, why didn't they just end it?' Everyone's lives might have been so much easier, I do not say.

'Stubbornness, mostly. My mother was determined to make my father pay for never having loved her. He was determined to prove her accusations that he was a worthless father incorrect.'

'Stubbornness again ...'

'And, of course, there was your mother.'

'What do you mean there was my mother? If anything, wouldn't that have made a divorce more likely?'

He winces. 'I don't think my mother would have given my father one. At least not without a fight. She told him he'd never see us again if he left and he wasn't willing to take that risk. She'd rather have been miserable with him than have him be happy with your mother.'

'You must hate her, my mother.'

'No.' He makes a bridge of his fingers and looks thoughtful. His cuticles are ragged, his nails nibbled to the quick. 'I don't think it ever occurred to me to mind. The letters seemed a low price for my father's happiness. They were just letters, after all. And I wanted to be part of it: that small happiness. Any small happiness. I spoke to Baby Tamasha ...' He hesitates.

I feel a prick of tears behind my eyes for the boy he must have been. A clumsy child with battered knees and bony wrists peeking from the cuffs of blazers always outgrown, hoping for a part in a small happiness, any small happiness. A lonely boy with a sick father and an acrimonious mother. It seems he's keen to tell me something, though, so I force a smile. 'Jam-filled biscuits?'

He chuckles. 'Raspberry. Baby Tamasha told me that my father tried to convince your mother to leave your father. She refused, Irenie. She loved your father. Maybe not the way she did mine, but there was love nonetheless,' he says in a breath, confirming what so many people have now told me, what in my heart I've known. 'And I'm glad of it, really I am,' he goes on. 'I never quite succeeded in imagining you as happy, particularly not after what happened, but I've always hoped you were at least not unhappy.'

'Did you really spend so much time imagining me?' I laugh, distracted. When he said I was just as he imagined, I thought he meant only that I am like my mother in the way he is like his father.

'All of my childhood. Ever since the day we first spoke.'

'But you've never said anything. You always hang up without a word.'

'You don't remember,' he says flatly. 'There are things for which you can't apologize. I should have known.'

'What do you mean I don't remember?' I remember everything, every detail, every smile that was ever forced or false and every lie.

'Maybe it's better this way.'

'What's better this way?' I demand. 'What are you talking about?' A fissure is beginning to open somewhere deep and dark at the back of my brain. Some long-buried mental baggage is about to tumble out.

He leans back and rubs his temples. 'I'd thought an apology might make it better but I see now I've been selfish. Apologies help no one but those who offer them.'

'An apology for what?'

'The first time I was just a kid. I didn't know any better. But the second time, I knew. I knew what would happen and I wanted her to come.' He put his head down on the table.

'Who, Firdaus?' I get up and walk around it. 'Who did you want to come?'

'Please. Sit.' He offers me his chair as though there aren't twenty-seven more. I shake my head. 'It was selfish of me. I knew it even then. But I wanted her to fix him. I really thought she could.'

To my alarm, his eyes fill up with tears. 'My mother?'

He nods miserably. I sit down next to him and, as gently as I can, I ask him to tell me. 'Just begin where it begins.'

He rubs his eyes and breathes in deeply. 'Okay.' He nods his head. 'I should have kept my mouth shut but now that I haven't, it's only fair you know. So you know about the letter smuggling. I never asked what they were, but you must remember, I already almost knew. I'd spent my whole life hearing accusations fly between my parents. One day when I got to the hospital my mother was still there. This was unusual because she was usually gone by tea, if she'd been at all. Neither my mother nor Khuram could stand hospitals. Nanny used to bring me after school. My parents were arguing that day. We could hear them in the corridor. 'I have to tell her,' my father kept repeating. 'You most certainly do not,' my mother yelled. She came storming out before Nanny had time to declare the conversation inappropriate for my hearing. Nanny went after her, but she was so angry she didn't notice us.

'I begged to be allowed to visit my father despite the argument and, I guess because she felt bad for me, Nanny agreed. He was half out of his mind that day, senseless with painkillers and grief. "I have to tell her," he kept saying.'

'My mother?' I ask again.

He nods. 'It didn't take me very long to guess. "You have to tell her this is it," he whispered when I did. "Tell her I say goodbye." Then he closed his eyes.'

Firdaus closes his as well. I feel I ought to do or say something, but I don't know what. I don't know what to do with any of their history. 'I didn't understand why he wanted to say goodbye,' he murmurs. 'I didn't understand what was wrong, not really. I didn't even know how to make an international call until I interrogated Nanny. I just knew my mother hated yours. In the end, I think that is why I did it. I was furious with her for upsetting my father when he was sick, for visiting him only occasionally and not really ever looking at him when she did. So I called the next time she went out. You answered on the first ring.'

'I remember doing that—answering on the first ring.' I'd been afraid if my mother let the phone go unanswered, my father would think something was wrong. Or worse, that she'd answer and he'd know it was.

'Do you remember telling me your mother was busy? You said she couldn't be disturbed.'

'I don't know.' I remember telling any number of people my mother could not come to the phone. But do I remember telling him? Somehow, I think, somewhere, I do. 'Maybe.'

'I could tell you were about to hang up so I blurted it out. "Who says goodbye?" you asked, and so I told you. "Ahmed says goodbye," you repeated. "This is it." Then we both hung up. I regretted it immediately even though I didn't fully understand what I'd done until I was older.'

'What do you mean?' I ask. Ahmed says goodbye. The phrase is so familiar. Hearing it now, I know I have said it. I know saying it has been something I regret. *I'm sorry. It's all my fault.*

'I'm so sorry, Irenie. I overheard some aunties discussing it. They said it was because of you that she survived.'

I'm sorry. It's all my fault. I remember that my hands were cold. I remember how my knuckles had grown stiff. I hadn't remembered my voice though, hoarse from this refrain. All this time, I'd thought she'd been frightened by a ghost. 'That was why she did it, wasn't it? Because of what I said?'

'No, not because of you. Because of me. I'm sorry, I'm so sorry.' I look up at the boy before me, a boy who might be handsome. His even features are twisted with grief and guilt. I see now there are circles beneath his eyes, darker than any I've ever seen. His skin is pallid and he's thinner than a fast-growing teenage boy should be.

'No,' I say, louder than I intend. It comes out almost a shout. He recoils at the sound. 'No, it wasn't because of you.' I hold up my hand, sensing he's about to protest. 'Don't apologize. Don't you dare. It was a terrible thing to ask of a little boy.'

'It was a terrible burden to place upon a little girl. I didn't realize it back then. I didn't understand. It was what my father needed me to do, so I did it without a second thought.'

I understand, though I'd rather not. My mother needed me to lead her to the tub, to rinse her coffee mug with Listerine, to see dinner didn't scald. 'We were just collateral,' I tell him quietly. 'Nothing we could have done would have made things worse or better.'

He shakes his head. 'You don't understand. I may have been an innocent kid the first time, but the second time I'd seen what she could do. She made him better so I called again.'

'What are you talking about? When?'

'The first time he was sick.' He pauses, sensing my confusion. 'I was sure you knew.'

'How could she have made him better? She couldn't even make herself better. She was a mess. Well, you know what happened. After that, she was sent away weeks.'

'She went away.'

'No, my father sent her. I saw the hospital.' I saw him with Jo Anne.

'That may well be, but at some point she came to London. I was at the hospital when she turned up. I've never seen Mum so angry. She didn't want to let her in, but eventually she did. Only for a few minutes, mind you, but long enough that four years later I guess she felt they'd already had time enough to say goodbye. A few days later, Abbu started to get better. I thought your mother was an angel.'

'The angel of death, maybe,' I mutter, livid that she flew halfway around the world to be an angel for other people when I'd been so worried for her back at home. When we'd been so worried, I amend. She'd left my father too. He hadn't locked her in a jail cell somewhere and thrown away the key: She had been the one to leave.

He goes even paler. 'Maybe. I should've known better than to call. I should've known by then that they wouldn't go on apart. He was going to die that time. I didn't want to see it and because of that your mother is dead too.'

'Firdaus,' I say, seizing his shoulders. 'That is the stupidest thing I've ever heard. It was an accident.'

'Was it?' he asks, searching my face for some sign of knowledge, some confirmation of what it was they'd intended.

'Wasn't it?' I whisper.

'He knew what a terrible driver your mother was. Everyone knew. Even I knew.'

'Well, it isn't as though he was fit to drive. I'm sure she did her best, but she lost control of the car. It said so in the newspaper.'

'Do you really think so?' I've never seen an expression so earnest, a person so eager to embrace supposition as certain fact. I know now why he's wanted to meet me and what he's wanted me to say.

'It was raining. The roads were bad.'

'Then why didn't they turn back?'

We stand in silence, neither of us wanting to be the one to admit that they couldn't, they never could. And then the lights go out.

17

I tried to remember what it felt like before I loved you and I found I drew a blank. I swore to you I'd give it up and I promise you I tried. But it seems to me no matter what I do, I cannot erase you from my mind. I don't know when I'll see you now; I don't know if I will ever again. So I'll tell you now and mean it always: no matter where we are and what we do, I'll love you till I die.

'Archibald Crowe,' the name came unbidden to James as he sat down to his lunch: a tuna salad sandwich with mayonnaise and mango chutney. He would have preferred pickle relish, but it wasn't something they kept on hand. Yasmeen had had no use for uniquely American condiments; Irenie even less. He sometimes thought his daughter was more Yasmeen than Yasmeen had been. The collars she ironed never got scorched. The meals that she made were never lacking in salt. She saw to it that the tablecloth was always spotless and starched, that the lamps in the living room were free of dust. James didn't know quite when it was the intricacies of his household began to change in small ways: the paintings set straight; the decades-old doorknobs no longer burnished with age. But he did remember just when Irenie first began to take control of the household.

Yasmeen had been gone almost a year. In a few months, Irenie would turn eleven. Already, she was taciturn as a teenager: shut away in her room when he was around, resolutely silent when they passed on the stairs. Christmas had come and gone; a sombre affair without Yasmeen's zeal for the holiday. James hadn't thought to get a tree. Irenie hadn't thought to remind him. He gave her a beautifully illustrated edition of the children's *Odyssey* by the fire they'd built in weak simulacrum of holiday cheer, knowing before she even opened it that she was too old. She silently handed him a bag of homemade popcorn balls on which he promptly chipped a tooth. Miserably, they ate their turkey TV dinners and wished for the first time for a television, a device Yasmeen had never allowed. They listened to the scratchy recording of *The Nutcracker* she always played after their Christmas meal and silently regarded the single sad string of lights James had draped over the mantle. Irenie toasted marshmallows, careful not to drip on her red velvet dress though the fabric was worn thin at the elbows and the lace collar was so in tatters it resembled a wisp of spider web caught around the neck of a careless adventuress. She needs new clothes, James thought, at once pleased he'd finally come up with something to give her and embarrassed it hadn't occurred to him earlier that children tend to grow.

The next day, she'd insisted on being dropped off at the shopping mall alone. Ten was too old to go shopping with one's father; though as he watched her tiny form meld into the masses he thought ten was too young to do anything alone. Instead of driving home to get some work done as he'd planned, he sat in the parking lot until she came out.

At home, she handed him his charge card and a sheaf of meticulously kept receipts. The total came to just under three hundred dollars. It seemed a lot to spend on a child's clothing, but James knew it was no more than Yasmeen generally spent. In fact, the receipts looked as though it had been his wife who'd done the shopping: pea coat, rain coat, five woollen skirts, five cotton, eight blouses, six sweaters, four dresses, two jumpers, patent leather Mary Janes, sandals, sneakers, galoshes, a pack of knee socks, two four-packs of tights, two each of panties and vests. The designer jeans Yasmeen had always been adamant against hadn't been snuck in, nor even had trousers, garments he knew Irenie had once complained all the other little girls got to wear to school. The only perplexing thing was a bill for $37.50 from a small supermarket next to the mall. Figuring he'd question his daughter later about the generous supply of sweets she'd indubitably secured for herself, James settled down to his work.

At half past seven, as was their custom, he knocked on his daughter's door to summon her for their evening meal, a meal invariably microwaveable in minutes. She didn't respond. He headed down to the kitchen, thinking perhaps she'd taken it upon herself to fix tonight's dinner. He was three minutes late, and Irenie was always punctual. Instead of the plastic trays he'd expected to greet him downstairs, he found the kitchen table set with their long-retired china and a neatly ironed tablecloth. Some sort of chicken dish Yasmeen often made when she was in a hurry steamed at the centre, surrounded by the little crystal dishes of yogurt and chutneys she always set out when they ate dinner as a family. For a wild moment, James thought his wife was back. She had done Irenie's school shopping; she had stopped by the supermarket to pick things up for dinner. But then he saw his daughter approaching from the stove, her thin arms trembling with the weight of an antique silver platter piled up high with rice. Wordlessly, she spooned food onto his plate, serving him first as Yasmeen always did, and then onto her own.

'It looks delicious, Irenie,' he said, touched by how she bit her lip while spooning salaan, worried it might drip. And it was delicious. He remembered how Yasmeen often gave their daughter credit when dinner came out especially well. For the first time, it occurred to James that she hadn't done so just to make the child feel that her having washed the rice had been indispensable a help. 'It tastes delicious too,' he added awkwardly.

Irenie looked at him, but didn't smile. She just picked up her fork and began to eat as though she'd never had any doubt it would.

Things changed at 437 Chestnut Hill Lane after that. Dinner was on the table every day at seven thirty whether James was there or not. Their stock of TV meals found its way into the garbage pail and grocery lists began to appear stuck to the fridge. Without James's really noticing it, laundry stopped piling up by the machine. The wrinkles in his clothes to which he'd long ago resigned himself, then resigned himself again, miraculously fell away. The curtains, drawn for the night until the housekeeper came and opened them one afternoon a week, were opened during daylight hours and shut when it was dark. The rose bushes along the front walk were pruned and the windows scrubbed sparklingly bright. When Irenie was twelve, he handed her his chequebook one morning, assuming correctly that she would rather not have to go through him for all minor expenses. Order established itself where there had been none and details long ignored found a diligent attendant. It wasn't until Faber invited himself over for a drink one spring evening that James registered the changes.

Just over three years had passed since Yasmeen left—James still couldn't bring himself to think 'died', it was always 'left' when he thought about his wife—and James was melancholic. He was always melancholic in April, though not even his daughter seemed to notice the subtle shift that differentiated his typical lugubriousness from the particular melancholy of that month. Then again, perhaps April found Irenie lost in a melancholy of her own. She had just turned thirteen; her fourth birthday without her mother, and incipient womanhood made her more distant that ever. Even the grief she carried around still was unknowable now. It no longer hung so heavy, but had, like his, sublimated into the hazy, grey illusion of alrightness. James had no idea what his daughter thought or felt beneath this blanket, in truth he never tried very hard to guess. He wasn't thinking of her as he half-listened to Faber's complaints about daughters with insufficient sense of duty, nor was he thinking of her when he let the old man talk him into going for a drink.

It had been years since James had seen the inside of a Crawford bar. Except for The Rose Room, a tavern known to be unwelcoming of non-septuagenarians, they were all student-centred establishments with ten-cent pint nights and walls pockmarked by darts. Early in his career, James sometimes allowed particularly persistent students to coax him out for nights of very minor debauchery, but those days had long passed. He wasn't about to let Faber drag him out to some sticky-floored bar populated by revellers hardly older than his daughter. Even if Faber didn't, James had some sense of dignity. Which left them with Crawford's restaurants: where respectable people did their drinking in tasteful vintages over expensive entrées. But James had even less desire to sit through a whole meal with the older man. Sensing as much, Faber had proposed that they pop by James's place for a quick nip. Before James could lie that he didn't keep a well-stocked liquor cabinet, Faber pulled a bottle of a twenty-five-year-old single malt from his filing cabinet and tucked it into the absurd monogrammed attaché case he insisted on carrying.

Faber was in a tizzy because not one of his three daughters was willing to fly home for the thirtieth anniversary of their mother's death. He had planned a small graveside ceremony and an elaborate dinner out, but they all claimed they were unable to travel on notice so short. 'The woman's been dead for thirty years,' he fumed, 'how much notice do they need?'

To be fair, two of the daughters were minor celebrities with obligations in Sacramento and the third was on a diplomatic mission somewhere in the Hague. James was surprised Faber had the sensitivity to plan anything at all; he wondered if the daughters had been as well. Although James had never quite come to like Faber, he had come to know him fairly well. After all, they were the two senior members of a dying department. Even then, it always caught James off guard when Faber wanted to confide in him. If James thought about it, he might have considered that Faber thought him a friend, but James did not think about it.

James did not have friends. Before he'd dislocated his shoulder during an especially fierce match several years back, he played tennis every Saturday with the doctor who once set Irenie's wrist. After having examined his shoulder, Dr Phelps ruefully recommended James give up strenuous sport. Though they met now and again for cups of coffee, without tennis, the relationship fizzled. Yasmeen had tried to rekindle it by inviting the Phelps family for dinner, but she found Mrs Phelps so insufferable she begged James not to force the association ever again. Though he dreaded having to decline the dinner invitation they were owed for several weeks, it was never offered. Perhaps Mrs Phelps had found Yasmeen as insufferable as Yasmeen had her. Or perhaps it had had something to do with Dr Phelps's inability to tear his gaze from his tennis partner's beautiful young wife. Either way, James's one and only almost-friendship had long since faded away. It was not a friendship he had solicited, nor was it one he endeavoured to replace. He certainly had done nothing to give Faber the impression that he wanted, needed, or even ever-so-slightly enjoyed his companionship.

But Faber seemed as oblivious to this as he rattled on about filial irresponsibility. In ancient Greece, they both knew, men were accorded the respect they deserved. Who ran to press papa's tired feet when he came home now? Who peeled him grapes, overjoyed by the responsibility, and entertained him each evening with sweet songs and dance? Not Faber's thankless daughters, that was for sure. By the time they reached Chestnut Hill Lane, James's melancholy had been replaced by the splitting headache of profound irritation. He would need that drink very much.

'Good god, man!' Faber exclaimed as they walked up the path. 'What's become of the jungle?' James saw now that the knee-high grass had been neatly trimmed. The flowerbeds had been weeded and the rose bushes were pruned. Someone had planted pansies along the porch, hung a quaint birdhouse from the maple tree. A trio of nymphets peered at James over the lilac bush; a fairy danced underneath the apple tree. Several exquisitely wrought toadstools had been placed around the stump of an ancient oak felled by lightning. Even the absurd baroque fountain Yasmeen had staunchly refused to get rid of had been repaired. The garden looked like a Victorian nightmare, a Lewis Carroll dream.

'I guess Irenie has a bit of a flair for gardening,' James muttered, embarrassed that he hadn't noticed earlier. He recalled signing cheques for a landscaping company, but none of sums so large that they would have accomplished this.

'What a miracle worker!' Faber commended. James agreed, proud to have a daughter so different from Faber's own. Although it seemed to him that the garden had transformed itself overnight, it had been a work in progress for years. Even before Yasmeen left, the figurines had been set out, the fountain raked of leaves. The garden was a project Celeste inspired, delighted by the outdoors after spending many years coaxing life from flowerpots in her grandmother's airless Upper East Side apartment. Irenie would have abandoned the venture after her mother left had not Celeste been so determined they continue. Hard work, she thought, would distract Irenie from thoughts of her lost mother. And to some extent it had. For years, exhausting herself in the mulch had been the only way Irenie could get to sleep. It was only a few weeks before that visit of Faber's that she had discovered it was a crutch of which she no longer was in need. James would have been surprised and not a little uncomfortable to learn that wild Celeste, the girl who would no doubt lead his daughter astray, stopped by most days in the springtime, to correct Irenie's half-hearted pruning and pull the weeds the housekeeper's indifferent son hadn't seen.

Leading Faber into the living room, James tried not to show how surprised he was at how, without his noticing, things had changed. But Faber was as astounded by the living room as he had been by the yard.

'What did you do, hire a decorator?' he exclaimed. 'The house looks great, old man, just great. You trying to impress those lady friends you've been seeing on the sly?'

Though James had escorted a visiting French lecturer to dinner less than a week ago, he was annoyed by Faber's insinuation. He was hardly a womanizer; the date hadn't even gone well. Besides, he thought, the inside of his house had hardly changed since Faber had seen it last. Then he realized that it had. Almost six years had passed since Yasmeen's last dinner party. The room was not so tidy then, the furniture not so gracefully arranged. Bit by bit, the room had been nudged into harmoniousness. Having once made the mistake of telling Irenie her koftas might just be better than her mother's, however, James knew better than to compliment her on the changes she made. Irenie didn't want to be better than Yasmeen. She wanted to be the same.

'Beautiful as ever,' Faber said almost to himself, examining the wedding photo of Yasmeen that James was relieved to see still sat where it always had been. He was unhappy as ever about Faber scrutinizing his wife, but decided to let it go.

'Let's have a drink, shall we?' he suggested.

By the time Irenie came home, James was drunk and Faber was drunker.

'Well hello there, my beauty,' he slurred, 'where have you been at this hour of the night?'

It was barely seven. They had been drinking since three. With each inch of quality scotch that slid down their throats, James, much to his surprise, had been finding Faber less and less aggravating. He almost felt sorry for the man: how sad for him to be so alone.

'The library,' Irenie replied, bemused. Faber gushed over her talent in the garden, how well she kept the house, how much prettier she was each time he saw her. He asked her about school, small questions she would skirt or ignore if James were to ask, and made her laugh. Before he knew what was happening, she'd invited him to stay on for dinner. Well, why not? She had done the cooking.

They kept up a steady stream of conversation all the while they ate, right until they showed an only slightly less inebriated Faber to the door. James was amazed that a teenage girl and an old man could find so much to say to each other.

'If you'd warned me we would have a guest, I would've come home early to cook something new for dinner,' his daughter told him later.

James just nodded, looked at the floor like a mildly shamed schoolboy. Henceforth, she always made something special on Thursdays, the day on which Faber was most wont to stop by. You don't have to do all this, he told her once. I'm happy with a banana and an egg. It was a thought James had had many times, a thought he'd only uttered aloud once. Irenie had regarded him so coldly, he'd never so much as thought to say so again. He'd understood then that in her own peculiar way, she did have to do it. It wasn't something she wanted, certainly not something she had asked for, but there was no one else to do it now. His telling her she didn't have to only reminded her that Yasmeen no longer could. To diverge from her mother's way of doing things would be to admit she would not be back. To Faber though, Irenie only laughed and said, 'It's biriyani, isn't it, that you like best?'

'Archibald Crowe, Archibald Crowe, how do I know that name?' James thought absently as he chewed his lunch with little interest. It became a refrain really, elevator music to which he no longer paid much mind. The bread of his tuna salad sandwich was soggy and stale. It had spent several months in the freezer behind a wall of neatly labelled aluminium trays, all laden with the remains of dinners Irenie had, unbeknownst to him, been making for weeks before she left. It had to have been weeks; there were so many trays. She'd left enough food frozen that he could easily have eaten her meals for lunch as well as dinner, but today he'd craved a tuna salad sandwich. It's a good tuna salad sandwich, James thought stubbornly, although it wasn't. Something more profound than just the chutney made it not-quite like his mother's. He considered throwing it out, heating up one of his daughter's homemade TV meals instead, but then decided he wouldn't. He had lived alone for most of his adult life. He could survive without a teenager tending to him. Still, it was thoughtful of her to have stocked the freezer before she left. Why had she, he wondered. Had her lifelong reticence simply been her waiting for him to make the first move? He'd begun to open up to her over the phone and she, in turn, had shared with him small details of her life he'd never known.

No, he wouldn't do her the disservice of assuming her motivations were or ever had been so simple. She had blamed him when her mother left, he knew, had considered him suspect even before then. His wife had been a great deal more depressed than he'd ever guessed, but surely Irenie couldn't blame him for that, could she? Not now that she knew about Ahmed, which she did, didn't she? She had to. Why else would she so suddenly decide to go to Pakistan? But then, James had to admit to himself that he had no idea whether the decision had been sudden. Perhaps it had seemed sudden only to him.

He wondered what his daughter was thinking, what she had found over there. Had she found peace? Had she been able to forgive her mother? Did she need to? James didn't know. She never knew that first time. When Yasmeen came back contrite and checked herself into the hospital, they'd agreed to let their daughter think everything had gone according to their plan. She hated James for having sent her mamma away, never knowing the part about how her mamma went away herself. The second time, she blamed James too. Of that he was sure. But was she mad at her mamma for never having come back?

'Archibald Crowe, of course!' it came to James so suddenly he dropped the piece of sandwich he was still trying to choke down.

Archibald Crowe: the man who made the figurines; the man whose house this was before he bought it; the man who hanged himself in the basement. The tale had troubled Yasmeen, though until she saw Irenie in the basement, jump rope around her neck, he hadn't known how much. All the hill station horror stories of backward-footed witches and beautiful, evil women seeking rides outside cemeteries came rushing back in such detail she began to scream and couldn't stop. James didn't know how many similar scenes their daughter had witnessed; he didn't want to know. Thus far, he'd elected to believe Yasmeen was perfectly fine until that very afternoon.

'What's wrong with Mamma?' Irenie asked him when he put her to bed. Not even James had it in him to explain to a six-year-old that her mother was losing her mind because the future she'd hoped for but hadn't got, the future that would have made Irenie's very existence impossible, lay dying in a hospital bed an ocean away. So he simply said Yasmeen was upset about the ghost.

It wouldn't have taken her long to conclude that her papa was lying, and if he was a liar who knew what else he had to hide? She had always been wary of him, but after that she'd been downright suspicious. His entanglement with Jo Anne the Sports Fan probably hadn't helped. Of course she hadn't said a word, not to him, or to Yasmeen. She could keep a silence indefinitely. Even at six, she'd kept it for over three hours on those stairs, those stairs beneath which a man had died, where it was too dark to see a thing. He was grateful she'd decided, finally, to speak.

18

Not long before we first met I was intrigued by solipsism. Could it be? Was there just me? How would I, could I, ever know? What if there was only me and the whole universe and I were eternally alone? It was only once I met you that I became sure this wasn't so.

It is darker in the conference room than anywhere I've ever been. It's the dark of a chalkboard wiped with a dampened eraser, the dark you find gazing into an old well on a night with no stars. Perhaps this is the dark of non-existence, under six feet of soil or somewhere. My mother is at once as close and as far as she's ever been.

Something grazes my hand then, grasps it. Neither of us speaks. There isn't any need. I know he feels the echoes in the endlessness as well. Our parents are everywhere around us: the ones who abandoned us and the ones who are still here.

When the light returns, millennia might well have passed. I'm surprised to find the carpet not crumbled, the paint unchipped and fresh. The flowers in the vase by the door ought, at least, to be dead.

'Well,' says Firdaus, blinking. He doesn't let go my hand.

'Well,' I echo. Something possesses me to take both of his in mine.

'I was so certain you'd know for sure,' he says, shaking his head as though clearing from it the last vestiges of an almost forgotten dream.

'You were?'

'Because of the letters.'

'Wait,' I exclaim, realizing at once what's been bothering me since the very start of this conversation. 'How do you know I had them?'

He looks slightly perplexed. 'Well I sent them to you, didn't I?'

'Why would you do that?'

'Because I trusted you more than anyone else in the world.'

I must look doubtful because he elaborates, 'After I made the call, my father told me everything. It was as though he'd spent years longing to say your mother's name and he finally had the chance. I was most interested in you, I confess. I made him tell me everything he knew. I'd heard something in your voice, something that made me think you'd understand me. You knew what it was like. I used to think about you all the time, pretend we were friends. We had all kinds of adventures in my head. This is so embarrassing …'

'You know,' I say, feeling I owe him this admission, 'I don't know if Baby Tamasha told you, but I imagined your father was my father. I wanted him to be.'

'Did you?' He laughs. Then grows serious. 'But my father is dead.' He pauses and takes my hand again. 'Oh, Irenie.'

I shrug. 'It was stupid. I know it was. After I read the letters, I felt closer to yours than I ever had to mine, but now that I've crossed the world I feel closer to mine than I ever have before. Isn't that funny?'

'Not particularly.'

He looks sad and sadness is the last thing I wish to cause him, not after all he's already endured. 'Not the brightest,' I joke, knocking my head. 'Perhaps you should have entrusted the letters to someone else.'

He grins feebly and shakes his head. 'Untrue. And anyway, there was no one else. It was my father's last request that I keep them safe. He said people would be hurt if they got out, so if anything ever happened to him I was to destroy them. After what happened, though, I couldn't bear to. I was sure they would explain.' He pauses. 'They don't, do they?'

I regard his ragged nails, his tired eyes. 'They would've found a way to share an ending no matter what we did.' For the first time, I am grateful for the letters' disappearance. He need never know that I don't know. If I live a hundred years I don't know if I'll tell any truths better than this lie.

He smiles. 'Are you going to tell me that every ending is a new beginning?'

'No,' I say, thinking of Shireen Khala. 'But maybe the endings aren't always where we think. Maybe there are infinite variations of every story.'

'And to think I'd imagined there were only seven!'

'Imagine all the characters in those seven whose story it isn't.'

Our hands fall to our sides then, leaving us suddenly awkward.

'There you are!' cries Naaz, exploding through the door. 'We were looking for you everywhere!'

'And who's this?' asks Shamim, looking Firdaus up and down.

I introduce them quickly, wanting to be somewhere, anywhere, else. Firdaus appears to feel the same. Somehow making small talk right now seems like sacrilege. As we pass back down the corridor, he whispers, 'And I suppose infinite outcomes exist for each of them?'

I smile and shrug. 'We can only hope.'

When my cousins and I return to the ballroom, everything is remarkably unchanged. No one seems to have noticed any of us were gone. We pose for one last round of pictures with Shezzie; raid the buffet of leftover gulab jamuns. Shamim gets into a minor fight with her mother about which tailor it was that stitched her suit; Naaz, distraught as always by argument, drops a cup of tea. I see Firdaus sitting next to his brother on the other side of the room, but Aamir Maamu demands to be taken home before we get a chance to speak.

'It's been five hours. How long can we possibly be expected to stare at the bride and groom?'

I leave my dupatta draped over a chair towards the back, not entirely by accident, and have to go back for it when we're already through the door. My cousins regard me knowingly, but it isn't what they think. She sits three feet from where I let my silk scarf fall, drinking a last cup of tea and smiling faintly at the bride. I clear my throat, but cannot bring myself to greet her. I cannot manage a 'Mehrunissa' or an 'excuse me' or even a 'hello'.

'I'm sorry,' I finally choke.

She looks at me, not disagreeably, and nods slightly just before I bolt.

In the car, I count the streetlights as they go by. Something needles at the edge of my mind. One dead sparrow on the road, two snoozing police at a checkpoint on their stools, three jacaranda trees no longer in bloom. Four child cyclists out much after they should be in bed, five models of Suzuki parked in a row along Margalla Road, six bats hanging from a tree. Seven buttons in a line down the front of Naaz's kameez. Now where to find eight things alike in the car or out of the window? Fortunately, my relatives are too busy discussing what so-and-so was wearing, how many kababs he-or-she ate in a single sitting to notice I've pressed my nose right to the glass.

I lose myself in the thought of order, of sets. I envision my neatly labelled childhood photographs down in the basement; a shelving system in an office so complex it appears chaotic at first; letters from my mother to my father arranged carefully by date and letters between my mother and Ahmed, arranged just the same. We're almost home before it occurs to me: what's been bothering me is something Firdaus has said, or rather something he hasn't: if he packed my mother's letters in a hasty parcel, who organized all of them by date?

19

*Were I to wake one day and feel your love gone, I'm sure I
would drop dead. My heart would stop still. Whatever remains
of what was once my soul would drift away. I know now I will
never have you; you and I will never build a life together. But
without the distant, sea-separated spark that is the ghost of
your love, I'm certain I would die.*

Irenie was still in Florida when the parcel came. Airmail.
Priority shipping. Addressed to Miss Irenie Eccles but with
no hint of the sender. Recognizing the Royal Mail sticker, James
for a moment thought it might be a birthday gift from his mother.
But Grace Eccles had been dead almost five years. Her last gift
to Irenie was a lace baptismal gown she'd tatted herself, a gift for
which unbaptized Irenie had never had any use.

'Think of her poor little soul drifting around in purgatory,' his
mother had begun tacking onto the end of each fairly format letter
accompanying each birthday of handkerchiefs. James thought of
it. Briefly. But he and Yasmeen had agreed not to indoctrinate
their daughter with any particular religious sentiment since both
their faiths had long since lapsed. Still, James had worried that
his mother never really took to her only grandchild. She'd read
to her from *The Children's Bible* for hours on end that time they'd
visited, but she hadn't had half the enthusiasm for Irenie that her
maternal grandparents had. Though Grace was never what anyone
would call demonstrative, James thought that his daughter and his

mother might have been closer if they spent more time together. As it had happened, Grace had keeled over in her garden shortly after that one ten-day-long visit. The predilection to guilt James had never fully been able to expunge, despite his disavowal of that religion with which it is particularly associated, had made it impossible for him not to wonder if his mother might just have lived longer if she'd had a grandchild in her life. It was thus that, seeing the parcel, he was momentarily overcome by relieved elation and then promptly plunged into a pit of overwhelming guilt.

If the parcel wasn't from his mother, it had to be from Yasmeen. Who else would have cause to send their daughter something from England? And that was where Yasmeen was, James knew. He'd known before the irate phone call from the woman whose voice sounded English but whose name had too many strange syllables to have been mistaken by a four-year-old for one of old Albion stock, before Heathrow had phoned to say a Mrs Yasmeen Eccles had somehow managed to leave her passport behind at the immigration desk. He'd known when he'd come home to find the house empty, known something was wrong when Yasmeen agreed to let Irenie go to Florida. But James hadn't said a word.

He knew Ahmed was dying, of course; he'd been told by Yasmeen. The first miracle recovery had been unexpected, unprecedented even. There wouldn't be a second. He'd seen this in the dullness of his wife's eyes when she met him at the door, in the indifference with which she'd regarded her reflection before leaving for the store, how she'd sighed and pulled a raincoat on instead of correcting the mis-buttoning of her dress. He'd known she would want to see Ahmed before he died, but he hadn't brought it up. The first time it had been easy for her: he'd tried to have her institutionalized, so she'd run away from him in response. But this time he'd done nothing. Yasmeen had no excuse to leave him now. And James truly thought she wouldn't. She had been a good wife to him for over a decade. For the most part, she had held true to her promise to never mention Ahmed; James knew she would hold true to it now. He just didn't expect she would do so by leaving without a word. This time, James was sure, she did not plan to return.

For weeks, she'd been berating herself for being a bad mother to their daughter; for months she'd been depressed. Once, she'd gone so far as to suggest Irenie would be better off without her. James had ignored it. How could I have ignored it, he fumed at himself, bringing in the parcel from the porch. If only he'd said something to her then. If only he'd told her to go see Ahmed, told her he'd be there for her when she came back. But he hadn't.

In a few days, James would learn of the car that had veered off a cliff outside Dover. He would learn it had carried two passengers, one female, and the other male. He would know the female passenger was Yasmeen before the rental company reported she'd kept a silver sedan three days beyond its scheduled return. He would know she was dead before Her Majesty's Coastguard called with the tentative suggestion that she was. While it would not be quite fair to say James had expected he would lose his wife, he had always regarded his marriage contract as something more closely resembling a lease. True, he had married the woman of his dreams but he had done so in full awareness that she would never really belong to him and that what is borrowed must some day be returned. James had managed to avoid thinking about this for almost the entire duration of his marriage, but the day he came home to an empty house, he knew at once that his lease had finally expired. Like many confronted with the unexpected loss of something in which they are heavily invested, he had blamed himself: first, for having allowed this long-avoided eventuality to occur and second, for being caught unawares when it did. On the day the parcel arrived, he was a complete and utter mess. So when he undid the packing that bore his daughter's name and slit through six untidy layers of packing tape, it was not done in complete consciousness.

What did James expect to find inside the parcel? Even he

couldn't properly have said. With deranged optimism, he had, for a brief moment, imagined it might contain a red t-shirt in children's size small emblazoned with that classic slogan: My Mother Went to London and All I Got Was This Lousy Shirt.

But that was not what it held at all. It held a sheaf of letters wrapped up in an old sheet.

'Dear Ahmed,' James read across the subject line of the first one, noting the casual untidiness of his wife's penmanship with the same surprise his daughter would feel when confronted with it five years in the future. Like Irenie, James knew exactly what these letters were. He was well aware that the enamelled box holding their responses was hidden somewhere in the house. Unlike Irenie, however, James had no desire to know what the letters said. Why Yasi, he wondered, why would you send these to Irenie?

In recent years, James had adopted his wife's habit of seeking solace in the empty bottom of a bottle. This is what he did the day the parcel came.

James set the rather mangled parcel on his desk and proceeded to empty out the liquor cabinet. He drank most of a fifth of whiskey, half a pint of gin, a vodka tonic Yasmeen had abandoned in the fridge some weeks ago. He then went about tidying the wine rack by finishing off all the bottles less than halfway full. For dessert, James drank two twelve-ounce bottles of home-brewed beer that he'd been saving either for an occasion or an emergency. Needless to say, he never knew if it had been as good as the grade-grubbing student who gifted it to him had promised. Irenie might well have found herself an orphan had James not been the man he was. The sheer extent of his excesses alone might have killed another man, and even if this hypothetical other man's basal brain function had somehow survived the alcoholic assault, he would most likely have thrown himself off a roof, across a set of railroad tracks, or into a paroxysm of seizures that would have killed him when they made disgorging the vomit in his windpipe altogether impossible.

But James was not this sort of man. James knew how to pace himself. He knew when it was time to eat a slice of bread and when whiskey wouldn't do for water. The fact of the matter is, James did not want to kill himself, nor did he want to drink himself into the courage to do so. All James wanted was a moment of absolute mental blankness, which, after fourteen hours of staring at the parcel on his desk and enough alcohol to kill a small rhinoceros, he got.

When James came to, he was on the living-room floor with his slipper for a pillow. He had scrawled the word 'no' all across his forearms in red ink, which he didn't remember doing, and clumsily buttoned himself into one of Yasmeen's maternity jumpers which, unfortunately, he did. The only time he'd ever felt so awful after a night of drinking was when he'd downed an entire pitcher of grain alcohol punch to which someone had forgotten to add the punch at a crew party in college. On that particular occasion, he'd stumbled into the street and woken up with his neck in a brace and his leg in traction. Though the injuries to his person were primarily in the form of self-inflicted humiliations when he woke up that morning, James's physiology punished him with the same ferocity it had all those long decades ago. It would be only a minor exaggeration to say he felt like he might die. It was in such a state that he stumbled over his wife's enamelled box en route to the kitchen. He had no recollection of where he'd found it or of whether he'd read the letters. He had no recollection either of how he'd identified the key: a tiny pendant on a chain Yasmeen had left hanging off their bureau. To his knowledge, she had never taken it off before. To his relief, he soon recovered the charm from the base of the espresso pot—oh the foresight of the drunk—but the fate Ahmed's letters had met, he couldn't begin to guess.

As James vainly tried to caffeinate his hangover away, he noticed that a piece of the parcel's wrapping had somehow entangled itself in the bowl of rotting pears currently serving as the kitchen table's centrepiece. The handwriting, he noticed with some alarm, was not Yasmeen's. Nor could it have been Ahmed's. Ahmed's penmanship, he knew, was so astoundingly bad he never wrote anything by hand. This handwriting was almost excruciatingly precise. It was the handwriting of children's writing assignments, the handwriting of one still penalized academically for letters slanting slightly to the left. The handwriting, unmistakably, belonged to a child.

In a sodden fit of bitter epiphany the night before, James had been struck by the answer to his question: Why, Yasi, why would you send these to Irenie? So some day she'll understand. Nothing doing, he had thought, enraged, you do not get to be the heroine when you've left her. He'd meticulously crumpled up every last letter, the ones from him, the ones from her, and amused himself for hours by aiming them, badly, at the bathtub. So that was where they were.

But Yasmeen hadn't tried to be a heroine, clearly the letters were sent by someone else. Knowing Yasmeen, she'd probably hoped to make Irenie hate her by leaving without a word. Or maybe she had planned to come back after all. Maybe the accident had been just an accident. He had resigned himself to the idea that his wife had left him, but would Yasmeen have left Irenie? Though he couldn't say for sure, it seemed unlikely that she would. He'd never once considered that anyone other than he himself was being left.

James devoted what remained of that day and the next two to seeking penance. Though his hangover lingered on like a nasty bug he couldn't quite shake, he drove from one end of town to the other in the dead of night depositing the evidence of his bender in disparate dumpsters. He set about rectifying the minor structural damages he'd done to the house, of which the most difficult to repair was an enormous oblong burn he'd somehow inflicted on the living room's hardwood floor. Eventually he just moved the couch. When he grew weary of hard labour and night-time jaunts behind the wheel, he endeavoured to repair the damage he'd done to the several thousand letters, which he was pleased to find was far less severe than he'd feared. He ironed every last one of them and put them in order: Yasmeen, Ahmed, Yasmeen, Ahmed, beginning with the first. Other than the dates, he did not read a single word. Just before he closed the lid, an idea came to him. He went into their bedroom—just his bedroom now—and took what remained of Yasmeen's painting class cash from the secret section at the back of her jewellery box. Without bothering to count it, he wrapped it in a Grace handkerchief and tied it up with twine. He taped the bundle into a crisp manila envelope and slipped it beneath the stack of letters without thinking too deeply about his actions. Then he locked the box and slid it as far back into the crawlspace above the bathroom as he could. The letters might have been addressed to Irenie, but Irenie was a child. And the person who had posted them was a child as well—Ahmed's, he assumed. Children weren't known for their good judgement. As a concession to his guilt, he gave Irenie the locket a few weeks after she'd come back.

'Your mother wanted you to have this,' he'd said. 'It was supposed to be a birthday gift.'

'But I am not grown up,' she said gravely.

For neither the first time nor the last, James suspected she'd been born adult.

20

Do you still believe all things are connected? Or do you feel alone? Do you believe a thought, a wish, a kiss, could somehow change the course of your journey altogether? Or do you think only what you do will take you where you go?

As a child, James had had a fondness for adventure novels. Adventure was the last genre he and Irene had enjoyed together and he continued reading them well into his teens. All through his adulthood, it might be said, if *The Hardy Boys* and *The Odyssey* can be considered fit for even the faintest comparison. The one thing James had always thought implausible in those tales of train heists and Aztec rings with secret maps inscribed inside the stones was the protagonist periodically awaking 'in an icy sweat'. James himself had never awoken in an icy sweat or, for that matter, in any kind of sweat not provoked by undue heat. On the morning of September eleventh, however, James woke up in an icy sweat. He had been dreaming of Irene again, this time of them swimming in a quarry somewhere the summer they were six. Grace was perched upon the rocky edge, not sunbathing as other mothers were, but knitting something red. She wasn't paying attention when Irene dove off the cliff. She didn't notice when her daughter didn't surface, gasping for air. Of this, only James had been aware.

He'd been playing a rather brutal rendition of water polo with some boys he knew from school. Since high points could be gained only by pulling off opponents' swimming trucks, his sister had been barred. It was rare that James was ever included in any game Irene hadn't been invited to, and he wasn't enjoying it. He didn't like being ducked underwater or having his shorts pulled off. He wished Irene had announced, as she would usually have done, that the two of them would play a much better game, but she had been angry that he'd just beat her in a race. He was thinking he'd let her win the next ten races if only she'd give him reason to escape this game when he felt something amiss. Just then, someone pounced on him from behind. James came up spluttering just in time to see his sister leap from the highest cliff. Perhaps she'd hoped to show the boys she was manlier than any of them; perhaps she'd just wanted to scare her brother, knowing how worried he could get. Whatever her reasons, James knew she would never have worried she might drown.

'Irene?' he called over the ruckus and splashing of the other boys. 'Irene,' he screamed when long seconds passed and she hadn't come up for air. No one heard him.

He swam around the edges of the quarry, dodging attempts to dunk and de-clothe him. But she was nowhere to be found

'Irene,' he called into the shadows. 'Irene?' he burbled underwater in the fish language only the two of them spoke. Then, just when he was about to give up and tell Grace, he saw a flash of green floating in the deepest shadows of the quarry, under the old oak tree where no one liked to swim.

'Irene,' he yelled again, but she didn't turn his way. By the time he got to the far edge where the roots formed a sort of nest, he saw her neck was oddly bent. No, cried out his dream-self, that isn't how it went. Irene was hiding behind our mother up on the rocky ledge. But dream-Irene was dead. He flipped over what he'd thought was his twin and the blank eyes staring up at him were Irenie's.

And James awoke in his first icy sweat.

In later months, he would hear the stories of school teachers who'd seen mushroom clouds in their coffee mugs that morning or of farmers whose well-trained horses had burst from the barn in a stampede, but James knew his icy sweat had not been an omen of that sort. His icy sweat had had nothing to do with the several thousand people about to die less than a hundred miles south of where he slept. James's icy sweat had been about his daughter; he'd known it the moment he woke up.

When the phone rang later that morning, he almost just let it ring. He was in no mood for their prank caller and it wasn't Irenie's day to phone. Later, he would tell her as much, and she would say with a cryptic grin that the caller would no longer be hanging up. That morning, though, she was calling to ask if he'd read the news. She knew he was well north of New York City but she worried nonetheless. In an instant, separations from those one loves can prove eternal. He had been prepared to beg. He had been prepared to plead. He had been prepared to demand and even threaten, but Irenie had agreed. Many years later, she would tell him that if he hadn't suggested it she would have proposed it herself.

They spoke for a while longer, mostly about the logistics of her return. He would pick her up, of course; he would even bring Celeste. No, she told him, I'll see her later. I'd like to talk to you. She said it shyly, almost tremulously, and before they said goodbye she thanked him very quietly. She hung up before he could ask what she was thanking him for, though deep in his heart, he knew.

21

I leave Pakistan on the twenty-third of September, 2001. The United States has not yet commenced its aerial assault of Afghanistan, but it is imminent. People have placed bets on when the first bomb will fall. I will not be here when it happens. I will be a world away, perhaps eating tuna sandwiches, which my father claims he's mastered, or hearing scandalous tales of love and lust from Celeste. Perhaps I will be speaking on the phone to my cousins or even to Firdaus. Perhaps I will be at the library, finally legally employed there, or sitting at a school desk, dreaming of the larger world. Whatever I am doing, it will be appropriately teenage and trite.

My flight leaves at four a.m., but despite the hour, everyone is here. Nani dabs her eyes with tissue and exhorts promises I will return. Naaz tells me she will visit: she has found a band in Princeton online and they want to use the lyrics she's been secretly writing all summer. Shamim grudgingly says she'll miss me and wraps her bony arms around me in a hug that hurts only a little bit. Aamir Maamu hands me a bag of sweets I know will be inedible. 'No Mintz,' he whispers with a wink, when Sairah Mumani is out of earshot. His wife, who has loaded me with costume jewellery and colourful silks, warns me to wash my face with ice-cold water every night and to protect my skin at all costs from the sun. Mehreen Khala snorts at this and tells me it's more important I remember to floss. Nana pats me on the head and quietly tells me he looks forward to hearing my opinion before slipping me a manuscript of *The Sinister Sultan*. If nothing else, it will help me sleep. They wait with me until it's time for me to go in. They wait outside behind the glass, waving wildly, until the security guard tells them they must leave. When I turn away, there are tears running down my cheeks. All these years I've never cried and now it seems my eyes are seldom dry.

Will I cry when I see my father, I wonder. Maybe when I step into the house? At some point during the journey home, a journey during which we'll speak for the first time in both our lives. I know he must think I want to talk to him about my mother, but he is wrong. For so many years, I've seen my mother as she never was, but I haven't seen my father at all. How much must it have cost him to straighten out those letters, to keep them in his house because they'd come addressed to me? How much must it have cost him to let me hate him for having let my mother leave? She left you too, Irenie, he'd said, but what I hadn't realized was that she'd left him as well.

After the clamour of check-in, the departure lounge seems silent and sparsely populated. I watch the airfield: dark and empty but for a single PIA craft beached to the far side of the runway. The monitors obstinately display a two-fifteen Qatar Airways flight to Doha (departed) and a seven a.m. PIA to Abu Dhabi (delayed). From what I can tell, the garbled PA announcements say nothing of my Emirates flight, though I do make out that smoking in the toilets is strictly forbidden and Pakistan won some match somewhere today. Though there's not a single airline official yet in sight, no one seems concerned. The three young men ahead of me during check-in nap happily in their seats. At half past four, a worried-looking Chinese businessman, apparently disheartened by the notion that this country will never let him go, approaches the snoozing gift store proprietor. The proprietor shrugs indifferently; my fellow passengers look amused.

At quarter to five, I think I hear my name announced. No, it can't be me, I think. It must be someone else. Then I leap up, new suitcase in hand. Could I have somehow missed my flight? I don't think I could stand to say my goodbyes again.

The young woman at the desk seems amused by my panic. Don't worry, she assures me, you haven't missed your flight. She smiles and tucks her hair back under her dupatta. From what I understand, it seems someone has found something that belongs to me. She leads me through a door and down some steps to where it seems baggage goes to die. There are a few mouldering crates and some cracked Samsonites and, behind them, a black suitcase with the luggage tag ripped off, 'I. Ecc' barely visible on the upper right. The young woman explains that when I checked in, the man who gave me my boarding pass recognized my peculiar name. She smiles again and asks me what it means. Was I the one who'd been calling every number listed for the airport about a missing bag? I stare at it, the broken wheel, the absurd padlock I secured it with all those weeks ago. I smile back at her and shake my head. 'This one isn't mine.'

Acknowledgements

My sincerest thanks to:
Laura Susjin and Priya Bora at the Susijn Agency, for taking a chance on an unknown. Working with you has been a joy. Your work on this book has made it more than I ever imagined it could be.

Manasi Subramaniam at HarperCollins India, whose incisive edits transformed the book.

My wonderful parents, Stephanie Bunker and Shahrukh Khan, who championed this endeavour even before I was sure of it myself. Without your love and support (and the lifetime of books you've gifted me) it never would have been possible. I am endlessly grateful for your faith in me.

Lila Kurosaka-Black, for devouring an early draft in days and telling me you couldn't put it down. I can't tell you how much that meant to me.

Gul Mawaz-Khan, for believing in me with all his heart. Also, for gracefully tolerating my glares and demands for quiet.

Arapaie Kurosaka-Black, your enthusiasm for invented worlds is contagious. My mind is always alive with new ideas after I speak to you.

Anum Ali Waheed and Rachel Sennett, for reading early drafts and sharing your invaluable insights.

Susan Striker, for giving me the most wonderfully flexible job. I can't imagine any writer has ever had a better one.

My professors and peers at Sarah Lawrence, who were so very kind about the shambolic early drafts of this book.

And the family and friends too innumerable to list here whose enthusiasm to see this book in print means more than they will ever know.